Ab...

Marion Lennox is a ... dairy farm. She m... weren't interested i... special doctor', she ... Trisha David. She's ... career teaching statistics. Finally, she's figured what's important and discovered the joys of baths, romance and chocolate. Preferably all at the same time! Marion is an international award-winning author.

Nina Milne has loved Mills & Boon, since as a child she discovered stacks of M&B books 'hidden' in the airing cupboard so is thrilled to now write for them. Nina spent her childhood in England, US and France. Since then she has acquired an English degree, one hero-husband, three gorgeous children and a house in Brighton where she plans to stay. After all she can now transport herself via her characters to anywhere in the world whilst sitting in pyjamas in her study. Bliss!

Barbara Wallace can't remember when she wasn't dreaming up love stories in her head, so writing romances for Mills & Boon is a dream come true. Happily married to her own Prince Charming, she lives in New England with a house full of empty-nest animals. Readers can catch up with Barbara through her newsletter. Sign up at www.barbarawallace.com

A Christmas Wish

MARION LENNOX

NINA MILNE

BARBARA WALLACE

MILLS & BOON

First Published in Great Britain 2020
By Mills & Boon, an imprint of HarperCollins*Publishers*
1 London Bridge Street, London, SE1 9GF

A CHRISTMAS WISH © 2020 Harlequin Books S.A.

Christmas with her Boss © 2010 Marion Lennox
Christmas Kisses with Her Boss © 2015 Nina Milne
Christmas with Her Millionaire Boss © 2017 Barbara Wallace

ISBN: 978-0-263-29842-0

MIX
Paper from
responsible sources
FSC™ C007454

This book is produced from independently certified FSC™ paper to ensure responsible forest management.

For more information visit: www.harpercollins.co.uk/green

Printed and bound in Spain
by CPI, Barcelona

CHRISTMAS WITH
HER BOSS

MARION LENNOX

CHAPTER ONE

'ALL scheduled flights have been cancelled until after Christmas. Charter planes are no exception. I'm sorry, ma'am, but nobody's going anywhere.'

Meg replaced the phone as if it was about to shatter. The air around her felt sharp and dangerous. She was trying hard not to breathe.

The door to her boss's inner sanctum was open. W S McMaster was clearing his desk, filing vital documents into his lovely calfskin briefcase. Suave, sleek and almost impossibly good-looking, the man looked what he was—a billionaire businessman moving on to the next important thing.

But the next important thing was in New York, and W S McMaster's personal assistant was about to tell him there were no planes for at least three days.

No-o-o-o-o-o.

'Oh, Meg, I'm so out of here.' Josie, Meg's assistant, was tugging off her office shoes and hauling on six-inch stilettos. 'Dan's meeting me in five minutes and I'm free. How cool to have Christmas fall on Monday. I have two solid days of partying until I need to sober up for the family Christmas Day.'

Meg didn't answer. She couldn't.

Josie and the rest of the office staff departed, calling Christmas greetings as they left. Yes, Christmas was on

Monday. It was Friday afternoon. The corporate world closed down, right now.

Except for Meg, whose job it was to be at hand as Mr McMaster's personal assistant at any time he was in Australia.

Mr McMaster was only in Australia for maybe ten or twelve weeks of the year, and there was little administration she had to do outside those times. It was a fabulous job. She'd been so lucky to get it. If she'd messed this up…

Don't go there. Focus on now. Focus on getting her boss out of the country. She gave a weak little wave to the departing staff and tried one last phone call.

Her boss was too far away to hear, but there was little to hear anyway; just more of the same.

'Helicopters depend on air traffic controllers too?' she asked bleakly. 'No, thank you; I understand. And there's no way the strike can be resolved until after Christmas? Of course I know the whole country closes down from five tonight, but this is vital. Can we…I don't know, take off from a paddock while no one's watching? Island hop to Indonesia and find a flight from there? I'm serious; I'll do anything.'

No and no and no.

She replaced her phone and stared at it as if it had personally betrayed her—and Mr McMaster was standing in the doorway, ready to go.

He looked ready to take on the world.

He always did, she conceded. William McMaster was thirty-six years old; he'd been born into money and he'd inherited the gene for making it. He headed a huge family corporation and the McMaster empire was growing by the day. For the last three years he'd spent two or three months a year here, growing the part of the firm that was opening mines all over Australia. He flew from one business meeting to another. While he was in Australia Meg flew with him, and as she did she realised why he had a different PA in every country. He'd wear one out in weeks.

She was worn out now, and he was ready to leave. He was leaning against the door, waiting for her attention. He was wearing a dark Italian business suit that screamed money and taste, with a crisp white shirt, new on this morning because the hotel laundry had sent his shirts back slightly yellowed. She'd had a frantic scramble to get new ones. His hotel was supposed to be the best in Melbourne—how could she top that? The hotel also had the best gym in Melbourne. He insisted on hotels with great gyms and his body proved it. Tall, dark, and far more good-looking than any man had a right to be, he was watching her now through dark, hooded eyes, as if he knew something was wrong.

Of course he knew something was wrong. You couldn't get to where he was without intelligence and intuition, and William McMaster had both in spades.

'My car to the airport?' he queried, but softly, as if he already suspected the answer.

'There's a problem,' she said, not looking at him. Her new three year contract was on her desk, waiting for her boss to sign on his way out. She shoved it under her fax, as if somehow hiding it could protect it.

She *so* wanted to keep this job. While Mr McMaster was overseas she wasn't needed, but when he was in the country she moved to total commitment. Seven days out of seven. Twelve hour days, or more.

He worked like this all the time, Meg knew. She was in touch with his three other PAs, one in London, one in New York and one in Hong Kong. Wherever he went, the work of a dozen people followed. The man was driven and he drove everyone around him.

He couldn't drive her now. She *must* go home.

'There's a delay,' Meg managed, trying desperately to sound

as if this was a mere hiccup to be sorted by six. Six, the time his plane took off and she could catch the train home and be free.

He didn't respond. He simply waited, his dark eyes barely flickering. He was a man of few words. He expected his people to anticipate his demands and sort them.

That was what she was paid to do, but this time she'd failed.

She couldn't hire a private jet. Helicopters needed airspace too. How long would it take a boat to get to New Zealand so he could fly from there? A week at least. No.

And hotels... They'd been booked out for months for this holiday weekend. When she'd settled his account this morning the manager already sounded tired in anticipation.

'It's great he's booked out early. I have people queuing. There's not a room to be had in the whole city. I have people offering bribes...'

'Are you intending to tell me?'

His eyes had narrowed—he knew by now that the problem was serious. To her surprise, though, there was a gleam of suppressed amusement in his dark eyes, as if he guessed the mess her thoughts were in.

'There's been a snap strike by air traffic controllers,' she said, feeling ill. 'The conciliation meeting ended twenty minutes ago, with no result. All airlines are grounded indefinitely.'

She could see the airport from this office. Meg snatched a fleeting glance outside. This was the penthouse suite of the most luxurious office block in Melbourne. The view was almost all the way to Tasmania, and normally there were planes between here and the sea.

Now the sky was empty, and her boss's gaze had followed hers.

'No planes,' he said slowly.

'Nothing that needs airspace until after Christmas. There's no guarantee even then. This is…'

'Absurd,' he snapped. 'A private jet…'

'Requires airspace.' She managed to meet his gaze full on. He liked direct answers; hated being messed around. She'd worked with him for three years now and she knew enough not to quail before that steely gaze. Sometimes this man demanded more than was humanly possible. When that happened she told him and he simply moved on.

He wasn't moving on yet.

'Organise me a car to Sydney. I'll fly from there.'

'The strike's Australia-wide.'

'That's impossible. I need to be in New York for Christmas.'

Why? There was enough space in her muddled thoughts to wonder what—or who—was waiting for him at home.

The gossip magazines said this man was a loner. He'd been an only child, and his parents were wealthy to the point of obscenity, long divorced and enmeshed in society living. As far as Meg knew, he never saw them. There'd been an actress on his arm last time he'd been in London but the tabloids had reported her broken heart at least three months ago. And it hadn't been very broken, Meg thought wryly. She knew how much the woman had received during their short relationship— 'Send this to Sarah… Settle Sarah's hotel bill…' and now Sarah had already moved on to the next high-status partner.

So who was waiting in New York?

'I can't get you to New York,' she said, trying to stay calm. To tell it like it was.

'You've tried everything?'

'Yes, sir.'

He stared at her for a long moment and she could see his cool brain assessing the situation. He trusted her—he'd trusted her from the moment he'd hired her—and she could tell by his expression that already he was in Melbourne for Christmas and making the best of it.

'I can work here,' he said, angry but seemingly resigned. Frequent flyers knew that sometimes factors moved out of their control, and she wouldn't be fired for this. 'I'll need to make some fast arrangements, though. We can use the time to sort the Berswood deal. That's urgent enough.'

Deep breath. Just say it.

'Mr McMaster, the Australian corporate world closes down at five this afternoon,' she said, meeting his gaze square on. 'This entire building will be shutting down. There'll be no air conditioning, no servicing; the place will be locked. The business district will be deserted. You pay me to be in charge of this office and I've already let the staff leave. And you can't sort the Berswood contract. There'll be no one at Berswood to sort it with.'

She was meeting her boss's gaze, tilting her chin, trying to sound calmly confident instead of defiant and scared.

She was definitely scared.

McMaster's gaze was almost blank, but she knew there was nothing blank about what he was thinking. This man sorted multi-million business deals in the time it took her to apply lipstick. Not that she had time to apply lipstick when he was around.

'Very well,' he conceded. 'You and I can work from my hotel suite.'

You and I can work from my hotel suite…

Her face must have changed again. He got it. He always knew.

'There's a problem there, too?'

'Sir, there's no rooms.'

'If I have to change hotels I will,' he snapped, but she shook her head. This was why she'd be fired. It was something she should have foreseen. At the first rumour she should have booked, but she'd missed the rumours.

She'd been frantic in the Christmas lead up, and she'd done her shopping in one crazy rush last night. The shops had been open all night. McMaster had let her go at eleven and she'd shopped until three. Then she'd fallen into an exhausted sleep—and been woken to a demand for clean shirts. She'd sorted it and been back in the office at seven, but her normally incisive scheduling had let her down. She'd missed listening to the morning news.

Fallback position... What was that?

There wasn't one.

'There really are no rooms,' she said, as calmly as she could. 'The country's full of trapped people. You left your hotel before seven this morning. Most people book out later. By eight the rumours had started and people simply refused to leave. If I'd figured this out this morning... I didn't and I'm sorry. There's a major Hollywood blockbuster being filmed on location just out of Melbourne. All the cast were due to fly out tonight. They've block-booked every luxury hotel in Melbourne and they're prepared to pay whatever it takes. The cheap places are overwhelmed by groups who can't get home. People are camping at the airport. There really is nothing.'

She hesitated, hating to throw it back to him, knowing she had no choice. 'Sir... Do you have friends? Your parents... There must be people you know?'

There was a moment's loaded silence. Then, 'You're telling me to contact my parents' friends?' The anger in his voice frightened her.

'No, I...'

'There is no way I will contact any friend of my parents—or anyone else. You're suggesting I ask for charity?'

'Of course not, but...'

'To impose myself on someone else's Christmas... I will not.'

'Sir...'

'So, taking away the personal option, where,' he said in a voice that dripped ice, 'do you suggest I stay?'

'I don't know,' she whispered.

'You're paid to know,' he snapped, his face dark with fury. He glanced at his watch. 'You have fifteen minutes. I'll get documents faxed from Berswood to give me work to do over the weekend. Meanwhile, find me something. Somewhere I can work in peace. Now.'

He turned and slammed back into his office and, for the first time in her entire life, Meg felt like having hysterics. Serious hysterics.

Hysterics wouldn't help. Where? Where?

Somewhere he could work in peace?

She could organise a mattress and a sleeping bag here, she thought, feeling more and more out of control. But even this office...without air conditioning...

No. Her job was so ended.

And more... In a little more than an hour, the train to Tandaroit would leave without her. Christmas was waiting. As well as that, there was hay waiting, ready to spoil if it wasn't harvested. She must go home.

She made one more miserable phone call, to a dealer in hotel rooms. Unless she'd take the absolute dregs there was nothing, nothing, nothing.

She sat and stared at her hands until exactly fifteen minutes later, when the door slammed open again.

'Well?' he demanded. His anger was back under control. He was icy calm, waiting for her solution. And there was only one solution to give.

'There are no hotels.'

'So?'

So say it. Just say it.

'So you can come home with me,' she said, trying desperately to make her voice bright and confident. 'It's the only solution, and it's a good one. We have a comfortable private spare room with its own bathroom, and we have the Internet. I'll be on call for your secretarial needs. We can't have you trapped in the city over Christmas. My family and I would be pleased if you could spend Christmas with us.'

If her boss's face had been thunderous before, it was worse now. It was as if there were a live hand-grenade ticking between them. The pin had been pulled. Who knew how long these things took to explode?

'You're offering me charity,' he said at last, slowly, carefully, as if saying the word itself was like taking poison.

'It's not charity at all,' she managed, feeling a faint stirring of anger. 'We'd love to have you.' Oooh, what a lie.

But what was the choice? Sleeping bags here was a real possibility, awful as it seemed. She could spend Christmas trying to make this office liveable, working around a situation which was appalling. Or she could try and resurrect Christmas.

If he accepted, then he'd spend the whole time in his room with his computer, she thought. Thank the stars she'd set up Internet access on the farm. It cost more than she could afford, but it had made Scotty jubilant and maybe...just maybe it would be the decider.

'I do not want to be part of anyone else's Christmas,' he snapped.

'You don't need to be. You can stay in your room and work. I can even bring your meals to your room, if you want to take it that far.'

'I can't believe this is the only solution.'

'It's the only one I can think of.'

No matter what she did, no matter what she offered, she

would lose her job over this, Meg thought miserably, and then she thought—why don't I quit now? She could walk away and leave this man to do whatever he wanted over Christmas.

But this was the best job. And maybe…maybe he'd even enjoy it. Letty put on a great Christmas. Miracles could happen.

Send me a miracle, she pleaded, starting her Santa list right now.

'It will work,' she said, managing to sound much more calm than she felt. 'This is a genuine offer and we'd be very pleased to have you.' She glanced at her watch, acting as if it was time to move on. Acting as if the thing had already been decided. 'You will be able to work. The room has a lovely view.' *Not exactly like this one.* 'You will be comfortable and you will be left alone. If you accept my offer, then my train leaves in an hour. I'm sorry you can't get home but this is the best I can do.'

His face was still dark with fury.

If he was so angry, why didn't he contact someone else? she thought. Any socialite in Melbourne would be pleased to be his friend. He was invited everywhere. Surely he didn't wish to spend Christmas with her.

But it seemed he did.

'Your house is large?'

That was easy. 'Yes, it is.'

'No young children?'

'No.' Scotty was fifteen. Surely that didn't count as young.

'And I will have privacy?'

'Yes, sir.'

'Right,' he said roughly, angrily. 'I'll pay your family for my accommodation and I'll work from there.'

'There's no need to pay.'

'This is business,' he snapped. 'Business or nothing.'

'Fine,' she said, accepting the inevitable. 'I'll get changed. We can walk to the station.'

'Walk?'

'It's Christmas,' she said. 'Traffic's gridlocked and it's four blocks.'

'I will have privacy at this place?' he demanded again, suddenly suspicious.

'At my home,' she said, goaded. 'Yes, you will.'

He hesitated. 'And your family...'

'They'll be glad of the extra income,' she said, knowing that this at least was true.

And it seemed it was the right thing to say. He was moving on.

'Don't think I'm accepting this with any degree of complacency,' he snapped. 'We'll discuss this debacle after Christmas. But for now...let's just get it over with.'

CHAPTER TWO

Where was she taking him?

Maybe he should have paid attention, but he'd stalked back into his office and worked until she'd decreed it was time to go. Then he'd walked beside her to the station and stayed silent as she organised tickets. He'd been too angry to do anything else, and too caught up in work. The Berswood faxes had come through just as he left, and he'd spotted a loophole that would have his lawyers busy for weeks.

Had they really thought he wouldn't notice such a problem?

As he walked to the station he was planning his course of attack—and maybe that was no accident. Burying himself in work had always been his way to block out the world, and he was not looking forward to the next three days. Three days immersed in his work, with little to alleviate it, with no hotel gym to burn energy… And missing Elinor and the kids… That hurt.

At least he had the Berswood contract to work on, he told himself as he strode beside his PA, trying to think the legal implications through as she purchased tickets and hurried to the train. Then as the train pulled out, the announcement came through that the train destination was four hours away. What the…?

He and Meg had been forced to sit across the aisle from each other. He looked across at her in alarm. 'Four hours?'

'We get off earlier,' she called. 'Two and a half hours.'

Two and a half hours?

He couldn't even grill her. He sat hard against the window with barely enough room to balance his laptop. Beside him, a woman was juggling two small children, one on her knee and one in a carrycot in the aisle. Meg had someone else's child on her lap. There were people squashed every which way, in a train taking them who knew where?

He was heading into the unknown, with his PA.

She didn't even look like his PA, he thought as the interminable train journey proceeded, and even the Berswood deal wasn't enough to hold his attention. It seemed she'd brought her luggage to the office so she could make a quick getaway. Once he'd grudgingly accepted her invitation, she'd slipped into the Ladies and emerged…different.

His PA normally wore a neat black suit, crisp white blouse and sensible black shoes with solid heels. She wore her hair pulled tightly into an elegant chignon. He'd never seen her with a hair out of place.

She was now wearing hip-hugging jeans, pale blue canvas sneakers—a little bit worn—and a soft white shirt, open necked, with a collar but no sleeves.

What was more amazing was that she'd tugged her chignon free, and her bouncing chestnut curls were flowing over her shoulders. And at her throat was a tiny Christmas angel.

The angel could have been under her corporate shirt for weeks, he thought, stunned at the transformation. She looked casual. She looked completely unbusinesslike—and he didn't like it. He didn't like being on this train. He didn't like it that his PA was chatting happily to the woman beside her about who knew what?

He wasn't in control, and to say he wasn't accustomed to the sensation was an understatement.

William McMaster had been born in control. His parents were distant, to say the least, and he'd learned early that nursery staff came and went. If he made a fuss, they went. He seldom did make a fuss. He liked continuity; he liked his world running smoothly.

His PA was paid to make sure it did.

Meg had come to him with impeccable references. She'd graduated with an excellent commerce degree, she'd moved up the corporate ladder in the banking sector and it was only when her personal circumstances changed that she'd applied for the job with him.

'I need to spend more time with my family,' she'd said and he hadn't asked more.

Her private life wasn't his business.

Only now it was his business. He should have asked more questions. He was trapped with her family, whoever her family turned out to be.

While back in New York...

He needed to contact Elinor, urgently, but he couldn't call her now. It was three in the morning her time. It'd have to wait.

The thought of contacting her made him feel ill. To give such disappointment...

'There's less than an hour to go,' Meg called across the aisle and, to his astonishment, she sounded cheerful. 'Dandle a baby if you're bored. I'm sure the lady beside you would be grateful.'

'I couldn't let him do that.' The young mother beside him looked shocked. 'I'd spoil his lovely suit.'

He winced. He'd taken off his jacket but he still looked corporate and he knew it. He had suits and gym gear. Nothing else.

Surely that couldn't be a problem. But...

Where were they going?

He'd had visions of a suburban house with a comfortable spare room where he could lock himself in and work for three days. He'd pay, so he wouldn't have to be social; something he'd be forced to be if he stayed with any of Melbourne's social set. But now... Where was she taking him?

He was a billionaire. He did not have problems like this.

How did you get off a train?

There was a no alcohol policy on the train, which was just as well as the carriage was starting to look like a party. It was full of commuters going home for Christmas, holidaymakers, everyone escaping the city and heading bush.

Someone started a Christmas singalong, which was ridiculous, but somehow Meg found herself singing along too.

Was she punch-drunk?

No. She was someone who'd lost the plot but there was nothing she could do about it. She had no illusions about her job. She'd messed things up and, even though she was doing the best she could, William McMaster had been denied his Christmas and she was responsible.

Worse, she was taking him home. He hadn't asked where home was. He wasn't interested.

She glanced across the aisle at him and thought he so didn't belong on this train. He looked...

Fabulous, she admitted to herself, and there it was, the thing she'd carefully suppressed since she'd taken this job. W S McMaster was awesome. He was brilliant and powerful and more. He worked her hard but he paid magnificently; he expected the best from her and he got it.

And he was so-o-o sexy. If she wasn't careful, she knew she stood every chance of having a major crush on the guy. But she'd realised that from the start, from that first interview, so she'd carefully compartmentalised her life. He was her boss. Any other sensation had to be carefully put aside.

And she'd learned from him. W S McMaster had compartments down to a fine art. There was never any hint of personal interaction between employer and employee.

But now there needed to be personal interaction. W S McMaster was coming home to her family.

He'd better be nice to Scotty.

He didn't have to be nice to anyone.

Yes, he did, she thought. For the next few days her boundaries needed to shift. Not to be taken away, she reminded herself hastily. Just moved a little. She needed to stop thinking about him as her boss and start thinking about him as someone who should be grateful to her for providing emergency accommodation.

She'd made a start, deliberately getting rid of her corporate gear, making a statement that this weekend wasn't entirely an extension of their work relationship.

He could lock himself in his room for the duration, she thought. She'd sent a flurry of texts to Letty on the subject of which room they'd put him in. The attic was best. There was a good bed and a desk and a comfy chair. It had its own small bathroom. The man was a serious workaholic. Maybe he'd even take his meals in his room.

'He's not singing,' the elderly woman beside her said. Meg had struck up an intermittent conversation with her, so she knew the connection. 'Your boss. Is he not happy?'

'He's stuck in Australia because of the airline strike,' Meg said. 'I suspect he's homesick.'

Homesick. She'd spoken loudly because of the singing, but there was a sudden lull between verses and somehow her words hit silence. Suddenly everyone was looking at William.

'Homesick,' the woman beside Meg breathed, loud enough

for everyone to hear; loud enough to catch William's attention. 'Oh, that's awful. Do you have a wife and kiddies back home?'

'I...no,' William said, clearly astonished that a stranger could be so familiar.

'So it'll just be your parents missing you,' the woman said. 'Oh, I couldn't bear it. Where's home?'

'New York.' The two syllables were said with bluntness bordering on rudeness, but the woman wasn't to be deflected.

'New York City?' she breathed. 'Oh, where? Near Central Park?'

'My apartment overlooks Central Park,' he conceded, and there was an awed hush.

'Will it be snowing there?' someone asked, and Meg looked at her boss's grim face and answered for him. She'd checked the forecast. It was part of her job.

'The forecast is for snow.'

'Oh, and the temperature here's going to be boiling.' The woman doing the questioning looked as if she might burst into tears on his behalf. 'You could have made snowmen in Central Park.'

'I don't...'

'Or thrown snowballs,' someone added.

'Or made a Snowman Santa.'

'Hey, did you see that movie where they fell down and made snow angels?'

'He could do that here in the dust.'

There was general laughter, but it was sympathetic, and then the next carol started and William was mercifully left alone.

Um...maybe she should have protected him from that. Maybe she shouldn't have told anyone he was her boss. Meg looked across at William—immersed in his work again—and thought—I'm taking my boss home for Christmas and all we're offering is dust angels. He could be having a white Christmas in Central Park.

With who?

She didn't know, and she was not going to feel bad about that, she decided. Not until he told her that he was missing a person in particular. If he was simply going to sit in a luxury penthouse and have lobster and caviar and truffles and open gifts to himself...

She was going home to Scotty and Grandma and a hundred cows.

That was a good thought. No matter how appallingly she'd messed up, she was still going home for Christmas.

She was very noble to share, she told herself.

Hold that thought.

Tandaroit wasn't so much a station as a rail head. There'd been talk of closing it down but Letty had immediately presented a petition with over five thousand names on it to their local parliamentarian. No matter that Letty, Scotty and Meg seemed to be the only ones who used it—and that the names on the petition had been garnered by Letty, dressed in gumboots and overalls, sitting on the corner of one of Melbourne's major pedestrian malls in Scotty's now discarded wheelchair. She'd been holding an enormous photograph of a huge-eyed calf with a logo saying 'Save Your Country Cousins' superimposed.

Tandaroit Station stayed.

When Letty wanted something she generally got it. Her energy was legendary. The death of her son and daughter-in-law four years ago had left her shattered, but afterwards she'd hugged Meg and she'd said, 'There's nothing to do but keep going, so we keep going. Let's get you another job.'

Meg's first thought had been to get some sort of accountancy job in Curalo, their closest city, but then they'd found Mr McMaster's advertisement. 'You'd be away from us almost completely for three months of the year but the rest we'd have you almost full-time. That'd be better for Scotty; better for all of us. And look at the pay,' Letty had said, awed. 'Oh, Meg, go for it.'

So she'd gone for it, and now she was tugging her bag down from the luggage rack as William extricated himself from his wedged in position and she was thinking that was what she had to do now. Just go for it. Christmas, here we come, ready or not.

Her bag was stuck under a load of other people's baggage. She gave it a fierce tug and it came loose, just as William freed himself from his seat. She lurched backward and he caught her. And held.

He had to hold her. The train was slowing. There were youngsters sitting in the aisle, she had no hope of steadying herself and she had every chance of landing on top of a child. But her boss was holding her against him, steady as a rock in the swaying train.

And she let him hold her. She was tired and unnerved and overwrought. She'd been trying to be chirpy; trying to pretend everything was cool and she brought someone like her boss home for Christmas every year. She'd been trying to think that she didn't care that she'd just ruined the most fantastic job she'd ever be likely to have.

And suddenly it was all just too much. For one fleeting moment she let her guard down. She let herself lean into him, while she felt his strength, the feel of his new-this-morning crisp linen shirt, the scent of his half-a-month's-salary aftershave...

'Ooh, I hope you two have a very happy Christmas,' the lady she'd been sitting near said, beaming up at them in approval. 'No need for gifts for you two, then. No wonder you're taking him home for Christmas.' And then she giggled. 'You know, I married my boss too. Best thing I ever did. Fourteen grandchildren later... You go for it, love.'

And Meg, who'd never blushed in her life, turned bright crimson and hauled herself out of her boss's arms as if she were burned.

The train was shuddering to a halt. She had to manoeuvre her way through the crowds to get out.

She headed for the door, leaving her boss to follow. If he could. And she wouldn't really mind if he couldn't.

The train dumped them and left, rolling away into the night, civilisation on wheels, leaving them where civilisation wasn't. Nine o'clock on the Tandaroit rail head. Social hub of the world. Or not. There was a single electric light above the entrance, and nothing else for as far as the eye could see.

'So...where exactly are we?' William said, sounding as if he might have just landed on Mars, but Meg wasn't listening. She was too busy staring out into the night, willing the headlights of Letty's station wagon to appear.

Letty was always late. She'd threatened her with death if she was late tonight.

She couldn't even phone her to find out where she was. There was no mobile reception out here. And, as if in echo of her thoughts...

'There's no reception.' Her boss was staring incredulously at his phone.

'There's a land line at the farm.'

'You've brought me somewhere with no cellphone reception?'

Hysterics were once again very close to the surface. Meg felt ill. 'It's better than sleeping at the airport,' she snapped, feeling desperate.

'How is it better?' He was looking where she was looking, obviously hoping for any small sign of civilisation. There wasn't any. Just a vast starlit sky and nothing and nothing and nothing.

'She'll come.'

'Who'll come?'

'My grandmother,' Meg said through gritted teeth. 'If she knows what's good for her, she'll come right now.'

'Your home is how far from the station?'

'Eight miles.'

'Eight!'

'Maybe a bit more.'

'It's a farm?'

'Yes.'

'So Tandaroit…'

She took a couple of deep breaths. Hysterics would help no one. 'It's more of a district than a town,' she admitted. 'There was a school here once, and tennis courts. Not now, though. They use the school for storing stock feed.'

'And your farm's eight miles from this…hub,' he said, his voice carefully, dangerously neutral. 'That's a little far to walk.'

'We're not walking.'

'I was thinking,' he said, 'of how long it might take to walk back here when I decide to leave.'

That caught her. She stopped staring out into the night and stared at her boss instead. Thinking how this might look to him.

'You mean if my family turn into axe-murderers?' she ventured.

'I've seen *Deliverance*.'

Her lips twitched. 'We're not that bad.'

'You don't own a car?'

'No.'

'Yet I pay you a very good wage.'

'We have Letty's station wagon and a tractor. What else do we need?'

'You like sitting on rail heads waiting for grandmothers who may or may not appear?'

'She'll appear.'

'I believe,' he said, speaking slowly, as if she was ever so slightly dim, 'that I might be changing my mind about travelling to a place that's eight miles from a train which comes… how often a day?'

'Three or four times, but it only stops here once.'

'Once,' he said faintly. 'It stops once, eight miles away from a place that has no mobile phone reception, with a grandmother who even her granddaughter appears to be feeling homicidal about.'

Uh-oh. She ran her fingers through her hair and tried to regroup.

'Not that it's not a very kind invitation,' he added and she choked. She was so close to the edge…

'I thought it was kind,' she managed.

'Kind?'

'I could have left you in the office.'

'Or not. It was you,' he reminded her, 'who got me into this mess.'

'You could have listened to the news on the radio this morning as well as me,' she snapped and then thought—had she really said that? What little hope she had of keeping her job had finally gone.

'That's what I pay you for,' he snapped back.

Well, if she'd gone this far… 'I left the office at eleven last night. I was at your hotel just after six. I don't get eight hours off?'

'I pay you for twenty-four hours on call.'

'I'm not fussed about what you pay me,' she snapped. The tension of the last few hours was suddenly erupting, and there was no way she could keep a lid on her emotions. 'I'm fussed about the ten minutes I spent washing my hair this morning when I should have been listening to the radio and hearing about the airline strike. I'm fussed about being stuck with my boss, who doesn't seem the least bit grateful that I'm doing the best I can. And now I'm stuck with someone who has the capacity to mess with my family Christmas if he doesn't stop making me feel guilty and if he spends the rest of Christmas playing Manhattan Millionaire stuck here, and it's All My Fault.'

She stopped. Out of breath. Out of emotion. Out of words. And it seemed he was the same.

Well, what could he say? Should he agree? He could hardly sack her here, right now, Meg thought. If he did…she and Letty really could be axe-murderers.

Or they could just leave him here, sitting on the Tandaroit station until the next train came through late tomorrow.

'Don't do it,' he growled, and she remembered too late he had an uncanny ability to read her mind. He hesitated and then obviously decided he had no choice but to be a little bit conciliatory. 'It's very…clean hair,' he ventured.

'Thank you.' What else was there to say?

'This…grandmother…'

'Letty.'

'She's backed up by other family members? With other cars?' He was obviously moving on from her outburst, deciding the wisest thing was to ignore it.

'Just Letty.'

'And…who else?'

'Scotty. My kid brother.'

'You said no children,' he said, alarmed.

'Fifteen's not a child.'

'Okay,' he conceded. 'Who else?'

'No one.'

'Where are your parents?'

'They died,' she said. 'Four years ago. Car crash.'

He was quick. He had it sorted straight away. 'Which is why you took the job with me?'

'So I could get home more,' she said. 'Ironic, isn't it?'

But he was no longer listening. Had he been listening, anyway? 'Could this be Letty?' he demanded.

Oh, please… She stared into the darkness, and there it was, two pinpricks of light in the distance, growing bigger.

Headlights.

'*Deliverance,*' she muttered and her boss almost visibly flinched.

'Just joking,' she said.

'Don't joke.'

'No jokes,' she agreed and took a deep breath and picked up her holdall. 'Okay, here's Letty and, while you may not appreciate it, we really are safe. We've organised you a nice private bedroom with Internet. You can use our telephone if there are people you need to contact other than over the Web. You can stay in your room and work all Christmas but Letty is one of the world's best cooks and here really is better than camping in the office.'

'I imagine it will be,' he said, but he didn't sound sure. 'And I am grateful.'

'I bet you are.'

'It's lovely hair,' he said, surprisingly. 'It would have been a shame to leave it dirty for Christmas.'

'Thank you,' she managed again. Cheering up, despite herself.

Letty was coming. She could send W S McMaster to his allocated room and she could get on with Christmas.

Anger was counterproductive. Anger would get him nowhere.

Yes, his PA had messed up his Christmas plans but the

thing was done. And no, he should never have agreed to come with her to this middle-of-nowhere place. If he'd thought it through, maybe he could have rung a realtor and even bought a small house. Anything rather than being stuck at the beck and call of one wiry little woman called Letty who seemed to own the only set of wheels in the entire district.

They hadn't passed another car. The car they were in sounded sick enough to be worrying. There was something wrong with its silencer—as if it didn't have one. The engine was periodically missing. The gearbox seemed seriously shot. They were jolting along an unsealed road. He was wedged in the back seat with both his and Meg's gear and Letty was talking at the top of her lungs.

'I'm late because Dave Barring popped over to check on Millicent. Millicent's a heifer I'm worried is going to calve over Christmas.' Letty was yelling at him over her shoulder. 'Dave's our local vet and he's off for Christmas so I wanted a bit of reassurance. He reckons she should be right,' she told Meg. 'Then I had to pick up three bags of fertiliser from Robertson's. Robby said if I didn't take it tonight the place'd be locked up till after New Year. So I'm sorry it's a bit squashed in the back.'

'I'm fine,' he said. He wasn't.

Anger was counterproductive. If he said it often enough he might believe it.

'We can swap if you want,' Meg said.

'You won't fit in the back,' Letty said. 'Not with Killer.'

Letty was right. The combination of Meg and Killer would never fit in the back seat with the baggage.

Killer looked like a cross between a Labrador and an Old English sheepdog. He was huge and hairy and black as the night around them. He'd met Meg with such exuberance that once more William had had to steady her, stopping her from being pushed right over.

While Killer had greeted Meg, Letty had greeted him with a handshake that was stronger than a man's twice her size. Then she'd greeted her granddaughter with a hug that made Meg wince, and then she'd moved into organisational mode.

'You in the back. Meg, in the front with Killer. I told Scotty I'd be back by nine-thirty so we need to move.'

They were moving. They were flying over the corrugated road with a speed that made him feel as if he was about to lose teeth.

'So what do we call you?' Letty said over her shoulder.

'I told you; he's Mr McMaster,' Meg said, sounding muffled, as well she might under so much dog.

'Mac?' Letty demanded.

'He's my boss,' Letty said, sounding desperate. 'He's not Mac.'

'He's our guest for Christmas. What do we call you?' she demanded again. 'How about Mac?'

Do not let the servants become familiar.

Master William.

Mr McMaster.

Sir.

Once upon a time a woman called Hannah had called him William. To her appalling cost...

'How about Bill?' Letty demanded. 'That's short for William. Or Billy.'

'Billy?' Meg said, sounding revolted. 'Grandma, can we...'

'William,' he said flatly, hating it.

'Willie?' Letty said, hopeful.

'William.'

Letty sighed. 'Will's better. Though it is a bit short.'

'Like Meg,' Meg said.

'You know I like Meggie.'

'And you know I don't answer to it. We don't have to call you anything you don't like,' Meg said over her shoulder. 'I'm happy to keep calling you Mr McMaster.'

'You are not,' Letty retorted. 'Not over Christmas. And why are you calling him Mr McMaster, anyway? How long have you worked for him? Three years?'

'He calls me Miss Jardine.'

'Then the pair of you need to come off your high horses,' Letty retorted. 'Meg and William it is, and if I hear any sign of Ms or Mr then it's Meggie and Willie for the rest of Christmas. Right?'

'Okay with me,' Meg said, resigned.

'Fine,' William said.

Define *fine*.

He was expecting hillbilly country. What he got was *Fantasia*. They sped over a crest and there it was, spread out before them, a house straight out of a fairy tale.

Or not. As he got closer…

Not a fairy tale. A Christmas tableau.

The farmhouse, set well back from the road among scattered gums, was lit up like a series of flashing neon signs. It was so bright it should almost be visible from the next state.

'Oh, my…' Meg breathed before William could even get his breath back. 'Grandma, what have you done?'

'We both did it,' Letty said proudly. 'Me and Scotty. You like our sleigh?'

The house had two chimneys, with what looked like an attic between them. The sleigh took up the entire distance between chimneys. There was a Santa protruding from the chimney on the left. Or, rather, part of Santa. His lower half. His legs were waving backwards and forwards, as if Santa had become stuck in descent. The movement wasn't smooth, so he moved gracefully from left to right, then jerked back with a movement sharp enough to dislodge vertebrae.

The house was Christmas City. There were lights from one end to the other, a myriad of fairy lights that made the house look like something out of a cartoon movie.

'It took us days,' Letty said, pleased with the awed hush. 'When you rang and said there was a chance you couldn't get home tonight Scotty and I were ready to shoot ourselves. We've worked our tails off getting this right.'

'I can see that you have,' Meg said, sounding as stunned as he was. 'Grandma...'

'And, before you say a word, we got it all over the Internet,' Letty informed her. 'Scotty found it. It was a package deal advertised in July by some lady cleaning out her garage. She'd just bought the house and found it, and she practically paid us to take it away. Some people,' she said, slowing the car so they could admire the house in all its glory, 'have no appreciation of art.'

'But running it,' Meg said helplessly. 'It'll cost...'

'It's practically all solar,' Letty cut in. 'Except Santa. Well, there's not a lot of solar Santa Claus's backsides out there. We haven't quite got the legs right, but I'll adjust them before Christmas. Still... What do you think?'

There was suddenly a touch of anxiety in her voice. William got it, and he thought maybe this lady wasn't as tough as she sounded. She surely wanted to please this girl, Meg, sitting somewhere under her dog.

'You climb up on that roof again and I'll give all of your Christmas presents to the dogs. But I love it,' Meg said as the car came to a halt.

'Really?'

'I really love it.' Meg giggled. 'It's kitsch and funny and those legs are just plain adorable.'

'What do you think?' Letty said, and she swivelled and looked straight at him. 'Will?'

'William. Um…'

'No lies,' she said. 'Is my Meg just humouring me?'

Meg swivelled too. She was covered in dog but somehow he managed to see her expression.

Mess with my grandma and I'll mess with you, her look said, and it was such a look that he had to revise all over again what he thought of his competent, biddable PA.

His hostess for Christmas.

'Adorable,' he said faintly.

'You're lying,' Letty said, and he found himself smiling.

'I am,' he agreed, and he met Meg's glare square on. 'There's nothing adorable about a pair of crimson trousers stuck in a chimney. However, it's fantastical and truly in the spirit of Christmas. As soon as we came over the crest I just knew this was going to be a Christmas to remember.'

'Better than being stuck in the office?' Meg said, starting to smile.

'Better than the office.' Maybe.

'Then that's okay,' Letty said, accelerating again. 'If you like my decorations then you can stay. The pair of you.'

'You're very generous,' William said.

'We are, aren't we?' Meg agreed, and hugged her dog.

And then the car pulled to a halt beside the house—and straight away there was more dog. Killer's relatives? William opened the door and four noses surged in, each desperate to reach him. They were all smaller than Killer, he thought with some relief. Black and white. Collies?

'Fred, Milo, Turps, Roger, leave the man alone,' Meg called and the dog pack headed frantically for the other side of the car to envelope someone they obviously knew and loved. Meg was on the ground hugging handfuls of ecstatic dog, being welcomed home in truly splendid style.

William extricated himself from the car and stared down at her. Any hint of his cool, composed PA had disappeared. Meg was being licked from every angle, she was coated with dog and she was showing every sign of loving it.

'Killer's Meg's dog,' Letty said, surveying the scene in satisfaction. 'Fred and Roger are mine. Turps and Milo belong to Scotty but they all love Meg. She's so good with dogs.'

Meg was well and truly buried—and the sight gave him pause.

In twenty-four hours he should be entering his apartment overlooking Central Park. His housekeeper would have come in before him, made sure the heating was on, filled the place with provisions, even set up a tasteful tree. The place would be warm and elegant and welcoming.

Maybe not as welcoming as this.

He would have been welcomed almost as much as this on Christmas Day, he thought, and that was a bleak thought. A really bleak thought. The disappointment he'd felt when he'd learned of the air strike hit home with a vengeance.

He didn't show emotion. He was schooled not to show it. But now…

It wasn't any use thinking of it, he thought, struggling to get a grip on his feelings. Elinor would make alternative arrangements. The kids were accustomed to disappointment.

That made it worse, not better.

Don't think about it. Why rail against something he could do nothing about?

Why was the sight of this woman rolling with dog intensifying the emotion? Making him feel as if he was on the outside looking in?

Back off, he told himself. He was stuck here for three days. Make the most of it and move on.

Meg was struggling to her feet and, despite a ridiculous urge to go fend off a few dogs, he let her do it herself, regain her feet and her composure, or as much composure as a woman who'd just been buried with dogs could have.

'No, down. Oh, I've missed you guys. But where's Scotty?'

Scotty was watching them.

The kid in the doorway was tall and gangly and way too skinny, even allowing for an adolescent growth spurt. He had Meg's chestnut curls, Meg's freckles, Meg's clear green eyes, but William's initial overriding impression was that he looked almost emaciated. There was a scar running the length of his left cheek. He had a brace enclosing his left leg, from foot to hip.

He was looking nervously at William, but as soon as William glanced at him he turned his attention to his sister. Who'd turned her attention to him.

'Scotty...' Dogs forgotten, Meg headed for her brother and enveloped him in a hug that was almost enough to take him from his feet. The kid was four or five inches taller than Meg's meagre five feet four or so, but he had no body weight to hold him down. Meg could hug as much as she wanted. There was no way Scotty could defend himself.

Not that he was defending himself. He was hugging Meg back, but with a wary glance at William over her head. Suspicious.

'Hi,' William said. 'I'm William.' There. He'd said it as if it didn't hurt at all.

'I'm Scott,' the boy said, and Meg released him and turned to face William, her arm staying round her brother, her face a mixture of defensiveness and pride.

'This is my family,' she said. 'Letty and Scotty and our dogs.'

'Scott,' Scott said again, only it didn't come out as it should. He was just at that age, William thought, adolescent trying desperately to be a man but his body wasn't cooperating. His voice was almost broken, but not quite.

And, aside from his breaking voice, his leg looked a mess as well. You didn't get to wear a brace that looked like scaffolding if the bones underneath weren't deeply problematic.

Meg had told him her parents had died four years ago. Had Scott been in the same car crash? The brace spoke of serious ongoing concerns.

Why hadn't he found this out? William had always prided himself on hiring on instinct rather than background checks. A background check right now would be handy.

'Did the car get you here all right?' the kid asked, and William could see he was making an effort to seem older than he was. 'It needs about six parts replacing but Grandma won't let me touch it.'

'You mess with that car and we're stuck,' Letty said. 'Next milk cheque I'll get it seen to.'

'I wouldn't hurt it.'

'You're fifteen. You're hardly a mechanic.'

'Yeah, but I've read…'

'No,' Letty snapped. 'The car's fine.'

'I tried messing with my dad's golf cart when I was fifteen,' William said, interrupting what he suspected to be a long running battle. 'Dad was away for a month. He came back and I'd supplied him with a hundred or so extra horsepower. Sadly, he touched the accelerator and hit the garage door. The fuss! Talk about lack of appreciation.'

Scott smiled at that—a shy smile but a smile nonetheless. So did Letty, and so did Meg. And his reaction surprised him.

He kind of liked these smiles, he decided. They took away a little of the sting of the last few hours. It seemed he could put thoughts of *Deliverance* aside. These people were decent. He could settle down here and get some work done.

And maybe he could try and make Meg smile again. Was that a thought worth considering?

'The Internet's down,' Scott said and smiling was suddenly the last thing on his mind.

'The Internet…' Meg said, sounding stunned. 'What's wrong with it?'

'There's been a landslip over at Tandaroit South and the lines are down. They don't know when it'll be fixed. Days probably.'

He was having trouble figuring this out. 'Lines?'

'Telephone lines,' Scott said, an adolescent explaining something to slightly stupid next-generation-up.

'You use phone lines for the Internet?'

'I know, dinosaur stuff and slow as,' Scott said. 'But satellite connection costs heaps. Mickey has satellite connection, but Meg's only just figured out a way we can afford dial-up.'

'And…' He checked his phone. 'There's no mobile reception here either,' he said slowly.

'No,' Meg told him.

'And now no fixed phone?'

'No.' Meg sounded really nervous—as well she might.

'So no Internet until the line's fixed?'

'Well, duh,' Scott said, sounding adolescent and a bit belligerent. Maybe he thought his sister was about to be attacked. Maybe she was.

But William wasn't focused on Meg. He was feeling ill. To be so far from contact… He should have rung Elinor before he left Melbourne. He should have woken her.

He *had* to contact her. Her entire Christmas would be ruined.

'I can't stay here,' he said through gritted teeth. 'The airport'd be better than this.'

'Hey!' Letty said.

He didn't have time or space to pacify her. All he could think of was Elinor—and two small kids. 'I need to use a phone,' he snapped. 'Now.'

'I have supper on,' Letty said.

'This is important. There are people waiting for me in New York.'

'But you're not due there until tomorrow,' Meg said, astounded. 'They'll hardly be waiting at the airport yet.'

'I still need a phone. Sort it, Jardine,' he ordered.

He watched her long thoughtful stare, the stare he'd come to rely on. This woman was seriously good. He depended on her in a crisis.

He was depending on her now, and she didn't let him down.

'Supper first,' she said at last. 'If it can wait that long.'

Maybe it could, he conceded. 'Supper first. Then what?'

'Then I'll take you over to Scotty...to Scott's friend, Mickey's. Mickey lives two miles north of here and his parents have satellite connection. You can use the Internet or their Skype phone for half an hour while I catch up with Mickey's mum. The weekend before Christmas she'll probably still be up.'

'I need it for more...'

'Half an hour max,' she said, blunt and direct, as he'd come to expect. 'Even that's a favour. They're dairy farmers and it's late now. But you should be able to talk to New York via Skype. Mind, it'll be before seven in the morning over there, so trying to wake anyone up...'

'She'll wake.'

'Of course she will,' she said, almost cordially, and he looked at her with suspicion.

'Miss Jardine...'

'I'm Meg,' she said. 'Remember? Meg until I'm back on the payroll, if that ever happens.'

'I don't believe I've fired you.'

'So you haven't,' she said. 'And Christmas miracles happen. Okay, I'll take you over to Mickey's and I will try and get you in touch with New York but let's not go anywhere until we've had some of Letty's mango trifle. You have made me mango trifle, haven't you, Grandma?'

'Of course.'

'Then what are we waiting for?' she demanded, and she grabbed her bag, manoeuvred her way through her dog pack and headed inside. 'Trifle, yay.' Then she paused. 'Oh, I'm sorry, sir,' she said, looking back. 'I mean… William. Do you want your mango trifle in your room? Do you want me to take you straight there?'

'Um…no,' he said weakly.

'That's a shame,' she said. 'If you're sitting at the kitchen table you'll want seconds. There's less for us that way, but if you're sure… Lead the way, Grandma. Let's go.'

CHAPTER THREE

AN HOUR later, fortified with a supper of huge ham sandwiches and a mango trifle which seemed to have stunned William, they were in the car again, heading for Mickey's. It was almost eleven but Meg knew enough of Mickey to believe he'd still be awake, Net surfing.

This was the only option for her boss to contact home. It had to work.

Who did he have waiting for him in New York? He wasn't saying, and she wasn't asking. They drove in silence.

She pulled up outside a farmhouse a lot less startling than Letty's. Instead of knocking, though, while William watched from the car, she tossed gravel at the lit end window.

Mickey hauled up the window. 'Bruce?'

That one word deflected her thoughts from her own problems. Once upon a time, Mickey would have expected Scott, Meg thought bleakly. The kids were the same age and they lived barely two miles apart. Four years ago, their bikes had practically created a rut in the road between.

But the rut had long been repaired. Tonight Scott had been too tired to come with them. He was always tired. He'd hardly touched his supper. His school work was slipping; he was simply uninterested. There were problems apart from his physical ones, she thought. In the New Year she'd have to talk to his doctors again about depression.

But how could she sort depression for a kid facing what Scott was facing? How long before he could ride a bike again? He believed he never could.

She hadn't accepted it, though. She'd fight it every inch of the way. But that meant staying employed so she could pay the bills. It also meant being nice to her boss over Christmas, or as nice as she could. Which meant throwing stones at a neighbour's window three days before Christmas.

'Bruce?' Mickey called again and she hauled her attention back to here and now. 'It's Meg,' she called to the kid at the window.

'Meg?' Mickey sounded pleased, and she liked that. She liked coming home. She liked it that every person in the tiny shopping town of Tandaroit East knew her, and she could go into every house in the district and find people she knew.

'The phones are out and I have a guest here who needs to contact New York,' she said. 'Scotty…Scott said you have Skype.'

'Hey, I do,' Mickey said, sounding inordinately pleased. 'I've never used it for New York, though. I don't know anyone there.'

'Would it be all right if Mr McMaster used it?'

'William,' said William.

'Hi, Will.' Mickey was clearly delighted to have company.

'Are your parents asleep?' Meg asked.

'Dad is. He's gotta milk at five. But Mum's making mince pies. You want me to tell her you're here?'

'Yes, please,' Meg said thankfully. 'I don't want to be caught creeping round the place at night without your parents knowing.'

'Yeah,' Mickey said in a laughing voice that said such an action had indeed been indulged in on more than one occasion before now.

And Meg thought sadly of how much of a normal kid's life Scotty was missing.

So her boss used Skype while Meg helped Mickey's mum scoop mincemeat into pastry shells. Jenny wasn't much older than Meg, but while Meg had gone to university and then to a career, Jenny had married her childhood sweetheart at seventeen and had Mickey nine months later.

She could have done the same, Meg thought, feeling nostalgic and a bit jealous as she took in the cosy farm kitchen, the muddle of Christmas baking, the detritus of a farming family, with twin girls of nine as well as Mickey.

'This place looks gorgeous,' Meg said, sitting on an ancient kitchen chair and scooping mincemeat.

'Nope,' Jenny said and grinned. 'Gorgeous is what's up in Mickey's room right now.' Jenny had been introduced before Mickey had taken William off to link him with the other side of the world, and Meg could see her friend adding two and two and making seventeen.

'You mean my boss.'

'I mean the man you've brought home for Christmas. Yum. I've seen him in the gossip rags and he's even more gorgeous in the flesh. He's a squillionaire. He's your boss. And you've got him for Christmas.'

'You can have him if you want him,' Meg said morosely. 'He might be happier here. You have a computer.'

'Yeah, and I have twins and Ian's extended family arriving tomorrow to stay for a week. There'll be eight kids in the house. Heaven help us.' But she was smiling as she said it and Meg thought, even though she had never understood Jenny's decision to marry and make a home so early, maybe... just maybe it made sense.

'You're not getting clucky,' Jenny demanded, following her gaze, and Meg realised she was staring at a pile of paper chains at the far end of the table. She remembered making them as a kid.

'I have spare paper,' Jenny said happily. 'You can help your boss make paper chains. Very bonding.'

'Very funny.'

'No, I think it's lovely,' Jenny said, getting serious. 'To have him here for Christmas... Oooh, Meg. But does he have a girlfriend?'

'I have no idea.'

'No idea?'

'Well, I'm his PA and I haven't been told to send flowers to anyone lately. But he was desperate to use the phone.'

'So who's he ringing?'

'I have no idea.'

'I'll ask Mickey.'

But Mickey, who wandered into the kitchen two minutes later, was no help at all.

'Yeah, he's talking but I put my headset on and left him to it. Nah, I didn't hear who to. Mum, you reckon it's too late to put another CD on my Christmas list? I've just found this sick new band...'

'Forget it,' his mother said. 'Santa asked for a list a month ago and you couldn't think of anything except a farm bike, which you know we can't afford. So what are you giving William for Christmas, Meg, love?'

Uh-oh. Here was yet another problem she hadn't thought through.

On Christmas morning she sat under the Christmas tree and opened presents. Lots of presents.

Meg's mother had always believed in...excess. She'd loved

Christmas with a passion and Meg had still been getting a Santa stocking at twenty-five.

The next year, with her parents dead, Meg had over-compensated, and so had Letty and, to their delight, so did Scott. He'd plundered his piggy bank and asked the nurses to help him.

They'd had a silly, over-the-top Christmas in Scotty's hospital ward, and the tradition had thus continued.

So Meg's last minute Christmas spree had filled her baggage with gifts but there wasn't a lot she could recycle for William.

'He has everything,' she said, feeling hopeless.

'He hasn't got Skype,' Mickey said.

'He will next week when he goes back to New York.'

'So buy him a satellite dish for the weekend,' Mickey said cheerfully. 'Then Scotty can use it after he leaves.'

Right. With what?

'That's just a bit more money than I had in mind to spend,' she retorted and Mickey screwed up his nose and sloped off to watch television in the other room. Grown-up problems. Not his.

'So how's the debt reduction going?' Jenny asked. Jenny had been one of the many who'd come to Meg's aid after the crash. She knew of Meg's debt. Scott's medical expenses were colossal, and on top of that they'd had to keep the farm going when there was no one to run it.

'It's okay,' she told her friend. As long as I'm not sacked, she added under her breath. But I'm probably sacked, so let's not go there.

'So it's just a present for Mr Sexy-Eyes. Can you knit?'

'No!'

'So that's home-made socks out of the question. Leaves only aftershave,' Jenny said. 'Ian gets some every year from his Aunty Merle, only Merle hasn't noticed that Ian's had a full beard for twenty years now. I'm happy to donate a gallon or six.'

'I suspect he uses his own.'

'I guess he would,' Jenny said, sliding one batch of mince pies out of the oven and another in. 'So there's nothing in the world he needs.'

'Except a plane out of here.'

'Out of your control, love,' Jenny said. 'It'll have to be aftershave.' She glanced up at the ceiling. 'I'd so love to be a fly on the wall, wouldn't you? I wonder who he's talking to?'

'It's not my business,' Meg said, a bit too primly, and Jenny laughed.

'You mean the walls are too thick and there's no way we can find out. Let's face it, you're interested, and why not? He's the most eligible man on the planet, as well as the most gorgeous. As well as that, he's your house guest for three days. You have him trapped. Meg darling, if you don't try and get him interested—seriously interested—you have rocks in your head.'

'Finished,' William's voice growled from the door and they both jumped and Meg did her blushing thing again. That was twice now. All I want for Christmas is my dignity, she thought desperately, as Jenny stifled laughter.

'Did…did you get onto who you wanted?' she managed, wondering how pink her face was.

'Yes, thank you.' How much had he heard? she thought. *The most eligible man on the planet…* And… *You have him trapped…* If he thought…

'Who did you need to talk to?' Jenny asked innocently and offered him a plate of mince pies.

'Friends,' he said shortly, his face expressionless. Meg knew that expression. It meant the McMaster displeasure was about to wreak consequences. There wasn't a lot of wreaking he could do right now, though, except wave away the mince pie plate as if it was poison.

'Eat my mince pies or I'll be offended for ever,' Jenny said. 'The price of my Internet café is a compliment for the cook.'

And he really was trapped, Meg thought. He was forced not to snap; he was forced even to be pleasant.

So he ate and he somehow managed to tell Jenny her mince pies were excellent, while Meg tried to get her face in order, and she almost managed it but then Jenny, dog at a bone, refusing to be deflected, said, 'So are you going to tell us who this friend is who's awake at six o'clock in the morning in New York?' and Meg blushed all over again.

'Jenny, he doesn't have to answer.'

'No, but I'm interested.'

'Thank you very much for your Internet use,' William said, clipped, tight and angry. He tugged his wallet out and laid a note on the kitchen table. A note so large it made Jenny gasp.

'What do you think you're doing?'

'Paying,' he said.

'Put it away,' Jenny said, angry to match now. 'There's no need for that.'

'Jenny's my friend,' Meg said. 'She'd never charge.'

'She's not *my* friend.'

Whoa. Line overstepped. She was home for Christmas and there were some things which she would not put up with. Hurting Jenny was one of them.

'She is because she let you use the Internet when she didn't have to. Without thought of payment. You won't have to walk back to the station. I'll drive you,' she snapped. 'Jenny, do you have a sleeping bag I can borrow? And a water bottle? Give him a couple more of those mince pies so he won't starve.'

'Hey, I wasn't that offended,' Jenny said, her flash of hurt disappearing and being replaced by her customary laughter. She took William's money and tucked it back into his suit pocket. 'It was very nice of him to offer.'

'It was not nice,' Meg said, glowering. 'He was being snarky.'

'Snarky?' William said.

'Don't look at me like I'm speaking some other language,' Meg retorted. 'You know what snarky is. Jenny. Sleeping bag.'

'You're not serious,' Jenny said. 'If you are, he can sleep here.'

'He's not your friend. He just said so.'

'He wasn't serious.'

'I was,' William said. 'But I'm having second thoughts.'

'You know, I think that's wise,' Jenny said, and grinned again and waggled her finger at the pair of them. 'Birds in their little nest agree…'

'Jenny!'

'Go on, get out of here, the two of you,' Jenny said cheerfully. 'Take him home, Meg, and don't even think of going via the station. Can you just see the headlines? Tomorrow's express train thundering through Tandaroit Station, with William McMaster sleeping off the effect of too many mince pies on a deserted platform? So be nice to her, William, and if you can possibly manage it, tell her who it is that you contacted tonight. She's dying to know, even if it isn't her business.'

She raised floury hands and shooed them out into the hall, out of the front door. She banged it shut after them, and then tugged it open again. An afterthought had just occurred.

'It's the season for peace on earth and goodwill to all men,' she called after them. 'So don't leave him on the railway station.'

* * *

They drove home in silence. Meg was too embarrassed to say anything. William simply…didn't.

She pulled up outside the house and made to get out, but William's hand came down onto her arm, making her pause.

'I'm sorry,' he said. 'But I don't take kindly to questions.'

'That's your right. But you will be nice to my family and to my friends.'

'I will be nice to your family and to your friends,' he repeated. 'Tell me about Scott.'

'Sorry?'

'I've employed you for three years. I've never asked about your family.

'I don't take kindly to questions,' she intoned and he grimaced.

'That's your right,' he conceded. 'Of course you're not obligated to tell me.'

'As you're not obligated to tell me who you just telephoned.' She relented then, sighed and put up her hands in mock surrender. 'No. Don't tell me. It's Jenny who wanted to know that one, not me.' And how about that for a barefaced lie? she thought, but some lies were almost compulsory.

But William's question still hung, unanswered, and he wasn't taking it back.

She glanced at the house. Apart from the Christmas decorations it was all in darkness. Letty and Scott would be long asleep. Even the dogs hadn't stirred on their return. They'd be sleeping in a huge huddle at the end of Scott's bed, she knew. Turps and Roger would be on the bed itself—Scott had trained them to lie still so he could use them as a rest for his brace. The others would be on the floor, as close as they could get.

She loved Scotty so much it hurt. It hurt so much she wanted to cry. And, all at once, it was easy to answer William's question. She wanted to talk.

'Scotty's my half-brother,' she said, staring ahead into the darkness. Speaking almost to herself. 'My mum was a single mum—she had me early and she raised me the hard way, with no parental support. Then, when I was nine, she met Scott's dad. Alex was a farmer, a fair bit older than she was. Mum was selling second-hand clothes at a market and Alex had come to town to check out some new, innovative water pump. He never bought the pump but he took one look at Mum and he fell hard.'

'Love at first sight,' William said, and he sounded a bit derisive. Meg glared at him. He was on shaky ground. Derision wasn't something she was putting up with tonight.

And apparently he realised it. 'Sorry,' he said. 'Sorry, sorry. Love at first sight. It happens.'

'So it does,' she said and glared at him a bit longer until she was sure he was remembering the railway station and the water bottle and the express train thundering through, crowded with people with cameras.

'So it did,' she reiterated as he attempted to look apologetic—not a good fit for W S McMaster but it was a start. Her glare faded. 'I remember the weekend Alex invited us here. He was a great big dairy farmer, in his forties. He hardly talked. That was okay. Mum was a talker, and I remember he just kept looking at Mum like she was some sort of magic. And then I met Letty and Letty was my magic. We arrived on the Friday night and Mum and Alex couldn't take their eyes off each other all weekend, and on Sunday Letty said "call me Grandma." It was like we'd come home. We had come home. Alex took us back to Melbourne and we threw our things into the back of his truck and we headed back here and stayed. Alex married Mum a month later. I was a flower girl. Letty made me the most gorgeous dress. We were so happy, and then five years later Scotty was born and it was perfect.'

'Nothing's perfect,' William said, as if he couldn't help himself, and she shook her head in disgust.

'And there's no such thing as love at first sight? Don't mess with my fairy tales, Mr McMaster. It was love at first sight and it was perfect for sixteen whole years. Sure, the farm's not big and we struggled a bit, but Mum still did markets and everyone helped. I was good at school and we knew there was no way the farm would support Scotty and me—or even one of us—but I was really happy going to university. I missed it more when I got a full-time job, but I was still pretty happy, having this place here as my backstop. And then four years ago a truck came round a bend on the wrong side of the road and it all crumpled to nothing.'

Silence.

'I'm so sorry,' he said at last.

'Yeah,' she said grimly. 'It makes you realise that when you have the fairy tale you hang on and you appreciate it every single moment. Just like that…' She shook her head, shaking away nightmares. 'Anyway, Mum and Alex were killed instantly. Scotty was eleven. He was in the back seat. He just broke…everything. For months we thought he'd be a paraplegic, but he had so much grit. He *has* so much grit. He's fought and fought. For ages neighbours kept the farm going for us. We thought we'd have to sell but then Letty and I figured maybe we could keep it. If we use my salary to augment the income, we can just get by. It's where Scotty's happy. It's where Letty's happy.'

'And your job with me…'

'See, there's the fairy tale again,' she said and smiled, but he didn't smile back. He looked intent, as if trying to see meaning behind her words. It disconcerted her, but no matter, she had to keep going. 'I thought I'd get a job in Curalo and commute the twenty miles,' she told him, 'but then along came your advertisement and it's been fabulous. We have a lady who comes and milks for us while I'm not here. Letty's still active. We've coped.'

'So if I sack you…'

Her smile faded. 'Then…'

'Then the fairy tale ends again?'

'It's not as bad as that,' she said and tilted her chin. 'We'll manage.'

'I won't sack you.'

'I don't need sympathy.'

'I'm not offering it. We'll put this behind us as an unfortunate aberration…'

'On my part.'

'On your part,' he agreed gravely. 'It's been a sad hiccup in your normally exemplary efficiency. We'll get this weekend behind us and then go back to where we were. You're normally an extremely competent employee.'

'Gee, thanks,' she said before she could stop herself. Who was being snarky now?

'If that's sarcasm…'

'No, I'm overwhelmed,' she said. 'Honestly I am.' She had to get herself under control here. Meek, she told herself. Do meek.

'I don't give compliments that aren't deserved,' he said stiffly and she thought—what am I doing, joshing with a guy who controls my life? But there was something about this day, or this night, this time, this season—maybe even it was just that Santa was still waggling dumbly overhead—that made her refuse to treat this as normal. She wasn't going back to being Miss Jardine; not just yet.

'You know you don't have to simply "get this weekend behind us,"' she said cautiously. 'You could enjoy it.'

'I'm hardly in a position to enjoy it.'

'Because you don't have the phone or the Internet?'

'Because I'm right out of my comfort zone,' he said honestly. 'And I want to be back in New York.'

'And I want my parents back,' she retorted. 'But that doesn't stop me enjoying what I have. The here and now.'

'That's very commendable.'

'It is, isn't it,' she said evenly. 'In fact, if I'm not mistaken, my boss just commended me. He said I was normally an extremely competent employee. So while I'm ahead I might just stop.' She swung herself out of the car and waited for him to do likewise. 'I have an early start, Mr McMaster, so I need to go to bed.'

'Why do you have an early start?'

'I milk cows,' she said, heading for the back door. 'If you can't sleep and run out of work, then you're welcome to join me at dawn. Instead of a gym workout. If I were you, though, I wouldn't wear a suit.' And she walked into the house and left him to follow—if he wanted.

What choice did he have?

None at all.

CHAPTER FOUR

HE WOKE to the sound of cows. Many cows. The window of his attic bedroom was open and the not-so-gentle lowing was filling the room. The old, comfortable bed, the faded furnishings and the unaccustomed sounds were so different from his normal environment that he struggled to take it in.

But he got it soon enough. He was trapped for Christmas. On Meg's farm.

Meg...

In the pre-dawn light the name felt strange, almost dangerous. He linked his hands loosely behind his head and stared upward, trying to assimilate how he was feeling. The planked ceiling ran up to a peak. He'd be right underneath Santa's sleigh, he thought, and that seemed so unnerving he unlinked his hands and swung himself straight out of bed.

He didn't intend to lie in bed and think about Santa. About what he'd promised. About what he was missing in New York.

Nor did he intend to lie in bed and think about Meg.

Miss Jardine.

Meg, he thought. The name suited her.

So why was Letty's order to use her name unsettling?

He knew why. As an adolescent blessed with enough insight to think about emotions, he'd struggled with reasons. He'd even wondered if one of the therapists his mother used might give him answers. But finally he'd worked it out himself. This had been a lesson taught early to a child by a jealous, vindictive mother, who believed employees and friends were to be strictly differentiated.

'They'll take advantage…'

It was a savage line, said with spite, and the memory of it still had the power to make him flinch.

Unsettled, he crossed to the attic window and peered below. It was barely daybreak; the sun wasn't yet over the horizon and the farm looked grey-green, barely lit from the night before. He could see the roof of what must be the dairy, and cows clustering beyond. A couple of dogs were fussing around them, but the cows were uninterested. The cows looked as if they knew what they were about, and the dogs were simply demonstrating their role.

A role other than licking Meg.

Meg. There it was again. The word.

'They'll take advantage…'

He'd been seven. His parents had been away, for who knew how long? It never seemed to matter because the house was much more fun with them gone. It was summer. School was out and Ros, their cook, had been teaching him to make pancakes. But she'd turned her back and he'd tried to flip a pancake before it was ready. The hot batter had oozed from the spatula and onto his hand.

Hannah, his nanny, had come running. She'd held him tight, rocking him, while Ros rushed to apply salve.

'There, baby, it'll be fine, see, Ros has ice and ointment all ready. Let Hannah see.'

His parents had walked in as they'd hugged him.

Maybe he hadn't reacted fast enough. He was shocked and his hand hurt, so instead of rushing to greet them with the pleasure he'd already begun to act instead of feel, he'd simply clung harder to his Hannah.

'What is this?' his mother had demanded with deep displeasure, and he'd sobbed then, with fright as well as pain. Already he knew that voice. 'William, stop that appalling crying and get over here. You do not get close to servants.'

'They're not servants,' he'd managed. 'They're Hannah and Ros.'

His mother's eyes had narrowed at that, and he'd been sent to his room without even salve on his hand.

Who knew where Hannah and Ros were now? They'd been given notice on the spot. He needed to learn independence, his mother had decreed, and he still remembered the sneer.

His next nanny had been nice enough, but he'd learned. His new nanny was Miss Carmichael. He did not get close.

Soon after that he'd been sent to boarding school. His parents had split and from then on his holidays had been spent with his grandparents. The only care he had there was from more servants—though eventually his grandfather realised he had a head for figures. That had resulted in a tinge of interest. William was deemed the new head of the McMaster Empire.

So there he had it, he thought ruefully, his one family use. His grandfather knew he'd make a good businessman and that was the extent of his importance. It was no wonder he was emotionally screwed.

He should be able to get over it—his dysfunctional family—their fierce focus on social hierarchy and fortune—their petty squabbles and personal vindictiveness—their total lack of sense of family. But how to get over a lifetime of dysfunction? Even now, he didn't really understand what family love or life was. He'd an inkling of it through friends and associates. At times he even envied it, but to try and achieve it… No.

He'd learned not to need it. He couldn't need something he didn't understand and the last thing he wanted was to hurt another human as his extended family had hurt each other. How could he undo so many years of family malice? He couldn't.

He told no one any lies about himself. The women he dated used his social cachet as pay-off, and that was fine by him.

And the kids? Pip and Ned? He was certainly fond of them, as fond as he ever allowed himself to be. But they called him Mr McMaster and he knew that soon he'd disappear from their lives as well. That was the way things had to be. Like now. He couldn't even be there for them at Christmas. A broken promise, like so many he'd been given as a child...

A whistle split the air, so loud it hauled him out of his reverie. Maybe that was just as well. There was little to be gained by trying to change at this stage of his life, and maybe a lot to lose. He shrugged, mocking something that was part and parcel of how he faced the world—and then he tried to figure who was whistling.

Meg had said she'd be helping with the milking. Who else was down there?

There was only one way to find out.

He checked his watch. It was five-thirty.

Early, even by his standards.

Whoever was down there knew how to work.

W S McMaster could be forgotten here. She was perfectly, gloriously happy. She was home.

Meg stomped across the baked dirt and whooshed her next cow into the bail. Friesian 87 plodded forward with resigned equanimity.

'That's Topsy,' Kerrie said. 'Her milk production's gone up twelve per cent this year. You're ace, aren't you, girl?'

'I thought Letty decided we should stop naming them.'

'That was only when she had to get rid of half the herd. It broke her heart. Now your income's so good she's decided we can name them again. She started with Millicent, and now she's moving onto the whole herd.'

Uh-oh.

'It's not so stable as you might think,' she said cautiously.

Kerrie released her cow and stretched and glanced across into the vat room, where her three little girls were playing in a makeshift playpen. 'We take one day at a time,' she said. 'We all know that.'

Maybe everyone did, Meg thought as she washed teats and attached cups. Last year Kerrie's husband had maxed out their credit cards and taken off with a girl half his age, leaving Kerrie with three babies under four. Milking here was now her sole income.

Kerrie's income was thus dependent on Meg's income. On Meg's job.

William had said he wouldn't fire her. She had to believe him. But first they had to get through Christmas.

We'll put this behind us as an unfortunate aberration…

Christmas. An aberration.

That wasn't what he'd meant, but it was how it seemed.

What was he intending to do with himself for the next three days?

'Can I help?'

She didn't have to show she was startled. The cows did it for her, backing away in alarm at this unfamiliar person in the yard. The cow Kerrie was ushering in backed right out again before Kerrie could stop her, and Kerrie swore and headed after her.

'You need to move,' Meg said swiftly. 'You're scaring the cows.'

He was in his gym gear. Black and white designer stuff with crisp white designer trainers. Very neat.

The cows weren't appreciating it.

He backed into the vat room, where the playpen was set up. The oldest of the little girls cried out in alarm and he backed out of there too.

Meg found herself smiling. Her boss, in charge of his world. Or not.

'Go back to bed,' she advised. 'It's early.'

'I don't like my PA working before me. Is there something I can do?'

'Really?'

'Really.'

Goodness. 'How are you at washing udders?' she asked, stunned.

'I learned it at kindergarten,' he said promptly and she found herself chuckling. He'd woken up on the right side of the bed, then. Maybe this could work.

'If you're serious…'

'I'm serious.'

'The cows don't like gym gear.'

'You think I should go back and put on one of my suits?'

'Um…no.' She chuckled and saw a flare of surprise in his eyes. Maybe she didn't chuckle around him enough.

Maybe she didn't chuckle at all.

'Kerrie's brother helps out here occasionally when the kids are sick,' she said. 'Ron's around your size. His overalls and gumboots are in the vat room.'

'Gumboots?'

'Wellingtons,' Kerrie said, entranced.

'This is Kerrie,' Meg said. 'Kerrie, this is William.'

'Your boss?' Kerrie asked.

'Not right this minute he's not,' she said firmly. 'Now he's offering to be a worker. You want to use Ron's gear? The cows will settle once you look familiar.' She pointed to the vat room.

'There's babies in there,' William said nervously, and both women burst out laughing.

'If you're going to give me a hard time...' William said but, to Meg's amazement, he was smiling.

'Nah, you're free labour,' Meg said, smiling right back. 'Kerrie, you're responsible for keeping Mr McMaster free of all babies. Get changed and come out and we'll introduce you to Cows One to a Hundred.

'Only now they all have names,' Kerrie reminded her. 'I'll teach you.'

'Teach us both,' Meg said. 'It seems we both need to get used to names.'

By the time they finished, the sun was already spreading warmth, promising a hot day to come. Meg set William to sluicing the dairy while she did who knew what with the equipment in the vat room. Sluicing was, William found, a curiously satisfying job, controlling a hose with enough water power to drive the mess off the ramp and into the drains. It was a manly sort of hose, he decided, and he set about enjoying himself.

Kerrie collected her kids and made to leave. 'I'll see you tonight,' she called to Meg and he thought suddenly, she looks tired.

Three kids, so small... What was she doing, milking twice a day?

'Are you milking over Christmas?' he asked, and Kerrie nodded.

'Letty and I milk twice a day. When Meg's here Letty gets time off. She needs it.'

'When do you get a sleep-in?' he asked and suddenly Meg was outside again, listening.

'With three babies?' Kerrie asked, as if sleep-ins were unheard of.

'Their dad…'

'He did a runner,' Kerrie said, with feigned indifference. 'Milking for Meg's the only thing between me and bankruptcy.'

And William glanced over at Meg, caught her urgent, unspoken message and knew it was true.

'So you're milking morning and night all over Christmas.'

'I like it,' Kerrie said.

'So if I said I'd do it for you…'

Both women drew in their breath. Meg's face went still. She obviously hadn't expected this.

'If it's okay with Meg, that is,' he said and swooshed a mess of stuff from the ramp. Swooshing felt excellent.

Meg smiled. He liked it when she smiled. How come he hadn't noticed that smile way before now?

'It's fine by me,' Meg said, 'but…'

'But I can't afford it,' Kerrie said, suddenly breathless. 'I mean…it's a lovely offer but…'

'But nothing,' Meg said, suddenly rock solid, smiling at William as if he was Santa in person. 'William's offering to do it for free. I'm sure of it. I've budgeted for your pay so this is his gift to you. Let the man be magnanimous.'

'Magnanimous?' Kerrie ventured.

'Manly,' Meg said, grinning. 'This is a very manly gesture.'

'If you're sure,' Kerrie whispered, sounding awed.

'Of course he's sure,' Meg said, smiling and smiling. 'There's so much women's work to be done over Christmas, and what do the men do? They buy a bottle of perfume at the last minute, if we're lucky. Even Scotty. He's left his Christmas shopping to the last minute and I have to take him to Curalo this morning. I'll stand outside the shop while he buys me the perfume I've told him I like and then I'll drive him home and that's his manly duty done. So here's one offering to be truly useful…'

'Wow,' Kerrie said.

'Yep, get and go before I change my mind,' William said. 'Or before I turn my hose on your boss. Happy Christmas, Kerrie.' He moved his hose so the water arced in a wide semi-circle. How long since he'd done something this hands-on? There was a pile of dried dung beside the fence. He aimed his hose and the dung flew eighteen inches in the air before heading for the drain. Deeply satisfying.

'Oh, wow,' Kerrie breathed again, and she abandoned the kids and hugged Meg. Then she eyed William—with caution—anyone would regard him with caution right now—but finally emotion got the better of sense and she darted over the yard and hugged him as well. Then she flew back to her kids and bustled them into the car and away before anyone had a chance to change their mind.

'Hey, that felt good,' Meg said, heading back into the vat room and replacing the dipstick sort of thing she was holding into the slot at the side of the vat. 'Did it feel good to you?'

He sent another cowpat into the air. 'Absolutely.'

'If you knew how much that means to Kerrie…' Then she hesitated. 'Um… Sir… What are you doing with that hose?'

Sir? She'd called him sir. Of course, that was what he was. Wasn't it? But she was looking bemused so he turned his attention back to the hose. It had made a left turn and was now aimed straight into the drain behind the cow's drinking trough, forcing the contents of the drain up and in.

Uh-oh.

'I guess the drinking trough now needs to be cleaned,' Meg said. 'We'll need to empty it, scrub it, rinse it three times and then fill it up again. We don't want contamination, do we?'

'Um…no,' he said and thought maybe there were a few skills he needed to concentrate on.

The milk tanker arrived just as he finished. The driver climbed from the cab and greeted Meg with delight.

'Hey, Meggie.'

'Meggie?' William said softly.

'Just try it…Willie,' she said with a glower that made him grin, and went to meet the driver. William listened in while they caught up. Their talk was all about milk yields and fat content and bacterial levels. Meg sounded as he was accustomed to hearing her, smoothly competent, in charge of her world. But it was such a different world.

They gossiped on while he cleaned the trough and cleaned the yard surely cleaner than it had ever been cleaned before. Then the driver started emptying the vats and Meg strode over and turned his hose off. He felt bereft.

'I was just getting good,' he said sadly.

'You can do it again tonight,' she said and he started winding the hose around the reel by hand. She leaned over and grabbed the wheel and started turning. She was showing him up here.

But there was something else happening. The angel…

Her little Christmas angel was still hanging around her neck, and it was sliding down her breasts. He noticed.

She was wearing grungy old overalls, sort of mud-brown. She was wearing…what had she called them? Gumboots. Her hair was pulled back with an elastic band and she had mud smeared down the side of her face.

The top three buttons of her overalls were undone. Her angel was nestling on the soft swell of her breasts.

Lucky angel.

Why had it taken him until now to realise how beautiful she was?

'Earth to William,' she said and he blinked and grabbed the wheel and started turning it himself, so fast the hose slipped off and he had to stop and start again.

Maybe this wasn't a good idea. Maybe he had to get away.
A thought…

'You need perfume?' he asked.

'No,' she said, bemused.

He didn't think so. Perfume would hardly fit with what she was doing right now. But…

'But Scott wants to buy you perfume.'

'He wants to go Christmas shopping. I promised I'd take him to Curalo. That's our closest major shopping centre—twenty miles from here.'

'But you have things to do here, right?'

'Right,' she said cautiously.

'So could I take him?'

'You,' she said, stunned, and he thought about whether he should take personal affront at the thought that she obviously thought him—and the rest of the male species—useless, and then he caught another glimpse of that angel and thought maybe not.

'Would he mind if I took him?' he asked. 'I could find an Internet place in town and do my contacting—kill two birds with one stone.'

'That'd be fantastic,' she breathed. 'Craig here says we should have signed the contract for our milk quota before Christmas. The manager's still at work, so Craig says I can get a lift back in with him. He can bring me back when he does the next farm. But then I promised Letty I'd help do the pudding. I need to check on Millicent. I need to see to the water troughs. I'm having trouble making everything fit.'

'So it's a good idea?'

'It's a fabulous idea,' she said admiringly. Her eyes were twinkling… Maybe she was manipulating him and it was such an odd experience…

People didn't manipulate him. Had she just manipulated him?

Who knew? This was one clever woman.

'Would you be confident driving Letty's car?' she said. 'I know you can drive on our side of the road.' More admiration?

'Yes, but...'

'Scotty would love to go with you. Christmas shopping with his sister, or go Christmas shopping with a guy, someone who won't make him wait outside lingerie shops? What a choice.'

'You don't!'

'He's always scared I might.' She hesitated, and the laughter died. 'I... he's had a tough time. He'd enjoy going shopping with you rather than with me.'

'His leg...'

She glanced across at Craig but Craig was bending down to pat Killer and was obviously not in too great a rush. She turned back to William and he realised he was being assessed. She held his gaze for a long moment and then gave a decisive little nod. Whatever test there'd been, it seemed he'd passed. Manipulation was past. It was time for honesty.

'Scott's been through hell and back,' she said bluntly. 'His leg was so badly smashed they had to put in a rod instead of bone. It healed but then they had to insert another rod because he grew. That got infected.' She swallowed. 'He almost died. Again. The leg still hasn't completely healed but it will and he's okay to get around. He's really good on crutches. If you could...just do what he wants. And if you can think of anything he'd like, I'd appreciate that too. I've bought him so many computer games he surely must be over them but I'm hopeless at thinking of what a teenage boy wants. He's so restricted—but he needs a manly present.'

Her frankness was working as manipulation never could. But he could do this. He even puffed his chest a little. 'So you'd like me to take your kid brother Christmas shopping for manly presents? I can do that.'

'Ooh, you're not my boss, you're my hero,' she said and before, he could begin to guess what she intended, she stood on tiptoe and kissed him. It was a feather kiss, almost a mockery, but not quite. It was a kiss of laughter and of sudden friendship, and why it had the capacity to make him feel...

How did it make him feel?

He didn't know and it was too late to find out. Craig was replacing his hoses and yelling, 'Are you coming or not?'

'I'm coming,' she called. 'I'll just go lose my overalls and check with Scott. But this is a great idea. My milking's sorted, my brother will be happy and I have a superhero in the dairy. What more could a girl want?'

It took Meg an hour to get to the factory and back, by which time William and Scott had been gone for an hour as well. Which left Meg back at home, with no way of knowing when they'd get back.

She was worrying about her brother. She was also worrying about why she'd kissed her boss. It had been an impulsive gesture, the sort she'd make to anyone who'd done her a big favour, but somehow...it seemed more.

She couldn't think of kissing her boss. That made her feel weird. She went back to worrying about Scott.

'You're worrying he's taken him back to New York?' Letty demanded as she caught Meg looking out of the window for maybe the twentieth time.

'He can't. There are no planes.'

'You've worked for the man for three years. Don't you trust him?'

'Of course I do.'

'Then why worry? Two hours is hardly time to Christmas shop.' But then she hesitated. 'Oh, but wait. These are guys.

Half an hour there, half an hour back, five minutes at the per-fume counter—yep, they should be back by now.' She grinned. 'But maybe they're doing some bonding. He misses his father, does Scotty. Pass the raisins.'

'You want me to mix the ingredients?'

'I handed you the bowl five minutes ago—so you could look at it?'

Whoops. 'Sorry.' She applied herself to her creaming. 'Why didn't you do this before?' she asked. 'Aren't puddings sup-posed to have been made a month ago?'

'You didn't get any time off and I was milking. I'm not getting any younger. But, back to your young man…'

'My *boss*.'

'He doesn't seem to mind hard work.'

'You say that like it's a compliment. He's addicted to work.'

'Plus he's really cute,' Letty said and eyed Meg sideways.

'He's my boss. I hadn't noticed.'

'Right,' Letty said dryly.

Right?

So, okay she had noticed. What normal warm-blooded woman wouldn't notice W S McMaster?

But what use was there in noticing? For the three years she'd worked for him their relationship had been totally busi-nesslike. Her boss worked far too hard for it to be anything else. He never noticed *her*, she thought. She was just one of his four PAs.

But sometimes… Sometimes when they'd been on a trip together, when they'd been working late, when she'd suddenly been a little too close, maybe even a little too familiar as tired-ness crept in at the edges, she'd thought he made a conscious decision not to notice her, as if there were some barrier he couldn't cross.

As, of course, there was. He was her employer.

He was a billionaire.

She mixed the ingredients with her hands, letting the warmth of her hands meld the mixture. She was still staring out of the kitchen window, but she was no longer looking for the absent Scott and William. She was thinking of William as he'd been this morning. Mucking round with his hose. Enjoying himself.

She'd kissed him.

It had been nothing but a silly gesture, she told herself. It meant nothing.

Only that wasn't quite true. Meg Jardine had kissed William McMaster. The lines between boss and secretary had blurred.

Leading where?

'You think that might be creamed enough?' Letty demanded and she looked down into the bowl and thought yep, it was getting so warm it was starting to melt.

There was an analogy somewhere here. Melting...

'You want me to chop some nuts?' she managed and Letty grinned some more and handed them over.

'Go right ahead. A girl's gotta vent her spleen on something. You're wondering how much perfume those boys are intending to buy, or are you wondering something else entirely?'

CHAPTER FIVE

THEY didn't appear for lunch and an hour later Meg was really starting to worry. 'I'll take the tractor over to Jenny's and phone him from there,' she muttered. 'They should be back.'

'You'll do no such thing,' Letty told her. 'They'll have found a football game or gone to the movies or chanced on something really interesting that only boys can understand. You didn't tell them a get-home-by time, for which I'm grateful because it's time we stopped mollycoddling our Scotty. Our Scott.' Then she spoiled it by glancing at the clock. 'But I hope Will's fed him. And he didn't take any painkillers. If his leg's hurting...'

'See,' Meg retorted and they both smiled, shamefaced.

'Shortbread next,' Letty declared, so they made a batch, and then another, and they were almost desperate enough to start a third when finally the car turned into the drive. Meg just happened to be looking out of the window when it did.

'What on earth have they got on behind?' she demanded, heading for the door.

The dogs were flying down from the veranda. Meg managed to stroll out with what she hoped was a little more dignity.

'Don't say we were worried,' Letty hissed beside her and she agreed entirely. They hadn't been worried at all.

What did they have behind the car?

A trailer. A really large trailer. And on the trailer…

'They've bought a car,' she muttered in amazement. Or… two cars?

'So much for perfume,' Letty muttered. 'This is never going to fit into a stocking.'

'Come and see, come and see.' Scott was out of the car, shouting his excitement, and the dogs were barking hysterically in response. William emerged from the driver's side, leaned back on the car door and crossed his arms—a genie who'd produced magic and was now expecting appreciation. He was wearing jeans and a short-sleeved open-topped shirt. He looked…great. He must have stopped at a clothes shop, Meg thought, and then she thought *I kissed him*—and then Scott's excitement tugged her attention back to what was on the trailer

At the front of the trailer was a Mini Minor, the kind that had been almost the coolest car on the planet back in the seventies. Though maybe it hadn't been quite as cool as the Volkswagen Combi.

Um…what was she thinking? She hadn't even been born in the seventies. This Mini, however, looked as if it had been. It was truly derelict. The little red and rust-red car had no wheels, no glass in its front windscreen and its hood was missing. What looked like grass was sprouting from where the engine should be.

And tied on behind was part of another Mini, in even worse repair. Instead of suffering from neglect, this one looked as if it had been smashed from behind. The back had been squashed almost to the front.

There was also a pile of assorted bits tied on top, meaning the trailer looked like a mini wrecker's yard.

'It's William's Christmas present to us all,' Scott shouted and her boss beamed and she thought again—he looks great.

Denim made him look *so-o-o-o* sexy—but somehow she managed to give her hormones a mental slap and ventured off the veranda to see.

William's Christmas present to us all…

'We saw a sign just out of town.' Despite his bad leg, Scott was practically jigging his excitement. 'It was in a paddock and it said For Sale. And parts as well. The guy restores Minis but his wife's put her foot down. He has three finished Minis in his garage and two more to restore and his wife says the rest have to go. So he sold us this. Two cars'll make one. He says there's enough here to make a complete one. He reckons if I start now, by the time I get my licence I'll have it on the road. If I get it going before then, I can practice in the paddocks. I can phone him any time I want, and if I'm really stuck he's even offered to come out here to help.'

'He really will,' William said, still smiling. 'This won't be any work for either of you. I promise.' His lovely, lazy smile lit his face and Meg thought frantically she'd have to give those hormones another slap.

'I have faith,' he went on. 'This'll mean eventually the farm has two cars. By the way, we also went to the motor place in Curalo and bought bits for your wagon, Letty. Your exhaust pipe has to be replaced and the silencer and so does the carburettor. If it's okay with you, I might make a start this afternoon.'

'You…' Meg said, dazed.

'I can fix cars,' he said neutrally. 'And Scott would like to learn.'

'You want to fix my car?' Letty said, while Meg simply stood with her mouth open.

'If it's okay with you.'

'Marry me,' Letty said, and Scott and William laughed—only, for some reason, Meg had trouble laughing. The sight of her boss in jeans was disconcerting enough, but she was looking at Scott's flushed face and his shining happiness and she thought, why hadn't she thought of this?

Scott was practically stranded here on the farm. His bad leg left him isolated. There were so many days when he simply gazed at his computer, in misery and in loneliness.

He now had a car to make. And it was an original Mini...

Mickey would come, she thought, and more. This project would be a magnet. Scott's mates would come, as they had before the accident.

She was blinking back tears.

'What's wrong?' William demanded, watching her face and clearly confounded.

She sniffed and tried desperately to think of something to say. Something to do rather than kiss him again, which seemed an entirely logical thing to do, but some germ of common sense was holding her back.

'I...I wanted perfume,' she managed, and her little brother stared at her as if she was out of her mind.

'Perfume...when you could have these!'

'They're not very...girlie,' she said and somehow she managed to sound doleful and Scott realised she was joking and grinned and hugged her. Which was amazing all by itself. How long since her seriously self-conscious brother had hugged?

'I'll let you drive my car,' he offered, magnanimity at its finest. 'Second drive after me, the minute I get it going.'

'What an offer,' she said and sniffed again and hugged him back and then smiled across at William through unshed tears.

'Thank you, Santa,' she said.

'Think nothing of it,' he said in a voice she didn't recognise and then she thought, no, she did know what she was hearing.

Her normally businesslike boss was just a wee bit emotional himself.

* * *

It was time for milking. Letty and Meg milked because, 'I'm not interfering with this, even if I have to milk the whole herd,' Letty declared in wonder. Meg could only agree, for kids were arriving from everywhere. It seemed William had detoured past Mickey's with their load—'just to show him,' Scott had told them, and Mickey had sent out word, and before they knew it a team of adolescents was unloading the heap of Mini jumble into the unused shed behind the dairy.

When milking was done Meg checked on Millicent—the little heifer was thankfully showing no signs of calving—then went to investigate. The teenagers were surrounded by Mini parts. William was under Letty's car.

'Sorry. I know I said I'd milk, but Letty assured me she could and someone had to supervise…'

Some supervision. All she could see of William was his legs. He was in his borrowed overalls again and his gumboots.

On the other side of the shed teenagers were happily dismantling the wreck, labelling pieces with Letty's preserving stickers. She had a bunch of gloriously happy teenagers, and the guy who'd caused it all to happen was apologising. Meg stared down at her boss's legs and thought she could totally understand where Letty's proposal had come from.

And she'd never realised until now how sexy a pair of grease-covered legs could be.

'So… So where did you learn mechanics?' she managed.

'I told you. Powering up my father's golf cart.' His voice was muffled, but she was aware of an undercurrent of contentment.

'And the rest?'

'My parents were away a lot. They had enough cars to warrant hiring a mechanic. He taught me.'

'Nice guy,' Meg said, deflected from thinking about legs—or almost. She thought instead of gossip she'd read about this man, about how appalling his parents sounded, how lonely his childhood must have been. 'Did this mechanic have a name?'

'Mr Himmel.'

'Mr Himmel.' She grimaced at the formality. 'He called you Mr McMaster?'

'Of course. Can you pass me under the tension wrench?'

'Tension wrench?'

'On the left with the blue handle.'

'That's a tension wrench?'

'And you a dairy farmer and all.'

'Dairy farmers aren't necessarily mechanics. Plus I'm a commerce graduate. And a PA.'

'Right, I forgot,' he said, but absently, and she knew his attention was on whatever he needed the tension wrench for.

She watched his legs for a little. His attention was totally on the car.

She watched the boys for a little. Their attention was totally on the car.

Guys doing guy stuff.

Befuddled, she headed back to the dairy, where Letty was sluicing. They cleaned almost in silence but she was aware that Letty kept glancing at her.

'What?' Meg said at last, exasperated.

'He's lovely.'

'So why are you looking at me?' She sighed. 'Anyway, he's not lovely. He's covered in grease.'

'You know what I mean.'

'Okay, I do,' she admitted. 'But you know who he is, so you can stop looking at me like you think I should do something about it. He's William McMaster, one of the wealthiest men on the planet. He's my boss and I have one of the best jobs in the world. If you think I'm messing with it by thinking he's lovely...'

'I suppose it would mess with it,' Letty said. 'Falling for the boss...'

'It'd be a disaster.'

'I don't know how you haven't before.'

'Because I've never seen him in overalls before.'

'They do make a man look sexy,' Letty said thoughtfully. 'That and carrying a grease gun. My Jack was always attached to a grease gun. Mind, once I had to get the grease off his clothes the novelty pretty soon wore off.' She sighed but then she brightened. 'But times have changed. Domestic equality and all that. He could get his own grease off.'

'You're seriously suggesting William McMaster could do his own laundry?' Meg even managed a chuckle. The idea merited a chuckle.

As was thinking of those legs, sticking out from under Letty's car. As was thinking that William McMaster was sexy.

Legs or not, even if the man carries a grease gun, he's still my boss, she told herself. A good servant knows her place. Just plaster that message across your box of hormones and leave it there.

They ate dinner on the run. The boys were in no hurry to go home. At dusk they took off, pack-like, whooping away on their bicycles, and Meg knew they'd be back first thing in the morning.

This was priceless.

Scott was almost asleep on his feet, but lit up almost as much as the Christmas tree in the sitting room. He fell into bed happier than she'd seen him for years.

Letty commandeered William to take him over to the shed to show her what he was doing with her car. Meg headed out behind the hay shed. Millicent was still doing little of interest, the small fawn and white cow chewing her cud and gazing placidly out at the fading sunset.

'Mind if I share your sunset?' she asked, and Millicent turned her huge bovine eyes on her and seemed to ask a question.

'He's only here until Monday. Then it's back to normal,' Meg said, as if Millicent really was asking the question. Only what was the question? And what was normal?

She hitched herself up on the fence and started sunset-gazing. But she wasn't seeing sunset. 'This is just a hiccup in our lives,' she said out loud. 'But it's a great hiccup.'

She was under no illusion as to how big a deal this was. Ever since the accident Scotty's mates had been drifting away. They were nice kids. They included him when they could, but increasingly he was off their radar.

Today they'd returned and they'd hated leaving. Here was a project designed to keep kids happy for months, if not years. A project with a working car at the end of it... A Mini. They'd be back and back and back.

And it was all down to William. William of the sexy legs. William of the sexy...everything.

And suddenly, inexplicably, she was tearing up. She sniffed and Millicent pushed her great wet nose under her arm as if in sympathy.

'Yeah, you'd know about men,' she retorted. 'Of all the dumb blondes...'

'Who's a dumb blonde?'

She hadn't heard him approach. He moved like a panther, she thought, startled. He was long and lithe and silent as the night. He leaned against her fence, and she had to hitch along a bit so he could climb up and sit beside her.

'Dumb blonde?' he said again.

'Meet Millicent,' she said. 'Dumb adolescent blonde.'

'That not a kind thing to say about an obviously sweet cow.'

'She's oversexed,' Meg said darkly, struggling not to react to the way his body brushed against hers. There was plenty of room. Why did he need to sit so close?

'Really?' It was William's turn to sound startled.

'Really.'

'So how do you tell if a cow is oversexed?'

'She got out of her paddock,' she explained. 'Not only did she get out, she got in again. We finally found her in our next door neighbour's bull paddock. Now she's pregnant and she's too young to have babies but that's what she's having, any day now. Letty's worried sick.'

'What's to worry about?'

'We don't know which bull it was.'

'You don't know which bull…'

'It could have been one of three.'

'You're telling me she's…loose?' he demanded, and she giggled and swayed on her perch and he put a hand out to steady her. He shifted closer and held on around the waist, making sure she was secure. She waited for him to let her go—but he didn't.

'So tell me all,' he demanded, and she thought, do you know what the feel of your arm around my waist is doing to me? Obviously not or it'd be gone in a flash.

Maybe she should tell him.

Or not.

She had to do something. She was getting close to melting here. 'I think you'd better let me go—Mr McMaster,' she managed, and he did. He shifted away a little, without comment, as if it meant nothing. As if holding her hadn't caused him any sort of reaction. Nothing like the sizzle that had just jolted through her.

'So are we waiting for the baby to be born so we can take DNA samples and enforce a paternity suit?' he asked, and they were talking about Millicent. Of course they were.

'Maybe not.' She was totally discombobulated. It wasn't just the feel of his arm. It was so much more. 'I... one of the bulls is a Murray Grey.'

'That's bad?'

'If you're a Friesian crossed with a Jersey, it's very bad. Have you ever met a Murray Grey?'

'I can't say I have.'

'They're about half Millicent's size again. She's still underdeveloped. If we'd found her straight away we could have done something, but she got out and we lost her and didn't find her for ages. What must have happened was that she got out onto the road, wandered along happily, we suspect, looking for bulls because she's that sort of girl. Whoever found her must have shooed her through the nearest gate to get her off the road—which, of course, happened to be Rod Palmer's bull paddock. There was plenty of feed in the paddock. It's hilly and mostly out of sight of the road and Rod lets his bulls be until he needs them. So Millicent might have been enjoying herself for quite a while. She certainly seemed content when Rod finally found her and called us.'

'Uh-oh,' he said. 'So now?'

'So now she's in the house paddock while we wait for the birth. Signs are any day now. I hope to heaven she doesn't drop over Christmas because there's no way we'll get a vet.' Then a thought occurred and she eyed him with hope. 'As well as cars... You didn't have a houseful of pets you practised on when you were a kid as well?' she enquired. 'Maybe a cow or two, and a resident vet?'

'Nary a goldfish.'

'Not even a dog?' she demanded, startled.

'My family don't do pets.'

'But you like them.'

'Just because I patted Killer...'

'No, but you do. When we're out on site… Every time we meet a dog you talk to it. You should have one.'

'And leave him in my Manhattan apartment alone, for months at a time?'

'You have staff. Is Mr Himmel still around?'

'Long gone.' That was said bleakly and she thought—don't go there. She was pushing past anywhere that was her business. Move on.

But move on where? Move onto where she wanted to go? Why not?

'So…so do you need to go over to Jenny's again later?' she managed.

'Jenny's?'

'Mickey's. To make more phone calls.'

'I rang Elinor while I was in Curalo.'

Elinor. First name. The word hung between them, loaded with unknowns.

Leave it, she thought, but then she thought if she was Letty she'd ask. She swung her legs against the fence rails and tried to look nonchalant. As if this was a lightweight question.

'So the gossip rags haven't caught up with Elinor?'

'I hope they never do.' It was said with such vehemence that she blinked.

'Um…it's serious then?'

He seemed disconcerted but then he shrugged. 'You could say that.'

'I'm sorry you'll miss Christmas with her, then.'

'I'm sorry, too.' He swung himself down from the fence and she knew the question had messed with whatever calm he'd been feeling. 'I believe I need to get that carburettor back in. Without it, we're dependent on the tractor as emergency transport so I'm not going to bed before it's in working order. It's okay. Twenty minutes work, tops. I'm not being a martyr.' He glanced down at his overalls and he smiled, with unmistakable all-boy satisfaction. 'I haven't looked this greasy since I was Scott's age. It feels great.'

'You are great,' she said as he reached up and took her by the waist and lifted her down to join him. He should let her go. He didn't.

'So are you.'

Uh-oh.

Keep it light, she told herself. *Keep it light.* 'If our office staff could see us now they'd have kittens,' she managed.

'Or a cameraman.'

The paparazzi. That was an appalling thought. She could see the headlines now: *McMaster Trapped with Secretary in Rural Hideway...* What would the unknown Elinor say if she saw such a headline?

'Does Elinor know you're stuck with me?' He was still holding her. She should step away—but she didn't.

'Yes,' he said.

'She doesn't mind?'

'She's upset for me. She knows I want to be home.'

For some reason that hurt, but she made herself respond. 'That's generous of Elinor.'

'She's a generous woman.'

What to say to that? And he was still holding her.

'I...I need to go to bed,' she managed and she tugged a little but still he didn't release her.

'Bed?'

'In case you hadn't noticed, it's nine, which is the witching hour when milking starts at five.'

'So you don't look forward to your morning milk?' he teased.

He was so close... She was having trouble making her voice work but she had to try. 'Getting up at five... Ugh,' she said. 'But while I'm here it's normal. For lots of people it's normal. You get up at five to check on your trade indices all the time. You don't mind.'

'So what do you want to do at five?'

'Sleep!'

He smiled, then put his head on one side, considering. 'So why stay on here? You're putting your life on hold for your little brother.'

'I haven't noticed much life-holding.'

'Where's the social life? When you work with me I demand twenty-four seven commitment. Then you come here and it seems the same. Milking from five to nine and milking from three to seven. Where's time for Meg in that?'

He sounded concerned, and that disconcerted her. He'd never sounded concerned. Their relationship was businesslike.

It had to stay that way.

'I have wild lunches,' she told him.

'Right.' He was watching her in a way that disturbed her. As if he was trying to figure her out.

'So…boyfriend?' he asked and she winced. Ouch. That'd do as far as personal questions went. He set his boundaries. She'd set hers.

'That's not your territory, Mr McMaster.' She tugged back and this time he did let her go. She made to turn away but his next question stopped her.

'Do you like working for me?'

That was an easy one. 'I love it.'

'Why?'

She hesitated. He was watching her in the fading light, and she knew her answer meant something to him.

'It's smart work,' she said slowly. 'I never know what my day's going to hold. I need to use my brain, and I love it that you treat me like I can.'

'Like you can what?'

'Rise to any challenge.' She managed a smile at that. 'Except get you home for Christmas.'

He didn't smile back. Silence. The sun had sunk well over the horizon and the light was disappearing fast. The night was warm and still. Millicent was right beside them by the fence, oozing the contentment of a soon-to-be mum who had everything she wanted in life.

Except she didn't have her bull, Meg thought, and then thought what was she thinking? *Her bull?*

'Bed,' she said.

'Sounds good,' he said and she blushed and stepped away so fast she tripped on her own feet. He put out a hand to catch her but she staggered and grabbed the fence and maintained her distance.

'Is there anything else you need?' she asked, stammering.

'I don't believe so.' He was laughing, she thought—not obviously, but there was laughter behind his eyes. 'So do we have a date with a hundred cows at five in the morning?'

'I can't believe you offered to milk.'

'It will be my pleasure.'

'In lieu of the world's trade indices.'

'In lieu of trade indices.' He hesitated. 'I really don't mind getting up early,' he told her. 'If you need to sleep… I wish I could milk them for you.'

He was serious.

'Yeah, well, I do have some affection for the cows,' she managed. 'Though it's a wonderful offer…' She took a deep breath. 'As was buying Scott the car. I'd like to pay.'

'Get off your high horse, Jardine.'

'It's not my high horse, it's my dignity,' she said with as much dignity as she could muster. 'By which I take it that you won't let me. In which case I'm very, very grateful. So thank you, Mr McMaster, and goodnight.'

'William,' he said, and it was a snap.

'William, then,' she said and met his gaze for as long as she dared—which wasn't very long at all.

'Sleep well,' he said and, before she knew what he was about, he reached out and touched her face. It was a feather touch, a fleeting brush of his finger against her cheek, but he might as well have kissed her. She raised her hand to her cheek as if he'd applied heat. Maybe he had.

'Sleep...sleep well yourself,' she whispered.

'I'll see what I can do,' he said. 'And Meg?'

'Yes?'

'Thank you for rising to my challenges. I appreciate it.'

He was still so close. She desperately wanted him to touch her again. She stood and stared up at him, but there was nothing to say.

She desperately wanted him to kiss her.

And where would businesslike be after that?

'Good...goodnight,' she managed, and then she turned and left him standing in the darkness leaning against a pregnant cow.

She knew that he watched her all the way back to the house.

He should move. He still had to get the carburettor in and he did have to get up at the same time as she did. Instead, he watched Meg's retreating figure and when she disappeared he stood and stared at the darkened house, lit only by its ridiculous decorations. Santa's legs were lurching at an even more alarming rate.

That was the morning's job, he decided. He'd do it after milking. Then he'd replace Letty's exhaust pipe. Then he'd help Scott with the Mini. He was looking forward to each of them.

So much for feeling trapped.

This was a weird sensation. The McMaster family business, a vast mining conglomerate, had been founded by his grandfather. William's father hadn't wanted to go near the business. His grandfather, however, had found his retiring grandson to be intelligent and biddable, and he'd thrown William in at the deep end.

That had been okay by William. He enjoyed the cut and thrust of the business world and in a way it made up for the lack of affection in his family. His grandfather had approved of him when he was doing well for the company, and on his grandfather's death he'd simply kept on with what he was good at. That was what the world expected. It was what he expected of himself.

But here… He'd forgotten how much he loved pulling a car apart. He'd loved his time with Scott.

As he'd love returning to Manhattan, he reminded himself.

When he finally arrived at Elinor's apartment, his reception would be just as crazy as Meg's had been. Or maybe not quite, he conceded. Ned was six years old and his little sister was four. They could bounce but they didn't quite equate to a five-dog pack, a grandma and a brother. And Elinor… Her smile would be as warm as it was possible for a smile to be, but Elinor was a sixty-two-year-old foster mother and she welcomed the world.

Like Letty.

Like Meg, too.

No. Don't think about Meg, he told himself. It's making you crazy. Meg was his PA. He was leaving in two days and he did not want to mess with their employer/employee relationship.

The problem was, though, that he was no longer able to think of her purely as his employee.

He'd called her Meg.

Don't think about her, he told himself again sharply as he headed for the shed. Think about people he could justifiably be attached to.

Like Elinor. Elinor expected nothing, which was just the way he liked it.

He'd been introduced to Elinor two years back, at the launch of New York's Foster-Friends programme. The programme was designed to give support to those who put their lives on hold for kids in need. He'd been approached to be a sponsor, he'd met Elinor at the launch and he'd been sucked right in by her commitment. Elinor was everything he wasn't—warm, devoted and passionate about Pip and Ned, the two kids in her care.

Tentatively, he'd suggested helping a little himself. Part-time commitment. Walking away when he needed to. It sounded… feasible. 'I'm not often available' he'd said and Elinor had beamed as if he were promising the world.

'Anything's better than what these two have been getting up to now,' she'd said simply. 'It breaks my heart their Mama won't put them up for adoption and they so need a Papa. You come when you can and you leave the rest to me.'

The thought of letting them down at Christmas had made him feel ill, but Elinor's big-hearted wisdom had come straight back at him.

'I have a turkey. We have candy and paper lanterns and a tree. We're going out today to see the fancy shop windows and then the kids are visiting Santa. You get home when you can and we'll love to see you, but don't you worry about us, Mr McMaster. We'll do fine.'

The relationship suited him fine. Elinor didn't depend on him. She gave her heart to the kids.

As Meg had given her heart to her half brother, and to a woman who wasn't really her grandmother.

Meg was a giver. His cool, clinical PA was just like

Elinor, and for some reason the thought had the capacity to scare him.

Why?

He didn't want to think about why. He reached the shed but he paused before flicking on the lights and going inside. He glanced back at the house—where Meg was.

Don't think about Meg.

Those Santa legs were getting on his nerves. Maybe he should try and fix them now.

And fall off the roof in the dark. They'd find him tomorrow, tangled in flashing Christmas lights, a cloud of self-pity hanging round his head.

'So maybe you'd better go to bed and stop thinking about fixing things,' he told himself.

Things? Plural?

What else needed to be fixed?

'Letty's car, the Mini and Santa's legs,' he said out loud. 'What else is there? Why would I want anything in my world to change?'

What indeed?

The Santa legs were seriously disconcerting. He turned his gaze upward where a million stars hung in the sky, brighter than he'd ever seen them.

'There are too many stars out here,' he told himself. 'They make a man disoriented. The world's the wrong way up. I've had enough.'

He flicked on the lights and went inside, but outside he knew the stars stayed hanging. Still the wrong way up.

They'd be the wrong way up until he could get out of here. Which should be soon.

Which had to be soon, because he was having trouble remembering what the right way up looked like.

* * *

She lay in her bed and she thought—I am in so much trouble.

Her boss wore jeans. He looked great with greasy hands. He smiled at her…

Do not fall in love with your boss.

How not to?

It's simply a crush, she told herself desperately. He's been touted as one of the most eligible bachelors in the world. When he finally smiles at you like you're a woman—like you're a friend—of course you're going to fall for him.

Any woman would.

So any woman must not make a fool of herself. Any woman had to remember that he moved in a different world to hers, that he was in Australia for three months of the year at the most and the rest he was with…

A woman called Elinor in Manhattan?

She so badly wanted the Internet. She wanted to check out any rumours. W S McMaster and a woman called Elinor.

You have it bad, she told the ceiling and when the door wobbled a little bit on its hinges and slowly opened she almost stopped breathing. Was it…?

Killer. Her dog had obviously decided his duty was with her rather than as one of Scotty's pack. He nosed her hand and then climbed laboriously up onto her bed, making hard work out of what was, for Killer, hardly a step.

'Your mistress is in trouble,' she told him and he whumped down on top of her and she had to shove him away a bit so she could breathe. He promptly turned and tried to lick her.

'Okay, you're the only man in my life. And if I was to think about admitting another one…'

Another lick, this time longer

'Yeah, no room, you're right. Forget it. We have to go to sleep. There's milking in the morning and tomorrow it's Christmas Eve.'

She hadn't written her Santa list. The thought came from nowhere. As a little girl, that was the major job before Christmas. In truth, as a child she'd usually started her Santa list in November.

'Well, it's no use asking for what I want now,' she told Killer and then she heard what she'd said and she winced.

But it was true. She did want it.

'Me and every single woman in the known universe,' she muttered. 'Especially someone called Elinor. Killer, get off me and let me go to sleep.'

She thought Elinor was his woman.

He lay and stared up at the attic ceiling and thought through the events of the day—and that was the fact that stood out.

He hadn't lied to her. But he had let her think…

'Defence,' he told the darkness and thought—how conceited was that? As if she was going to jump him…

He'd had women trying to jump him before. He knew how to defend himself.

He wasn't the least worried about Meg overstepping the line.

The line.

Meg.

See, there was the problem, he told himself. He'd let himself call her Meg. He'd let himself think about her as Meg. She was his employee, his wonderful, efficient PA. All he had to do was go back to thinking of her as Miss Jardine and all would be well.

But she'd felt…

And there was another problem. He could give his head all the orders he liked, but his body was another matter entirely. When he'd tugged her down from the fence she'd fallen against him. Her body had felt soft, pliable, curving into him, even if only for a fraction of a second before she'd tugged away. And she smelled of something he couldn't identify. Not perfume, he thought, and he knew most, but something else. Citrusy, clean…

She'd spent most of the day surrounded by cows. How could she smell clean?

She did, and this wasn't getting him anywhere. He needed to sleep. He had a big day tomorrow, milking cows, fixing things… Trying not to think about Meg.

Miss Jardine.

Why not think of her? It was a tiny voice, insidious, starting from nowhere.

Because you don't.

The thought of Hannah was suddenly with him, Hannah, holding him, loving him, and suddenly…not there. The pain had been unbelievable.

His world was hard. He had no illusions as to what wealth could do to people, marriages, relationships. Wealth had destroyed his parents, turned them into something ugly, surrounded by sycophants in their old age. It took enormous self-control to stop himself from being sucked down the same path.

And he had no idea how to cope with an emotional connection.

It didn't matter. His work was satisfying. His life was satisfying, and if there were spaces…Elinor and the kids were enough.

They took what he had to give.

Maybe Meg…

'Don't even go there,' he said savagely into the night. 'You're not as selfish as that. She deserves so much more.'

CHAPTER SIX

IT TOOK Meg a while to wake up on milking mornings. She liked working in silence for the first half hour or so, and that suited the cows. They usually seemed to be half asleep too, ridding themselves of their load of milk before getting on with their daily task of grazing, snoozing and making more.

But, eventually, Meg woke up. Whether she was working with Letty or Kerrie, by the time milking ended she usually had the radio on, she was chatting to whoever was around, singing along with the radio; even the cows seemed more cheerful.

But not this morning. Her boss seemed to have left his bed on the wrong side. He worked methodically, swabbing, attaching cups, releasing cows from the bales, but answering any ventured conversation with monosyllables. Yes, no, and nothing more was forthcoming.

It was probably for the best, Meg decided as they worked on. Yesterday had threatened to get out of hand. She wasn't quite sure what it was that was getting out of hand, but whatever it was scared her. She knew enough to retreat now into her own world and let W S McMaster get on with his.

It was disconcerting, though. With milking finished, William handled the hose with none of yesterday's enjoyment. She found herself getting irritated, and when Craig arrived to pick up the milk and gestured towards William and said, 'So who's the boyfriend?' she was able to shake her head without even raising colour. Who'd want someone like this for a boyfriend?

'He's someone I work with. He's stuck here because of the airline strike.'

'And he bought the kid the Minis?' It seemed the whole district knew about the Minis. Craig's son had been under the car pile last night and would be back here this morning.

'Yeah.'

'Good move,' he said approvingly. He glanced across at William, obviously aching to talk cars, but William was concentrating on getting the yard hosed and nothing was distracting him. 'Seemed happier yesterday,' he noted.

'He's homesick.'

'Wife? Kids?'

'No.'

'Then what's he whinging about?' Craig demanded. He yelled over to William, 'Hey, Will. Merry Christmas. There's no dairy pick-up tomorrow, so have a good one.'

William raised a hand in a slight salute and went on hosing. Craig departed and Meg surveyed her boss carefully.

'We've offended you?'

He shrugged.

Oh, enough. 'It's Christmas Eve,' she said. 'Lighten up.'

'I'll finish here. You go do something else. Don't you have to stuff a turkey or something?'

'Right,' she said and stalked out of the yard, really irritated now. She was hungry. She'd intended to wait for William before she ate breakfast, but he could eat his toast alone.

She detoured via Millicent, and that made her pause. Millicent was standing in the middle of the home paddock, her back arched a little and her tail held high. Uh-oh. When Meg slipped through the rails and crossed to check, the cow relaxed and let Meg rub her nose, but Meg thought the calf would be here soon, today or tomorrow.

Here was another factor to complicate her Christmas. Letty would worry all day.

Every now and then a cow came along you got fond of. Millicent was one of those. Born after a difficult labour, she'd been a weakling calf. A hard-headed dairy farmer would have sold her straight away. Letty, however, had argued the pros and cons with herself for a week while tending to her like a human baby, and after a week she'd decided she had potential.

She'd named her before she'd decided to name the rest of the herd, and she'd been gutted when she'd been lost. Finding her had been a joy.

'So let's do this right for Letty,' Meg told her and went and fetched her a bucket of chaff and shooed her closer to the trough. 'No complications for Christmas.'

There was nothing more she could do now, though. Labour in cows didn't require a support person, at least in the early stages.

Breakfast. Hunger. And don't think about William, she told herself; he was yet another complication she didn't need.

And then a scream split the morning, a scream so high and terrified Meg's heart seemed to stop. She forgot all about William, forgot about Millicent's complications, and she started to run.

The concrete was as clean as he could make it. No speck of dirt was escaping his eagle eye this morning and he finally turned off the tap with regret. Move on to the next thing fast, he thought. He had today and tomorrow to get through while keeping things businesslike.

Meg would be in the kitchen, having breakfast. Yesterday he'd watched her eat toast. Before yesterday he'd never watched her eat toast. Yes, he travelled with her often, but when he did he ordered breakfast in his room. He wasted less time that way.

But yesterday he'd decided he liked watching her eat breakfast. Dumb or not, it wasn't a bad way to waste time.

A man could waste a lot of time watching Meg.

And that was exactly what he was trying not to think. He wound the hose back onto the reel with more force than was necessary and thought he'd see if Scott was in the shed yet. It was after eight. He could talk to Scott for a while and then maybe Meg would be finished in the kitchen.

What sort of coward was he? What was to be afraid of, watching Meg eat toast?

Meg. Miss Jardine.

Meg.

He sighed and ran his hand through his hair. Two days…

He could do this. He turned towards the house, irritated with himself. All this needed was a bit of discipline. Containment.

And then…a scream.

Forget containment. He ran.

It was Letty. Where? Where?

As Meg neared the house Letty screamed again.

Dear God…

She was high up on the roof, right by the Santa chimney. Had she been trying to fix him? But now wasn't the time for questions. Letty was dangling from the ridge, tiny and frail and in deadly peril.

The roof had two inclines, the main one steep enough, but the attic gable rising even more steeply. The roof was old, the iron was rusting, and the capping on the high ridge had given way. Or was giving way. It hadn't given completely.

It was all that was holding Letty up.

Scotty burst out of the house as Meg arrived. 'Grandma!'

'She's on the roof.'

The capping tore again, just a little, iron scraping on iron. Letty lurched downward but somehow still held.

'Grandma,' Scott screamed, his voice breaking in terror. 'Hang on!'

Meg was too busy to scream. How had she climbed? The ladder… Where? By the gate.

But then William was beside her, reaching the ladder before she did. 'Hold it,' he snapped. 'Scott, hold the other side.'

The capping tore more, and Letty lurched again.

'Letty, hold on,' William ordered her, in a voice that brooked no argument. 'Fingernails if you must, but do not let go. I'm coming.'

'H…hurry.'

He was already climbing. 'Keep still.'

How could you defy that voice? Why would you?

Nobody moved. Meg and Scott held to the ladder as if their lives depended on it.

Their lives didn't. Letty's did, and so did William's.

The roof was high pitched, curved, dangerous, and the ladder only reached part way to the top ridge. William clambered over the main eaves as if they weren't there. It was impossible to climb further, Meg thought numbly from underneath. The second gable was far too steep—but somehow William was doing it.

'You'll fall,' she faltered.

'Not me,' he said, finding footholds she knew couldn't exist. 'Mountaineering 101—Basic skills for your modern businessman. Watch and wonder.'

She watched, and yes, she wondered, but it wasn't admiration she was feeling. It was blind terror.

Please. Please.

And then somehow, unbelievably, William was on the upper ridge, edging himself toward Letty. Santa's sleigh was between them. He shoved; it tumbled back behind the house and no one noticed its going.

He edged closer…closer…while below him Meg and Scott forgot to breathe.

He'd reached her. He was steadying, stabilising himself over the ridge, grasping Letty's wrists and holding.

He had her.

'Don't move. Just lie limp and let me pull you up.'

Scotty choked on a sob. Meg gripped his hand and held, taking comfort as well as giving it. Letty wasn't safe yet. William was still balanced on a ridge with an already broken capping.

The ladder only reached to the eaves of the main roof, so what now? William might be able to climb up like a cat burglar. It was impossible that he climb down holding Letty.

'Meg?'

'Y…yes?'

'I can't get us down,' he told her. 'Not the way I came up. If I overbalance we'll both go.'

She knew it. They needed the fire brigade, she thought. They needed help.

They had no phone. The nearest neighbour was a mile away, but William already knew that.

'I'm buying you a satellite phone for Christmas,' he muttered. 'If it costs a million bucks you're still having one.' He had Letty solidly under the arms now and was hauling her upward like a limp doll. 'So Letty, are you going to argue?'

'N…No.'

'Good woman.' One last heave and he had her on the ridge, into his arms.

She was safe, Meg thought. Or…safeish. With the capping gone the whole attic roof looked unstable but at least Letty was no longer dangling.

But… Her wrist looked hurt. She could see a crimson stain from here. She was losing blood?

William was inching backward along the ridge, heading for the chimney. He could lean on the bricks. Safeish was turning to safe.

Sort of. Until he came to get her down.

'This cut's not looking good,' he said, almost conversationally, and Meg thought he was trying not to scare Letty. But she knew this voice. It meant he wanted action, fast. He tugged Letty hard against him, leaned back against the chimney to make them both stable, then ripped the sleeve from his overalls, as if it was gauze instead of industrial-strength cotton. He wound the fabric round her arm and held her close.

'So how did you get up here?' he asked.

Letty didn't answer. Not a good sign.

He stared downward, seemingly as mystified as Meg. That Letty could have scrambled up the way he had seemed incredible.

'There…there's another ladder,' Scott ventured. He was shaking, and Meg's hand firmed over his.

'Another ladder?'

'When I put the sleigh up I used two.'

'You used two…'

'It fell,' Letty muttered, her voice barely above a whisper. 'As I reached the top. I grabbed, but it went and then I grabbed the capping.'

Meg was no longer listening. She was searching the undergrowth, and here it was. Another ladder, buried behind the banksias.

Scott and Letty had both climbed up on this ancient roof using two ladders. Alone.

Were they out of their minds?

She shouldn't have left them. She should've been here. She should…

Just get a grip, she told herself. Blame needed to wait.

'I'll get the ladder back up,' she called to William. 'Hold on.'

There was no time for hesitation. She moved the main ladder along the wall so it was wedged against the yard gate, so Scott could hold it steady by himself. Then she headed up, tugging the smaller ladder with her.

'Meg…' William sounded appalled. 'What do you think you're doing?'

'Scott's done it. Letty's done it. If all of my stupid family is intent on self destruction I might as well join them. There's no alternative.'

There wasn't. He knew there wasn't.

'You fall and you're fired,' he snapped.

'That's right. Resort to threats under pressure. You fall and I quit,' she snapped back, and caught the flash of a rueful smile.

But… How had Letty and Scotty done this, she thought, as she struggled upward. They'd climbed the first ladder dragging the next, each doing it alone?

She'd looked at Santa's legs last night and she'd thought the same as Letty obviously had—that she'd have a go at fixing him. But Letty was in her seventies, and that Scott could have tried with his leg in a brace…

She shuddered and she paused, half way up the ladder.

'You can do it,' William said strongly and she looked up and met his gaze and took a deep breath.

During the years she'd worked for William she'd been given the most extraordinary orders. She'd done the most extraordinary things.

You can do it.

She loved working for William.

You fall and you're fired.

What did he think she was? A wuss? She climbed on.

She reached the first eave. She balanced herself, took a deep breath and swung the second ladder up to the next eave.

'No,' William said.

'No?'

'It won't hold.' He sounded calm now, back in control. He'd obviously been using the time while she struggled to think the scenario through. 'I can see where it fell. The guttering's broken and there's no guarantee it won't break again. You'll need to lie a plank along its length so the ladder's weight's on half a dozen fastenings instead of one.'

'I'll get a plank,' Scott said.

'Scott!' William's voice would have stopped an army.

'What?'

'Let that ladder go before your sister's down and you're fired, too. Meg, leave the ladder where it is and go find the plank with Scott. You do this together. My way or not at all.'

Meg looked at her boss. He looked straight back.

'Let's do what the man says,' she told her little brother. 'He's the boss.'

They found a beam, ten foot long. Scott heaved from below and she tugged. She laid it along the length of guttering. She shifted the second ladder so it was balanced on the midpoint and it was as safe as they could make it. Done.

All William had to do was edge Letty back along the ridge—and let Meg take her down.

'You can't.' William's voice was agonised as they faced this final step, but he knew the facts. Meg was five foot five; he was six feet two. He weighed at least forty pounds more than she did. Everything depended on the guttering holding.

Letty couldn't climb herself. It was Meg who'd support Letty on the way down.

Slowly William edged back along the ridge, lifting Letty

a little at each move. She was so limp, Meg thought. She couldn't get her down if she lost consciousness. But…

'I'm saving my strength,' Letty whispered.

'You're a woman with intelligence as well as courage,' William said, and he met Meg's gaze, and she thought…

She thought…

Yeah, well, there wasn't a lot of use going down that path. Of all the inappropriate things to think right now. He looked lean and mean and dangerous. He had torn overalls, blood-stained chest, one arm bared. His expression was grim and focussed. He was totally intent on what he was doing. He looked… He looked…

She knew how he looked. She also knew how he was making her feel, and somehow it made things…

Scarier? That she'd decided she loved a man who was balanced on a crumbling ridge, with her injured grandmother in his arms and her little brother underneath, and if they fell…

Um…get a grip.

She gripped.

William was moving so slowly there was no risk of him overbalancing. He was shifting Letty a few inches at a time.

The wait was interminable.

'I have you steady.' It was Scott from underneath them. He'd climbed the first ladder and was holding the second.

This was safer—except it meant Scotty was right beneath her.

'Scott…' she started and she knew her voice quavered.

'Scott's fine. No one's going to fall,' William said. It was his 'no one's going home until this is sorted' voice. Meg blinked. Okay, she couldn't defy him on this one.

'Letty, you need to trust us all,' William said. 'Meg will catch your legs while you find a footing on the ladder. She'll be right under you, pressing you into the rungs. You'll hold as best you can with one hand. That's all you'll need. Meg will be guiding your feet, holding you firm. Don't release the first rung until you feel totally stable; stable enough to reach under for the next. If you can't do it then stop until you feel you can. There's no rush. We have all the time in the world.'

All the time in the world. Except Letty looked dreadful. If she fainted...

If she fainted then Meg would catch her and hold her and somehow get her down. No one's going to fall. The guy in the bloodstained overalls had said so.

'As soon as you have her I'll slide down the ridge the way I came up,' William said. 'I'll be beneath you.'

'What, slide and jump?' Meg retorted. 'You want a broken leg? Scotty's underneath and he'll do any catching.'

'I will,' Scott said, and Meg looked up and met William's gaze and saw agony. William McMaster depended on no one. For him to depend on a kid like Scott...

No choice. No one's going to fall.

And somehow no one did. Somehow William got a limp and trembling Letty onto Meg's ladder. Somehow Meg held her, guiding her every step of the way. Somehow they climbed down, rung after rung.

'Women are awesome,' Letty muttered as they reached the lower guttering and manoeuvred across to the next ladder. Meg even managed a smile.

'You bet. You ready for the next bit, Grandma?'

'Bring it on.' Letty's voice might be a thready whisper but her spirit was indomitable.

And then it was done. As they reached the ground Letty sagged but Scott was there. It was Scott who lifted his grandmother from the ladder. He had his Grandma in his arms, and then Meg was there, too, hugging them both.

And William was down, as well. He stood back, and Meg saw him over Letty's head, and she reached out and tugged him in as well. Her big, bloodstained hero. Her boss.

William.

They hugged together. Sandwich squeeze, she'd called this when she was little, when the family was celebrating, or something dreadful had happened, or sometimes simply because they could. Because they were family.

And this felt the same. It felt… Family?

Except William wasn't. She knew he wasn't, so it shouldn't hurt when he was the first to pull away.

It did. Even though he must.

'Let's have a look at that arm,' William said in a voice that was none too steady, and she knew he was feeling the whole gamut of emotions she was feeling. Only maybe not the family one.

There was a woman called Elinor?

Letty's knees had given completely. Scott brought cushions and blankets while Meg and William assessed the damage as best they could. Letty's arm was bound tightly with William's sleeve, but the crimson bloom was spreading.

'I don't think we should disturb it,' William said. 'Where's the nearest hospital.'

'I'm not going to hospital,' Letty quavered and for an answer William simply scooped her up, blankets and all.

'Car keys,' he snapped at Meg. 'You sit in the back seat with your grandmother. Scott, are you coming?'

Someone had turned into the drive. Mickey and his Dad, Meg thought, recognising the car, come to play with the Minis.

'Maybe…maybe I should stay,' Scott managed and then tried to get his voice down a quaver or two. 'I…Mickey can help me clean up.'

That Letty hadn't squeaked a second protest was scary, but William had her in his arms, heading for the car, and Meg could spare a moment to think things through. Scott loathed hospitals, for good reason. She could see he was torn. She needed to give him a reason to stay, and she had one. One pregnant cow.

'I need you to keep an eye on Millicent,' she said.

'Why?'

'She's showing the first signs of calving.'

'My Millicent…' Letty squeaked over William's shoulder.

'Your Millicent,' Meg retorted. 'Who's staying in the care of your grandson, and Mickey and Mickey's Dad. There's two for you and three for Millicent. So who's arguing, Grandma?'

'No one's arguing,' William said. 'Let's go.'

CHAPTER SEVEN

THE gash on her arm was deep and jagged. The doctors wanted to keep Letty in overnight, an option she wouldn't consider.

'Just pull it together and let me go. I have a turkey to stuff.'

Finally, they conceded that she could go home, but only after they were sure she was okay. 'She's lost a lot of blood, she's elderly and she's shocked,' the doctor on duty told them as they wheeled her off to Theatre. 'We'll tie her down for a couple of hours to make sure there aren't complications. Can you wait?'

'We can wait,' William said and he and Meg went to sit in the waiting room. Meg picked up a glossy magazine and stared sightlessly at its pages.

He shouldn't go near her, William decided.

Her hands were still shaking.

How could he not go to her? He moved to the seat next to hers and touched her hand.

She put her magazine down and blinked back tears.

So much for not going near her. He put his arm round her and tugged her close.

Her whole body was shaking.

'It's okay. Baby, it's okay.'

'I'm not…' She gulped and tried to pull away. 'I'm not b… baby.'

'Miss Jardine, it's okay,' he said, and pulled her closer still.

That brought a chuckle, but a watery one. She sniffed and reached for a tissue in her overalls pocket. She blew her nose, hard, and he thought, how could he go back to calling her Miss Jardine? This wasn't his super-efficient PA. This was someone he no longer knew.

Or maybe... Maybe it was just that he hadn't known his super-efficient PA, because it was starting to feel as if he did know this woman, and he wanted to know more.

'If...if the paparazzi could see us now,' she muttered and he winced. What a thing to think.

They'd come straight from the cow yard. They'd been filthy to begin with and Letty's blood had added a layer that was truly appalling.

'I think the chances of me being recognised are about zip,' he said. 'We're safe.'

'We are,' she whispered. 'Thanks to you. How did you ever get up on that roof?'

'I have skills you can't even begin to imagine,' he said, trying to make her smile.

'Can you fix Santa when we get home?'

'What?' He looked at her and discovered she was smiling—she was joking. She was still shaking but there was no way she was sinking into self-pity.

'I have a better idea,' he said unsteadily. 'Let's toss a grenade into the fireplace and blast him right out of there. All I've seen so far have been legs. A life without a head can't be all that satisfying. Let's put him out of his misery.'

She choked on something that could be a bubble of laughter or it could be tears, he couldn't decide which, and he hugged her closer and he simply held.

Eventually, the tremors stopped. He didn't let her go,

though. It felt okay to sit here and hold her—as if he had the right.

Did he want the right?

What sort of dumb thing was that to think? The shock of the morning must be getting to him.

She felt right, he thought. Holding her felt right.

But then a nurse came through the door and said, 'Miss Jardine?' and he was no longer holding her. His side felt cold without her there.

'Yes?' Meg was still frightened, he thought. She'd risen to face the nurse as if she was bracing for the worst.

She'd seen the worst, he thought. She'd have been here when her mother and stepfather were killed; when Scotty had been so appallingly injured.

She knew what happened when you let people get close.

He rose and stood beside her, and held her as the nurse approached.

But it was okay. 'Your brother's on the phone,' the nurse said. He watched as she took a deep steadying breath and nodded and moved away from the support of his arm and walked across to the nurses' station to take the call.

He watched her as she spoke. She seemed totally unconscious of how she looked. How many women did he know who could be so unaware of what they were wearing? His comment about her clothes had made her smile but she certainly wasn't thinking about them.

He watched her talk; he watched her as she replaced the receiver. He watched the quiet dignity as she thanked the nurse. He watched her walk back to him and he thought, she's a woman in a million. A woman to change your life plans for?

How crazy a thought was that?

'Our phone's back on,' she told him. 'It came back on just after we left. The line must be mended. Mickey's mum and dad are both there now and Jenny's stuffing our turkey and making brandy sauce. Millicent's calving hasn't progressed any further—Ian thinks the calf's a while off. The boys are playing with the cars. Jenny's called in the neighbours and three men are up on the roof putting tarpaulins over the capping in case there's rain before we can get a builder in. Oh, and they've fixed Santa Claus.'

'They've fixed...'

'But his sleigh's broken beyond repair. There's nothing they can do about that so Santa's escape route's gone. We're stuck with him.' She was smiling now, though her smile was a bit watery.

'Hooray,' he said faintly, and he couldn't keep his gaze from her face. Why hadn't he realised just how beautiful she was? He'd been blind.

'Hooray at last,' she repeated and her voice softened. 'It's all okay again. I have help. Scott says there's no rush to get home. Christmas is back on track. And...and it's thanks to you,' she said, and choked a bit again. 'You saved Letty. You saved us.'

'There's no need for hyperbole,' he said, embarrassed. 'You did some saving as well.'

'There's no way I would have got up on that roof in time to stop her falling.'

'You don't know what you can do until you must.'

'Indeed you don't,' she said, and her eyes were shining and she was close enough to touch. Close enough to...

She backed away, as if suddenly something had touched her, reminded her. 'I... that's all I wanted to say,' she faltered.

Was it all he wanted to say? He wanted more. He wanted to kiss her. In the middle of the emergency waiting room. With patients, medics, relatives everywhere.

He definitely wanted to kiss her.

'No,' she said, and he met her gaze with a jolt of shock. Of course. This woman was seriously good. She anticipated his needs. That was what he paid her for.

She'd anticipated this one and she was refusing.

'I... I don't think we need to stay here,' she managed. She glanced at her watch, and that tiny movement put more distance between them. It made what he wanted to do even more impossible. 'We should do something while we wait. Go down and look at the sea?'

'How about shopping?' he suggested. 'I checked yesterday—every shop in the city will be open today.'

'You're joking,' she said, startled. 'Walk through the Christmas crowds looking like this? We look like something out of *Chainsaw Massacre*.'

'Hence my shopping plan. Are you hungry?'

Her eyes widened at that, as if remembering something important.

'Yes,' she said. 'Yes, I am. Whatever happened to breakfast?'

He grinned. 'I guess it's still waiting beside the toaster at home.' *Home?* The word seemed to jar, and he corrected himself. 'Back at the farm.'

'We could grab a sandwich at the hospital cafeteria. I guess there is a hospital cafeteria.'

'I refuse to have hospital sandwiches on Christmas Eve. What I suggest...'

'Here we go.'

'What?'

'What you suggest...'

'What's wrong with that?'

'It's just *What I suggest* is McMaster for *What's going to happen.*'

'I'm open to discussion,' he said, wounded, and she was smiling again. More. She was laughing at him.

It was such a weird sensation that he felt winded.

No one laughed at him.

He kind of…liked it.

He grinned, and she grinned back, and suddenly there was such a frisson of tension between them that if a nurse hadn't approached he would have thrown reserve, caution, sense to the wind and taken her in his arms and kissed her, right on the spot. He still might…but the nurse was walking right up to them, speaking to Meg but glancing at him, as if he was included in this too.

Almost as if he was family.

'The stitching's done,' she said. 'The doctors used a very light general anaesthetic—they thought it was more appropriate, given how shocked she is—and we're popping in a little plasma to get her blood pressure up faster. I suspect she'll sleep for two hours at least. Can you give us that time before you take her home?'

'Yes,' William said before Meg could answer. 'Yes, we can.' He glanced at his cellphone and smiled. 'Hey, I have reception. I'll give you my number. Can you ring us when she wakes? Meanwhile, I suggest Miss Jardine and I find something decent to wear and then eat.'

'And if I want hospital sandwiches?' Meg muttered but she was smiling too.

'I'm your boss,' he said. 'That has to count for something.'

It counted for a lot, and so did money. Meg was simply led by William's 'suggestions'.

First, he took her to what the nurse had told him when he'd enquired was 'the classiest clothes shop in town'.

'She needs a frock,' William said to the bemused assistant. 'Or more. I suggest she buys three and everything that goes with them. Shoes, whatever.' He laid his credit card on the counter. 'Whatever it takes.'

'This feels like *Pretty Woman*,' Meg muttered. 'I'm not for sale.'

'I'm not buying.'

She met his gaze. Something passed between them, changed. *I'm not buying.*

Of course he wasn't, Meg thought. He had Elinor and women of her ilk. He escorted women from the pages of glamour magazines.

And, again, he knew what she was thinking. 'You're my PA,' he said, his tone softening. 'Nothing more. Don't get any ideas, Jardine. It's just that I don't like my PA in blood-spattered overalls.'

He sounded suddenly formal and she shivered. The warmth that had been growing inside, the comfort she'd felt as he'd held her, the bud of an idea, shrivelled.

The idea had been stupid—but she had to move on.

'And I don't like my boss in blood-spattered overalls,' she managed and tilted her chin.

'Which is why I'm heading to the place Scott showed me yesterday to buy even more jeans,' he said. 'So I'll leave you to it. No shaking while I'm gone. Everything's fine.'

And, before she could guess what he intended, he took her hands, tugged her towards him and kissed her lightly on the lips. Only it wasn't how she wanted to be kissed. It was back to where she'd started. It was a *Pretty Woman* kind of kiss. Take my plastic and buy what you need. I'll comfort you and care for you, because you're part of my entourage.

'Don't look like that, Miss Jardine,' he said softly. 'I'm not buying your soul. I'm only returning you to respectability.'

'Meg,' she said, and if she sounded forlorn she couldn't help it.

'I believe it should be Miss Jardine.'

'Willie,' she snapped and, before he could guess what she intended back, she grabbed his hands, tugged him toward her

and kissed him as well. Harder. Defiant. 'Willie,' she said
again and glowered.

His lips twitched. There was laughter behind his eyes. And
admiration.

And something more?

Something quickly quelled. Something he didn't want to
admit?

No matter, it was gone, he was gone, and she was left with
his plastic.

'Wow,' the sales assistant breathed as he disappeared into
the crowd of last minute Christmas shoppers. 'I wish my boyfriend would do something like this.'

'He's not my boyfriend.'

'Oh, but he's gorgeous.'

'In blood-stained overalls?'

'He'd be gorgeous in anything,' the girl breathed. 'Oh,
miss… Oh, let's find you the prettiest dress in the shop. With
a guy like that letting you use his credit card, you want to be
gorgeous.'

'With a guy like that I should wear a faded bag over my
head,' Meg muttered but the sales assistant was already hauling out offerings.

She should not accept his money. But…

I suggest…

This was W S McMaster talking. Her boss, giving orders.
If she put things back on their rightful footing, she'd accept.

Miss Jardine would accept. It was only Meg who was
having stupid quibbles.

'Show me what you have,' she said, resigned. Two more
days of autocracy and he'd be gone. Or sooner. She should
check the news on the air strike.

Why didn't she want to?

'What about this?' the sales assistant asked, and held up
a dress that made her gasp. It was pretty in the real sense of

the word. It was a nineteen-fifties halter neck, cinch-waisted frock with a full circled skirt. It was white with red dots. It was young, frivolous and so far away from what Meg always wore that she shook her head before she thought about it.

She wore sensible black skirts and white shirts, or she wore overalls, or she wore jeans, and somewhere at home she had a pale grey skirt for church and funerals.

She did not wear polka dots.

'Something sensible,' she said.

'It's Christmas,' the girl said and then she looked at Meg's overalls. 'And…excuse me for asking, but that looks bad.'

'It nearly was bad.'

'So it could have been bad,' the girl said and Meg realised she was in the hands of a master saleswoman. 'And, if it had been, you'd never have got the chance to wear polka dots. And he…' she looked meaningfully in the direction William had gone '…would never have seen you in polka dots.'

'Perish the thought,' Meg said, trying to sound sarcastic, but it didn't come off.

'So will you try it?'

No, Meg thought. But she couldn't say it.

She looked at the dress, and then she also glanced in the direction William had gone. She could no longer see him.

He'd be back.

Tomorrow or the next day he'd be gone.

What the heck. It was his plastic. *I suggest…*

She was merely following her boss's orders. Only he no longer felt like her boss. He felt like something else completely.

So did she. She stared into the mirror and saw the woman she'd been two days ago behind the woman she was now. And she thought of the impossibility of going back to what she had been.

I'll be one of those elderly secretaries, she thought, totally devoted to the boss, taking whatever he'll give. 'Good morning, Mr McMaster, of course I'll take dictation, certainly I'll send flowers to Sarah, I suggest tiger lilies because they're what the gossip columnists say is her favourite flower.'

Meanwhile...

Meanwhile, Scotty had climbed on the roof to put Santa up himself and Letty had tried to fix it. If she'd had a regular job, where she could go home every night...

She'd told herself this was better. Working twenty-four seven for short bursts and then staying home.

She'd loved twenty-four seven. She loved working for W S McMaster. But now...

Now she'd seen William clinging to the roof, holding her grandma. Now William had held her at the hospital and she'd needed him to hold her.

Two days ago she'd been able to draw a line—that life, this life.

The lines had blurred and it frightened her.

Decisiveness had always been her strong point. She didn't have to like it but she knew when a decision had to be made. She made one now. Oh, but it hurt.

She took a deep breath. She glanced once more in the direction William had gone. Before he came back, she had to find some resolution.

She took the polka dots and disappeared into the changing room...to change.

She was wearing polka dots.

He'd left her wearing bloodied overalls and truly disgusting boots. She was now wearing what could only be described as a happy dress, a Christmas dress. Her boots had been replaced with white strappy stilettos and her hair, caught back with an elastic band while she'd done the milking, was now a riot of bouncing curls, caught on the side with a tiny red rosette.

She looked about ten years younger.

She looked breathtakingly lovely.

Meg was gazing into the mirror as if she, too, hardly recognised herself. She met his reflected gaze and turned slowly to face him, and he thought if he hadn't caught her in this she might have fled and taken it off.

'It's…it's silly,' she said.

'It's lovely,' the shop assistant said definitely. 'We've found two more that are just as pretty, only she won't buy three. She's reluctant to buy even this one, but I persuaded her to try it on again. With shoes.'

'Well done,' he said, walking closer. 'I can see it needs shoes.'

'It's silly,' Meg said again.

'It's not,' William said, somehow managing to smile at the shop assistant without taking his eyes off Meg. 'You look lovely.'

She flushed. 'I feel like something out of Hollywood.'

'Great things come out of Hollywood. We'll take it.' He still hadn't taken his eyes from her. 'And the other two. Wrap the others. She'll leave this one on.'

'William…'

'Say "Yes, Mr. McMaster".'

'No!'

'You're intending to go to a classy restaurant wearing overalls?'

'I'm not going to any classy restaurant.' Her new resolution hadn't included socialising. She'd have a sandwich on the run and then go back to the hospital. Then she'd get through Christmas. She'd tell him her decision as she put him on the flight back to New York.

A withered spinster gazing adoringly after her boss… She hauled the conjured vision back into her head and held on to it.

Her decision was right, no matter how much it hurt. She had to move forward.

But he was still thinking restaurants. 'Of course we need to go to a restaurant,' he said, sounding wounded. 'I've bought new clothes too, so we're both dressed up. You like my chinos?'

He was smiling at her. Oh, that smile…

'They're fine, but…'

'Hey, I said you're lovely.'

'Okay, you're lovely too,' she muttered. 'But we don't need to match.'

'Better that we don't, I think,' he said softly. 'But we'll buy the dresses anyway.'

CHAPTER EIGHT

MEG walked out of the shop feeling as if she were in a freeze-frame from a fifties movie. William put his hand in the small of her back to guide her through the crush of shoppers and the feeling of unreality deepened.

'Don't think about it,' he said, obviously sensing how self-conscious she felt. 'The crowds were looking when you were covered in blood. They're still looking, but now they're smiling. Let's concentrate on the important things. Like breakfast.'

She'd given up fighting. A sandwich on the run felt good, but anything would do. She was so hungry she was likely to keel over. If he had to take her to a restaurant, then so be it.

'Yes, please,' she said, expecting him to take her into one of the small local restaurants. But instead he ushered her back into the car—how did this man manage to get a park when the whole world was looking for a park today?—and she almost groaned. She wanted to eat *now*.

But she'd worked for too long for this man to complain when meals took too long coming, so she stifled her groan and folded her hands in her lap and thought she looked ridiculous. She should be smiling and waving. But then they should be driving an expensive sports car instead of Letty's farm wagon. At least the silencer was fixed, she thought, and then she saw where they were going and she forgot about anything else.

He was driving up to the cliff above the town. He was taking her to the most expensive restaurant in the district.

She'd never been here.

'This place is… Oh, it's where you go to celebrate wedding anniversaries. When you're rich. They don't do breakfast,' she breathed.

'They do today. I rang them. I spoke to the chef personally. Bacon and eggs and fried bread and strawberries and fresh juice and sourdough toast and home-made butter… We had a long discussion. Anything we want, we can have.'

'If we pay.'

'If I pay,' he said gently and he was out of the car, striding round to her side and handing her out as if she was one of his dates instead of Miss Jardine, his PA.

He never handed her out of his car. He opened doors for her, the natural courtesy of a polite man, but to walk around and help her out of the car… no. She was his employee and the extra cosseting was reserved for…his women?

She no longer fitted either category, she thought, as she brushed past him and his touch made her feel even more as if this was not real, it was something out of a movie. The lines were blurring.

But if the lines were blurring… The question was huge and for some reason it was drumming in her head—insistent, urgent. There was never going to be a good time to ask—so why not now?

'Who's Elinor?' she asked, and he looked at her for a long moment and then smiled and shrugged and led her inside.

Maybe the lines were blurring for him too, she thought, and then she thought, all the more reason why her decision was the only possible one.

'I'll tell you over breakfast,' he said simply, and she knew she was right.

The restaurant was almost empty. This place started lunch

at what it deemed a respectable hour and this didn't quite qualify. Maybe they wouldn't have taken his booking if he hadn't…thrown his credit card around? Thrown his name around?

'You'll have the paparazzi in your face before you know it,' she said darkly and he shook his head.

'You think the paparazzi has nothing better to do on Christmas Eve than take photos of me? I'm low-key in the celebrity world.'

He was, she thought, but only because he created little stir. He didn't do the society thing. Even though his name was known worldwide, for the most part he deliberately kept away from cameras. He was seen in the celebrity magazines, stepping back into the shadows as his woman of the moment smiled and posed. If the women he escorted started to like the limelight too much, he moved on. Was this why she hadn't heard of Elinor until now? Did the woman have sense enough to stay low profile?

She shouldn't have asked. She had no business asking.

She really wanted to know.

The head waiter was leading them to what must surely be the best table in the house, in an alcove which gave a semblance of privacy but where the view stretched away across the ocean, as far as the eye could see. There were windsurfers on the waves below them. Meg thought suddenly, how long had it been since she'd swum?

Their farm was almost an hour's drive from the sea. There was never any time to indulge in anything so frivolous.

Maybe *when* she changed jobs…

The thought was inexorably bleak.

'Eggs and bacon and toast and fruit and juice and coffee,' William said to the waiter. 'Any way you want to serve them, as long as it starts coming fast. Is that okay with you, Miss Jardine?'

Miss Jardine. It sounded wrong. Maybe it sounded wrong to William too, because he was frowning.

'Yes. Wonderful,' she managed.

The waiter sailed off as if he'd just been given an order which was a triumph of creation all on its own—how much had William paid to get this table, to get a breakfast menu, to simply be here? To take his woman somewhere beautiful.

She was not his woman.

Neither was she Miss Jardine.

Deep breath. Just do it. 'Mr McMaster, this might not be the time to tell you, but I think I should,' she said and she faltered. Was she mad? Yes, she was. She knew it, but she still knew that she had no choice. 'I need to resign.'

William had glanced out to sea as a windsurfer wiped out in spectacular fashion. He turned back to face her and his expression had stilled.

'Resign?'

'I'll train my replacement,' she said hurriedly. 'I won't leave you without anyone. But you're going back to the States anyway. If you're gone for a couple for months I'll have someone sorted before you return. I'll work side by side with her then for a couple of weeks until I'm sure you're happy, but...'

'I hire my own PAs,' he snapped.

'So you do. Then, please, you need to find my replacement.'

'Can I ask why?'

There was the question. A thousand answers crowded in but he was watching her face—and this was William... No, this was W S McMaster...and she knew him and he knew her and only honesty would do.

'The work we do...we need to travel side by side. We need to be totally dependent on each other but we need to stay detached. Today... Up on the roof I got undetached.'

'Meaning?'

'Meaning I don't think of you as Mr McMaster any more. I think of you as the man who saved my grandma.'

His gaze didn't leave her face. 'So take a pay cut,' he said at last. 'I don't see how abandoning me is showing your gratitude.'

'You know what I mean.'

He did. She saw a flicker behind his eyes that might almost be read as pain if she didn't know how aloof this man was. How he stood apart.

'There's no need to leave.'

'I think there is.'

'You're under contract,' he snapped.

'No.' She met his gaze calmly, hoping he couldn't guess the tumult behind her words. 'My contract's up for renewal. It expires next month.'

'You're responsible for keeping contracts up to date.'

'So I am. So I have. My contract expires. It's not to be renewed, so we move on.'

'So you tell me now?' he snapped. 'And you expect us to calmly go on sharing Christmas when you no longer work for me?'

She flinched, but there was no avoiding what needed to be said. She knew him well enough now to accept the only way forward was honesty.

'It's the only way I can go on sharing Christmas,' she said simply. 'Feeling the way I do.'

'Feeling...'

'Like you're not my boss any more.'

'This is nonsense.'

'It's not nonsense,' she said stubbornly. 'I'm sorry but there it is. I've quit. If you want me to keep working until you get a replacement...'

'That means you'll still be working over Christmas.'

'I'm returning my Christmas bonus.' She glanced down at her dress. 'I'll take these in the form of severance pay. You won't be out of pocket.'

'What nonsense is this? You can't afford the grand gesture.'

'It's not a grand gesture,' she said stiffly. 'It's what I need to do. I can't afford not to.'

'What's that supposed to mean?'

'It means not everything's about money.' She hesitated. 'Who's Elinor?' she asked again and his brows snapped down in a sharp, dark line of anger.

'Is that what this is about?'

'You mean am I, your PA, jealous of a woman called Elinor?' She managed a smile at that one. 'Of course I'm not. All I'm saying is that the lines between personal and professional have been blurred. Last week I wouldn't have dared ask that question—I wouldn't want to. However, suddenly I want to know why you never had a dog when you were a kid. I want to know how you learned to climb when you were a boy. And, yes, I do want to know about Elinor.' She hesitated. 'Maybe this can't make sense to you, but a week ago I didn't mind…that you seemed aloof and a bit…unhappy.'

'I'm not unhappy,' he said, startled, and she thought about it.

'Okay, not unhappy,' she conceded. 'Wrong word, but I don't know what the word is. Just…holding yourself tight against the world, when letting the world in could make you happy.'

And he got it, just like that. 'Like caring about Scott and Letty?'

'Like caring about Scott and Letty.'

'And if anything happens to them?'

'Then my world falls apart.'

'Then that's dumb. You can't afford to think like that.'

'Why not? That's all there is.'

'Emotional nonsense.'

'So who's Elinor?'

'It's none of your business.'

'It's not,' she agreed. 'And as my boss you can tell me to mind my own. As a casual acquaintance you can tell me that as well. But now I'm your hostess for Christmas, and you saved my grandma's life. So I owe you and you owe me and I really want to know that there's someone in your life who can take that horrid, reserved look away from your face.'

He stared at her, nonplussed. She managed to meet his gaze and hold. This wasn't just about her, she thought. There was something she had to reach…something it was important to reach.

He'd saved Letty. She owed it to him to try.

But then breakfast arrived. The smell reached her before the meal, wafting across the room as a delicious, tantalising siren call. A couple of early lunch diners were being ushered to their tables. She saw their noses wrinkle with appreciation and she thought—mine, hands off.

She turned back to William, and the same thought flickered. *Mine…* Only it was a stupid, stupid thought. It was why she had to get out.

Maybe she didn't want to know who Elinor was. Personal or not, boss or…friend?…she didn't have the right.

But she wasn't retracting and her question hung.

And it seemed he'd decided to tell her. The meal was set before them and he started to talk even before he started to eat. There was anger beneath his words, an edge of darkness, but the words were coming out all the same.

'Elinor's a foster mother in Manhattan,' he said. 'She's a lovely, warm Afro-American lady with a heart bigger than Texas. She's old enough to retire but there are always children who need her. Right now she's fostering Ned and Pip.

Two years ago she took them in while their mother suppos-edly undertook a court-ordered rehab, but instead she robbed a drug store, with violence. She's been in prison ever since and she doesn't contact them; she treats them with complete indifference. Elinor's trying to persuade her to give them up for adoption but she won't. So Elinor's the only mother they know.'

'And...you?' she asked, stunned.

'I met Elinor when I agreed to sponsor the Manhattan Foster-Friends programme. It's an organisation designed to give foster carers support, for people who'd love to help but who only have limited time to give. So Elinor and the children have become my... Foster-Friends. I'd promised to take them out for Christmas.'

'I see,' she whispered, and she did see. Sort of. So the image of a sleek, sterile Manhattan apartment wasn't right. Or maybe it was right; it was just that he moved out from it in a way she hadn't expected.

'So what will they do now?' she asked, feeling dreadful—for Elinor, for Pip and Ned, and for William himself.

'Elinor has said not to worry. She'll give them Christmas. They don't depend on me.'

'Oh,' she said in a small voice.

'Eat your breakfast, Meg,' he said gently and she turned her attention to her plate, though the enjoyment wasn't in it now. Or not so much.

It did, indeed, look wonderful. Pleasure laced with guilt.

'I'm sorry I didn't get you home,' she said.

'It's not your fault. Eat.'

Eat. She'd almost forgotten she was hungry. Or maybe not. She was fickle, she thought, piercing an egg and watching the yolk ooze across the richly buttered toast. Mmm.

She glanced up and William was watching her and she thought, with a tiny frisson of something she was far too sensible to feel—*Elinor's a retirement age foster mother. And William cares about kids.*

But William only cared about these kids part-time. In the bits he had available. She knew he was out of the country eight months out of twelve.

The coldness settled back—the bleak certainty that this man walked alone and would walk alone for ever. There was nothing she could do about it. She'd resigned. She didn't have to watch him self-destruct.

But maybe he was right. Maybe he wasn't self-destructing— maybe it was she who was putting herself out there to be shot down with emotional pain.

The whole scenario was too hard. There was only one thing to do here.

She looked back down at her egg—firmly—and concentrated—firmly—on her truly excellent breakfast.

There wasn't a lot of conversation after that. After their third coffee William rang the hospital while Meg stared into the dregs of her cup. He put it onto speaker so Meg could hear the nurse's response.

'She's still asleep. Yes, she's fine. I promise we'll ring you the moment she wakes.'

'So let's walk,' he decreed and Meg could only agree. She didn't want to go back to the hospital and wait. And think.

Think of what she was walking away from.

So they walked down to the beach, and Meg slipped off her sandals and headed for the shallows.

William watched her from further up on the sand. He kept his shoes on. He'd swapped his boots for a pair of casual loafers but he wasn't taking the next step. W S McMaster with bare feet, walking in the shallows? Unthinkable.

She walked along, letting the last run of the waves lick over her toes, kicking sprays of water up in front of her.

William walked parallel to her but fifteen feet up the beach. She was in the shallows. He was on solid sand.

Solid sand?

There was no such thing, she thought. Nothing was solid. Everything was shifting.

Why wasn't he taking his shoes off? Why wasn't he coming close?

She knew why. She even agreed it was sensible that he shouldn't.

The wind was warm on her face. The sand and salt between her toes felt fabulous. All it needed was for William to take fifteen steps and take her hand and life would be…

A fairy tale.

So get real, she told herself and kicked up a spray of water so high she soaked the front of her dress. This guy is a billionaire from Manhattan—my ex-boss. I'm unemployed, with a hundred dairy cows, a little brother and a grandma who needs me and will need me for years.

She kicked the water again and glanced sideways at William.

He wasn't looking at her. He was striding along the beach as if he was there to walk off his too-big breakfast and that was that.

And why shouldn't it be that? The man hadn't been to the gym for two days. He'd be suffering from withdrawal.

'You go on by yourself,' she called to him. 'Burn some energy. I'm happy to stay here and kick water.'

He glanced at her and nodded, brisk, serious.

She turned to watch the windsurfers and he headed off along the beach. Alone.

He was being a bore.

He didn't know what else to be.

There were a thousand emotions crowding into his head right now and he didn't know what to do with any of them.

She was beautiful. There was a really big part of him that wanted to head into the shallows—with or without shoes— and tug her to him and hold.

How selfish would that be?

She wasn't like any woman he'd dated. He'd selected her with care as his Australian PA and that was what she was qualified to be. She was smart, efficient, unflappable. Loyal, honest, discreet. Sassy, funny, emotional.

Trusting and beautiful.

He didn't have a clue what to do with all these things. He moved in circles where women knew boundaries; indeed, they wanted them. He was an accessory, a guy with looks and money who was good for their image. No one had ever clung.

Meg wasn't clinging. The opposite—she was walking away.

That was good. She knew the boundaries. She knew they'd overstepped them so she was protecting herself. She had the right.

And if he stepped over the boundaries after her, like walking into the water now and taking her hand, pretending they could just be a normal couple, boy and girl...

He didn't do boy and girl. He had to leave; he knew no other way of living.

Do not depend on anyone.

He could depend on Meg.

No. She'd resigned. The thought hurt. He tried to drum up anger but it wasn't there. All that was left was a sense of emptiness, as if he'd missed out on something other people had. How to change? If he tried... If he hurt her...

He walked faster, striding along the hard sand, trying to drive away demons. He stopped and looked back, and Meg was a red and white splash of colour in the shallows, far behind.

In a day or two she'd be further away. She'd get some sort of hick job and be stuck here, milking her cows. Taking care of Letty and Scott.

It was her choice.

He picked up a heap of seaweed and hurled it out into the shallows, as if it'd personally done him injury. That was what this felt like, but he couldn't fault Meg. She was protecting herself, as he protected his own barriers.

She had the right.

He'd choose another PA and move on.

But first…he had to get Christmas over. Bring on Santa Claus, he thought grimly, followed by a plane out of here.

And then they'd all live happily ever after?

CHAPTER NINE

IT WAS a subdued trio who returned home. Letty was stretched out on the back seat, dozing. The doctors had been inclined to keep her; she'd woken enough to be stubborn but she was sleeping now.

Meg sat in the passenger seat, staring straight ahead. As if she was enduring something that had to be endured.

He'd made a few desultory attempts at conversation but had given up. So much for his smart, sassy PA. Now she was just…Meg. Someone he once knew?

Just concentrate on driving, he told himself. When he got back to the farm he'd move onto evening milking. The phone line was working again so after milking he could use the Internet; keep himself busy.

'By the way, I've organised your satellite connection,' he said and Meg cast him a glance that was almost scared.

'You what?'

'While you were dress shopping. It only took me minutes to buy what I needed, and the Internet place was open for business. It seems satellite dishes make great Christmas gifts. Even I couldn't get them to erect it today, but first working day after Christmas it'll be here.'

'I can't afford…'

'It's paid for. Three years in advance.'

'No, thank you,' she said in a tight, clipped voice. 'Three dresses are enough.'

But… 'Are you out of your mind?' Letty was suddenly awake, piping up from the back seat in indignation. 'Meg, what sort of gift horse are you looking in the mouth here? Scotty will love it. You know there'll be times still when he's stuck at home in pain. You can't say no to that.'

'Letty, I'm no longer working for Mr McMaster,' Meg said. 'So I can't take expensive gifts.'

'You're not working for him?'

'She's resigned. Tell her she's daft,' William said.

'No,' Letty said, surprisingly strongly. 'My Meg's not daft. If she's quit there's a good and sensible reason. But a satellite connection…that'd be a gift to Scotty and me, not to Meg, wouldn't it, Mr McMaster?'

'William,' he said and he almost snapped.

'William,' Letty said. 'Scott's friend. My friend. Meg, dear, William has more money than he knows what to do with, and he's just given us a very fine Christmas gift in return for a bed for Christmas. And…' She hesitated, but she was a wise old bird, was Letty. 'And you don't want anything in return, do you, Mr McMaster?'

'William!'

'William,' Letty said obediently. 'But you're not buying Meg with this. She doesn't owe you anything, right?'

'Right,' he said and glanced across at Meg. Her face was drawn, almost as if she was in pain.

He hated that look. He didn't know what to do about it.

'Then I accept on Scotty's behalf,' Letty said across his thoughts. 'And your bed for Christmas is assured.'

When they'd left the farm it had been almost deserted. When they turned back into the driveway there were more than a dozen vehicles parked under the row of gums out front.

'Uh-oh,' Letty said, peering dubiously out of the window. 'This looks like a funeral.'

'If it hadn't been for William, it would have been,' Meg said, and once again William thought she sounded strained to breaking point. 'If Scott's done something else stupid…'

But it seemed he hadn't. When they pulled up, women emerged from the house, men appeared from the yard, kids appeared from everywhere.

'They called a working bee,' Scott said, limping across to the car on his crutches and tugging open the back door to make sure for himself that his grandmother was in one piece. 'They said you had enough on your plate, Meg. And they knew you'd left the hay till after Christmas, so they brought slashers and they've done three whole paddocks. They're bringing in the last of it now.'

'You're kidding,' Meg whispered, but she was staring across to a hay shed which had stood almost empty this morning and now looked three-quarters full. 'In what—four hours?'

'We can work when we want to.' It was Jenny, coming forward to give her friend a hug. 'We were thinking we'd help after Christmas but when this happened I said to Ian, why not now?' She cast a curious glance at William. 'She needs looking after, our Meg.'

'I do not,' Meg said, revolted.

'She doesn't,' Scott said and Jenny grinned and hugged him as well until he turned scarlet in embarrassment.

'Okay, she doesn't. As long as you and Letty stop doing darn fool things when she's not around,' Jenny retorted.

'I'm going to be around,' Meg said. 'I'll try and find a job locally. I… I don't want to be away any more. But for now… thank you all so, so much. I'm incredibly grateful. But I need to get Letty inside. She needs to sleep.'

'I'll carry her,' William said but one of the neighbours

stepped forward and lifted Letty from the car before he could.

'We're local,' he said to William, quite kindly, but firmly for all that. 'We look after our own. Cows are on their way up now, Meg. You want some help with tonight's milking?'

'You've done enough,' Meg said.

'This guy'll help?' It seemed everyone was looking at William.

'He's promised to.'

'Is he any good?'

'At milking? He has untapped potential,' Meg said and people laughed and gathered their kids and said their goodbyes and left.

Meg tucked Letty into bed and fussed over her. Scott limped over to the cow yard and William followed.

'We should start,' Scott said.

William looked at the brace on Scott's leg and said gently, 'Is that okay? That you help with milking?'

'It has to be. I'm tired of waiting for it to heal.'

'So it's not okay.'

'Meg and Grandma fuss that if my leg gets kicked we have to start over again. But I'll be careful.'

'Or not. How about you supervise while I do the hands on?' William eyed the mass of cows pressing against the yard gate. He eyed the waiting bales. Nothing to this. Except... Maybe you had to do stuff to the vat for pasteurisation or... or something. He didn't want to waste a whole milking. 'Do you know how this works?'

'Course.'

'Then you give me instructions and leave me to it.'

'I can help.' Scott squared his shoulders. 'I know I was dumb trying to put that Santa up. I never dreamed Grandma'd try and fix it. But I'm not completely helpless. This leg'll soon be better. I can look after them.'

William looked into his drawn face. He saw reflected horror from this morning's accident. He saw the unmistakable traces of years of pain and he saw tension, worry, the pain of being a kid without a dad, an adolescent trying desperately to be an adult.

'I know you can,' he said softly. 'If you must. But I'm at a loose end right now, and it seems everything else is taken care of. So you sit on the fence and tell me your plans for your car restoration and in between plans you can tell me how to turn this milking machine on and let these girls get rid of their load.'

Scotty must be exhausted. Meg arrived at the dairy, back in her milking gear, and one glance at her little brother told her he was close to the edge. Physically, he was still frail. This morning would have terrified him and, with all the neighbours here helping, his pride wouldn't have let him stop.

She wanted to grab him down from the fence, hug him and haul him off to bed. But he was talking to William, who appeared to be underneath a cow, and she knew that pride still played a part here.

'So you two reckon you can run this place without me?' she enquired and William emerged from behind the cow and grinned.

'Nothing to this milking game. I'm about to add Milker to my CV.'

'How is he, Scotty?' she asked and then corrected herself. 'Sorry, Scott.'

'You can still call me Scotty if you like,' her brother conceded. 'In private.'

'In front of William's not private.'

'No, but he's okay.'

That was a huge concession, Meg thought. There'd been

a few guys in her past—of course there had—but Scott had bristled at all of them. *He's okay.* Huge.

'Just because he bought you bits of cars…' she managed, feeling choked up.

'No, he really is okay. Is Grandma asleep?'

'Almost,' she said and here was a way to let him off the hook without injuring any more of that fragile manly ego. 'She wants to say goodnight to you. Do you reckon you could stay with her while we milk? I'm still a bit worried about her.'

'Sure,' Scott said and slid off the fence and again she had to haul herself back from rushing forward to help. 'Watch William with those cups, though. Four teats, four cups. It's taking him a bit of time to figure it out.'

'Hey!' William said, sounding wounded, and Meg laughed and watched her little brother retreat and thought this was as good as it got.

But it was so fleeting. Tomorrow or the next day, William would be gone.

It was okay. This was the right thing to do. She had no choice but to resign. A PA, hopelessly devoted to her boss? That was pathetic and she knew it.

She glanced at him and thought, dumb or not, she was hopelessly devoted. She had no choice but to get as far from William as possible.

'He's a great kid,' William said and she flushed and started milking and didn't answer.

'You don't agree?' he asked after she'd cupped her first cow.

'Of course I agree.'

'But you're not talking.'

'It's been a big day.'

'But it's normal again now,' he said gently. 'Though it's a shame you felt the need to change. I liked your dress.'

'I'll wear it again tomorrow.' She gathered her emotions

and told them firmly to behave. Two days max and he'd be gone. 'Tell me about Pip and Ned. Do you have Christmas gifts for them?'

'I do.'

'What?'

'Bubble guns,' he said. 'Battery powered. Ten bubbles a second and they're seriously big.'

'You sound like you tried them out.'

'Why wouldn't I?'

Whoa… The thought of W S McMaster with a bubble gun… 'Whereabouts did you try them out?'

'On my balcony. I sent bubbles over Central Park.'

She giggled. Then she remembered he was going home and she stopped giggling.

'Meg?' he said softly from behind a cow.

'Yes?'

'Reconsider.'

'Quitting?'

'Yes.'

'No.'

'Why not?'

'Not negotiable,' she said. 'Being your assistant means being aloof.'

'You were never aloof.'

'I was aloof in my head.'

'And you're not now?'

'No,' she said shortly. 'Can we keep on milking?'

'Of course we can. As long as you keep on thinking about reconsidering.'

'I can't.'

'Don't think can't. Think of all the reasons why you just might can.'

'That's a crazy thing to say.'

'Resigning's a crazy thing to think.'

* * *

Only of course she was right and it was non-negotiable. They both knew it.

They finished milking, they cleaned the yard, they worked in tandem and mostly they worked in silence. Then they headed inside and ate the last of the trifle and bread and ham in that order because Letty and Scott were both deeply asleep and it didn't seem to matter what order they ate in.

William thought back to Christmas Eve meals he'd had as a child. Christmas had been an excuse for socializing, which meant huge parties of very drunk people. Because it was Christmas his parents had insisted he be part of it. At Christmas they had to pretend to be a family.

Here...for the past two days they'd lived on Letty's vast trifle and chunks of the huge Christmas ham and fresh bread and butter, eating as they felt like it, and it had felt... okay. Sensible. Delicious, even. But not...right?

The world seemed out of kilter somehow, William thought as he washed the dinner dishes and Meg wiped beside him. It felt so domestic, and domestic was something he'd never felt. Doing the washing-up with his PA was weird. All of today had been weird.

He'd lost his PA.

He'd lost Meg.

'We have the Internet back on,' Meg said as she put away the last plate. 'There's a phone connection in the attic—I use the attic as an office when it's not a spare bedroom—so you can catch up on the outside world before you go to sleep.'

'And you?'

'I'm checking on Millicent and then I'm going to bed. Christmas or not, it's still a five a.m. start. Goodnight, William.'

'Do you want help with Millicent?'

'She's not looking much different to this morning. I doubt if anything's happening tonight. Goodnight,' she said again, and she took the torch and headed out through the back door. The day was ended.

He'd check the Internet. He'd see what was happening with air traffic. He hadn't even checked today; maybe it was resolved.

Maybe he could leave.

Meg had already left.

Maybe things *were* happening tonight. She'd started again. Millicent was back to being uncomfortable, or more than uncomfortable, Meg thought. Her tail was constantly high, her back was arched and her eyes told Meg that she was in pain.

'Hey, it's okay,' Meg told her, fondling her behind the ears, scratching her, letting her rub her big head against her chest. This cow had been raised as a pet. She was a big sook and Letty loved her.

A normal dairy farmer would go to bed now, set the alarm and check her in a couple of hours. But, when she stepped back, Millicent's eyes widened in fear. Meg sighed and went back to the house and fetched a folding chair, a lantern, a book and a rug.

'Happy Christmas,' she told Millicent as she settled down to wait. 'You and me and hopefully a baby for Christmas. We should do this in a manger. Or, at the very least, at the bottom of the haystack.'

But Millicent wasn't going anywhere. Trying to move her now would only add to her distress and the night was warm enough.

'Who needs a manger, anyway?' Meg muttered and glanced upward to where a thousand stars glittered in the clear night sky. 'This is where babies should be born. So get on with it.'

Millicent rolled her eyes.

'I know, sweetheart, it's hard,' Meg said. 'Or I don't actually know. I've heard it's hard. You should have its daddy holding your hoof.'

She was being ridiculous.

She was thinking of William. The book she'd brought out to read was a romance. She and William. Having a baby. William coaching her through…

'Well, pigs might fly,' she muttered and tossed her romance aside and snuggled under her blanket. 'We're two single ladies, Millicent, and we need to get on with it together. You do your bit and I'll do mine.'

There'd been a last minute offer to the air traffic controllers. The union officials had deemed it worth considering and had sent out urgent contact to its members. Because this was Christmas they'd vote online. If enough members voted by midnight, planes could start flying as soon as tomorrow morning.

Great. He might get home almost by Christmas, he thought. He'd gain a day flying from Australia to the States. If he left on Christmas Day, then he'd arrive on Christmas Day.

He could give Ned and Pip their gifts. He could see them again; take them out to dinner, maybe.

Leaving Meg?

She was his employee. His ex-employee. So what was the problem leaving her?

No problem at all.

He intended to help with milking at five. He needed to go to sleep.

He lay in bed and stared at the ceiling and thought of…

Meg.

He thought of Meg for a long time. He tried to think of anything but Meg but she was superimposed, like a veil through which he saw everything else.

Or maybe…maybe everything in his life was a veil and Meg was behind. The only substantial thing.

What sort of crazy thinking was this? Where was the logic? Furious with himself, he threw off his covers and paced over to the attic window.

Two o'clock. The stars were amazing.

There was a light in the paddock beside the dairy. A faint light from a lantern. Someone was beside it.

Millicent? Was she calving?

Meg would be down there, making sure things were okay.

What business was it of his? He didn't know the first thing about birthing calves. He'd be no help at all.

But, now he knew she was there, doing nothing was impossible. He'd help if he could, he thought grimly, and then he'd leave.

He tugged on his overalls and headed downstairs.

What sort of life was this? Meg had been awake since five this morning. She'd be asleep on her feet, he thought as he made his way across the yard towards the lantern, but then he thought of all the times he'd demanded she stay up late, that she be awake for an early flight, that she continue until the work was done.

That was different. She was Miss Jardine then. He paid her to work when he worked.

He had three PAs. He thought of them now, and thought how hard did he work them? They never complained.

He paid them not to complain.

But, for the first time, he felt a niggle of guilt. He treated his employees fairly; he made it clear at the outset what he expected and he paid well. He had a loyal and long-serving staff because of it. But his demand that they stay impersonal…

His PAs told him what he needed to know about his staff. But his PAs themselves… Miss Darling, Mrs Abraham, Miss

O'Connell? He'd have to look up their staff profiles to find out what their family background was.

What was happening to him? His staff were turning into people. And you got attached to people. *Do not get attached to people you pay.*

Meg was messing with his head, that was what it was. The sooner he was out of here, the better.

Only she was in trouble. As he neared, he could see…

Millicent was down, flat on her side, her body arched and her neck stretched up as if straining to the limit.

Meg…yes, it was Meg…was lying behind her, a dark shadow behind the light. He could see a mat laid out to the side, a couple of buckets, rags, ropes…

'Problem?' he asked as he came up beside her and she didn't react. He looked more closely—and discovered why she didn't react. She was hardly in a position to concentrate on anything but the cow.

What was she doing?

'What's happening?' he asked, squatting beside her.

'Dystocia,' she said, gasping. 'I can't.'

She was lying flat, hard against Millicent's rear. Her arm…

'Dystocia?'

'Birth problems.' She sounded as if she'd been running. 'First calf. Bull was too big and now this. I knew it. I can't…'

'What can't you do?' he said, feeling helpless. He'd never seen a birth. He never wanted to see a birth.

Obviously, he was going to see this one.

Or more than see. 'Maybe you can help,' she gasped, and he thought maybe he should head back to his nice safe attic right now. Only a coward would run.

He surely felt like a coward.

'You're stronger than I am,' she gasped and he thought, uh oh.

'Can we call the vet?'

'He's away until after Christmas. He warned us.'

'Surely there's more than one vet.' He was taking in the whole scene now and, as he did, Millicent strained. Her whole body heaved and Meg moaned, and moaned again.

'What are you doing?'

'I can't…' She gasped, not able to continue until the contractions subsided. Then… 'Yes, we need a vet but we only have one locally. And the calf's leg's tucked backward instead of forward, meaning there's a ridge of shoulder stopping the birth. So I need to get the head back in the birth canal so there's room to turn it. But I can't. I don't have the strength.' She pushed and pushed again—and then seemed to make a decision. Her arm was suddenly free. She dunked it in the nearest bucket and looked up to him. 'Can you?'

'Can I what?'

'Push the head back far enough so you can get the leg forward.'

He felt as if someone had punched him. Milking was one thing, but this? 'You want me to…'

'I'm not strong enough,' she said simply. 'Please.'

'You think I…'

She wasn't listening. 'Rip your shirt off—it'll be ruined. Shove your arm into the disinfectant and I'll lubricate it. Hurry, before the next contraction.'

'You want me to…'

'Just do it,' she snapped and he was hauling his shirt off, thinking…thinking…nothing.

He dunked his arm in disinfectant. Meg wiped it and then started lathering him with some sort of jelly. He felt too winded to object.

'Lie flat,' she told him. 'If a contraction hits, don't try to do anything except stop the head coming further forward. But the foreleg on the right is lying back instead of hoof-forward. You need to push the head back far enough so you have space to feel the foreleg and tug it forward. There's no way she can get the calf out with it back.'

'I have no idea how to do that.'

'Simple,' she snapped. 'Cows have two forelegs. To calf they both need to be forward with the head between. So you pull a leg forward.'

'How do I know what everything is?'

She wasn't listening to his panic. She was intent only on instructions. 'It's not brain surgery. A hoof's easy to feel. Think about it. Think what you're looking for and then find it. Gentle as you can—do no damage—but you have to move fast. Before the next contraction. Go.'

So he lay full length on the grass and he did the unthinkable. To his astonishment, he could feel… What? He could feel the head. He could feel one small hoof on the left.

He needed the matching one.

Another contraction rippled through and he discovered why Meg had moaned. He almost moaned himself.

'Don't try and do anything during the contraction. Just hold it,' she snapped from above him and he held with all the strength he had and he knew that if he hadn't been holding the head would be emerging.

With one hoof and not the other.

So he held and finally, blessedly, the contraction eased.

'Now push,' Meg said urgently. 'All the force you can. You need to get it back.'

He didn't need to be told. He pushed, gently at first and then, as his grip tightened, as he became more sure of what he was holding, he pushed with more force. Then he pushed with all his strength.

The head moved…and then more…

'Now.' Meg would have seen by his arm that the head had shifted. 'Before the next contraction. Find the leg.'

He had to loosen his grip on the head, slide his fingers to the side… It was so tight….

But there it was, a bony joint, surely the leg. He felt along it, conscious of the need for speed…

He had it, hooked by two fingers, and he was tugging it forward.

'Careful not to rip anything,' Meg said urgently. 'Take care.'

Another contraction. He felt it coming, released the leg, held the head. Just held.

Then, as the contraction eased, he moved again, only this time he knew what he was looking for.

He had it. He pulled, hard, hoping he wasn't doing more harm than good, but the limb was slithering round, shifting, and there seemed to be room…

He had it!

'It's round,' he muttered and Meg's hand was on his shoulder, pressing him in a move of exultation. She was lying against him, full length on the dirt.

'Aligned?'

He knew what she meant and he could feel it. He had two neat hooves with the head between.

'Yes. Here's another….'

'Let it come,' she said. 'It'll come now.'

And it did, the next contraction shoving everything forward. Two hooves were out, and Meg was fastening them before the head appeared, tying them carefully with some sort of soft rope.

'What…'

'Just in case we need to help her,' she said. 'She's been straining for too long already and this calf is big. I'll loop this above and below the fetlock so we can pull without doing damage.'

'Where did you learn to do this?' he demanded, dazed, and he felt her smile rather than saw it.

'You mean why wasn't it on my CV? I can't think why I didn't include it. Here we go.'

Another contraction. Meg let it pass but the head didn't emerge.

'Okay, let's give her a hand,' she said. 'Can you take the rope? Tug with the contraction, not too hard, not enough to hurt the calf, I'm happy with an inch or two at a time.'

He nodded. Meg's hands were lubricated again. She was feeling…

'Now,' she said and he tugged.

A little further.

'Man, this head's big,' Meg said. 'With the size of this brain, you must be having the smartest baby on the planet, Millicent. He'll take a lot of knitting for a baby bonnet.'

Her voice was low and even and, with a sense of shock, William realised that, even though most of Meg's attention was on the calf, there was solid affection and worry for the cow as well.

She'd given her heart to a cow? How nuts was that? Where was his clinically efficient, unemotional PA now?

Gone. And the sense of loss was gut-wrenching.

'Now,' she said again, and then moaned because her hand was cupping the head, shoehorning it, and William was tugging on the hooves and there was only so much room…

'Keep going,' she managed as the contraction lengthened and he tugged some more, slowly, insistently and suddenly the head was there, the rope was no longer needed, the calf was half out.

Millicent gave a long bovine moan and Meg cleared membrane from the tiny nose and then laid her hand on Millicent's flank.

'Nearly there, girl. One more push. You can do it.'

One more contraction and the thing was done. The calf slithered out into the lantern light, a long wet bundle of spindly legs and black nose and rag-like tail. Meg cried out in delight and checked its nose was still clear and then lifted it around a little so Millicent could reach her baby with ease.

And she did. She turned and nosed her baby and she started to lick it clean. And William looked at Meg and saw her eyes were filled with tears and a man would have to be inhuman not to be moved. Not to take her into his arms…

Millicent had taken over, licking her calf with solid maternal ownership. Meg shifted away and her body collided with William's—and she didn't move any further.

He'd slipped the loop from the calf's hooves. He'd done all he could. Meg had done all she could. Their calf was alive and well—and Meg was hard against him.

He'd helped birth a calf. He and Meg. The feeling was awesome.

They were still half lying on the ground, and Meg was warm and beautiful, stained, filthy, her face tracked with tears…

She was trembling, her body reacting to the combined terrors of this day. How could he bear her trembling? How could he bear not to put his arms round her and tug her closer? So he did and, as he felt her yield, he tugged her closer still. Her hair brushed his face and he kissed the top of her head, just lightly, no pressure, nothing.

The awe from the birth was all around them—the stars, the warmth of the night, the feeling that a miracle had happened. New life… Did she feel this every time she delivered a calf? he wondered, but then he forgot to think more because she was turning in his arms and she was looking straight at him, her eyes huge and shadowed, vaguely troubled, but nevertheless…sure.

Sure that he'd kiss her. Sure that she wanted him to kiss her. He knew it and it was one more thing to add to the glory of this night—or maybe the whole night had been building to this kiss.

Maybe his whole life had been building to this kiss.

That was a crazy thing to think—but how could he think it was crazy when his hands were cupping her face and he was drawing her in to meet him? How could he think he was crazy when his mouth was lowering to hers and she was so sweet, so beautiful, so right?

She melted in to him, her mouth seeking his, her hands taking his shoulders so she could centre herself, be centred. Her need was as great as his. He could feel it in the urgency of her hold, in the fire he felt the moment he found her mouth.

She wanted him. He felt her need and his whole body responded. Their kiss was suddenly urgent, hard, demanding. It was as if a magnetic field had been created, locking them to each other, two force fields meeting as they must, with fire at the centre.

He wanted her. He wanted her fiercely, with a passion that rocked him. He felt…out of control.

Maybe he was out of control. It was Christmas Eve. He was in the centre of a paddock somewhere in Australia—he didn't truly know where—with a woman he'd thought he knew but he now realised he hadn't known at all.

His Meg.

No. Just Meg. Her own beautiful self.

He deepened the kiss and she responded with heat and need, her lips opening, her tongue searching. Oh, but he wanted her… His hands were on her breasts, but she was wearing overalls. How did you get through overalls?

She was buttoned to the throat. No. Not buttons. Studs.

They unfastened with satisfactory pops. Underneath the overalls was a lacy bra, and underneath the bra… His breath drew in, with awe and wonder.

His hands were cupping her, and he'd never felt such beauty. He'd never wanted a woman so much as he wanted Meg right now.

No woman before had been Meg.

He rolled back with her and she came, smiling down into his eyes. They were lying full length, wanting each other with a desperate heat they could read in each other's eyes.

She was above him, smiling in the moonlight. Meg, his beauty. Her skin was pale and luminous, she almost seemed to shine.

They were on a horse rug or somesuch, something she'd spread in the middle of a cow paddock. No pillowed bed could feel better. No bed could feel more right.

'You're not taking your overalls off,' she whispered and he realised with a shock that she was laughing. 'Not fair.'

His overalls were all in one. He'd pulled them on in a rush. Underneath… Well, there wouldn't be a lot of finesse in his undressing.

'You're wearing a bra,' he managed. 'I don't believe I'm wearing anything.'

Her chuckle was so sexy it took his breath away. 'I think that's good.'

'You don't want me out of my overalls,' he said but he couldn't say it with any degree of certainty. This night…anything was possible this night.

'And if I do?'

There was a statement to take his breath away. But a man had to have sense, even if finding it almost tore him in two. 'I'm not…' Hell, it was so hard to get his voice to work. 'I'm not carrying condoms.'

She paused at that. She stilled. He kissed her again, a

gentle, wondrous exploration that left him wanting more. Much more.

Why hadn't he thought of condoms? Of all the stupid… He didn't even have them in his bag back at the house.

He'd hardly packed thinking he was about to seduce his PA.

And Meg was tugging away, propping herself up on her arms, considering him in the dim light. 'How big's your head?' she asked and he blinked.

'Pardon?'

'Millicent operated with no condoms,' she said, her voice husky and shaken. 'Look what happened to her.'

He laughed, but it was a shaken laugh. He pulled away a little, sense returning. A little.

'We can't,' he managed. 'Unless Santa arrives right now.'

'I didn't put condoms on my Santa list,' she whispered, her voice laced with a thousand regrets.

'That's not efficient of you.'

'I'm not feeling efficient.'

'You don't look efficient,' he said and he tugged her to him again and held. He just held. 'My obstetrician extraordinaire.'

'Hey, you turned the leg. Maybe you've found your new calling.'

'I'm not ready for a new career. If it's all the same to you, I think I'll stick to the old one,' he said. But, the moment he said it, he knew it was a mistake.

Or maybe it wasn't a mistake. Maybe it was simply the truth, which had to be put out there.

It had killed the moment. Meg moved back, squatted back on her heels and looked at him for a long moment, as if searching his face. And, whatever she was looking for, she didn't find it. She smiled again, a wry little smile with all the regret in the world, and she tugged her overalls up to decency.

'Well, that was fun,' she said and suddenly he had Miss Jardine back—clinical, cool, ready to move on. 'Birth does crazy things to your head. Imagine how I'd feel if ever I was around a human birth. Lucky I'm not. But enough. It's three hours till milking. I need some sleep.'

'Meg…'

'No,' she said.

'No?'

'No.' She met his gaze, calm and cool in the moonlight, and if there was bleakness behind it there wasn't anything he could do about it. 'This was moon madness. We both know it, and it bears out my decision that I need to quit. What if there'd been a condom round tonight? We'd have been lost.'

Lost. The word hung between them, loaded with too many meanings.

'Will you help me pack up?' she said. 'Millicent will be fine for what's left of the night. It's lovely and warm. She has a fine heifer calf to clean and she'll do it better without us.'

'Heifer?'

'A little girl. I think we'll call her Milly. Millicent, mother of Milly. It has a fine ring to it, don't you think?'

She was talking for the sake of talking, he realised. She was putting emotion aside.

'I don't want to leave you,' he said simply and she looked at him for a long moment, considering, and then she shook her head.

'You can't take me with you. I don't fit. I did when my role was PA. No more. Somehow we've messed this and all there is now is for us to get on with our lives. You've got Ned and Pip and Elinor waiting for you back in New York, and you have your life there. I have a grandma and a little brother, and dairy cows and dogs and one brand new calf. That's enough to keep any girl happy.'

'Is it?'

'Yes,' she said, rising and dumping ropes into buckets. 'Yes, it is. Yes, it must be.'

CHAPTER TEN

WILLIAM woke to an operatic soprano belting out *Silent Night* right underneath his attic. Letty was singing along, almost louder than the soprano. A couple of dogs were joining right in.

Five-thirty. He'd been in bed for what—two and a half hours—and he'd lain awake for at least one of them.

He groaned and put his pillow over his head and then Scotty started singing too, and more dogs joined in, full howl.

Christmas. Hooray.

Feeling more like Scrooge every minute, he hauled his jeans on and staggered downstairs. The kitchen table was groaning with food in various states of preparation. Letty was wearing a truly astonishing crimson robe and a Santa hat. Scotty was sitting in his pyjamas, shelling peas. The difference between now and yesterday was astonishing.

'Happy Christmas,' Letty said, beaming. 'Great pecs.' Then, as he tried to figure whether to blush, she motioned to the sound system in the corner where, mercifully, *Silent Night* had just come to an end. 'My favourite carol. You want us to play it again?'

'She'll make you sing,' Scotty warned and William looked at the pair of them and saw exactly why Meg loved them to bits. A blushing adolescent and an old lady with her arm bandaged to her elbow, a lady who had almost died yesterday, who was now stirring something vaguely alcoholic, or possibly more than vaguely.

'Eggnog,' Letty said, following his gaze. 'Just on finished. You want first glass?'

At five-thirty in the morning?'

'Yeah, it's late,' Letty said. 'Meg's already milking, without her eggnog. You want to take some over to her?'

'No,' he said, revolted.

'What's wrong with my eggnog?'

'If I'm going to help her milk, I need to be able to count teats.'

'He has trouble getting to four, Grandma,' Scotty said kindly. 'We'd better let him off eggnog till the girls are milked.' He hesitated. 'You will help milk, won't you? Meg said you helped so much last night that she wouldn't wake you, but she'll be ages alone.'

'I could help,' Letty said darkly. 'Only she won't let me.'

'With your arm? You're as dodgy as I am,' Scott retorted and once again William was hit with the sensation that he was on the outside, looking in. Family?

'Okay, toast and coffee and no eggnog until afterwards, but there's home-made raspberry jam,' Letty told him, moving right on. 'And real butter. None of that cholesterol-reducing muck this morning.'

'Grandma...' Scott said and Letty grimaced and held up her hands in surrender.

'I know. Back to being good tomorrow. You needn't worry, young man; I intend to be around to boss you for a long time to come.'

'So no more Santa rescues.'

'I'll be good,' she said and William saw a flash of remembered terror from yesterday and he thought she wasn't as tough as she was making out. She was brave, though. And he saw

Scott worrying about her and he thought that courage came in all guises.

They were all brave. And Meg... What she'd been trying to do for all of them since her parents' death...

'So you know about Millicent's calf,' he ventured, feeling really off centre, and they both grinned, happiness returning.

'Of course we do,' Scott said. 'She's gorgeous. And Meg said you got a backward hoof out. I wish she'd called me. I could've have helped.'

'There'll be lots of calves for you to help in the future,' Letty said roundly. 'We'll get *your* leg right first. We're just lucky William was able to help. We're very pleased to have you here,' she said to William. 'Now, Meg checked the news before she milked and she says the planes are running again. She and Scott checked flights and there are some available. She said to tell you when you woke up. But you don't want to leave yet, do you?'

'I...'

Did he want to leave? They were looking at him expectantly. Over in the dairy, Meg was milking, alone.

His world was twisting, as if it was trying to turn him in a direction he hadn't a clue about.

'I do need to go,' he said at last and it was as if the words were dragged out of him. 'If I help with the milking now, Scott, would you mind making me a list of flights and times?'

'*Today?*'

'Yes, please.'

'You really want to leave?' Scott demanded incredulously, and William thought about last night, thought about holding Meg. Thought about holding Meg again.

If he got any closer...

If Letty had fallen yesterday... If Scotty had been killed in that accident...

If anything happened to Meg…

Do not get close. Do not open yourself to that sort of pain.

'I don't want to go,' he said, striving not to let his voice sound heavy. 'How could I want to leave Letty's eggnog? But I do need to get back to Manhattan as soon as possible. So please let me know which flight might be available.'

'Okay,' Scotty said and, even if the kid did sound disappointed, William couldn't let that stand in the way of a decision that must be made.

He headed back upstairs to dress and, as he did, Letty adjusted the sound system. Next on the playlist was *Deck the Halls* and she turned the sound up even louder.

This place was crazy.

Of course he had to get out of here.

Meg was milking, head down behind a cow. When he reached the yard she didn't emerge, just kept on doing what she was doing. Killer and the rest of the dog pack greeted him with pleasure but there wasn't a lot of pleasure emanating from Meg.

That had to be okay by him. Maybe it was even sensible. He ushered the next cow into a bale and started doing what had to be done. He was getting good at this. Where could he use this new skill when he left?

Would he ever milk a cow again?

'Happy Christmas,' Meg said at last from behind her cow and he thought she sounded exhausted. Had she slept at all?

He wanted to tell her to go back to bed, that he'd take over. He couldn't. Yes, he'd learned new skills but he couldn't milk by himself yet.

If he left today… Would she be milking the cows alone?

'Happy Christmas,' he replied at last. Cautiously.

'The airlines are back. I'm sorry but I didn't have time to check flights before milking.'

'Not good enough,' he growled, trying for a smile, but she stiffened and said nothing.

'I was joking.'

'I know.'

'I'm sorry,' he said. 'Bad joke.'

'I'm sorry too,' she said, straightening and heading out to fetch another cow in. 'Last night…it should never have happened. It was like… I'd been so worried. It was reaction; nothing more.'

'It felt like more.'

'Well, it wasn't,' she snapped. 'Fortunately, the airlines are operating. We'll see if we can get you a flight out tonight.'

'What about milking?'

'What about milking?'

'Who's going to do it?'

'I will,' she said. 'I've done it alone plenty of times before. It just takes longer.'

'You're exhausted already.'

'Kerrie's back tomorrow—she's coming for lunch today so maybe she can even help tonight—and I can sleep in the middle of the day.'

'And then you need to job hunt.'

'I believe I'm still employed by you until my contract expires.'

'So you are.'

'So I'll keep the office operating here as my contract specifies. That'll give me time to find something else.'

They were being absurdly formal, he thought, but maybe formal was the only thing to be.

'What sort of job do you want?' he asked.

'I'm a qualified accountant.'

'You'll do accountancy in a provincial city?'

'What's wrong with that?'

'What a waste.'

She didn't bother responding. She just kept right on milking.

'You don't need to keep the office operating,' he said at last.

'You can't dismiss me without notice.'

'I'm not dismissing you. I'll pay you till the end of your contract.'

'Then I'll work till the end of my contract. I've taken enough from you. I can't take any more.'

'I'd like to give more.'

'Like what?' she said from behind her cow and he thought about it. What would he like to give her?

Money. Security. The knowledge that she wouldn't have to get up to milk a cow unless she wanted to.

The ability to drop everything and be with Scott when and if he needed further operations. The ability to care for Letty as she needed to be cared for. Financial freedom to call the vet whenever she needed the vet.

Freedom to have a bit of fun.

But this was nothing he could do. He'd given Scott his old cars. He'd given Meg dresses and he'd given them all the satellite dish. He knew without asking that she'd accept nothing else.

So there was nothing more he could do. There was nothing more he should do. As soon as his flight was confirmed, he could walk away and not look back.

That was what he wanted, wasn't it? Anything else was way too complicated.

Dogs. Cows.

Family.

'We'd best get a move on,' she said across his thoughts.

'We don't do Santa until the cows are done and then there's church and then there's eggnog.'

'You don't do eggnog until after Santa and church?'

'Not very much,' she said and managed a smile. 'Grandma doesn't tip up the brandy bottle until we're all safe home.'

Milking finished, William swished the dairy while Meg went to check on Millicent and the brand new Milly. They were standing contentedly in the home paddock, Milly at her mother's teat, no sign of the trauma associated with her birth.

If she was a hard-headed businesswoman, she'd remove the calf now, Meg thought ruefully as she looked down at the pretty little calf. After the first few hours, when the calf had taken the all important colostrum, efficient dairy practice was to remove the calf and get the cow straight into mass production.

Only neither Letty nor Meg were hard-headed. The calves stayed with their mothers until Letty decreed they were ready to be independent, which lost them milk production but probably made them a healthier herd. Or possibly made them a healthier herd. Or not.

It was a decision of the heart, not of the head.

'Like me stopping working for William,' she told Millicent and sat on the edge of the trough while she watched the cow and her new little calf. Killer nosed up beside her and shoved his head against her ribs. She hugged him tight and suddenly she felt like crying.

'And that's also dumb,' she told Killer. 'Why cry? For that matter, why quit? Working for the McMaster empire's the best job I've ever had. Why can't I keep on doing it? Why can't I ignore how I feel about him and get on with it?'

She knew she couldn't.

He was watching her. He was sluicing the yard but she could feel his gaze. She hugged her dog hard, then straightened her shoulders and rose and tried to look professional, as if she was examining cow and calf as a proper dairy farmer should. In terms of what she could make from them.

Millicent's eyes were huge and contented and maybe a little bit wondrous. While Meg watched, she started to lick her calf and the little calf kept right on feeding.

Drat, those tears kept right on welling.

'Happy Christmas, you great sook,' she told herself angrily and swiped at her cheeks with venom. 'Get a grip. And stop crying right now.'

She had to stop crying. William was finished in the yard. She should wait for him and walk him back to the house.

He was helping her. It'd be only civil to walk back.

But the feeling of that kiss of the night before was too huge, too raw, too real. It was threatening to overwhelm her.

'If I head back now I get first shower,' she told Killer. 'That's what a hard-headed, professional dairy farmer should do. And that's what I am.'

Right.

'Go fast before he catches up.'

Even more right. Or not.

He'd never seen a Christmas tree like it.

They'd been so busy, William had hardly been in the sitting room until now, but after a second breakfast and a little eggnog—yes, the serious stuff would come after church—Letty bossed them into the sitting room for present opening.

The tree was real but it wasn't pine. 'There are no pines here and there's no way I'm spending money importing one,' Letty growled, following his gaze. 'This might not be what you're used to, but it's okay with us.'

It was a small gum tree in a vast pot on wheels. 'We pull it in and pull it out every year,' Letty said while Meg said nothing. 'This year's the last for this tree; she's getting too big. We'll plant her out but there's already a new one coming on to take her place.'

And that made him feel weird as well. The thought of such continuity. A long line of trees, each taking its turn as a Christmas tree before growing to be one of the huge gums that surrounded the farm. Fantastic. And sort of…grounded. Good.

The decorations were great as well, all home-made, some wonderful, some distinctly corny.

'They date from the time Meg arrived here,' Letty said proudly. 'She made paper chains, her mum made the balls and lanterns, then Scotty came along and here's his kindergarten things…'

'Grandma…' Scott said, revolted, and Letty chuckled and tossed him a gift.

It was a sweater. Home knitted. Scott made a truly manful effort to look pleased and the hug he gave his grandma was genuine. He put it on. Red and green stripes. Just the thing…

'For winter,' he said, and Letty beamed with pleasure.

Meg said, 'But take it off before you faint in the heat.'

Scott threw his sister a look of such gratitude that William had trouble not to laugh out loud. As he did with so many of the gifts they were opening, small jokes, trivia, fun.

And then there was a gift in his hands. He stared down at the box—small, flat, red and tied with gold ribbon.

'You've done enough for us,' Meg said softly. 'We can't possibly repay you, but this is the least we can do.'

He opened the box, feeling disoriented, as if he'd been transported to another world. Inside was a certificate, folded neatly.

He read through, trying to make it out.

He'd been given…a part-time dog?

'Scott and I found it on the Internet,' Meg said as he looked up, astounded. 'It's an animal shelter in Manhattan, and it's not far from where you live. This gives you visiting rights. More. What you do is adopt a dog whenever you're in town. If you're based in New York for three months, then you take a dog for three months. You can take her back to the shelter at night if you want, or you can keep her at home, or you can simply take her out for a run each day. Whatever you want. You give your time and the shelter takes over what you can't provide. The only stipulation is that she's still available for permanent adoption. This plan means the shelter can take far more dogs than they could otherwise care for, and they don't have to put them down. But if someone wants to adopt one permanently, then you need to choose another.'

A part-time dog, he thought. Like Ned and Pip and Elinor. His part-time family. Good. Excellent.

So why did it make him feel empty?

Luckily, Scott was filling his silence. 'The dog you've semi-adopted is Sheeba,' he told William. 'Her photograph's in the bottom of the box. She's part greyhound, part Dalmatian. I reckon she should be your first.'

'Because every man needs a dog,' Letty said solidly.

William glanced out towards the kitchen. The dogs weren't permitted in the sitting room. There were five dogs squashed in the doorway, each nose managing to claim an inch of sitting room carpet.

Every man should have a dog. A part-time dog.

He watched as Meg opened yet another extraordinary knitted object and hugged Letty and giggled, and then watched as Scott and Letty were both ordered to open their gifts from Meg together, so they did, and they were bazooka-like machine guns loaded with foam balls. Christmas immediately became a running battle between grandmother and grandson. Who'd have thought Letty had been close to death yesterday, and who'd have ever thought of giving a grandmother a foam ball-shooter?

He looked at Meg and Meg was giggling like a kid—and he thought he was never going to see her again.

He started gathering wrapping paper, and then Letty remembered the turkey and Scott remembered flights.

'Oh, whoops, sorry,' he said, firing a foam ball at Killer, who caught it neatly in his mouth, bit it in two and then looked expectantly for more. 'Killer!'

'Sorry, what?'

'Your flights.' He looked to Meg, as if to confirm he was doing the right thing. 'I checked while you were milking. If you really want to go…'

'What have you found?' Meg asked.

'There's a flight at nine tonight. You could catch the four o'clock train back to Melbourne and take the skybus to the airport. It all fits. Is that okay, Meg?'

'He's used to private cars,' Meg said, not looking at William. 'But it sounds okay.' She rose and headed out to the kitchen after Letty, tossing her words over her shoulder. Still carefully not looking at him. 'Is that okay with you, William? You can have Christmas dinner and we'll drive you to the train.'

'He'll need extra weight allowance after Grandma's pudding,' Scott joked and Letty hooted from the kitchen, but William didn't laugh.

He couldn't see Meg any more. She was behind the kitchen door, but he was willing to bet she didn't laugh either.

'You don't need to come to church,' Meg said, but sitting back at the farmhouse without them seemed unthinkable. So he went and Meg orchestrated things so she sat with Letty and Scott between them. She was wearing another of her new dresses—lilac, simpler than yesterday's, but just as pretty.

Or more pretty. Or maybe it was that he was looking at her more often.

The service was lovely, a tiny community coming together in happiness, belting out beloved Christmas hymns with enthusiasm and as much tunefulness as they could muster. William could only stand for the first two hymns because, some time between the second and the third, Letty leaned against his shoulder and went to sleep. Meg saw why he wasn't standing and she smiled at him, the smile he'd worked with for three years and hadn't noticed, and he thought it was worth holding Letty to receive that smile.

Though, if he'd had a choice... He still would hold Letty, he thought, memories of yesterday's terror flooding back. She was an indomitable old lady and he could see why Meg loved her.

So he sat while the rest of the congregation sang and there were approving looks from many, and curious looks from more, and he thought Meg was going to get the full inquisition after he left.

After he left...

Maybe he could stay a few days more. Make sure Letty was okay. Give Kerrie a few more days off milking.

Get closer to Meg?

She was sharing a song sheet with Scott, and her voice was true and pure. He could hear her through the rest of the congregation—he knew her voice.

He wouldn't hear it again.

He shouldn't be here. This wasn't his place. If he got closer...

He'd hurt her. He didn't know the first thing about family.

He'd go home to his part-time dog, his part-time Foster-Friends role, his full-time career.

What was he doing? Surely he wasn't thinking he could stay here and milk cows for ever?

Maybe he could take Meg with him.

She wouldn't go.

'Collection,' Scott hissed, and he looked at him in incomprehension.

'Money,' Scott said and grinned and William realised he was being handed the collection plate. Everyone in the pew was looking at him. They must have thought he was as sleepy as Letty.

Before he could react, Meg dropped a note into the plate and handed it back to the server. 'He's a bit tight,' she said, in a make-believe whisper which carried through the church. 'He hasn't had any work since before Christmas, you know.'

He stared at her in open-mouthed astonishment and she grinned and then chuckled and Letty stirred against him and opened her eyes.

'Have we sung *O Little Town of Bethlehem* yet?'

'No,' he said, confounded.

'Then why don't we?' she demanded. 'Don't they know our turkey's waiting?'

Dinner came next. Kerrie arrived with her three children and it was hard to know who whooped louder, the children or Letty. Far too much food was consumed. The pudding flamed magnificently. Crackers were pulled. Silly jokes were read. Meg checked her watch for about the hundredth time and finally said, 'It's time to go.'

'It is,' William said. 'You'll drive me to the station?'

'I'll drive you,' Letty said with alacrity and grinned. 'Meg can do the washing-up.'

'Let Meg take him, Grandma,' Scott said with rare insight. 'She'll want to say goodbye.'

'I want to say goodbye,' Letty retorted.

Scott said, 'Grandma,' in a meaningful voice and Letty gave a theatrical sigh and started clearing the table. But she wasn't exactly martyred. Kerrie and Scott were helping clear. Kerrie would stay on for milking—they'd organised that at some time over pudding. It'd only take Meg twenty minutes to take William to the station. Ten minutes there, ten minutes back and life would go on without him.

As it should.

He'd already packed his bag. He rose from the still laden table and felt… empty.

'Thank you,' he said simply and Letty looked at him as if he was a sandwich short of a picnic.

'Thank us? After what you've done for us?'

'I'll send you pictures of my car,' Scott said shyly. 'As it takes shape.'

'I'd like that.'

There was nothing else to say. Meg was already at the door, keys in her hand.

Ready to move on?

CHAPTER ELEVEN

WHY didn't he speak? The tension seemed unbearable. Thankfully, the station was only ten minutes' drive, otherwise she'd explode. Or something. She flicked on the radio and there were the inevitable Christmas carols. William flicked them straight off.

'What's wrong with my carols?' she demanded, trying to sound offended.

'I'm crossing the time line tonight. I'm facing another twenty-four hours of Christmas. Enough is enough.'

'Two Christmases in a row. How appalling.' So much for offended. She knew she sounded miserable.

'My Christmas isn't like your Christmas,' he told her. 'Two of my normal Christmases would be appalling.'

'Will you see your parents?'

'No.'

'You should. Even the media says they're lonely. Call them.'

'You're telling me how to run my life?'

'I forgot,' she said, suddenly contrite. 'I'm still employed. I shouldn't tell you anything.'

'But when you're not employed?'

'When I'm not employed I won't be anywhere near you,' she whispered. There was more silence and then, thankfully, they arrived. She pulled up beside the platform—it really was in the middle of nowhere. But this was where she had to leave him.

'Here you are,' she managed, feeling ill. 'The train will be here in six minutes.'

He looked around him in doubt. 'How do I know you're right with your timetable?'

'Trust me.'

'Trust you to leave me standing on a platform in the middle of nowhere, waiting for a train, when I only have your word for it that it'll come?'

She sighed. 'Okay, I'll wait. Sir. Do you want me to carry your bag onto the station?'

'No,' he said. 'Meg…'

'We need to be on the station. If the driver can't see us from a way ahead he won't stop.' She headed onto the platform, leaving him to follow.

He followed.

More silence. They stood side by side in the middle of nowhere and he tried to think of something to say. So many things, but none of them suitable. None of them possible.

'Reconsider your job,' he said at last and she shook her head.

'I can't.'

'Because I kissed you?'

'I believe I resigned before that.'

'Because I wanted to kiss you, then? And because when I did kiss you, it was wonderful?'

'William, I can't cope with an affair,' she said simply. 'And I can't cope with loving my boss.'

'Loving…' The word made him feel as if he'd been punched.

'I don't, of course,' she said hastily. 'It's just that I might. Given time and enough…heat.' There was a faint speck on the horizon, a distant rumble and they both knew the train was on its way. 'So…so it's been fabulous. I've had the best time working for you and I can't begin to thank you for what you've done for my family this Christmas.'

'There's no need to thank me.' Did he take her hands or did she take his? He didn't know. All he did know was that suddenly they were linked. The train was growing closer and she was just…*here*.

He was holding Meg. Not Miss Jardine. He was definitely holding Meg. And he knew what he most wanted to say.

'Come with me,' he said urgently, and her eyes widened.

'What?'

'To New York. You could have a second Christmas too.'

'I've had Christmas.' The train was closer now. The driver had seen them and was starting to slow.

'I want you to come.'

'And leave Letty and Scott? Ring them up and say sorry, I won't be home for tea, can you get someone to cover the milking?' She sounded a little hysterical. Panicked. Her hands tugged back, but he didn't let her go. 'What are you saying? Christmas in New York… That's crazy.'

He knew it was. 'Crazy or not, I mean it.'

She met his gaze square on, and the flare of panic settled. 'No,' she said, sounding sure. 'My place is here. As yours is in Manhattan. Or Hong Kong. Or London. Wherever your business takes you. And here's your train. Say hello to Sheeba for me.'

'Sheeba?'

'Your part-time dog,' she chided and he stared down at her and thought—part-time dog, part-time life; he so didn't want to leave this woman.

But the alternative?

She couldn't go with him. There wasn't an alternative.

'Goodbye, William,' she said gently and pushed his hands

a little, pushing him to let her go. Only the train hadn't quite stopped yet and his hold on her tightened.

'Goodbye, Meg.' There was a blast from the train's horn, as if the driver was saying get on fast; the train surely didn't want to waste time sitting at this windswept, sunburned country railway siding. No one would want to waste time here. Least of all him.

He had to leave.

But how could he leave when he was holding Meg?

He must.

He looked down into her eyes for one last time, and then, because there was no way he couldn't, he pulled her tight against him. He cupped her chin, he tilted her face—and then he kissed her.

It was a fast kiss, fast by necessity as the train had now stopped. But still the kiss was strong and searching, and it ached to be more. For one precious moment she yielded against him, her mouth opened under his and she melted. Her body moulded against his and she was crushed against him.

Meg.

But the doors of the train were sliding open and the conductor was stepping onto the platform.

'All aboard,' he snapped, straight at them, and there was no avoiding the inevitable. For one last moment Meg clung and he held, and then she was standing back and there was nothing he could do but lift his bag and board the train.

She drove home feeling sick. Life as she knew it was over.

Well, that was a stupid thing to think. She had cows to look forward to. And finding a local job. Plus there was a rather nice young farmer who'd been interested before she'd left to take the McMaster job. Letty told her every time she came home that he was still single. Maybe she could drum up some enthusiasm.

Only she'd taken the job with William for a reason and the reason still stood. She loved the farm, but it wasn't enough.

She'd adored working for William. For Mr McMaster.

For William. He could never be Mr McMaster again. She knew that. He was too cute, too warm-hearted, too...hot.

And too needy. See, there was the problem. What really hurt—or, if she was honest, what hurt almost as much as missing him—was the thought of him going back to his sterile life in Manhattan. Sure, he had his part-time kids and now he had his part-time dog. Sure, he thought he was happy. He was rich and confident and a powerful figure in the world's economy.

But he wouldn't call his parents and she guessed they wouldn't call him. He'd probably call one of his Cool-To-Be-Seen-With women to fill in the gaps in his life, and that made her think dark thoughts about life in general and Cool-To-Be-Seen-With women in particular. She dredged up an image of the erstwhile Sarah, and imagined the picture as a dartboard.

How childish was that?

She *was* being childish. But there was more behind what she was feeling than childishness, and she knew what it was.

For she'd fallen in love. Some time over the last two days, she'd fallen hard. Maybe it had been latent, waiting in the wings to strike when the time was right. Maybe she'd been in love with W S McMaster for years; she just hadn't known it.

And he was going home alone and she felt sick—and sad for him as well as for her. He'd go back to the life he knew and she didn't envy him one bit. He might be rich and powerful but she had Scotty and Letty and the dogs.

She didn't have William.

He'd asked her to go with him. How crazy was that? Oh,

but she'd wanted to. To board the train and leave, flying to Manhattan with William, stepping into his life...

His part-time life. For she was under no illusions as to what an affair with William would be. She'd made arrangements for too many such affairs in the past. Glorious indulgence and then mutual parting, no hard feelings.

She pulled the car off the road and got out. She walked round the car, then round again. It was no use going back to the farm until she had her head in order.

William was gone, and she had to move on. She had to walk into the kitchen at home and be cheerful.

Right. One more round of the car, or maybe two, and she could do it.

She must.

He heaved his bag up onto the luggage rack and he thought for the first time—he *had* been preoccupied until now—that his bag was heavier than usual. And, almost as he thought it, the zip burst open.

His luggage was quality. Zips did not burst.

Nor did plastic bags and plastic containers spill out onto the floor of the train.

But, over Christmas, W S McMaster had become William, and someone had packed leftovers in William's bag. The transparent containers held turkey, plum pudding, grapes, cherries, chocolates and more. There was also a plastic bottle labelled Brandy Sauce.

Meg would never do this. It must have been Letty. Meg was far too sensible to pack him leftovers.

Or was she?

He'd get rid of it at the airport, he thought, gathering the containers while bemused passengers watched. He travelled first class. Leftovers compared to the airline's best haute cuisine?

But then he thought, this was Letty's cooking and Jenny's cooking. Maybe there was even Meg's cooking in there somewhere. She'd definitely stirred the pudding.

Maybe he wouldn't get rid of it.

He started shoving the containers back into his bag and realised there was something deeper. He delved and found…a bazooka. Complete with foam bullets. It was the same as the ones Letty and Scott had found in their stockings, orange, purple and gold. A note was attached.

To William. I had huge trouble finding you one of these at short notice but I knew you'd be jealous of Letty and Scott so, with Mickey's help, here's your very own. I thought it might cheer you up when you reach home. You and Pip and Ned can play with it in Central Park. Just don't take it on board your plane as hand luggage. You could get into Very Serious Trouble. Love Meg.

Ridiculous.

But… He *had* been jealous this morning as Letty and Scott had shot each other. As if he was on the outside looking in.

Pip and Ned would think this was cool. *He* thought it was cool. He wanted to try it out now.

Or not. Mature businessmen did not shoot foam bazookas on trains.

He read the note again.

Love Meg.

Don't go there.

He stowed the bazooka. He managed to get his bag refastened, and finally sank into his seat.

The train was almost empty. Of course. It was Christmas night. Who'd be travelling tonight except people going from one family to another?

There was a young mother in the seat opposite, hugging

her baby. Maybe she wasn't going from one family to another. She looked wan and tear-stained.

The W S McMaster of Friday would hardly have noticed. But now… 'Are you okay?' he asked.

'I…yes. Thank you.' She managed a watery smile; she clearly wanted to talk. 'My husband's working on an off-shore oil rig so we can save a deposit for a house. We only have one week together a month. It's only for a year but I hate being a part-time family. And I have to go back to my parents tonight… Night's my favourite time. When the day's over, snuggling down and talking about it… Oh, I miss him. I love him so much.'

She sniffed and blew her nose and there was nothing he could say to make her feel better. He retrieved some of his leftover chocolates. They shared their chocolate and their silence, and neither of them was happy.

I love him so much…

There was a lot in that statement to avoid thinking about. He decided he'd think about the rest.

Night's my favourite time…

He hated Christmas night. Christmas Day was usually bearable—there were always social functions, and last year he'd had Pip and Ned. Only at the end…

When the day's over, snuggling down and talking about it…

That was what was missing. He'd never figured it out. How could he miss what he'd never known?

Christmas night alone… He always did Christmas night alone.

Maybe he'd be home in time to see Pip and Ned.

He checked his phone and then remembered. No reception.

'You can ring when we go through towns,' the girl told him. 'Only you need to talk fast.'

When the day's over, snuggling down and talking about it...

The last twenty-four hours had been huge. Who could he talk about it with?

They were approaching a town. Sure enough, reception bars appeared on his cellphone. He rang Manhattan. Elinor. She answered on the first ring.

'What's wrong?' She sounded breathless and he realised it was one in the morning back home. Night-time.

When the day's over, snuggling down and talking about it...

'I'm sorry,' he said. 'I've woken you.'

'Oh, Mr McMaster, it's you,' she said. 'No, I was just stuffing stockings, so you didn't wake me. I'm glad you rang. I have such good news.'

'You do?'

'The children... Their mother's finally agreed to their adoption. The agency contacted me this morning. There's a couple... They lost their children in a car accident five years ago and they so want a family. They sound lovely and there's grandmas and grandpas; everything these children most need. So tomorrow, after Christmas lunch, they're coming to visit. It's only first contact, but oh, they sound nice. These children so need a family.'

'They do,' he said and somehow he managed to keep his voice from sounding bereft. Bereft? Of all the stupid sensations...

And Elinor heard it—he knew she did. 'There's so many needy children out there,' she said, her voice growing sombre. 'You know that. There's always more to be looked after.'

And he heard her pain as well. She'd be giving up these children and moving on. 'Oh, Elinor.' She loved with all her heart. You didn't love without hurting. Where had he learned that? Was he just starting?

'Yeah, it hurts,' she said across his thoughts, and he could almost see her steeling herself. 'But, if you don't love, then you might as well stop living. This family live right nearby so we'll see each other in the park. So how about you? Will we see you tomorrow? I mean, today?'

'My flight won't get in until late.'

'Oh, the children will be disappointed,' she said, but in a tone that said not too disappointed; they were about to meet their new mommy and daddy. What more did children need for Christmas?

'So you'll be flying all Christmas,' she said. 'I'm so sorry.'

'There's no need to be sorry,' he said, startled.

'Well, there is,' she said, and she sounded truly concerned. 'It's time you stayed put. I know you're important and I know you're busy but you have a good heart, Mr McMaster, and it's time you found somewhere to park it. I've done my share of parking in my time, but have you? You need to find somewhere you can leave it for good.'

The train had streamed through the town and out the other side. Reception was starting to break up. He could barely hear.

Maybe it was just as well, William thought. What sort of advice was this? He wished her Merry Christmas, but he didn't hear a response. He clicked off his phone and stared out of the window. Trying not to replay her words.

'Bad news?' the young mother asked.

'I…no. Good news, really.'

'You don't look like it was good news.'

'It's okay.'

He wanted to tell her about it. Only…if he told her…how could he make it sound like good news? She'd guess how he felt, he thought, as Elinor had guessed. As Meg would guess?

He wanted to tell Meg.

When the day's over, snuggling down and talking about it...

Such a thing wasn't for him. For a McMaster to...snuggle... Unthinkable.

He stared out at the sparse Australian landscape, so unlike Manhattan, and he thought of his family—the McMaster dynasty. Damaged people all. Deeply unhappy. Poisoned by wealth and by social expectations. Unhappy unions had created unhappy children, and on it went, for generation after generation, spreading outward.

How could he ask someone to join such a family?

He couldn't. He'd sworn he never would. But, if not...

The thought came from nowhere, and it started as a jumble. A Christmas tree with decorations from childhood. Letty's mango trifle. Cows and dogs. Gumboots parked at the back door. Meg's laughter...

Crazy Santa legs. Scott amid a jumble of Mini parts. The feel of Meg against him in the emergency room.

This was a family so unlike his own it was unbelievable, and the jumbled thought unravelled, settled and finally left a clear thought that was amazing.

If his family was unworkable...

Maybe he could join another?

The conductor was coming through now, checking tickets and, before he could take the thought any further, he found himself asking, 'Is there another train tonight?'

'To where?'

'To where I got on.'

'To Tandaroit? You have to be joking. Once a day to Tandaroit. Next train leaves tomorrow night from Melbourne.'

'Do you want to go back?' the woman across the way asked as the conductor moved on.

'Maybe,' William said, feeling dazed.

'To the girl you were kissing on the station?'

And there it was, front and centre. The girl he'd been kissing on the station.

'Who is she?' the woman asked and he managed a smile.

'She was Miss Jardine,' he said softly. 'But now…her name is Meg.'

CHAPTER TWELVE

MEG liked Christmas night, or she always had. Christmas was huge, busy, noisy, fun, and it left her happy. Even the first appalling Christmas after the accident, she and Letty had managed to make it fun and she'd slept that night feeling just a little bit optimistic about the future.

So why wasn't she feeling optimistic now?

Kerrie stayed and helped with the milking while Letty and Scott cleaned up inside and minded the children. After tea, they loaded the sleeping children into Kerrie's car and bade them goodnight. Kerrie drove off and Meg found herself feeling jealous. Kerrie would be snuggling the children into bed.

Um… Kerrie was a struggling single mother who worked herself raw. Was she jealous because she had babies?

Was she jealous of what they represented?

Scott and Letty went to bed, tired and happy after what they decreed had been an awesome Christmas. 'We should invite William every year,' Scott said sleepily and Meg felt even more bereft.

The dogs had eaten too many leftovers. They were asleep; useless as company.

She went across to the home paddock to talk to Millicent, but Millicent was snoozing as well.

She walked back to the house, kicking stones, disconsolate. Santa was still waving back and forth in his chimney.

'I wonder if I can shoot him down with one of the bazookas?' she asked herself but she couldn't dredge up a smile.

She didn't want to smile. She wanted to wallow.

She climbed into her pyjamas and went to bed. She thumped her pillows for a while, then gave up and headed back into the kitchen to pour herself the last of the eggnog. She stared into its depths and then carefully tipped it down the sink.

'Let's not drown our sorrows here,' she told herself. 'We need to be nice and sober to read the Job Vacancy ads tomorrow.'

She sniffed. 'Ooh, who's maudlin? And I haven't even drunk my eggnog.'

William would be back in Melbourne now. She looked at her watch. No. William would be in the sky.

She glanced out of the window at the stars beyond. Nothing and nothing and nothing.

And…something. A tiny light, growing brighter.

It was a small plane, she thought, low in the east. Some private charter, going places now the restrictions were lifted. Good for them.

The light was getting brighter. Brighter still. And the sound…

Not a plane, then. A helicopter.

Closer still. Low and fast.

Who…?

And then she thought…

No.

Yes?

This was stupid. She was imagining things. Maybe there'd been an accident somewhere close and this was an air transfer. That'd be it.

But it was over their land now. Hovering. Lights were beaming down.

It'd panic the cows.

But, even as she thought it, she realised it wasn't hovering over the cow pastures. The paddock underneath was at the eastern extremity of the property, where the hay had been slashed only yesterday.

Whoever was in the chopper knew the paddock was bare. Knew the paddock was safe.

It'd be… It'd be…

She daren't think who it'd be.

It wouldn't be William.

But the chopper was on her land.

The dogs had heard. Killer was at the kitchen door, his head to one side, listening.

'I'll take you with me,' she told him, and then as the rest of the pack appeared, she nodded. 'Okay, maybe I do need protection. Let's all go and investigate.'

He stood in the paddock and he thought, whoa, it's a long way to the house. He knew he couldn't scare the cows; he knew this paddock would be a safe place to land, but still…

'Where's a limousine when you need it?' The pilot was enjoying himself. Yes, he'd been pulled away from his family Christmas, but he'd had his Christmas dinner and the bonus he'd been promised made him very happy indeed. 'Maybe I could take you over the house and lower you on a rope,' he told him, grinning, and William thought, where's the respect? He'd made the mistake of chatting to Steve about his family, and look where it got him.

And then he saw Letty's wagon bumping across the paddocks and he stopped thinking about Steve—he stopped thinking of anything but Meg.

Was it Meg? The car came to a halt, the driver's door

opened, but, before he could see who it was five dogs tumbled out, enveloping him in a sea of canine ecstasy.

He'd been at the farm for three days. By the dogs' reaction, they were his lifelong friends and he'd been gone for years.

He kind of liked it. But still… Hopefully, Meg was behind them. He managed to shove the dogs aside. The pack descended on Steve, who backed into his cockpit. The dogs jumped right up after him. Hopefully, the machine was hard to start, otherwise they risked flight by dog. Whatever, William was too busy looking at Meg to do anything about it.

For she was here.

She was wearing…pyjamas? Pink silk with tiny stars and moons all over. Silver stars. His sense of unreality deepened. Her hair was messed as if she'd been asleep. She looked rumpled and sexy and so fabulous he wanted to scoop her into his arms right then and there.

Think of something to say, Stupid, he told himself but he was having trouble. Tonight had made sense to him at the planning stage. Now he was having trouble getting started.

'You had to bring the dogs,' he managed, as a muffled grunt emerged from the cockpit.

'Anyone could be landing in our hay paddock. On the chance that you could be enemy alien cow poachers…'

'You came wearing pyjamas?'

'I have a loaded bazooka under these pyjamas.'

He eyed the pyjamas. They were silky and clinging and…

No. Don't think of what might or might not be under those pyjamas. Definitely not a bazooka.

What to say? He gazed at Meg, at her adorably confused face, at her wonderful stars and moons, at her dishevelled hair. This was Meg, the woman he loved with all his heart, and he knew he had to go forward.

The woman he loved with all his heart…

When had he figured this out? Just then, he thought. He'd known he had to come. He'd planned to come. But now, looking at her, he knew for sure.

All those corny movies he'd watched as a lonely child... they were right. Throw your hat into the ring.

Jump.

'I had to come back for you,' he said simply, his gaze not leaving her face.

'I said I couldn't come with you,' she whispered, sounding awed.

'You don't need to come. I didn't come back to fetch you. I came back to be with you.'

'P...pardon?'

'I came back because I love you,' he said, strongly now, more sure. 'I came back because when it came down to it I couldn't leave.'

'You love me?' She said it wonderingly, and he knew the alien thing was still in her mind. She said it as if his words were some sort of fantasy that had no connection to reality.

It was up to him to make her see this was real. That this was true.

'I do love you.' It was as serious as any wedding vow. He took a step towards her but she held up her hands as if to ward him off. As if she was afraid.

Behind him, Steve was still surrounded by dogs. He couldn't be holding five collars, yet the dogs were all still. It was as if they sensed how important this was.

Was this important to a chopper pilot? To dogs?

Why not? It was the whole world to him.

'Meg, I need to know,' he said roughly, because he couldn't bear to wait a moment longer. 'When you talked about loving... Did you mean it? That you could love me?'

'I might,' she whispered, and his world settled. Things were falling into place that he'd never realised were out of kilter until now. That he'd known this woman for three long years and not loved her… How could he have been so blind?

How could he waste another moment? It was killing him not to take her into his arms but he knew he shouldn't.

Do not rush this.

As if falling in love in three days, hiring a helicopter in the middle of the night, telling her he wanted her right now, wasn't rushing things.

Okay, do not rush this even more.

So say it. Lay the whole plan on the line.

'I can move here,' he said and Meg's face froze.

'Here?'

'It's not impossible.'

'I think I need to sit.'

'Can I hold you up?'

'Not until I figure what you're talking about.'

'My plans.'

'I like plans,' she said faintly. 'Okay, talk.'

So he talked. 'I'll explain fast,' he said, and it had to be fast because if he didn't hold her soon he'd go up in smoke. 'I propose to base myself here. No, wrong, I propose we base ourselves here, because I need you, Meg, in business, in every facet of my life. You're smart and intuitive and funny and I want you with me every step of the way. So what I'd really like is to build here, set up headquarters here. Keep the farm but add to it. We'd need a helicopter pad. I fancy a swimming pool. And I bet a gymnasium would really help Scott.'

'Scott…'

'He's part of it. He's part of your life. Family.'

'William…'

'I know,' he said hurriedly, afraid to stop, afraid of how she'd respond. 'It's just it was a really long train ride back to Melbourne, and making plans is what I'm principally good at. I thought we could restore the old cottage on the other side of the dairy and ask Kerrie if she'd consider living here. Letty told me it was a dream of yours and it sounds good to me. That means we'd always have a milker on hand. Then… maybe we could employ a nanny…'

'A nanny,' she said, astonished.

'For Kerrie's kids,' he said hurriedly. 'And for…for whoever else might come along. That means you and I can travel, whenever we wish. There's so much… It'll take us years to sort it out, but we will. We can. If we want to. If you want to. What…what do you think?'

There was a long, long pause. The enemy alien cow poacher was still in the back of her mind, he thought, but slowly, slowly, he watched her expression change. She was searching his face and what she saw seemed to change things.

'I think…' she whispered, but then her voice firmed. 'I think I'd never leave our kids with a nanny,' she said, and suddenly the woman in the pink silk pyjamas was smiling.

His heart gave a leap. *I'd never leave our kids…* There were all sorts of assumptions in that statement, and he liked them all.

'How many kids would you like?' he asked tenderly.

'William!'

Maybe he had to throw in a few more inducements. Maybe he still didn't have it right. How to talk of love… It seemed so fragile—and all he had was words. Not now.

'You know, Letty and Scotty could travel with us too, if they like,' he said hurriedly. 'They could see Manhattan. And London and Hong Kong. I think they'd like it. But I'm serious about only travelling when I must.' He hesitated. 'You know, I didn't get this right. My parents taught me personal stuff was a disaster so I buried myself in work. But you…you enjoy what you do for me, yes?'

'I love it,' she said simply.

'Yet you love the farm.'

'Yes.'

'As I like pulling silencers off cars.'

'Do you?'

'I do,' he said and it was a vow. She was looking at him very strangely but he'd started—he had to explain. And he was struggling to explain it to himself.

Words... Find the right words, he told himself. Get it right.

Say the love word.

'I've been thinking...if I could mix grease guns with business, then maybe I could mix loving in there somewhere as well,' he tried, but it didn't sound right.

'In the spare bits?'

'No,' he said, sure of himself on this one. 'In all my bits. In my business. In my spare time, in my hobbies, in my dreams. I want loving in all of it. Meg, I want you.'

She looked stunned. She looked star-struck. 'You're truly serious?'

And there was only one answer to that. 'I've never been more serious about anything in my life,' he said simply. 'No matter what happens, at the end of every day of my life I want to lie in bed with you.'

'And...talk?' she managed, and there was the beginning of laughter in her lovely eyes.

'Or anything else that might occur to us,' he told her, smiling, loving her with all his heart, and suddenly she chuckled, a lovely deep ripple of wonder, and he thought he might just have got this right.

'So will you marry me?' he asked, for what else was there to say?

She gasped. 'You want to marry me?'

'Yes.' Then... 'But I do have a problem,' he was forced to admit. 'Try as I might, Christmas night is not a time to buy a ring.'

'Not?' she said and she laced her voice with such a depth of disappointment that he wasn't sure where the chuckle ended and sincerity began.

Aargh. He had everything right except this. But then Killer took a leap from the chopper and lumbered over. Dangling from his collar was his dog tag. It was a ring—of sorts.

'Excuse me, Killer,' he said and flicked off the collar and removed the tag. 'Can I borrow this until the shops reopen?'

'I don't believe this,' Meg said faintly.

'We need to organise new tags, anyway,' William said, refastening the collar. 'I'm shipping Sheeba out here as soon as I possibly can.'

'You're shipping Sheeba…'

'I figure you have one dog; Letty has two and Scott has two. When I decided to stay, I took out my Christmas card and stared at the picture of Sheeba and thought—how could I turn my back on such a fine gift? But I'm not doing part-time anything any more, so she gets to be full-time. I'm hoping she likes being a farm dog, but how could she not?' And then, because this seemed as good a time as any, he dropped on one knee and held out the dog tag. 'So, Miss Jardine…'

'Meg,' she said sharply.

'Meg,' he said, suitably chastened. 'My love.'

'That's much better.' She was smiling mistily down at him. *My love* is way better than Meg.'

'Hey!' It was a piercing shout and he turned, groaning. But the shout and the associated rumble couldn't be ignored.

For it was Letty and Scott, bouncing over the paddocks towards them on the ancient farm tractor. 'Don't you dare propose until we get there,' Letty yelled in a voice that was truly scary.

'Am I so obvious?' he demanded of his love and his love chuckled and behind them Steve laughed and Killer started barking.

'My love…' he started urgently, but Meg put her finger on his lips and hushed him. She tugged him up and she smiled.

'I wouldn't have it any other way,' she whispered. 'In front of witnesses.'

'You have to be joking.'

'You've been a loner all your life, William McMaster. No more.'

So he waited. With a promise like that, a man could wait. He waited until Letty and Scott were in full earshot and they'd introduced themselves to Steve and they were holding the dogs back and then Letty said, 'Okay, get on with it.'

And William, who was feeling absurdly self-conscious, suddenly thought no.

'No,' he said.

'No?' Meg said.

'Steve, how many does that chopper hold?'

'Six,' Steve said.

'Three people and five dogs?'

'At a push.'

'Then there are free chopper flights on offer,' he said. 'Starting now. You guys can watch, but from above. Take it or leave it. Witnesses from above, but not right here.'

'Oh, cool,' Scotty said, high with excitement. 'Come on, Grandma, who wants to listen to a soppy proposal when we can ride in a chopper? And it is,' he added conscientiously, 'their business anyway.'

So, before Letty knew what she was about, her grandson had bundled her into the chopper. The dogs were tossed up after. The doors were clanged shut and the chopper rose into the night sky.

But not very far. William might have intended that Steve take them far away. Steve had other ideas.

The chopper simply hovered. Its downlight nailed them.

'You were saying?' Meg yelled at the top of her lungs,

laughing, and William thought he was never, ever going to be able to do this better than he could right now. He was standing in the middle of a hay paddock. A helicopter was practically blasting him to bits with its down-draught. The moon was high in the night sky, and over at the house Santa's legs moved steadily back and forth, back and forth, back and forth.

'Happy Christmas,' he shouted, and he tried again for the third time. Third time lucky? 'Will you marry me?'

'What?' The sound of the chopper was deafening.

'With this ring, I thee wed?' he shouted back and he placed the tag on her finger and he scooped her up and lifted her high into his arms, holding her hard against his heart. And finally he kissed her as he needed to kiss her, as she needed to be kissed, as he intended to kiss her for the rest of her life.

'I'll give you diamonds,' he yelled when they could finally bear to pull apart.

'Who needs diamonds?' Meg said lovingly. He could barely hear her words but he knew what her lips were saying. It was what his heart was saying.

'Merry Christmas, my love,' she told him. 'Diamonds or not, I just need you.'

* * * * *

CHRISTMAS KISSES WITH HER BOSS

NINA MILNE

This one is for my dad,
because I always remember him at Christmas
and always lift a glass to his memory.

CHAPTER ONE

LOITER. SKULK. PANIC. Who knew it was possible to do all three at once? Ruby Hampton shoved her hands into the pockets of the overlong padded coat, worn for the purpose of disguise as well as to keep the bite of the December wind out.

This was nuts. All she had to do was cross the bustling London street and enter the impressive skyscraper that housed Caversham Holiday Adventures HQ. Easy, right? Clearly not, because her feet remained adhered to the pavement.

On the plus side, at least there didn't seem to be any reporters around. Unless they were camouflaged as one of the Christmas vendors touting anything from chestnuts to reindeer-daubed jumpers. Not that she'd studied them too closely as she'd walked through Knightsbridge, head down, in desperate hope that her furry hood and sunglasses would save her from recognition and the mortification of a public lynching.

But so far so good, and maybe the fact there were no paps in hot pursuit meant they had finally got the message and realised that not a single comment would fall from her zipped lips, effectively sewn shut by Hugh's threats.

His American drawl still echoed in her ears.

'One wrong word and my publicity machine will chew you up, spit you out and leave your remains for my lawyers to kick.'

So the paps were better off camping on Hugh's doorstep, where comments flowed in a stream of lies from his glamorous Hollywood lips. No change there. Mind you, she couldn't even blame his legions of fans for their implicit belief in him. After all, she had fallen hook, line and sinker for every honeyed word he'd conned her with. And now…

Now the headlines screamed across her brain.

> *Ruby Hampton—exposed as two-timing gold-digger!*
> *Hugh Farlane: Hollywood megastar. Heartbroken!*
> *Christmas Engagement Extravaganza off!*
> *Ruby Hampton vilified by Farlane's adoring public!*

'Vilified' was an understatement—Hugh's besotted fans were baying for her blood. No one believed in her innocence—instead they believed she had broken Hugh's heart whilst in hot pursuit of filthy lucre. The idea made her toes curl in abhorrence—she'd vowed in childhood never to exist on someone else's handouts and it was a promise she'd faithfully kept. Her parents had produced child after child to reap state benefits to fuel their addictions—had cadged and lied and cheated. No way could she do that.

For a moment shades of the past threatened. Tom… Edie… Philippa… Siblings she'd never see again.

Whoa, Ruby.

The past was over. Done with.

Right now she needed to haul ass and get herself to this job interview—it was time to do what she did best: pick up the pieces and move on. Put Hugh Ratbag Farlane and the past firmly behind her.

Ah…

Therein lay a cracker of a problem—an explanation for

her skulk, loiter and panic manoeuvre in blustery December on a London kerbside.

A piece of her past awaited her inside Caversham HQ—a veritable blast from the past was about to interview her.

Ethan Caversham.

The syllables unleashed another onslaught of nerves. The last man she'd ever expected to lay eyes on ever again. The last man she'd *wanted* to lay eyes on ever again.

Get a grip, Ruby—Ethan was so far in her past he was history. She was no longer that wide-eyed teenager with a ginormous crush. Ginormous and short-lived. She still cringed at the memory of that crush exploding into smithereens, bombed by Ethan's words.

'*Stop following me around. I don't want your gratitude. I don't want your help. I don't want* you. *So please just leave me alone.*'

Clearly times had changed, because fast-forward ten years and Ethan had contacted her to offer her an interview. His email, via a business media site, had been short and to the point—no hint of whether he remembered her, not much clue as to what the job even entailed. But that didn't matter. Right now she needed a job—*any* job.

She had been a fool to quit her previous job, but she had believed Hugh.

Frustration at her own idiocy clogged her throat—she'd free fallen for Hugh's persuasive words—had let him mess with her head, believed he needed her by his side. As a result she had given up an incredible job. *Idiot.*

Work was her lifeline—her salvation, her security—and right now no one else would give her so much as an opportunity to ask the time of day. They didn't want to be tainted by all the negative publicity, and she didn't want to sit around and wait until the public furore died down. Not her style.

So… Time to walk the walk, talk the talk and nail this role.

Ethan Caversham meant nothing to her any more—he had walked out on their friendship and as far as Ruby was concerned he was simply a prospective employer with the potential to offer her a job that would enhance her CV.

It would do more than that—crystal-clear determination solidified in her gut. This job would provide her with money and security…the wherewithal to start the adoption process—to have a family. By herself.

Pulling her hands out of her pockets, she urged her feet into walk mode, crossed the street and entered the glass revolving door of the sleek glass-plated building. An elevator ride to the third floor allowed her just enough time to take off her coat and check that the severe professional chignon was still in place, the subtle make-up intact.

The doors slid open, and with a deep in-haul of breath Ruby entered the lobby of Caversham Holiday Adventures.

She braced herself as the receptionist looked up, and on cue there was the expected glare of condemnation. Clearly the svelte blonde woman was yet another of Hugh's legion of fans.

No way would she cower—instead she smiled, and took courage from her carefully chosen outfit: a grey woollen jacket that nipped in at her waist over a tailored black jersey dress. Severe, smooth, *professional*.

'I have an interview with Ethan Caversham.'

The receptionist nodded, tight-lipped. 'I'll let him know you're here.'

'Thank you.'

Adrenalin started to spike and Ruby focused on her surroundings. It was an old childhood trick that had always grounded her in tricky times—helped her concentrate on reality and the importance of the tasks ahead—how to convince social workers that all was well, how to angle a bottle of milk so that the baby didn't cough it up, how to keep her siblings safe...

This backdrop was way different from the squalid environment of her youth—here there was marble flooring, lush green exotic plants, and a lustrous glass reception desk. Imposing photographs graced the walls. Glorious rugged mountains. The turquoise-blue of the sea. A surfer cresting the swell of a wave. The pictures exuded energy and exhilaration.

After a brief telephone conversation the receptionist rose to her considerable height. 'I'll take you to him,' she said.

'Thank you.'

Ruby followed her down a corridor and curiosity, panic and anticipation mingled in her tummy. *Ethan Caversham. Ethan Caversham. Ethan Caversham.* The syllables beat a tattoo in her brain that matched the click-clack of her heels on the parquet floor. Even as she tried to remind herself that he meant zilch to her now.

The receptionist pushed the door open. 'Ethan. Your ten o'clock appointment is here.'

'Thank you, Linda.'

One more censorious look and Linda withdrew, the door snapping shut behind her.

Heart pounding so hard it was a miracle her ribcage remained intact, Ruby stepped forward as a man rose from behind the curved cherrywood desk.

Oh.

Sure, she'd researched him. Sure, the internet had revealed that present-day Ethan Caversham was hot, rugged and handsome. Come to that, teenage Ethan had been no slouch in the looks department.

But now... Now she was adhered to the plush carpet, mouth agape, as she took in his chiselled features, thick brown hair, cool blue-grey eyes. Six foot plus, with a body that had been honed over the years into muscular perfection. The angry vibe of a decade ago had been muted into an edgy aura of toughness; this wasn't a man you'd mess with.

Nerves that had already been writhing serpent-like in her tummy renewed their snaking.

Come on, Ruby. Don't blow this.

Uprooting her feet, she moved towards the cherrywood desk and held her hand out. 'Ruby Hampton.'

The feel of his fingers round hers brought back a blast of memory and an undefinable, ridiculous sense of safety, and for an insane second she wanted to hold on to his broad, capable hand. For a lingering second his eyes met hers and something glinted in their blue-grey depths.

'Good to see you again,' he said.

'You too.'

His eyebrows rose. 'You don't sound convinced.'

'I…I…'

Oh, for heaven's sake. This was ridiculous. She'd known the past would come up and she'd planned to deal with it with brightness and breeze. Unfortunately the plan hadn't allowed for the poleaxed effect on her of this version of Ethan. What was the matter with her? Instant attraction wasn't something she believed in. Any more than she believed in instant coffee.

'I wasn't sure you knew who I was, given we didn't exactly part on the best of terms.' The words escaped her lips with a lot more tartness than she'd intended—more ice-cold than bright and breezy.

'No.'

There was a pause, but it soon became clear that Ethan wasn't planning to vouchsafe any more. For a moment the urge to berate him—to force an apology for a decade-old insult, a hurt she hadn't deserved—tempted her vocal cords.

Bad idea, Ruby.

The past needed to remain firmly anchored in the past.

Plus, no way did she want Ethan to know he could still incite such a seething of emotional turmoil. Truth be told, she wasn't that happy about it herself.

Forcing a cool smile to her lips, she nodded. 'I guess the important thing is that we've both come a long way this past decade.'

He gestured to the chair opposite his desk. 'That we have. Please—have a seat and let's get started.'

Easier said than done.

Annoyance flicked in Ethan at his inexplicable reaction to Ruby Hampton.

Inexplicable? Get real.

Ruby was dynamite. Somewhere in the past decade she had morphed from street urchin to professional beauty—dark hair swept up in a chignon, flawless skin glowing translucent and cheekbones you could climb. The problem was his response was more than physical.

Physical attraction he could deal with—attractive women were ten a penny. But Ruby had awoken something else. Because he'd glimpsed a flash of quickly masked vulnerability in her sapphire eyes. The very same vulnerability that had been there all those years ago. An indefinable yet familiar emotion had banded his chest, and for an instant he could taste those youthful emotions—anger, confusion, panic.

Back then her eyes had held incipient hero-worship too. A look he'd loathed. He had known then, as he knew now, that he was no hero, and the idea of adoration had flayed his soul. Sudden guilt thumped his chest. Pointless guilt. Ten years ago he'd done what had been right for Ruby—ripped her fledgling crush out at the roots before it developed into more. Because then, as now, he had known he couldn't offer more.

Enough, already.

That had been then—this was now. And right now all Ruby's eyes held was a cool wariness as she waited for him to start the interview.

So... 'How did you end up in the catering industry?'

'After you and I...' a small hesitation '...went our separate ways I started a waitressing job and enrolled on an adult education course. I worked every shift I could and studied the rest of the time.' Sheer determination etched her features. 'I wanted out of the hostel and out of the care system. I wanted to make my own way in the world and I wanted to do it as fast as possible.'

'I get that.'

He totally understood the need to spend every second busy, busy, busy, until you fell into bed so exhausted that the past didn't dig its talons into your dreams. He fully grasped the necessity of achieving success for your own salvation.

'Once I got some qualifications the owner of the café I worked in offered me promotion to manager and I took it. From there I moved into hotel work, and...'

As she continued to outline her impressive career trail admiration touched him.

'And your last job was front-of-house manager at Forsythe's?'

Forsythe's being one of London's most prestigious restaurants. Graced by the rich and famous, it adjoined Forsythe's Theatre, run by the Forsythe family for centuries.

'Tell me about your experience there.'

'I worked closely with the manager to give the restaurant a new touch. I introduced a Regency theme—spent hours trawling the internet, art shops and markets, finding some incredible items.'

All wariness clearly forgotten, she leant forward; her hands flying the air as she made a point, her classical features illuminated by enthusiasm as she described finding a genuine two-hundred-year-old sketch of the theatre.

'I researched new menus…liaised with customers—' She broke off and a shadow crossed her face as she sat back in her chair.

'Like Hugh Farlane,' Ethan stated.

'Yes. And many others.' Her tone was noncommittal, her dark blue eyes once again guarded. 'I hope that my experience at Forsythe's ties in with whatever role you have in mind for me?'

'Yes, it does. Let me tell you more about the position.'

And then, if she was interested, he would return to the subject of Hugh Farlane.

'So, how much do you know about Caversham Holiday Adventures?'

'A holiday company with a twist, Caversham offers very high-end packages that incorporate extreme sports and hotels with a difference around the world. Your clients include billionaires, jetsetters and celebrities. Your latest project is a castle in Cornwall.'

'Correct.'

For a second Ethan lingered on his vision for the castle and adrenalin buzzed through him. The brooding Cornish castle had captured his imagination, fired him with a desire to do something different—to mix his business life with his charity work.

'Renovation there is nearly complete, and I'm ready to get the restaurant up and flying. I need a restaurant manager to work with me on the design, the menus and the staff, and to plan a grand New Year's Eve opening. The hotel opens for normal business January fifteenth. I know that's a tight deadline. Especially with Christmas. Can you do it?'

'Yes.' There was not a sliver of doubt in her tone. 'But I'm not sure I understand why you don't already have someone in place.'

'I did. We didn't see eye to eye and he quit.' It had turned out that the guy hadn't bought into Ethan's vision for the castle. 'I've been interviewing for a week or so and no dice. This is an important project and I need the right person. You could be it.'

Her eyes lit up and for the first time since she'd entered the room a small, genuine smile tugged her lips up and sucker-punched him straight in the chest.

'That's great.' Then a small frown creased her brow. 'I can do the job,' she said with utter certainty, 'but as I am sure you are aware I am currently not the public's most favourite person. Social media and the tabloids are awash with vitriol aimed at me—if you hire me there may be a backlash.'

Although her voice was even there was a quickly veiled shadow in her eyes that jolted him. Her words were an understatement—the comments being aimed at Ruby were vicious, awash with menace, and in some cases downright obscene.

Ethan's lips tightened in distaste even as his brain clouded with a black shadow. The knowledge of the tragic consequences that could ensue after such unconscionable bullying twisted his very soul.

Pushing the dark memories away, he focused on Ruby. 'I realise that. It's not a problem. I stand by my employees because I trust them. Which brings me to my next question.'

Her credentials were excellent. Now all he had to do was confirm his gut instinct and make sure he could believe in her.

'Go ahead.' Her body tensed in palpable anticipation.

'Obviously I read the papers, and I've seen the accusations that you are a gold-digger who used your position at Forsythe's to attract Hugh Farlane. At Caversham you would be on the front line, liaising with my clients, so I need to trust that you will be delivering customer service without an eye on their wallets. You haven't denied any of the allegations in the press. Could you clarify the situation for me?'

He leant back and waited for her to do just that.

Instead the smile plummeted from her lips with maximum velocity. Her hands twisted together so tightly that her knuckles clicked in protest, the sound breaking the depth of silence.

Then, 'No comment.'

CHAPTER TWO

RUBY BRACED HERSELF as his brown eyebrows rose. 'You're sure you don't want to expand on that?'

What was she supposed to do? Frustration danced in her tummy even as her brain scrambled for a way to salvage the situation. She knew she was innocent, but logic indicated that she could hardly expect Ethan to give her the benefit of the doubt without some semblance of an explanation.

But there was no way she could risk discussing Hugh Farlane—she *knew* the power he wielded. All it would take was for Ethan to go to the papers with her 'story' and *whoomph*—her life would go further down the toilet.

But, she wanted this job. The thought of a return to her solitary apartment for another ice-cream-eating stint was not an option. However much she liked double-double choc-chip.

Ugh. How had this happened? Ah—she knew the answer. The reason she was in this mess was because she had been a fool—had allowed herself to do the unthinkable and dream. *Again.* Dream that she could have it all—love and a family. *Stupid.* Dreams were fantasies, fiction. In real life she had to concentrate on real goals. Such as this job.

The drumming of Ethan's fingers on the cherrywood desk recalled her to the fact that he was awaiting a response. The slight slash of a frown that creased his brow looked more perplexed then judgemental.

Come on. Answer the man.

'I would like to expand further but I can't risk it. Anything I say could be twisted, so it seems best to me that I say nothing. If you decide to quote me, or post something on social media, it will spark off another barrage of hatred.' And consequences from Hugh that she didn't want to contemplate. 'And I... I don't want that.' She hated that quiver in her voice; she didn't want Ethan to think her scared. 'But I give you my word that if you give me a chance I'll do a fabulous job for you and won't let you down.'

His frown deepened. 'And I give you *my* word that I won't betray your confidence. There is no way that I would aggravate the situation.'

A shadow crossed his eyes and for a second Ruby saw a depth of pain in his eyes that made her want to stretch her hand across the desk. Then it was gone, and yet the deep sincerity of his words echoed in her brain.

For an insane second she felt the urge to tell him the whole truth. 'I...'

Stop, Ruby.

Had she learnt nothing from the debacle of Hugh Farlane? She'd trusted him and look where it had landed her—up to her neck in metaphorical manure.

Yet it was impossible to believe that Ethan Caversham was cut from Farlane cloth. The man had saved her life ten years ago.

Yes, and then he'd vanished from her life without trace. Cut and run.

But he'd also bothered to call her for an interview.

Head awhirl, she hauled in breath. It wasn't as if she'd be a contender for any Best Judge of Character awards right now. There were times when she still felt enmeshed in the illusions and lies Hugh had woven. So the best rule of all was *Trust no one*.

'Okay.' Ethan raised his hands. 'Think about what I've said. If we're going to work together there has to be an element of trust. On both sides. Now let's consider another of my concerns. I need to know that you would be fully committed to this job.'

That was easy. 'I would be. All yours. One hundred per cent.'

For an instant his gaze locked on hers and the *double entendre* of her words shimmered over his desk. She gulped.

'Yet you left Forsythe's after just two months.'

A flush heated her cheeks. 'That was what I believe is known as "a career mistake".' Of monumental proportions. 'I'd got engaged, and at the time it seemed like the right course of action. The Forsythe sisters were very understanding.'

'I get that. Most women would get carried away by the lifestyle of fiancée to a Hollywood movie star compared to working in an all-hours pressured job. I saw the press coverage of those swish parties—you're clearly a natural partygoer.'

'No!'

The world might believe that of her, but she felt affront scrape her chest at the idea that Ethan should join that bandwagon of opinion.

'I loathed those parties. I'm so used to fronting events or serving tables that being a guest was hard. All that glitter and glam and there was nothing for me to do except—' She broke off.

Except play the part of Hugh Farlane's besotted girl-friend.

How could she have fallen for it? For *him*? At first she hadn't been interested in a man with his playboy heart-breaker reputation. Certainly she had wanted zilch to do with his fame, the limelight, his money. But slowly he'd chipped away at her resistance, and then he'd confessed that he needed her, that she was the one woman who could heal him, and his honeyed voice had called to something in her very soul.

After all, she'd failed to heal her family on so very many levels—with heart-rending consequences.

So when he had gone down on bended knee, when he had poured out his desire to turn his life around, her heart had melted and she'd known she would do whatever it took to help Hugh. And if that meant she'd have to embrace a lifestyle she disliked, play the part of the glamorous girl-friend and smile at the paps, then she would do that. After all, playing a part was second nature to her—and Hugh had needed her.

Yuck! Talk about deluded…

'Except what?' A hint of unexpected compassion soft-ened his eyes as he picked up a pencil and rolled it between his fingers. 'Except be Hugh Farlane's girlfriend? Guess it must have been hard to lose your identity…'

For a second her brain scrambled, mesmerised by the movement and the broad capability of his hand, and shocked by his understanding. For a second the impulse to confide in him returned. To tell him just how hard it had been, and how much worse it had made Hugh's sub-sequent betrayal.

Swallowing it down, she met his gaze. 'If possible I'd like to keep Hugh out of this. I get that I'm asking a lot, but I promise you can trust me. I will do a brilliant job and I will not leave you in the lurch. Give me a chance to convince you.'

This job was perfect for her—exactly up her street—and her fierce desire to achieve this role had nothing to do with the man offering it. *At all.* All she wanted was to put the last few weeks behind her, to consign the whole Hugh debacle to oblivion and move on.

The pencil thunked down on the table with finality and she felt panic glimmer. She'd blown it.

Silence stretched and yawned as his blue-grey eyes bored into her. Then he blinked, and a slight hint of ruefulness tipped up his lips. 'Okay. I'll give you the job. Trial period until the grand opening. Then we'll take it from there.'

Triumph-tinged relief doused her and tipped her own lips up into a smile. 'You won't regret it. Thank you.'

'Don't thank me yet, Ruby. I'm a hard task master and I'll be with you every step of the way.'

'You will?' Just peachy—the idea sent a flotilla of butterflies aswirl in her tummy.

'Yes. This project is important to me, so you and I will be spending the next few weeks in close conference.'

Close conference. The businesslike words misfired in her brain to take on a stupid intimacy.

'Starting now. I'm headed down to the castle this afternoon. I'll meet you there, or if you prefer I can give you a lift.'

Common sense overrode her instinct to refuse the offer of transport. The only other alternative was a train journey, where the chances of recognition would be high.

'A lift would be great.' The words were not exactly true—the whole idea of time in an enclosed space with Ethan sent a strange trickle of anticipation through her veins. 'Thank you...'

Ethan gave his companion a quick sideways glance and then returned his gaze to the stretch of road ahead. Dressed now in a pair of dark trousers, a white shirt and a soft brown jacket cinched at the waist with a wide belt, she still looked the epitome of professional. Yet his fingers *still* itched to pull the pins out of her severe bun and then run through the resultant tumble of glossy black hair. Even as her cinnamon scent tantalised...

This awareness sucked.

An awareness he suspected was mutual—he'd caught the way her eyes rested on him, the quickly lowered lashes. So why had he hired her? This level of awareness was an issue—he didn't understand it, and the niggle of suspicion that it was more than just physical was already causing his temples to pound.

Employing someone from his past was nuts—he should have known that. The woman next to him triggered memories of times he would rather forget—of the Ethan Caversham of a decade ago, driven to the streets to try and escape the harsh reality of his life, the bitter knowledge that his mother had wanted shot of him made worse by the knowledge that he could hardly blame her.

Shoving the darkness aside, he unclenched his jaw and reminded himself that Ruby was the right person for the job.

But it was more than that.

The quiver in her voice had flicked him on the raw with the knowledge that she was scared—he'd looked across his desk at Ruby and images had surged of Tanya…of the beautiful, gentle sister he'd been unable to protect.

Of Ruby herself ten years before.

A far scrawnier version of Ruby stood in a less than salubrious park trying to face down three vicious-looking youths. He'd seen the scene but the true interpretation of the tableau had taken a moment to sink in. Then one of the youths had lunged and sudden fear had coated his teeth as adrenalin spiked. Not fear of the gang but fear he wouldn't make it in time.

Once he got there he'd take them on—bad odds but he'd weathered worse. Flipside of growing up on a gang-ridden estate meant he knew how to fight. Worst case scenario they'd take him down but the girl would escape. That was what mattered. He couldn't…wouldn't be party to further tragedy.

The element of surprise helped. The youths too intent on their prey to pay him any attention. The jagged sound of the girl's shirt rip galvanised him and he launched knocking the youth aside.

'Run,' he yelled at the girl.

But she hadn't. For a second she had frozen and then she'd entered the melee.

Ten vicious minutes later it was over—the three youths ran off and he turned to see a tall, dark haired girl, her midnight hair hacked as if she'd done it herself. Her face was grubby and a small trickle of blood daubed her forehead. Silhouetted against the barren scrubland of the park, she returned his gaze; wide sapphire blue eyes fringed by incredibly long lashes mesmerised him. Their ragged breaths mingled and for an insane second he didn't see her there—instead he saw his sister. The girl he hadn't managed to save.

He held his hand out. 'Let's go. Before they come back with reinforcements. Or knives.'

'Go where?' Her voice shaky now as reality sunk in.

'Hostel. You can bunk in with me for the night. You'll be safe with me. I promise.'

She'd stared at his hand, and without hesitation she'd placed her hand in his, that damned hero worship dawning in her brilliant eyes.

Present day, and the end result was he'd offered her a job. Because every instinct told him that Hugh Farlane had done her over somehow. Because he would not leave her prey to the online bullies. Because—somehow, somewhere that protective urge had been rebooted.

The dual carriageway had reduced to a single lane. Dusky scenery flashed past the windows—a mixture of wind turbines and farmland that morphed into a small Cornish hamlet, up a windy hill, and then...

'Here we are,' he said, and heard the burr of pride as he

drove down the grand tree-spanned driveway and parked in the car park.

He turned to see Ruby's reaction—hoped she would see in it what he saw.

She shifted and gazed out of the window, her blue eyes fixed to where the castle jutted magnificently on the horizon. 'It's…*awesome*. By which I mean it fills me with awe,' she said.

He knew what she meant. Sometimes it seemed impossible to him that he owned these mighty stone walls, these turrets and towers weighted with the history of centuries, the air peopled by the memory of generations gone past.

Ruby sighed. 'If I close my eyes I can see the Parliamentarians and the Royalists battling it out…the blood that would have seeped into the stone…the cries, the bravery, the pain. I can imagine medieval knights galloping towards the portcullis—' An almost embarrassed smile accompanied her words. 'Sorry. That sounded a bit daft. How on earth did you get permission to convert it into a hotel? Isn't it protected?'

'Permission had already been given, decades ago—I have no idea how—but the company that undertook the project went bust and the castle was left to fall into disrepair. I undertook negotiations with the council and various heritage trusts and bought the place, and now…'

'Now you've transformed it…' Her voice was low and melodious.

Lost in contemplation of her surroundings, she shifted closer to him—and all of a sudden it seemed imperative to get out of the confines of the car, away from the tantalising hint of cinnamon she exuded, away from the warmth in her eyes and voice as she surveyed the castle and then him.

'So, let me show you what I've done and hopefully that will trigger some ideas for you to think about.'

'Perfect.'

The gravel of the vast path crunched under their feet as they walked to the refurbished ancient portcullis. Ethan inhaled the cold, crisp Cornish air, with its sea tang, and saw Ruby do the same, her cheeks already pink from the gust of the winter breeze.

They reached the door and entered the warmth of the reception area. A familiar sense of pride warmed his chest as he glanced round at the mix of modern and ancient. Tapestries adorned the stone walls, plush red armchairs and mahogany tables were strategically placed around the area, with Wi-Fi available throughout.

'This is incredible,' Ruby said.

'Let me show you the rest.'

Ethan led the way along the stone-walled corridors and into the room destined to be the restaurant.

'We believe this was once the banqueting hall,' he said, gesturing round the vast cavernous room also with stone walls and floor.

'Wow…' Ruby stepped forward, her eyes wide and dreamy. She walked into the middle of the room and stood for a moment with her eyes closed.

Ethan caught his breath—Ruby *got* it. She felt the thrill of this place and that meant she'd do her best.

Opening her eyes, she exhaled. 'I can see how this hall would have been in medieval times. Jugglers, singers, raconteurs—a great table laden with food…'

'Let me show you the other rooms.'

Ruby paused outside a large room adjoining the hall. 'What about this one?'

'You don't need to worry about that one.'

Ethan knew his voice was guarded, but he had no wish to share his full vision for the castle with Ruby. There would be time enough to explain, as and when it was necessary. Right now she was on trial.

'But it looks perfect for a café. Your guests won't always want to dine in splendour—they might just want a sandwich or a bowl of soup. I could—'

'I said you don't need to worry about it.'

Seeing the flash of hurt cross her face, he raised his hand in a placatory gesture and smiled.

'Right now I want you to see the parts of the castle that I have renovated—not worry about the ones I haven't. Let's keep moving.'

Another length of corridor and they reached a bar. 'I want the castle to be representative of all periods of history. This room shows the Victorian era,' he explained.

'It is absolutely incredible!' Ruby enthused as she stood and gazed around the room before walking to the actual bar, where she ran a hand along the smooth polished English oak.

Ethan gulped, mesmerised as her slender fingers slid its length. He turned the sound into what even *he* could hear was a less than plausible cough. 'Would you like a drink? The bar's not fully stocked yet, but I do have a selection of drinks.'

'That would be really helpful.'

'Helpful…?'

'Yup. Lots of your guests will sit in here before coming into the restaurant. I want their movement to segue. So if I can just soak up the atmosphere in here a bit that would be helpful.'

'Fine by me. What would you like to drink?'

'Tomato juice with tabasco sauce.'

Ethan went behind the bar, ridiculously aware of her gaze on him as he squatted down to grab a bottle, deftly opened the tomato juice, shifted ice and peppered the mix with the fiery sauce.

A blink and she stepped away from the bar. 'You're a natural.' Her voice edged with added husk.

'I make sure I can stand in for any of my staff,' he said,

placing her drink on the bar, unable to risk so much as the brush of her hand. He gestured towards an area near the Victorian fireplace, with two overstuffed armchairs.

Ruby sat down and looked round the room, blue eyes widening. 'You have done such a *fabulous* job here—I can't really find words to describe it. I know I've never been to any of the other Caversham sites, but I did do a lot of online research and...' Slim shoulders lifted. 'This seems different. I can't quite put my finger on it but this feels more...*personal*. Does that sound daft?'

No, it didn't. It spoke volumes for her intuitive powers. His vision for the castle *was* personal. And it was going to stay that way. An explanation too likely to open him up to accolades—the idea set his teeth on the brink of discomfort. Even worse, it might pave the way to a discussion as to his motivations and a visit down memory lane. That was enough to make his soul run cold and he felt his mouth form a grim line.

Ruby twirled a strand of hair that had escaped its confines. 'I'm not trying to pry, but if you do have a different idea for the castle restaurant then I need to know, so I can come up with the right design.'

Time to say something. 'I feel proud of what I've already done here, and I'm sure we can work together to come up with a concept that works for the castle.'

Another glance around and then she smiled at him, a smile that warmed him despite his best attempts to erect a wall of coldness.

'You're right to be proud, Ethan—you have come so far. You said ten years ago you would make it big—but this... it's gigantically humungous.'

There it was again—the tug back to the past. Yes, he'd vowed to succeed—how else could he show his mother, show the whole world, that he was worth something? That he was not his father.

'I'm truly honoured to be part of it. So if there is anything I need to know, please share.'

Share. The word was alien. Ethan Caversham knew the best way to walk was alone. Ten years ago Ruby Hampton had slipped under his guard enough that he'd *shared* his dream of success. And instantly regretted the confidence when it had seemed to make her want more—now here she was again with a request that he share, and once again the promise of warmth in those eyes held allure, a tempt to disclosure.

Not this time—this time he'd break the spell at the outset.

'I do have an attachment to the castle—I think it's because it does feel steeped in history. That's why I've gone into such detail. You may want to take note of the stone floors. Also the reason the room is predominantly ruby-red and dark green is that there were limited colours actually available then. And did you know that it was only in the eighteen-forties that wallpaper was first mass-produced?'

Excellent—he'd turned into a walking encyclopaedia on Victorian restoration.

Ruby nodded. 'You've got it exactly right with the birds and animals motif, and the faux marble paint effects are spot-on too. As for the fireplace…it's magnificent—especially with all the dried flowers.'

Clearly Ruby had decided to humour the boss and join in with the fact-bombardment.

'I love the brass light fittings as well. And all the ornaments. The Victorians *loved* ornaments.' She rose from the sofa and crouched down in front of one of a pair of porcelain dogs on either side of the fireplace. 'These are a real find. A proper matching pair.'

'They are,' Ethan agreed. 'How come you're so knowledgeable?'

'We looked into the idea of going Victorian in For-sythe's.'

That seemed to cover Victoriana, and suddenly the atmosphere thickened.

Rising to her feet, Ruby reached out for her glass, drained it and glanced at her watch. 'Would it be okay if I clocked off for today? I need to sort out somewhere to stay—I've got a list of places to ring.'

For a fraction of a second a shadow crossed her sapphire eyes. Then the hint of vulnerability was blinked away as she straightened her shoulders and smiled at him.

'I'll call them, find somewhere, and then grab a taxi.'

Realisation crashed down. She was scared—and who could blame her? Right now the idea of an encounter with the public was enough to daunt the staunchest of celebrities.

That instinctive need to protect her surged up and triggered his vocal cords. 'Or you could stay here.'

CHAPTER THREE

'HERE?' RELIEF TOUCHED RUBY, but before she could succumb she forced her brain to think mode. 'Why?'

Ethan shrugged. 'It makes sense. It's a hotel. There's plenty of room. You'll have to make your own bed, and there's no housekeeping service, but you can have a suite and work more effectively here. I'll be staying here too, so you won't be on your own.'

Thoughts scrambled round her brain. Truth be told, she would feel safer here. *Because of Ethan.* The thought sneaked in and she dismissed it instantly. This was zip to do with Ethan—sheer logic dictated she should stay in the castle. Nothing to do with his aura, or the slow burn of the atmosphere.

'Thank you, Ethan. If you're sure.'

'I'm sure. Let's find you a bedroom.'

'Um… Okay.' *Freaking great*—here came a tidal wave blush adolescent-style at the word. How ridiculous. As preposterous as the thud of her heart as she followed him up the sweep of the magnificent staircase to the second floor, where he pushed open a door marked 'Elizabethan Suite' and stood back to let her enter.

'Whoa!' The room was stunning, a panorama of resplendence, and yet despite its space, despite the splendour of the brocade curtains and the gorgeous wall-hangings that depicted scenes of verdure, her eyes were drawn with mesmerising force to the bed. Four-poster, awash with luxurious draperies—but right now all she could concentrate on was the fact that it was a bed.

For a crazy moment her mind raced to create an age-old formula; her body brazenly—*foolishly*—wanted to act on an instinct older than time. And for one ephemeral heartbeat his pupils darkened to slate-grey and she believed that insanity must be contagious...believed that he would close the gap between them.

Then Ethan stepped back and the instant dissolved, leaving a sizzle in the air. A swivel of the heel and he'd turned to the door.

'I'll meet you in the morning to finish showing you around. If you're hungry there's some basic food stuff in the kitchen.'

'Okay.' Though her appetite had deserted her—pushed aside by the spin of emotions Ethan had unleashed.

'If you need anything you've got my mobile number. My suite is on the next floor. No one knows you're here, so you can sleep easy.'

For the first time in the two horrendous weeks since she'd walked in on Hugh and a woman who had turned out to be a hooker she felt...safe...

'Thank you. And, Ethan...?'

'Yes?'

'Thank you for today. For...well, for coming to my rescue again.'

A long moment and then he nodded, his expression unreadable. 'No problem.'

'Ethan?'

'Yes.'

'Can I ask you something?'

Wariness crossed his face and left behind a guarded expression. 'You can ask...'

'Why did you call me to an interview?'

Silence yawned and Ruby's breath caught. Foolish hope that he had wanted to make amends for the past unfurled.

'Everyone is entitled to a chance,' he said finally. 'And everyone deserves a second one.'

The words were a deep rumble, and fraught with a connotation she couldn't grasp.

'Sleep well, Ruby. We've got a lot of work ahead.'

The door clicked shut behind him and Ruby sank down onto the bed.

Enough. Don't analyse. Don't think. Don't be attracted to him. In other words, don't repeat the mistakes of the past.

Ethan Caversham had offered her a chance and she wouldn't let the jerk of attraction mess that up. Wouldn't kid herself that it was more than that—more like a bond between them. Ruby shook her head—this was an aftermath…an echo of her ancient crush on the man. Because he'd rescued her again.

Only this time it had to play out differently. Instead of allowing the development of pointless feelings and imaginary emotional connections she would concentrate on the job at hand. Get through the trial period, secure the job as a permanent post and then she would be back on track. Heading towards her goal of a family.

One week later

Ethan gave a perfunctory knock and pushed the door open. Ruby looked up from her paper-strewn makeshift desk in the box room where she'd set up office. His conscience panged at her pale face and the dark smudges under her eyes. She'd worked her guts out these past days and he'd let her. More than that—he'd encouraged it.

Get a grip, Ethan.

That was what he paid her to do—to work and work hard. He had high expectations of all his employees and made no bones about it. Ruby was no different.

Sure. Keep telling yourself that, Ethan. Say it enough times and maybe it will become true.

'Earth to Ethan. I was about to call you with an update. I've got delivery dates for the furniture for the banqueting hall and I've found a mural painter. I've mocked up some possible uniforms—black and red as a theme—and…'

'That's all sounds great, but that's not why I'm here. There's something else I need you to do.'

'Okay. No problem. Shoot.'

'Rafael Martinez is coming for dinner and I need you to rustle us up a meal.'

Her dark eyebrows rose. 'Rafael Martinez—billionaire wine guru, owner of the vineyard of all vineyards—is coming for dinner? Why on earth didn't you mention it before?'

'Because I didn't know. I'd scheduled to meet him later this month, but he called to say he's in the UK and that tonight would suit him. I realise it's not ideal. But Rafael and I are…'

Old friends? Nope. Acquaintances? More than that. Old schoolmates? The idea was almost laughable—he and Rafael had bunked off more school than they had attended.

'We go back a while.'

'Maybe you should take him out somewhere?'

'I'd rather discuss business in private. But if it's too much for you…?'

He made no attempt to disguise the challenge in his tone, and she made no attempt to pretend she didn't hear it, angling her chin somewhere between determination and defiance.

'Leave it with me.'

'You're sure?'

'I'm sure.'

'Look on this as a test of your ability to handle a restaurant crisis.'

'Yippee. An opportunity!'

A snort of laughter escaped his lips. 'That's the attitude. I'll leave you to it.'

Whilst he figured out the best way to approach Rafael with his proposition… Rafael Martinez was known more for his playboy tendencies and utterly ruthless business tactics than his philanthropic traits. But Ethan had been upfront in his preliminary approach—had intimated that his agenda was a business deal with a charitable bent—and Rafael had agreed to meet. Somehow it seemed unlikely that he'd done so to reminisce over the bad old days of their more than misguided youth.

He'd reached the doorway when he heard Ruby's voice. 'Actually…I've had an idea…'

Ethan turned. 'Go ahead.'

'Okay. So it's best if you eat in the bar—it's a pretty impressive room, and I think we should make it a little bit Christmassy.'

'Christmassy?' Somehow the idea of Christmas and Rafael didn't exactly gel. 'I don't think so, Ruby. My guess is that Rafael is even less enamoured with the schmaltz of Christmas than me.'

A shake of her dark head and an exaggerated sigh. 'I'm not suggesting schmaltz. If we were open we would be playing the Christmas card—of course we would.' For a second a hint of wistfulness touched her face. 'Can't you picture it? An enormous tree. Garlands. Twinkling lights—' She broke off and frowned. 'I assume all your other business ventures offer Christmas deals and a proper Christmas ambience?'

'Yes, but I don't do it myself.'

He wouldn't have the first clue how—he hadn't celebrated Christmas Day in the traditional sense since… since Tanya was alive.

For a second he was transported back to childhood. His sister had loved Christmas…had made it magical—she had made him help her make paper chains and decorate the tree, and although he'd protested they'd both known the protest to be half-hearted. She'd chivvied their mum into the festive spirit and the day had always been happy. But after Tanya… Well, best not to go there.

'To be honest, I'm not much of a Christmas type of guy. And I'm pretty sure Rafael isn't either.'

'Well, luckily for you I'm a Christmas type of gal. I'm thinking a tasteful acknowledgement of the time of year so that Rafael Martinez gets an idea of how Caversham Castle would showcase his wine. The Martinez Vineyards offer plenty of Christmas wines. Plus, if we do it right the whole Christmas edge might soften him up.'

Difficult to imagine, but given he hoped to appeal to Rafael's charitable side maybe it was worth a shot. And he believed in encouraging staff initiative and drive.

'Knock yourself out,' he said.

'Fabulous. I'll hit the shops.'

Ruby crouched down and carefully moved the small potted tree a couple of centimetres to the left of the hearth. She inhaled the scent of fir and soil and felt a small glow of satisfaction at a job well done. Or at least *she* thought so—Ethan clearly had reservations about the whole Christmas idea, and her research into Rafael Martinez had shown her why.

Like Ethan Caversham, he had a reputation for ruthlessness, and an internet trawl had revealed images of a man with a dark aura. Midnight hair, tall, with a dominant nose and deep black eyes. Unlike Ethan, he'd left a score of girlfriends in his wake—all glamorous, gorgeous and very, very temporary. For a second Ruby dwelled on Ethan, and curiosity about his love-life bubbled. But it was none of her business.

He's your boss, nothing more.

'Hey.'

Ruby leapt up and swivelled round. *Chill, Ruby.* Ethan was many things, but he was not a mind-reader.

'Hey. Sorry. You startled me.' She gestured around. 'What do you think? I was just making sure the trees don't overshadow Dash and Dot.'

'Dash and Dot?'

Ruby chewed her bottom lip. *Idiot.*

Ethan's lips turned up in a sudden small smile and her toes curled. For a second he'd looked way younger, and she could remember her flash of gratification at winning a rare smile all those years ago.

'You named the china dogs?'

'Yes. In my head. I have to admit I didn't intend to share that fact with anyone. But, yes, I did. Queen Victoria had a spaniel called Dash, you see.' Ruby puffed out a sigh. 'And then I thought of Dot because of Morse code. Anyway, what do you think?'

'Excellent names,' he said, his features schooled to gravity, though amusement glinted in his eyes.

Ruby couldn't help but chuckle, despite the clawing worry that he'd loathe what she'd done. 'I meant the decorations.'

Hope that he'd approve mixed with annoyance at her need for approval. A hangover from childhood, when approval had been at high premium and in short supply.

Surely he had to like it? Her gaze swept over the small potted trees on either side of the fireplace and the wreath hanging above. Took in the lightly scented candles on the mantelpiece and the backdrop of tasteful branch lights casting a festive hint.

'It's incredible.'

'No need to sound surprised.' Sheer relief curved her lips into a no doubt goofy grin. 'Admit it. You thought I would produce something ghastly and flashy.'

'I should have had more faith.'

'Absolutely. Don't get me wrong, I can do tacky schmaltz—in fact I have done. A few years back I worked in a café called Yvette's. Yvette herself was lovely, but she was incredibly sentimental. On Valentine's Day you could barely move for helium-filled heart balloons, and as for Christmas… I provided gaudy tinsel, baubles, mistletoe—and this absolutely incredibly tacky light-up Father Christmas that had to be seen to be believed.'

Ethan glanced at her. 'You're a woman of many talents. But what about you? What kind of Christmas is *your* kind?'

The question caught her off guard and without permission her brain conjured up her game plan Christmas. 'Me? Um… Well… I've spent every Christmas working for the past decade, so I go with my employers' flow.'

'So it's just another day for you? You said you were a Christmas kind of gal.'

'I am.' His words pushed all her buttons and she twisted to face him. 'It's a time of celebration. I'm not overly religious, but I do believe it is way more than just another day. It's a time for giving—a magical day.'

His lips were a straight line as he contemplated her words. 'Giving, yes. Magic, no. That's idealistic. Christmas Day doesn't magically put an end to poverty or disease or crime.'

'No, it doesn't. But it is an opportunity to strive for a ceasefire—to try and alleviate sadness and spread some happiness and cheer. Don't you believe that?'

He hesitated, opened his mouth and then closed it again. Waited a beat and then, 'Yes, Ruby. I do believe that.'

'Good. It's also about being with the people you care about and…'

The familiar tug of loss thudded behind her ribcage… the wondering as to the whereabouts of her siblings, the hope that their Christmas would be a joyful one. It would.

Of course it would. They had a loving adoptive family, and the thought encased her in a genuine blanket of happiness.

Seeing Ethan's blue-grey eyes resting on her expression, she went on. 'And if you can't do that then I think it's still wonderful to be part of someone else's happiness. That's why I've always worked Christmas Day; watching other families celebrate is enough for now.'

'For now?'

'Sure.' *Keep it light*. 'One day I'll have a family, and then…'

'Then all will be well in the world?' His scathing tone shocked her.

'Yes.' The affirmation fell from her lips with way too much emphasis. 'And when I have a family I can tell you the exact Christmas I'll have. An enormous tree, the scent of pine, crackers, decorated walls, holly, ivy, stockings with a candy cane peering over the top. The table laid with cutlery that gleams in the twinkle of Christmas lights. In the centre a golden turkey and all the extras. Pigs in blankets, roast potatoes, roast parsnips, stuffing and lashings of gravy. But most important of all there'll be children. My family. Because *that* is what Christmas is about. And that is magical.'

Ruby hauled in breath as realisation dawned that she might have got a tad carried away.

'Anyway, obviously that is in the far distant future and not something I need to worry about right now.'

It would take time to save enough money to support a family—time to go through the lengthy adoption process.

'No, it isn't.' Ethan's voice was neutral now, his eyes hooded. 'And now isn't the time to dream of future Christmases.'

'It's not a dream. It's a goal. That's different.'

Dreams were insubstantial clouds—stupid aspirations that might never be attained. Goals—goals were different. Goals were definitive. And Ruby was definite that she would have a family. By hook or by crook.

'But you're right. I need to be in the kitchen—or you and Rafael will be eating candle wax for dinner.'

'Hang on.' His forehead was slashed with a deep frown. 'I meant now is the time to think about present-day Christmas. What are your plans for this year?'

His voice had a rough edge of concern to it and Ruby frowned. The last thing she wanted was for Ethan Caversham to feel sorry for her—the idea was insupportable.

'I'll be fine. I have plans.'

Sure. Her plan was to shut herself away in her apartment and watch weepy movies with a vat of ice cream. But that counted as a plan, right? It wasn't even that she was mourning Hugh—she was bereft at the loss of a dream. Because for all her lofty words she had been stupid enough to take her eye off the goal and allow herself to dream. And Hugh had crushed that dream and trampled it into the dust. Further proof—as if she'd needed it—that dreams were for idiots. Lesson learnt. *Again*. But this time reinforced in steel.

'But thank you for asking.'

Ethan's eyes bored into her and the conviction that he would ask her to expand on the exact nature of her plans opened her lips in pre-emptive strike.

'What about your plans?'

His expression retreated to neutral. 'They aren't firmed up as yet.'

Obscure irrational hurt touched her that he didn't feel able to share his plans with her. Daft! After all, it wasn't as if she was sharing hers with him.

'Well, I hope they sort themselves out. Right now I must go and cook. Prepare to be amazed!'

CHAPTER FOUR

ETHAN HANDED RAFAEL a crystal tumbler of malt whisky, checked the fire and sat down in the opposite armchair.

Rafael cradled the glass. 'So, my old friend, tell me what it is you want of me?'

'To negotiate a wine deal. You provide my restaurants worldwide at a cost we negotiate. All except here at Caversham Castle—here I'd like you to donate the wine.'

'And why would I do that?' Rafael scanned the room and the slight upturn of his lips glinted with amusement. 'In the spirit of Christmas?'

'Yes,' Ethan said. 'If by that you mean the spirit of giving and caring. Because I plan to run Caversham Castle differently from my other businesses. As a charitable concern. The castle will be open to holidaymakers for nine months of the year and for the remaining three it will be used as a place to help disadvantaged youngsters.'

For a second, the image of him and Rafael, side by side as they faced down one of the gangs that had roved their estate, flashed in his mind. They had both been loners, but when Rafael had seen him in trouble he'd come to his aid.

'I plan to provide sporting holidays and job-training opportunities. Run fundraisers where they can help out and help organise them. Get involved. Make a difference.' He met Rafael's gaze. 'Give them a chance to do what we've both done.'

After all, they had both been experts in petty crime, headed towards worse, but they had both turned their lives around.

'We did it on our own.'

'Doesn't mean we shouldn't help others.'

Before Rafael could reply the door swung open and Ruby entered.

Whoa. She looked stunning, and Ethan nearly inhaled his mouthful of whisky. Her dark luxuriant hair was swept up in an elegant chignon, clipped with a red barrette. A black dress that reached mid-thigh was cinched at the waist with a wide red sash, and—heaven help him—she wore black peeptoe shoes with jaunty red bows at the heels. Clearly she was giving the new uniform an airing.

A small smile curved her lips as she glided towards them and placed a tray on the table. 'Appetisers to go with your pre-dinner drinks,' she said. 'Parma ham and mozzarella bites, and smoked salmon on crushed potato'.

'Thank you, Ruby.' Attempting to gather his scattered brain cells, Ethan rose to his feet and Rafael followed suit, his dark eyes alight with interest.

'Rafael, this is Ruby Hampton—my restaurant manager.'

'Enchanted to meet you.' Rafael smiled. 'The lady who knocked me off the celebrity gossip pages.'

Colour leached from her face and Ethan stepped towards her.

'I…I hope you enjoyed the respite,' she said, her smile not wavering, and admiration touched his chest. 'I'm not planning on a repeat run.'

Rafael gave a small laugh. 'Well said.' He reached down and picked up one of the canapés and popped it into his mouth. 'Exquisite.'

'Thank you. I'll leave you to it, and then I'll be back with the starters in about fifteen minutes.'

'So…' Rafael said as the door swung shut. 'You've hired Ruby Hampton?'

'Yes.'

'Why? Because you want to give her a second chance?' Rafael gestured round the bar. 'That's what this is about, right? You want people to be given a chance?'

'Yes. I do. I want youngsters who've had a tough time in life to see there is a choice apart from a life of truancy and mindless crime.'

Images of the bleak landscape of the council estate they'd grown up on streamed in his mind.

'And I want society to recognise that they deserve a chance even if they've messed up.'

Rafael leant back. 'You see, *I* think people should make their own choices and prove they deserve a chance. So let's talk business, my friend, and let me think about the charitable angle.'

'Done.'

Ethan placed his whisky glass down. Time to show Rafael Martinez that he might have a philanthropic side, but it didn't mean he wasn't hard-nosed at the negotiating table—helped by the fact that said table was soon occupied by melt-in-the-mouth food, discreetly delivered and served.

In fact if it wasn't for the ultra-sensitive 'detecting Ruby' antennae he seemed to have developed he doubted he would have noticed her presence.

Once the dessert plates were cleared away Ethan scribbled some final figures down and handed them across to Rafael. 'So we're agreed?'

'We're agreed. I'll get it drawn up legally and the contracts across to you tomorrow.'

'And the wine for Caversham Castle?'

Rafael crossed one long leg across his knee and steepled his fingers together as Ruby entered with a tray of coffee.

'Ruby, I'd like to thank you. Dinner was superb. Why don't you join us for coffee?' His smile widened and Ruby hesitated, but then Rafael rose and pulled out a chair for her. 'I insist. I'm sure you and I will have some contact in the future.'

Half an hour later Ethan resisted the urge to applaud. Conversation had flowed and Ethan could only admire the fact that somehow Ruby had found the time to research Rafael sufficiently to engage him on topics that interested him.

Eventually Ruby rose to her feet and held a hand out to Rafael. 'It's been a pleasure—and now I'll leave you two to get back to business.'

Ruby stood in the gleaming chrome confines of the state-of-the-art kitchens and allowed one puff of weariness to escape her lips as she wiped down the final surface.

Tired didn't cover it—she was teetering on the cliff of exhaustion. But she welcomed it. The past week had been incredible. Sure, Ethan was a hard taskmaster, but the man was a human dynamo—and it had energised her. There were times when she could almost believe the whole debacle with Hugh Farlane had been a bad dream. The only whisper of worry was that it wasn't the work that provided balm—it was working with Ethan.

As if her thoughts had the art of conjure, the kitchen door swung open and there he stood. Still suited in the charcoal-grey wool that fitted him to perfection, he'd shed his tie and undone the top button of the crisp white shirt. Her gaze snagged on the triangle of golden bare skin and her breath caught in her throat as he strode towards her.

Cool it, Ruby.

Will power forced the tumult of her pulse to slow. 'All signed on the dotted line?'

'Yes.' His eyes were alight with satisfaction and she could feel energy vibrate off him. 'Rafael just left and I've come to thank you.'

'No problem. Just doing my job.'

'No. You went the extra mile and then some. The meal, the décor…and then you—you charmed the pants off him.'

His words caused a flinch that she tried to turn into another swipe of the counter; panic lashed her as she reviewed their coffee conversation.

'What's wrong?'

She shrugged and straightened up. 'I guess I'm hoping Rafael didn't think that was my aim in the literal sense.'

Comprehension dawned in his eyes. 'He didn't. You did your job. You liaised.'

His matter-of-fact assurance warmed her very soul. 'Thank you for seeing that. Problem is, I'm not sure everyone will. The world believes I trapped Hugh whilst *liaising* on the job.'

He stepped towards her, frustration evident in the power of his stride, in the tension that tautened his body. 'Then deny the allegations.'

'I can't.'

'Why not? Unless you do feel guilty?' Blue-grey eyes bored into her. 'If he dazzled you with his wealth and charm that doesn't make you a gold-digger. When you start out with nothing it's easy to be swept off your feet— to welcome the idea of lifelong security and easy wealth. There is no need for guilt.'

'I wasn't dazzled by his wealth. I always vowed that I would earn my keep every step of the way.' Wouldn't set foot on her parents' path. 'I wasn't after Hugh's cash.'

And yet…

A small hard lump of honesty formed in her tummy. 'But I suppose with hindsight I am worried that I was dazzled by the idea of a family. He said he wanted kids, and…'

Yes, there had been that idea of it being within her grasp—the idea that she'd finally found a man who wanted a family. Not a man like Steve or Gary but a man who could provide, who needed her and wanted her help to heal him… What a sucker she'd been. Never again—that was for sure.

'I assume he lied? Like he's lying now? That is his bad. Not yours. So fight him. I had you down as a fighter.'

'I can't win this fight. Hugh Farlane is too big to take on. It's unbelievable how much clout he has. He has enough money to sink a ship…enough publicity people to spin the Bayeux Tapestry.'

'What about right and wrong?'

'That's subjective.'

It was a lesson she had learnt the hard way. She'd fought the good fight before and lost her siblings. Lord knew she was so very happy for them—joyful that Tom and Edie and Philippa had found an adoptive family to love them all. But it had been hard to accept that they would never be the happy family unit she had always dreamed they would be.

So many dreams…woven, threaded, embroidered with intricate care. Of parents who cleaned up their alcohol and drug-fuelled life and transformed themselves into people who cared and nurtured and loved… And when that dream had dissolved she had rethreaded the loom with rose threads and produced a new picture. An adoptive family who would take them all in and provide a normal life—a place where love abounded along with food, drink, clothes and happiness…

She'd fought for both those dreams and been beaten both times. Still had the bruises. So she might have learnt the hard way, but she'd sucked the lesson right up.

'Yes, it is.' His voice was hard. 'But you should still fight injustice. You owe it yourself.'

'No! What I owe myself is to not let my life be wiped out.' *Again.* 'I've worked hard to get where I am now, and I will not throw it away.'

'I don't see how denying these allegations equates to chucking your life away. Unless…'

A deep slash creased his brow and she could almost hear the cogs of his brain click into gear. For a crazy moment she considered breaking into a dance to distract him. But then…

'Has he forced you to silence? Threatened you?'

Ethan started to pace, his strides covering the resin floor from the grill station with its burnished charbroiler to the sauté station where she stood.

'Is that why you aren't fighting this? Why you haven't refuted the rubbish in the papers? Why Farlane knows he can slate you with impunity and guarantee he'll come up drenched in the scent of roses.'

Just freaking fabulous—he'd worked it out. 'Leave it, Ethan. It doesn't matter. This is my choice. To not add more logs to already fiery flames.'

His expulsion of breath tinged the air with impatience. 'That's a pretty crummy choice.'

'Easy for you to say. You're the multimillionaire head of a global business and best mates with the Rafael Martinezes of the world.'

'That is irrelevant. I would take Hugh Farlane down, whatever my bank balance and connections, because he is a bully. The kind of man who uses his power to hurt and terrorise others.'

Ruby blinked; the ice in his voice had caused the hairs on her arms to stand to attention.

'If you don't stand up to him he will do this to someone else. Bully them, harass them, scare them.'

'No, he won't.'

'You don't know that.'

'Yes, I do…'

Ruby hesitated, tried to tell herself that common sense dictated she end this exchange here and now. But, she couldn't. Her tummy churned in repudiation of the disappointment in his gaze, the flick of disdain in his tone.

'The whole engagement was a set-up.'

The taste of mortification was bitter on her tongue as the words were blurted out.

Ethan frowned. You two were faking a relationship?'

'No. *We* weren't faking. Hugh was. It was a publicity stunt—he needed an urgent image-change. His public were disenchanted with his womanising and his sex addiction. Hugh was keen to get into the more serious side of acting as well, and he wanted to impress the Forsythe sisters, who are notorious for their high moral standards. So he figured he'd get engaged to someone "normal". I fell for it. Hook line and sinker.'

His jaw clenched. 'So it was a scam?'

'Yup. I thought he loved me—in reality he was using me.'

Story of her life.

'I resigned because he asked me to—so that I could be by his side. He told me it was to help him. To keep him from the temptation to stray. But really it was all about the publicity. I can't believe I didn't see it. Hugh Farlane…rich, famous…a man who could have any woman he wanted… decided to sweep *me* off my feet, to change his whole lifestyle, marry me. He said we would live happily ever after with lots of sproglets.' She shook her head. 'I of all people should have known the stupidity of believing *that*.'

Her own parents hadn't loved her enough to change their lifestyles—despite their endless promises to quit, their addictions had held sway over their world. Rendered them immoral and uncaring of anything except the whereabouts of their next fix.

'How did you find out?'

Ethan's voice pulled her back to the present.

'He "confessed" when I found him in bed with another woman. A hooker, no less. Turned out he'd been sleeping around the whole time. He'd told me that he wanted to wait to sleep with me until we got married, to prove I was "different".'

Little wonder her cheeks were burning—she'd accepted Hugh's declaration as further evidence of his feelings for her, of his willingness to change his lifestyle for her, and her soul had sung.

'In reality it was so that he could be free at night for some extracurricular action between the sheets.'

For a second a flicker of relief crossed his face, before sheer contempt hardened his features to granite. Both emotions she fully grasped. If she'd actually slept with Hugh she would feel even more besmirched than she already did. As for contempt—she'd been through every shade, though each one had been tinted with a healthy dose of self-castigation at her own stupidity.

'Anyway, once I got over the shock I chucked the ring at him, advised him to pay the woman with it and left. Then his publicity machine swung into action. Hugh's first gambit was to apologise. It was cringeworthy. Next up, ironically enough, he offered to pay me to play the role of his fiancée. When I refused, it all got a bit ugly.'

Ethan halted, his jaw and hands clenched. 'You want me to go and find him? Drag him here and make him grovel?'

'No!'

But his words had loosed a thrill into her veins—there was no doubt in her mind that he would do exactly that. For a second she lingered on the satisfying image of a kowtowing Hugh Farlane and she gave a sudden gurgle of laughter.

'I appreciate it, but no—thank you. The point is he said he'd never bother to pull a publicity stunt like this again. So I don't need to make a stand for the greater good. To be honest, I just want it to blow over; I want the threats and the hatred to stop.'

Ethan drummed his fingers on the counter and her flesh

goosebumped at his proximity, at the level of anger that buzzed off him. It was an anger with a depth that filled her with the urge to try to soothe him. Instinct told her this went deeper than outrage on her behalf, and her hand rose to reach out and touch him. Rested on his forearm.

His muscles tensed and his blue-grey gaze contemplated her touch for a stretch. Then he covered her hand with his own and the sheer warmth made her sway.

'I'm sorry you went through that, Ruby. I'd like to make the bastard pay.'

'It's okay.' Ruby shook her head. 'I'm good. Thanks to you. You gave me a chance, believed in me, and that means the world.'

Lighten the mood. Before you do something nuts like lean over and kiss him on the cheek. Or just inhale his woodsy aroma.

'If it weren't for you I'd still be under my duvet, ice cream in hand. Instead I'm here. Helping renovate a castle. So I'm really good, and I want to move forward with my life.'

'Then let's do exactly that.' Ethan nodded. 'Let's go to dinner.'

'Huh?' Confusion flicked her, along with a thread of apprehension at the glint in his eye. 'Now? You've had dinner, remember?'

'Tomorrow. Pugliano's. In the next town along.'

'Pugliano's? You're kidding? We'd never get in at such short notice.'

'Don't worry about that. We'll get a table.'

'But why do you want us to go out for dinner?' For a scant nanosecond her heart speeded up, made giddy by the idea that it was a date.

'To celebrate making your appointment official. You're off trial.'

'I am?' A momentary emotion she refused to acknowledge as disappointment that it was not a date twanged. To be succeeded by suspicion. 'Why?'

Shut up, shut up, shut up.

This was good news, right? The type that should have her cartwheeling around the room. But…

'I don't want this job out of pity.'

'Look at me.' He met her gaze. 'Do I look like a man who would appoint someone to an important business role out of pity?'

'Fair point. No, you don't. But I think your timing is suspect.'

'Nope. You've proved yourself this past week. You've matched my work drive without complaint and with enthusiasm. Tonight you went beyond the call of duty with Rafael and now you've told me the truth. No pity involved. So… Dinner?'

'Dinner.'

Try as she might the idea sizzled—right alongside his touch. His hand still covered hers and she wanted more.

As if realisation hit him at the same instant he released his grip and stepped backwards. 'It will be good for you as well. To see how Pugliano's works.'

'Good…how?' Hurt flickered across her chest. 'I've researched all your places. I've talked to your restaurant managers in Spain and France and New York. Plus I know how a top-notch restaurant works already.'

'Sure—but as a manager, not as a guest.' He raised a hand. 'I know your engagement to Hugh was filled with social occasions in glitzy places, but you said it yourself you didn't enjoy them and now I get why. I want you to see it from the point of view of a guest. Experience it from *that* side of the table.'

Despite all her endeavour, the bit of her that persisted in believing the date scenario pointed out that she would positively *revel* in the experience alongside Ethan.

The thought unleashed a flutter of apprehension.

Chill, Ruby. And think this through.

This was *not* a date, and actually… 'I'm not sure it's a good idea. What if it reactivates the media hype? What if people think that I'm moving in on *you*, shovel in hand, kitted out in my gold-prospecting ensemble?'

His broad shoulders shrugged with an indifference she could only envy. 'Does it matter what people think?'

'It does if it starts up a media storm.'

'We can weather the storm. This is a business dinner, not a date, and I don't have a problem going public with that.'

'Well, *I* do. I can picture it—sitting there being stared at, whispered about…the salacious glances…'

'But once they see two people clearly in the process of having a business dinner they will lose interest and stop gawping.'

'What about the negative publicity viewpoint?'

'You are my *restaurant manager*. You do your job and I will deal with any negative publicity. I stand by my employees. Look, I get that it will be hard, but if you want to move on you need to face it. I'll be right there by your side.'

'I get that it will be hard… You need to face it…I'll be right there by your side.'

The phrases echoed along the passage of a decade—the self-same words that the younger Ethan Caversham had uttered.

Those grey-blue eyes had held her mesmerised and his voice, his sheer presence, had held her panic attacks at bay. It had been Ethan who had made her leave the hostel, who had built her confidence so she could walk the streets again, only this time with more assurance, with a poise engendered by the self-defence classes he'd enrolled her in.

Yes—for weeks he'd been by her side. Then he'd gone. One overstep on her part, one outburst on his, and he'd gone. Left her. Moved out and away, leaving no forwarding address.

Ruby met his gaze, hooded now, and wondered if he had travelled the same memory route. She reminded herself that now it was different—*she* was different. No way would she open herself to that hurt again—that particular door was permanently closed and armour-plated.

So Ethan was right—to move forward she needed to put herself out there.

'Let's do this.'

CHAPTER FIVE

ETHAN RESISTED THE urge to loosen his collar as he waited in front of the limo outside the castle's grand entrance. This strange fizz of anticipation in his gut was not acceptable— not something he'd experienced before, and not something he wanted to experience again.

Fact One: this was *not* a date. A whoosh of irritation escaped his lips that he needed a reminder of the obvious. The word date was not in Ethan Caversham's dictionary.

Fact Two: Ruby was an *employee* and this was a business dinner, to give her a guest's viewpoint and to show her—an *employee*—his appreciation of a job well done. Perhaps if he stressed the word *employee* enough his body and mind would grasp the concept…

Fact Three: yes, they had a shared past—but that past consisted of a brief snapshot in time, and that tiny percentage of time was not relevant to the present.

So… Those were the facts and now he was sorted. Defizzed. Ethan Caversham was back in control.

A minute later the front door opened and every bit of his control was blown sky-high, splattering him with the smithereens of perspective. Moisture sheened his neck as he slammed his hands into his pockets and forced himself not to rock back on his heels.

Ruby looked sensational, and all his senses reeled in response. Her glorious dark hair tumbled loose in glossy ripples over the creamy bare skin of her shoulders. The black lacy bodice of her dress tantalised his vision. A wide black band emphasised the slender curve of her waist and the dress was ruched into a fun, flirty skirt that showcased the length of her legs.

But what robbed his lungs of breath was the expression on her face and the very slight question in her sapphire eyes. That hint of masked vulnerability smote him with a direct jab to the chest.

'You look stunning.'

'Thank you.' Her chin angled in defiance. 'I decided that if people are going to stare I'd better scrub up.'

'You scrub up well.'

With a gargantuan effort he kept his tone light, pushed away the urge to pull her into his arms and show her how well, to try to soothe the apprehension that pulsed from her.

'Your limo awaits.'

'You didn't need to hire a limo.'

'I wanted to. We're celebrating, and I want to do this in style—tonight I want you to enjoy the experience of being a guest.'

To make up in some small way for what Hugh had put her through. All those high society occasions where he'd groomed her to act a part she'd disliked. Sheer anger at the actor's behaviour still fuelled Ethan—to have messed with Ruby's head like that was unforgivable. So tonight it was all about Ruby. As his *employee*. His temple pounded a warning—perspective needed to be retained.

'So that you can use the experience to help you at Caversham Castle. Speaking of which…I've issued a press statement.'

'Good idea.' The words were alight with false brightness as she slid into the limousine. Waited for him to join her in sleek leather luxury. 'What did it say?'

'"Ethan Caversham is pleased to announce the appointment of a restaurant manager for his new project, Caversham Castle in Cornwall. Ruby Hampton has taken on the role, and both Ethan and Ruby are excited at the prospect of creating a restaurant that sparkles with all the usual Caversham glitter and offers a dining experience to savour.'"

'Sounds good.'

After that, silence fell, and Ethan forced his gaze away from her beauty and instead gazed out at the scenery. A quick glance at Ruby saw her doing the same. There was tension in the taut stance of her body and in the twisting of her hands in her lap.

'You okay?' he asked.

'Sure.' The word was too swift, the smile too bright.

'It's all right to be nervous. You've been in hiding for weeks.'

'I'll be fine.' Slim bare shoulders lifted. 'I just loathe being gawped at. You know…? Plus, you *do* realise there is every chance people will chuck bread rolls at me, or worse?'

'Not on my watch,' he said as the limo glided to a stop. 'But if they do we'll face it together.' The words were all wrong. 'As employer and employee—colleagues…professionals.' Okay… Now he was overcompensating. 'You can do this, Ruby.'

A small determined nod was her response as the car door was opened by the driver. Ethan slid along the leather seat and stepped out, waited as Ruby followed suit. Before she could so much as step from the car a bevy of reporters flocked around them. Quelling the urge to actually move closer to her, Ethan turned to face them, angled his body to shield Ruby.

'So, Ruby, have you decided to break your silence about Hugh Farlane?'

'Ethan, is it true that you've *hired* Ruby, or is this something more personal?'

Ethan raised his hands. 'Easy, guys. Give Ruby some space, please. We get that you're pleased to see her, but she needs to breathe. I need my new restaurant manager to be fully functional.'

Next to him, he sensed the shudder of tension ripple through her body, heard her inhalation of breath—and then she stepped forward.

'Hey, guys. I'm happy to chat about my new role—which I am *very* excited about as the next step in my career—but I have nothing to say about Hugh.'

His chest warmed with admiration at the cool confidence of her tone and the poise she generated.

'That's old news,' he interpolated. 'Our concern is with the future and with Caversham's new venture. Ruby is already doing an amazing job, and I'm looking forward to continuing to work with her.'

'Best keep an eye on your wallet, then, Ethan!'

'What about you, Ruby? Is this a new game plan? To get your mitts on Ethan and the Caversham bank balance?'

She flinched, and Ethan swivelled with lethal speed, the urge to lash out contained and leashed, his tone smooth as ice.

'My wallet is perfectly safe, but many thanks for your concern. I have no doubt that Ruby has the same game plan as me. Right now I'm concentrating on the grand opening of Caversham Castle—the guest list is shaping up nicely. My plan is to grant exclusive coverage to a magazine—though I haven't decided who yet. Perhaps we'll discuss it over dinner.'

The implication was clear. *Drop the gold-digger angle and you might be in with a chance.*

The reporters dispersed, oiled away with ingratiating smiles, and satisfaction touched him. They would stop ripping Ruby to shreds, Hugh Farlane would in turn back off, public interest would die down and the bullies and the nutcases would retreat.

His aim was achieved—his anger channelled to achieve the desired result. Control was key—emotions needed to be ruled and used. When you let your emotions rule you then you lost control. And Ethan was never walking that road again.

Without thought he placed his hand on the small of her back to guide her forward and then wished he hadn't. *Too close, too much*—a reminder that the physical awareness hadn't diminished.

It was with relief that he entered the warmth of the restaurant and Ruby stepped away from him. Her face flushed as her gaze skittered away from his and she looked around.

'Wow!'

'Tony Pugliano is a fan of Christmas,' Ethan said.

The whole restaurant was a dazzling testament to that. The winter grotto theme was delicate, yet pervasive. Lights like icicles glittered from the ceiling and a suspended ice sculpture captured the eye. Windows and mirrors were frosted, and each table displayed scented star-shaped candles that filled the room with the elusive scent of Christmas.

'It's beautiful…' Ruby breathed.

'You like it?' boomed a voice.

Ethan dragged his gaze from Ruby's rapt features to see Tony Pugliano crossing the floor towards them.

'Ethan.' Tony pulled him into a bear hug and slapped his back. 'This is fabulous, no? Welcome to my winter palace. Ruby—it's good to see you.'

'You too—and it's glorious, Tony.'

The grizzled Italian beamed. 'And now, for you, I have reserved the best table—you will be private, and yet you will appreciate every bit of the restaurant's atmosphere. Anything you want you must ask and it is yours, my friends.'

'Thank you, Tony. We appreciate it.'

'We really do,' Ruby said as they followed in Tony's expansive wake to a table that outdid all the other tables in the vicinity.

Crystal glasses seized the light and glittered from each

angled facet, a plethora of star candles dotted the table, and the gleam of moisture sheened the champagne already in an ice bucket.

'Sit, sit…' Tony said. 'I have, for you, chosen the best—the very best of our menu. You need not even have to think—you can simply enjoy.'

Ruby watched his departing back and opened her mouth, closed it again as a waiter glided towards them, poured the champagne and reverently placed a plate of canapés in front of them.

'Made by Signor Pugliano himself. There is *arancini di riso* filled with smoked mozzarella cheese, radicchio ravioli, bresaola and pecorino crostini drizzled with truffle oil, and Jerusalem artichokes with chestnut velouté, perfumed with white truffle oil.'

'That sounds marvellous,' Ruby managed.

Once the waiter had gone she met Ethan's gaze, clocked his smile and forced her toes to remain uncurled. It was a smile—nothing more.

'This is almost as miraculous as what I just witnessed. I am considering how to lift my jaw from my knees.' She shook her head. 'Tony Pugliano is renowned as one of the toughest, most brusque, most temperamental chefs in the country and round you he's turned into some sort of pussycat. How? Why? What gives?'

His smile morphed into a grin. 'It's my famous charm.'

'Rubbish.' However charming Ethan was—and that was a point she had no wish to dwell on—it wouldn't affect Tony Pugliano. 'Plus, I know Hugh eats here, so I'm amazed he seemed so happy to see me.'

'You are underrating my charm capacity,' Ethan said.

Picking up a canapé, she narrowed her eyes. Nope—she wasn't buying it. This was zip to do with charm, but clearly Ethan had no intention of sharing. No surprise there, then.

'Especially given his less than accommodating attitude when I applied for a job here after my break-up with Hugh. Whereas now, if you asked him to, he'd probably give me any job I asked for.' Seeing his eyebrows rise she shook her head. 'Not that I *want* you to do that!'

'You sure?' There was an edge to his voice under the light banter.

Disbelief and hurt mingled. Surely Ethan couldn't possibly think she would go after another job. 'I am one hundred per cent sure. You gave me a chance when no one else would give me the opportunity to wash so much as a dish. So you get one hundred per cent loyalty.'

'I appreciate that.'

Yet the flatness of his tone was in direct variance to the fizz of champagne on her tongue. 'Ethan. I mean it.'

His broad shoulders lifted and for a second the resultant ripple of muscle distracted her. But only for a heartbeat.

'There isn't such a thing as one hundred per cent loyalty. Everyone has a price or a boundary that dissolves loyalty.'

The edge of bitterness caught at her. Had someone let him down? All of a sudden it became imperative that he believed in her.

'Well, *I* don't. You're stuck with me for the duration.'

His large hand cradled his glass, set the light amber liquid swirling. 'If you had an opportunity to have a family then your loyalty might lose some percentage points. Likewise if I stopped paying your salary your allegiance would be forfeit.' He pierced a raviolo. 'That's life, Ruby. No big deal.'

'It is a *huge* deal—and I think I need to make something clear. I do want children, but that does not take precedence above this job. Right now my top priority is to see Caversham Castle firmly ensconced as the lodestar of Caversham Holiday Adventures. I have no intention of starting a family until I am financially secure, with a house, savings in the bank and the ability to support one. But even if I won the Lottery I would not let you down. As for you not paying me—I know you would only do that in a crisis. I would always believe that you'd turn that crisis around, so you'd still have my loyalty.'

Ethan didn't look even remotely moved—it was as if her words had slid off his smooth armour of cynicism.

Dipping a succulent morsel of artichoke into the chestnut velouté, she savoured the taste, wondered how else she could persuade him. She looked up and encountered an ironic glint in his eyes.

'Forget the Lottery. What if Mr Perfect turns up and says he wants a family right now? I wouldn't see you for dust.'

The words stung—what would it take to show him that he could trust her? 'That won't happen because I'm not planning on a meeting with Mr Perfect. I don't *need* Mr Perfect—or Mr Anyone. My plan is to be a single parent.'

His grey-blue eyes hardened, all emotion vanishing to leave only ice.

The advent of their waiter was a relief and a prevention of further conversation. As if sensing the tension, he worked deftly to remove their used plates and replace them.

'Here is langoustine cooked three different ways. Roasted with a hint of chilli and served with puy lentils, grilled with seared avocado and manuka honey, and a langoustine mousseline with manzanilla,' he said swiftly, before making a dignified retreat with a discreet, *'Buon appetito.'*

Ethan didn't so much as peek down at his plate, and Ruby forced herself to hold his gaze even as regret pounded her temples. Of all the idiotic conversational paths to take, telling Ethan about her single parenthood aspirations rated right up there as the Idiot Trail. Her intent had been to prove her loyalty was genuine, to *reassure* him. Which was nuts.

Ethan was a billionaire…head of a global business—he did not need reassurance from one restaurant manager minion.

'This looks delicious,' she ventured.

'Enjoy it whilst you can. Single parenthood doesn't offer much opportunity to eat like this.'

Was he for real? A trickle of anger seeped into her veins. 'That's a bit of a sweeping statement, don't you think?'

His snort of derision caused her toes to tingle with the urge to kick him.

'No. Do you have any idea of the reality of single parenthood? How hard it is?'

Swallowing down the threat of a mirthless laugh, she slapped some of the langoustine mousse onto some bread and took a bite. Tried to concentrate on the incredible hit to her tastebuds instead of the memories that hovered before her—memories of those childhood years when she had effectively looked after her siblings. Dark-haired Tom, blue-eyed Philippa and baby Edie…

Yes! she wanted to shout. Yes, she did know how hard it was—but she also knew with all her being that it was worth it.

'I fully understand how enormous a responsibility parenting is and I know it will be hard. But I also know it will be incredibly rewarding.'

Ever since she'd lost her siblings, understood she would never be with them again. Ruby had known with every cell of her body and soul that she wanted a family.

Desperately she tried to neutralise her expression but it was too late—his blue-grey eyes considered her and his face lost some of its scowl.

'Those are words, Ruby. Easy to say. But the reality of caring for a family and supporting them at the same time on your own is way more daunting.' His voice sounded less harsh, yet the words were leaden with knowledge.

'I know it won't be easy.'

'No, it won't. Plus it's not all about babies and how cute and sweet they are.'

'I get that.' Her teeth were now clenched so tightly her jaw ached. 'I am not a fool, basing a decision like this on a baby's cute factor.'

Given her plan to adopt, it was more than possible that she'd opt for older children. Children such as she and her siblings had been.

'Babies grow up—into toddlers, into schoolchildren and into teenagers. Sometimes when you're on your own, trying to do it all, it can go wrong.' A shadow darkened his features and he scoured his palm over his face as if in an effort to erase it.

For a heartbeat doubt shook her—Tom had been five, the girls even younger when social services had finally hauled the whole family into care. If that hadn't happened would it all have gone wrong for them? Maybe it would—but that was because back then she'd been a child herself. This time she had it all *planned*.

'I told you. I won't embark on having a family until I have sufficient resources to make it possible. I will make sure I can work part-time, I will have the best childcare known to mankind, and—' Breaking off, she picked up her fork and pulled her plate towards her. Shook her head. 'I have no idea why I am justifying myself to you. Who made you the authority on single parenthood?'

'No one. But I am concerned that you are jumping the gun. Just because Hugh Farlane turned out to be a number one schmuck it doesn't mean you have to dive into single parenthood. Maybe this desire for kids on your own is a reaction to how badly it worked out with Hugh. I don't think you should make any hasty decisions, that's all. It's a mighty big step to take.'

His deep tone had gentled, the concern in it undoubtedly genuine, and that was worse than his scorn. That she could have dismissed, or countered with anger. But care triggered in her an alarming yearn to confide in him, to explain that her desire for a family was way more than a whim activated by Hugh's perfidy.

Bad idea. Yet she had to say something.

'I know that.' She did. 'But this is not a rebound decision from Hugh. Truly it isn't. It feels right.'

'Why?'

Ruby hesitated, picked up her glass and sipped a swirl of champagne, relieved to see their waiter approaching. Her brain raced as he placed the next course in front of them, rapidly explained that it consisted of crispy skinned chicken breast with black truffles, spinach and a white port sauce, and then discreetly melted into the background.

This would be the perfect opportunity to turn the conversation. Yet surely there was no harm in answering the question—maybe it was time to remind herself of her goals and her motivations…set it all out.

A warning chime pealed from the alcoves of her mind. This was meant to be a professional dinner. It was hard to see that this conversation was anything *but* personal. But for some indefinable reason it seemed natural. The ding-dong of alarm pealed harder. This was how it had felt a decade before. Curled up in a chair in the beige metallic confines of a hostel room, the temptation to talk and confide had ended up in disaster.

But it was different now, and…and, *truth be told*—she wanted him to know that she was all grown up…not some daft girl who hadn't thought through the idea of going it alone into parenthood. So one last explanation and then she would move the conversation into professional waters.

CHAPTER SIX

ETHAN KNEW THAT the whole discussion had derailed spectacularly and that it behoved him to push it onto a blander path.

But, he couldn't. Intrigue and frustration intermeshed at the idea of Ruby launching herself into the murk of single parenthood through choice.

Chill, Ethan.

There were many, many excellent single parents—he knew that. But it was a tough road; he knew from bitter personal experience exactly how difficult it was—had seen how it had played out for his mother.

'So why single parenthood?' he repeated.

Ruby carefully cut up a piece of chicken and for a moment he thought she would change the subject, then she put her cutlery down and shrugged.

'Because I'm not exactly clued up at choosing good father material.'

'Just because Hugh didn't work out…'

Ruby snorted. '"Didn't work out" is a bit of an understatement. But the point is that it's not just Hugh. You see, Hugh wasn't the first person to tug the wool over my eyes. Being taken in is my speciality—I could write a thesis. When I was nineteen there was Gary. I believed Gary to be a misunderstood individual who had been wrongfully dismissed. Turned out he was a drunken layabout who'd been quite rightly fired. Then a few years later there was Steve—a self-confessed gambler who swore himself hoarse that he was trying to quit. In reality he was keen on extracting as much money from me as possible to fund the local betting shop.'

A wave of her fork in his direction.

'Hugh you know about. So surely you can see the theme here. I am not a good judge of character. So it makes sense to do this alone.'

'But why do it at all? Or at least why do it now? You're twenty-six.'

'You are thirty. Most thirty-year-olds aren't billionaire CEOs of their own global business. Ten years ago I knew I wanted a family and you knew you wanted to make it big. You've done that through grit and hard work and drive. Well, now I am doing the same to get a family.'

A frown slashed his brow. 'Children aren't an acquisition.'

'I am not suggesting they are.' She gave an expressive roll of her eyes as she huffed out a breath that left her exasperation to hover in the air. '*Sheesh*. What is wrong with wanting to have children?'

'Nothing.'

For Pete's sake—he'd muttered the word, and now his lips had pressed together as a barrier to the further words that wanted to spill from his lips with unprecedented freedom. To stem the explanation that having children could lead to devastation not joy.

His mother had been deprived of her daughter—her pride and joy. For an instant the image of Tanya's lifeless body assaulted his brain. His sister—driven to take her own life. And he hadn't known—hadn't been able to protect her.

His mother had been left with him, her son, a mirror image of her violent criminal husband. The son she had never been able to love but had done her duty by. Until he'd driven her to snap point and she'd washed her hands of him.

For a split second the memory of the packed case and the hand-over to social services jarred his brain. No fault of hers—in her eyes he'd been on the road to following his father's footsteps. His impassioned pleas for forgiveness and promises to reform would have simply been further shades of the man she despised.

Ethan shut down the thought process and concentrated on Ruby's face. Those sapphire eyes, delicate features and that determined chin. Her expression of challenge had morphed into one of concern and he forced his vocal cords into action and his face into neutral.

'There is nothing wrong with wanting children. I just think you need to give single parenthood a lot of thought and not enter the whole venture with rose-coloured spectacles. That's all.'

End of subject, and Ethan picked up his knife and fork and started to eat.

Ruby twirled a tendril of hair around her finger. 'What about you? Where do you stand on the venture into parenthood? Don't you hope for a family one day?'

'No.'

The idea of a family was enough to bring him out in hives. Family had brought him nothing except a one-way channel to loss, heartbreak and rejection. So what was the point?

'Never?' Surprise laced her tone.

'No.' Perhaps monosyllables would indicate to Ruby that this wasn't a topic he wished to pursue.

'Why not?'

Clearly the indirect approach hadn't worked—so it was time to make it clear.

'That's my personal choice.'

Hurt mingled with anger flashed across her features. *Fair enough, Ethan.* He'd been mighty fine with a personal conversation when it was *her* personal life under discussion.

'In brief, it's not what I want. Like you. I've worked hard to get to where I am and I don't want to rock the boat. I'm exactly where I want to be. And I know exactly where I'm going.'

'Isn't that a bit boring? I mean, will that be your life for ever? Buy another property…set up another venture? What happens when you run out of countries?'

Ethan blinked at the barrage of questions. 'Boring? I run a global business, travel the world on a daily basis, have more than enough money and a pretty nifty lifestyle. So, nope. Not humdrum.'

'But…' A shake of her head and she turned her attention back to her plate.

Following suit, he took another mouthful, tried to appreciate the delicacy of the truffles, the infusion of port, the tenderness of the meat. To his own irritation he couldn't let it go.

'But what?'

Her shoulders lifted and for a second his gaze lingered on the creamy skin, the enticing hint of cleavage.

'That world of yours—that non-rocking boat of yours—only contains you, and that sounds lonely. Unless you're in a relationship that you haven't mentioned?'

'Nope. It's a one-man vessel and I'm good with that.'

'So you don't want a long-term relationship or kids? Ever?'

'I don't want any type of relationship. Full stop. I make sure my…my liaisons are brief.' Like a night—a weekend, tops.

Ruby's eyed widened and his exasperation escalated as he identified compassion in her.

'But you've worked so hard to build up Caversham. What's the point if you don't have someone to hand it over to?'

'That's hardly a reason to have a child.'

'Not a reason, but surely part of being a parent is the desire to pass on your values or beliefs. A part of yourself.'

The very idea made him go cold. 'I think that's a bit egocentric. You can't have children just to inculcate them with your beliefs.'

'No!' She shook her head, impatience in the movement. 'You're making it sound as if I want to instil them with questionable propaganda. I don't. But I *do* believe we are programmed with a need to nurture. To love and be loved.'

'Well, I'm the exception to the rule.'

Her chin angled in defiance. 'Or your programming has gone haywire.'

Ethan picked his glass up and sipped the fizz. No way would he rise to that bait.

'The point is, even if you're right, it is wrong to put that burden on someone. That responsibility. You shouldn't have a child just because you want someone to love and love you back. There are enough people out there already. The world doesn't need more.'

'Actually…' Ruby hesitated.

'Actually, what?'

'Nothing.'

Before he could respond the boom of Tony Pugliano's voice rang out. 'So, my friends. It was all to your liking?'

Ruby's thoughts whirled as she strove to concentrate on Tony's question, primed her lips to smile. Maybe this was an intervention from providence itself—a reinforcement of her decision to cease with the confidences.

'It was incredible, Tony!' she stated.

'How could it be anything else?' the chef declared. 'And now we have the perfect end to the perfect meal—I have for you a sample of the very best desserts in the world.'

He waved an expansive hand and the waiter appeared with an enormous platter, which he placed in the middle of the table.

'I, Tony Pugliano, prepared these with my own hands

for your delectation. There is praline mousseline with cherry confit, clementine cheesecake, almond and black sesame pannacotta and a dark chilli chocolate lime *torta*.' He beamed as he clapped Ethan on the shoulder. 'And of course all this is on the house.'

There went her jaw again—headed kneewards. *On the house.* She doubted such words had ever crossed Tony's lips before.

'You look surprised. No need. Because never, *never* can I thank this man enough. You saved my Carlo—my one and only child. You are a good man, Ethan, and I thank you with all my heart.'

Tony seemed sublimely unaware of Ethan's look of intense discomfort. Yet the shadow in Ethan's eye, the flash of darkness, made her chest band in instinctive sympathy.

'I think this meal goes a long way towards thanks,' she said. 'It was divine. I don't suppose you would share the secret of the truffle sauce in…?'

The tactic worked. As if recalled to his chef persona, Tony gave a mock roar and shook his head.

'*Never.* Not even for you would I reveal the Pugliano family secret. It has passed from one generation to the next for centuries and shall remain sacrosanct for ever. Now—I shall leave you to enjoy the fruit of my unsurpassable skills.'

Once he had made a majestic exit, Ethan nodded. 'Thanks for the change of subject.'

'No problem.' Ruby reached out and selected a mini-dessert. 'I knew it took more than charm to get Tony Pugliano grazing from your hand. Whatever you did for his son must have been a big deal.'

Ethan shrugged his shoulders, the casual gesture at variance with the wariness in his clenched jaw. 'I was in a position to help his son and I did so. Simple as that.'

'It didn't sound simple to me. More like fundamental.'

'How about another change of subject?'

Picking up a morsel of cheesecake, he popped it in his mouth. His expression was not so much closed as locked, barred *and* padlocked—with a 'Trespassers Will Be Prosecuted' sign up to boot.

'I think our dinner conversation has gone a bit off the business track.'

He wasn't wrong. In fact she should be doused in relief that he didn't want to rewind their conversational spool. Because she had been on the cusp of intimacy—tempted to confide to Ethan that her plan was to adopt, about to spill even more of her guts. And a girl needed her intestines to survive. Something she would do well to remember.

Her family plans were zilch to do with Ethan Caversham. And similarly there was no need for her to wonder why he had decided to eschew love of any sort from a partner or a child. Over the past week she'd gained his trust, they had built up an easy working relationship, and she would not risk that. She mustn't let this man tug her into an emotional vortex again. Ten years ago it had been understandable. Now it would be classed as sheer stupidity.

'So,' he said. 'How about we start with what you think of this restaurant? With your guest's hat on?'

'Modern. Sweeping. The glass effect works to make it sleek, and his table placement is extraordinary. I love the balcony—it's contemporary and it's got buzz. Those enormous flower arrangements are perfect. As for the Christmas effect—it is superb.'

Maybe she could blame the glitter of the pseudo icicles or the scent of cinnamon and gingerbread that lingered in the air for flavouring their conversation with intimacy...

'Definitely five-star. But is this what you want for Caversham?'

'Five stars? Absolutely.'

'I get that, but I have an idea that you're holding some

information back. About your plans for the castle.' Something she couldn't quantify made her know that what Tony Pugliano had achieved wasn't exactly what Ethan was after. His body stilled and she scooped up a spoonful of the cheesecake, allowed the cold tang of clementine to melt on her tongue. 'Am I right?'

Ethan drummed a rhythm on the table. 'Yes,' he said finally. 'But it's on a need-to-know basis.'

'Don't you think that as your restaurant manager I "need to know"?'

'Yes—and when it's the right time I will tell you. For now, I'd like to discuss the grand opening.'

Determination not to show hurt allowed her to nod, relieved that the movement shook her hair forward to shield her expression from those all-seeing eyes.

'Fair enough.'

An inhalation of breath and she summoned enthusiasm—she *was* excited about her ideas for the event and she would not let Ethan's caginess shadow that.

'I thought we could have a medieval theme—maybe even a ball. And what do you think about the idea of making it a fundraiser? I know we've already confirmed the guest list, but I think people will happily buy tickets for a good cause. Especially if they also get publicity from it. We could offer exclusive coverage to one of the celebrity gossip mags and—'

Ruby broke off. Ethan sat immobile, his silence uninterpretable.

Then… 'It's a great idea,' Ethan said. A sudden rueful smile tipped his lips and curled her toes. 'In fact it ties in perfectly with my ideas for the castle. So I guess you now "need to know".' His smile vanished and left his lips in a hard straight line. 'In brief, I want to run Caversham Castle as a charitable venture. So kick-starting it with a fundraiser would work well.'

It was as if each word had been wrung from him and confusion creased her brow. 'I love the idea, but can you tell me more? Is it a particular charity you want to raise money for? The more information I have the more successful I can make the event.'

'The money raised will go to a charity that helps troubled teens. Gets them off the streets, helps them back on their feet if they've been in juvie.'

It took a few moments for the true meaning of his words to make an impact, and then it took all her will-power not to launch herself across the table and wrap her arms around him. Only the knowledge that they were in a public place and the suspicion that Ethan would loathe the display kept her in her seat. But the idea that Ethan Caversham, renowned tough guy and entrepreneur, had a different side to him made her tummy go gooey. He'd experienced life on the streets, been a troubled teen himself and now he wanted to help others.

'I think that is an amazing idea. Brilliant. We will make this the best fundraiser ever.' Her mind was already fizzing with ideas. 'How about we go back to my suite for coffee and a brainstorm?'

Ethan bit back a groan and tried to get a grip. Better late than never, after all. Somehow he'd utterly lost his grasp of events—the conversation had spiralled out of control and now he could see more than a flicker of approval in Ruby's eyes. An approval he didn't want.

Time to try and relocate even a shard of perspective.

Ruby was his employee—one who could help make this fundraiser work. Therefore he should be pleased at her enthusiasm and accept her approval on a professional level, not a personal one.

So... 'Coffee and a brainstorm sound good.'

'Perfect.' A blink of hesitation and then she reached out

and covered his hand with her own. 'I will make this *rock*. I remember how it felt to be a teenager on the streets. It was like being shrouded in invisibility. Even the people who dropped a ten pence piece in front of me did it without even a glance.'

A small shiver ran through her body, and her eyes were wide in a face that had been leached of colour.

'The idea of subsisting on people's charity made me feel small and helpless and angry and very alone.'

The image of Ruby huddled on the streets smote his chest.

'It is an endemic problem. I know there are hostels and soup kitchens and the like, and that is incredible, but I want to do something more hands-on, more direct—' He broke off.

The image of a homeless Ruby had set him galloping on his hobby horse.

'Like what?' She leant forward, her entire being absorbed in their conversation. 'Come on, Ethan—spill. I want to help.'

Her sincerity was vibrant and how could he quench that? It would be wrong.

'My idea for the castle is to open it as a luxury hotel for nine months of the year and then use the proceeds to utilise it differently for the remaining three months. As a place for troubled teens. Surfing holidays but also training courses, so they can learn job skills—maybe in the hotel industry.'

He'd explained his idea to Rafael, but somehow the words were much harder to utter now—maybe because Rafael understood his need for redemption, retribution, second chances. Ruby didn't. And there it was—the dawning of approbation, the foretaste of hero worship simmering in her beautiful eyes.

'That is an awesome idea,' she said quietly. 'Truly. Tony was right. You are a good man.'

The words were not what he wanted to hear—there was too much in his past for him to have earned that epithet.

'I'm not quite ready for a halo—all I plan to do is use the profits from a business venture to try and do some good. That's all. Don't big it up into more than it is.'

A push of the nearly empty dessert plate across the table.

'Now, eat up and then let's go brainstorm.'

There went her chin again. 'You're not just raising money—you have a hands-on plan that will help some of those homeless kids out there. That's pretty big in my book, and nothing you say will change my opinion. Now, we'd better find Tony and say goodbye.'

One effusive farewell later and they were outside. Next to him, Ruby inhaled the cold crisp air and looked up into the darkness of the sky. 'Do you think it will snow?'

'Unlikely.'

'So no white Christmas?' Ruby said with a hint of wistfulness. 'It's a shame, really—can you imagine how beautiful Cornwall would be covered in snow?' She shook her head. 'On the subject of Christmas…how do you feel about a Christmas party at Caversham? Not on Christmas Day, obviously, but maybe Christmas Eve drinks? Or eve of Christmas Eve drinks? For suppliers and locals. A lot of the staff we've taken on are local, so I think it would be a nice idea. Bank some goodwill…show the Caversham community ethos.'

Ethan considered—it was a good idea. But not in the run-up to Christmas.

'It doesn't fit with my plans.' More plans he didn't wish to share. 'Maybe we could think about it later? After New Year? Anyway, I know you said you had Christmas plans as well. So take some time off. From the twenty-first—that's not a problem.'

'Okay. Thanks.'

Enthusiasm was not prominent in her voice and Ethan

swallowed the urge to ask her exactly what her plans were. Not his business—and not fair, as he didn't want to share his own.

The limo pulled up and he held the door open for Ruby to slide in, averted his eyes from the smooth length of her leg, hoped the tantalising cinnamon smell wouldn't whirl his head further. *Employee, employee, employee.*

As soon as the car started she leant forward; now her enthusiasm shone through the dim interior of the car.

'So—for the medieval banquet…I've already done loads of research and I've got some fab dishes we could use. What do you think about eels in a thick spicy purée, loach in a cold green sauce and a meat tile—which is chicken cooked in a spiced sauce of pounded crayfish tails, almonds and toasted bread, garnished with whole crayfish tails. Or capon pasties—or even eel and bream pasties. I've spoken to a medieval re-enactor and I reckon he'll know someone who will come along and cook us some samples. We could even put together a recipe book and sell it—raise some extra funds.'

'Excellent ideas. Though…what is loach?'

'It's a freshwater fish. Mind you, I'm not sure you can get it here.' A quick rummage in her evening bag netted a small notebook and pen. 'I'll check. What about an auction?' A sudden grin illuminated her face. 'Hey! You could talk to Tony. Auction off a cooking lesson with Antonio Pugliano. What do you think?'

His breath caught as his lungs suspended their function. One thought only was in his mind—Ruby was so beautiful, so animated, so unutterably gorgeous, and all he wanted was to tug her across the seat and kiss her.

CHAPTER SEVEN

RUBY BROKE OFF as all her ideas took flight from her brain in one perfect V-shaped swoop, evicted by an across-the-board sweep of desire. Ethan's pupils had darkened and the atmosphere in the limousine morphed. Words withered on her tongue she shifted towards him, propelled by instinct, pulled by his mesmerising eyes.

His features seemed ever so slightly softened by the shadows in the dim interior. Or maybe it was because now she had gained some insight. This man cared about so much more than profit and business domination. He hadn't let ambition consume him to the point where he forgot people in need. Forgot the Ethan and Ruby of a decade ago.

'Ethan…' she whispered.

Somehow they were right alongside each other, her leg pressed against the solid strength of his thigh, and she let out a small sigh. The closeness felt right, and she twisted her torso so she faced him, placed a hand over his heart, felt the steady beat increase tempo. Then his broad, capable hand cupped her jaw oh so gently, his thumb brushed her lip and she shivered in response.

His grey-blue eyes locked onto hers with a blaze of desire that melted all barriers, called to something deep inside her. She parted her lips, sheer anticipation hollowed her tummy—and then with precipitous speed his expression changed.

'What am I doing?'

The words were muttered with a low ferocity as his hand dropped from her face, left her skin bereft.

He hauled in an audible breath. 'This is not a good idea. I wish it were, but it isn't.'

It took a few seconds for the words to register, to make sense, and then reality hit. Forget Ethan. What was *she* doing? This was her boss…this was Ethan Caversham… this was a disastrous idea.

The idea that a reporter with some sort of lens able to penetrate tinted windows might have caught them on camera made her cringe. But even worse than that was the sheer stupidity of getting involved in any way with Ethan. There was an edge of danger—a foreshadow she recognised all too well and that urged her to scramble back to her side of the seat.

'You're right. I…I guess we got carried away. Food, champagne, limo… It's easily done. We'll forget it ever happened, yes? But would you mind if we took up the brainstorming tomorrow?'

She needed time to detonate that near-kiss from her psyche, scrub it from her memory banks. Right now the idea of Ethan in her suite was impossible to contemplate. A few hours by herself and she would rebuild the façade, resume the role of Ruby Hampton, Restaurant Manager. Then all would be well—because this time the mask would be uncrackable, fireproof, indestructible…

Unable to stop herself, she glanced nervously out of the window, checking for reporters.

Ethan noticed, and his lips pulled into a tight, grim line. 'Worried about the paps? You're safe in here, you know.'

'I know.'

And she did—deep down. Thanks to Ethan, who had neutralised the reporters with smooth, cold ease and rendered them powerless. The memory triggered a small thrill that she hastened to suppress. Yes, Ethan had protected her—but he had done so on principle. To him, the Hugh Farlanes and the paps out for a story at any price were scum and he would shield anyone from them. It wasn't personal. He would champion anyone broken or wounded or hurt.

But that near-kiss was pretty personal, pointed out a small inner voice. Which was exactly why he'd shut it down. And she should be grateful for that—would be once she'd escaped this limousine, where the air swirled with might-have-beens and what-ifs.

When they arrived back at the castle Ruby practically shot from the car through the grand entrance. 'I'll see you in the morning,' she called over her shoulder.

An expletive dropped from Ethan's lips, making her pause and turn on the stairs. He scrubbed a hand down his jaw, looking weary.

'Listen, Ruby, we need to get rid of the awkwardness. We have a lot to do in a minimal amount of time to upgrade the opening dinner to a ball. So we must manage it—nothing happened and nothing will happen. It was one fool moment and I will not let that ruin the professional relationship we have established.'

'You're right. It wasn't even a kiss. No big deal, right?'

An infinitesimal hesitation and then he nodded. 'No big deal.'

Ethan's head pounded as he looked across at Ruby. Seated at her desk she was back in professional mode—glossy black hair pinned back into a svelte chignon, dressed in dark grey trousers and a pinstripe jacket over a crisp white shirt. Her posture spoke of wariness and her eyes held a matching guard. The spontaneous trust, the spark doused and if Ethan could have worked out a way to kick himself round Cornwall he would have.

She straightened some papers on her desk, the action unnecessary. 'If it's OK with you rather than brainstorm I'll put together a presentation.'

Which meant he'd miss out on seeing her features light

with enthusiasm as she came up with ideas. Mind you it was that illumination that had led to his disastrous impulse the night before. Impulses never ended well—he knew that to bitter cost.

Ruby was a woman with a plan to have a family—she was barely out of a demoralising relationship, and he had no business kissing her. 'Sounds good. Come down to my office when you're ready.' Maybe he'd rustle up some stilts to shore up the conversation. As he clicked the door shut he vowed to himself that by hook or by crook he'd win back their former camaraderie. It was necessary in order to maximise their productivity and their ability to pull of this ball. It was zip to do with a desire to see her lips curve up into a genuine smile.

So first he'd throw himself into work, get himself back on track and then he'd charm Ruby back to the status quo. But one conference call later a perfunctory knock heralded the appearance of Ruby and camaraderie looked to be the last thing on her mind—in fact she could have personified the cliché spitting mad.

'I have a message for you.' Annoyance clipped each syllable.

'Shoot.'

Her chest rose and he could almost see metaphorical steam issuing from her. 'It's from Tony Pugliano.'

Ah... 'Why didn't you put the call through to me?'

'Obviously I tried to, but you were engaged, and then Tony said it didn't matter—he could discuss it with me. Which was when he informed me that he will make a delivery of super-special pizzas on the twenty-second of December. Explained how happy he is to support such a worthy cause and how much he admires your plan to give these teens in care a wonderful time over the Christmas period. So there you go—message delivered.'

With that she swivelled on one black-booted foot and headed for the door.

That wasn't just anger that radiated off her—there was hurt as well.

'Ruby—wait.'

A heartbeat of hesitation and then she turned to face him. 'Yes.'

'I should have told you.'

Her shoulders lifted. 'It's your business—you don't have to tell me everything.'

'No. But I should have told you this.'

'So why didn't you?'

'We have been and will be working full-time until the ball. I figured you'd deserve a break—those days will be pretty full-on. Plus the kids will be here from the twenty-second to the twenty-fourth, and I know you have Christmas plans. I didn't want you to feel obliged to cancel them, or to feel guilty. It's no big deal.'

All the truth—though nowhere near the complete truth. But it was difficult to explain his utter disinclination to let her see the full extent of his charitable activities.

Her expression softened as she studied his face, though a small frown still nipped at her wide brow. 'Your idea of what is a big deal and mine is different. But you're right—you should have told me. Now I know, I would like to help.'

Bad idea… The previous night had amply demonstrated that a break would do them good. 'No need. I have it all covered here. There is nothing for you to do—so go and enjoy yourself.'

'Ethan, I don't want to go and enjoy myself. I know I can help. Why don't you want me to? Is it because…?' Her voice faltered for a second and then she met his gaze full-on. 'Because of what happened last night.'

'No. I don't want you to help because I don't want you to

get burn out. There is a huge amount of work to be done in the next few days. You'll need a break. I've got it covered.'

Ethan could feel the grooves in the floor where his heels were dug in. Instinct told him that if they weren't careful, complications would abound.

'I bet you haven't.' Her chin angled, pugnacious. 'Tell me your plans and if I can work out how to improve them I get to help. Deal?'

Great! Instinct had made another express delivery—this was über-important to Ruby and it went deep, though he wasn't sure why.

Expelling a sigh of pure exasperation, he shrugged. 'Fine. I wanted to do it all actually on Christmas Day, but that didn't work out. So…a busload of teenagers will arrive here on the twenty-second. They are all either in children's homes or in foster care and they've all got a chequered history. We'll have a pizza, DVD and games night. I've ordered a billiards table and a darts board. On the twenty-third I and a few surf instructors will take them out for a day of water sports. We'll come back and I'm having caterers in to serve up a Christmas dinner. Another relaxed games evening, then to bed. Another morning's water sport on Christmas Eve and then they head back.'

There—you couldn't say fairer than that surely? So who knew why Ruby was shaking her head?

'What you have scheduled is brilliant, but I can make it better,' she said flatly.

'How?'

'Can I sit?'

Once he'd nodded she lowered herself onto a chair, rested her elbows on the desk and cupped her chin.

'I think you've missed something.'

'What? Another game? A…?'

'The magic of Christmas. You've mentioned Christmas dinner, but otherwise it could be any weekend. This is about the spirit of Christmas even if it's not actually Christmas Day. So what about a tree?'

'I thought about that and I figured the last thing they'll want is a tree and lots of schmaltz. These kids are tough and they've been through the mill. They'll want to obliterate Christmas—suppress the tainted memories it evokes.'

'Maybe some of them think like that—maybe that's what they need to think in order to get through Christmas. Dissing Christmas is their method of self-defence. But deep down they are still kids, and they deserve to be given a real Christmas—to see that Christmas doesn't always have to suck, that it can be wonderful and magical. It could be that what they're going back to is dismal, or lonely, or grim, so this two days you give them has to be something precious. Maybe to help them dilute those tainted memories.'

Her words strummed him... They spoke of a deep, vibrant sincerity and an underlying genuine comprehension, and Ethan knew that such empathy could only come from one place.

'Were you ever in care?' he asked. 'Is that why this is so important to you?'

She blinked, as if the question had zinged out of nowhere and caught her completely on the hop, skip and jump.

A flush seeped into her cheeks and then she shrugged. 'Yes—and yes. I was in care, and that's why I want to be part of this. I was eleven when it happened, and although I know that foster care can sometimes work out well it didn't for me. Looking back, I can see I was a difficult child to care for—so no surprise that I was moved from place to place. Including a stint in a residential home. I empathise with these kids. Because I remember vividly how awful holiday times were. Especially Christmas. But that doesn't mean I've given up on Christmas. And I don't want these kids to either.'

'I'm sorry the care system didn't work for you.'

'Don't be. I'm not after sympathy. I'm after your agreement to let me loose on this Christmas break. What do you think?'

Ethan drummed his fingers on the table. Of course he could shut this down and tell her no, but what kind of heel would that make him? To turn away someone who fervently wanted to help with a cause he fervently believed in?

'Go for it. You have carte blanche.' His smile twisted a little 'If you can give these kids some of the magic of Christmas then that would be a great thing. But I'm not sure it'll be easy. Some of these kids come from a very notorious estate and they have all been in serious trouble at one time or another.'

Images of the estate dotted his retina like flash photography. Depressing grey high-rise buildings, tower blocks of misery, with the smell of urine up the stairs, lifts that never worked. Vandalised park areas daubed with graffiti where kids roamed in gangs, so many of them caught in a vicious cycle of young offenders' units and truancy, the product of misery and neglect. Guilt stamped him—because he hadn't had that excuse for the road he'd chosen to walk.

Suddenly aware of Ruby's small frown, he shook his head to dislodge the thoughts. 'Just keep it in mind that you may need more than a magic wand and sprinkle of glitter,' he said.

'Sure…'

The speculative gaze she planted on him sent a frisson of unease through him. It was as if she were considering waving that wand and glitter pot at him.

He tugged his keyboard across the desk. 'Now you're here let's start that brainstorm session and get down to business.'

Time to make it clear this was a non-magical, glitter-free zone.

CHAPTER EIGHT

'THROUGH HERE, PLEASE.'

Two days later Ruby directed the three men toting the most enormous Christmas tree she'd ever seen into the library—the room Ethan had designated as Teen Base.

'That's perfect,' she stated, refusing to allow the battalion of doubts that were making a spirited attempt to gain a foothold in her brain.

It was the tyrannosaurus rex of spruces. Once the delivery men had left she contemplated the sheer enormity of actually decorating the tree, and for a second considered enlisting Ethan's help.

No. The tree had been her idea—plus she had vowed not to orchestrate any time with Ethan that could be avoided. Somehow she had to squash the urge to try to entice him into the idea of liking Christmas—had to suppress the urge for closeness that threatened at every turn.

The problem was the more they discussed the medieval ball and ways to raise money and publicity for their cause, the more she learnt about his ideas for Caversham Castle and the worse her gooey tummy syndrome became. The more he spoke about the youths he wished to help, the more sure she was that his empathy came from his own experiences. Which in turn led to her nutty desire to enmesh Ethan in the magic of Christmas.

Only it was clear he had no wish to enter her net. In the past two days his demeanour had been always professional, with the high expectations she'd become accustomed to, alleviated by a polite charm and appreciation for her work. But there was a guardedness, a caginess that kept her at a distance.

A distance she needed to respect—to welcome, even. Because Ethan Caversham was synonymous with danger. It was an equation she had to remember—because linked to her desire for emotional intimacy was the ever-present underlay of attraction. It was a lose-lose situation all round.

So she'd better get on with the decorations herself.

Inhaling the evocative spruce aroma that now tinged the air, Ruby opened the first box of ornaments with a small sigh of pleasure. This tree would exude Christmas and be the Christmassiest tree ever seen. Or at least the bits she could reach would be...

'Ruby.'

The sound of Ethan's deep voice nearly sent her tumbling from the stepladder.

'Here you are. We're meant to be doing the final run-through of the seating plan.'

Ruby twisted round to face him. 'I am so sorry. I lost track of time.'

'No worries.' His glance rested for a second on the tree. 'Looks good.'

'Good? Is that all you can say.' Ruby stepped backwards to assess her handiwork so far. 'It's flipping marvellous, if I say so myself. I know I've only managed to get less than half done, but I think the bold and beautiful theme works.'

Reds, purples and golds abounded, though she had made sure that the lush green of the pine was also on display. The ornaments were tasteful, but with a vibrant appeal that she thought would at least mean the tree would be noticed.

'So come on. Surely you can do better than "good" as an adjective.'

'Eye-catching,' he said, and she frowned at the obvious effort.

The syllables sounded forced. It was almost as if he didn't want to look at the tree or at her. Well, tough! He'd agreed to her plan to try to offer these youths some Christmas spirit, so the least he could do was be polite.

Better yet... 'Do you want to help me finish decorating it? As you can see it's pretty big—and you're taller than me. Plus it might be fun.'

The challenging smile slid from her lips as she clocked his sudden leaching of colour, his small step backwards. As if he'd seen a ghost.

He scraped a hand down his face as if to force his features into a semblance of normality. 'I'll pass, thanks. Trust me—you wouldn't want me bah-humbugging about the place.'

It was a credible attempt to lighten his expression, marred only by the wary ice-blue flecks in his eyes and the slight clenching of his jaw.

Every instinct told her he was hurting, and without thought she moved towards him and placed her hand over his forearm—the texture of his skin, the rough smattering of hair embedded itself into her fingertips.

'Look what happened to Scrooge. The ghosts of Christmases Past do not have to ruin the possibilities of Christmas Present.'

She'd expected him to scoff at the concept of ghosts—instead he simply shook his head. There was something intangible about him that she didn't understand—the way his blue-grey eyes zoned in on her, haunted, glittering with something elusive, as if they could see something she couldn't.

'Leave it, Ruby. The tree is incredible; you're doing a great job. Find me when it's done. No rush.'

His voice was so flat that instinct told her his spectres hovered close. It seemed clear what she ought to do— let him go, remember his disinclination to get close, the danger signs she had already identified, his need for distance. But she couldn't… She didn't know what had triggered his reaction, doubted he would tell her, but maybe she could help.

'Don't go.'

A frown descended on his brow at her words and she clenched her fingers into her palm and forced herself to hold her ground.

'Ethan. Stay. Try it. Let's decorate together.'

Gathering all her courage, she squatted down and hefted a box of purple baubles.

'Here. I get that you don't want to, and I get that sometimes the past taints the present, but these kids will be here the day after tomorrow and there's lots to be done.'

'You're suggesting tree decoration as some form of therapy?' He was back in control now—on the surface at least—and his voice was a drawl. 'Or have you bitten off more than you can chew?'

'A bit of both… This tree needs help. So—are you in?'

Was he in? Ethan stared down at the box of purple ornaments. Why was he even considering this idea?

Because Ruby had a point. From a practical point of view this gargantuan tree did need to be finished, and if he left Ruby to it she probably wouldn't get it done until past midnight.

And that was a problem because…?

Ruby was the one who had ordered the tree in the first place—and since when had he cavilled at the thought of his staff working overtime? Ethan gusted out a sigh. Since now, apparently. Because—tough business guy or not— if he walked out of this room now he would feel like an A-class schmuck.

He'd have to get over the memories and get on with it. The shock had hit him with unexpected force. For a vivid second the memory of Tanya had been so stark he might have believed he'd been transported back in time. He'd heard his sister's voice persuading him to help decorate the tree, remembered arranging the tinsel and the scruffy, cheap but cheerful decorations under her instruction.

The memory had receded now, and as he looked at Ruby's almost comically hopeful expression he shrugged.

'I'm in.'

That way maybe there'd be a chance of getting some actual work done that day.

Whoa, Ethan, play fair. He'd agreed to this whole magic of Christmas idea; he just hadn't reckoned on the extent of Ruby's enchantment scheme.

'Excellent,' she said. 'So you're in charge of purple. I'll do the red.'

For a while they worked in a silence that seemed oddly peaceful. To his own irritation he found himself stepping down at intervals, to check the effect of his handiwork. A snort of exasperation escaped his lips and Ruby's subsequent chuckle had him glaring across at her.

'Sorry. I couldn't help it. You look so…*absorbed.*'

'Yes, well. If I do something I make sure I do it properly.'

For no reason whatsoever the words travelled across the pine-scented air and took on an unintended undertone… one that brought an image of kissing Ruby with attention to every detail. It was an effort not to crane his neck in a search for mistletoe. Instead his eyes snagged on the lush outline of her lips and desire tautened inside him.

Her fingers rose and touched her lips. He heard her intake of breath and forced his gaze to return to the tree.

'So…' His voice resembled that of a frog. *Try again.* 'So, believe me, my share of this tree will rock and roll.'

A small shake of her head and then her lips tilted into a full-wattage smile. 'See? It is kind of fun, isn't it?'

Ethan blinked—to his own surprise, it was…but it would be a whole lot better if he could tell himself that the reason had zip to do with his fellow decorator. Maybe her palpable belief in the magic of Christmas was contagious. Dear Lord—he'd lost the plot big-time. If he didn't take care he'd find himself with a pillow round his middle in a red suit.

'Could be worse,' he muttered as he stretched up his arm to thread a silver-spangled ball on to a branch.

Hmm… Alarm bells started to toll in his brain. If Ruby had gone this over the top with the tree, what other schemes were afoot?

'So…any other magical plans apart from the tree?'

Ruby expertly unhooked a strand of tinsel and rearranged it. 'I've planned a bake-off.'

'A bake-off?'

'Yup. I think they'll go for it because of all the TV shows. My plan is that everyone has a go at Christmas cookies and gingerbread. It will be friendly—they can judge each other. Or the ones who really don't want to bake can judge. It will make a nice start to the festivities. Then they can eat Tony's pizzas and chill, play some games, maybe catch a Christmas movie. I'll make popcorn.'

'That sounds like a lot of work for you.' Ethan hesitated; he didn't want to hail on her parade or dim her enthusiasm, but… 'You do know that these kids…they may not appreciate your good intentions.'

'Don't worry. I know I'm coming across all Pollyanna, but I have kept a reality check. I've got in extra fire extinguishers, plus I've cleared out all the sharp knives, though I've decided cookie cutters won't be lethal. I know there is a chance none of them will engage. But…' Reaching up, she attached a gold bauble. 'I've got to try. Because if we get through to even one of these kids and create a happy memory of Christmas then it will be worth it. Even if they aren't in a place to show their appreciation.'

'The "dilute the tainted memories" approach?' he said.

'Yup.'

For a second Ethan wondered if that were possible— then knew he was deluded. It wasn't. He wasn't even sure he wanted it to be.

Once he'd believed the best thing to do was obliterate the chain of memories with mindless anger. Beat them into oblivion. Especially the memory of the Christmas after Tanya's death. His mother, him, and the ghost of Tanya. In the end rage had overcome him and he'd hurled the micro-waved stodgy food at the wall, watched the gravy trickle and blend in with the grungy paint. Once he'd started he hadn't been able to stop—had pulled the scrawny tree from its pot, flung it down. Stamped on it, kicked it—as if the tree had been the bully who had driven Tanya to her death.

His mother hadn't said a word; then she had left the room with a curt, 'Clean it up.'

Seconds later he'd heard the sound of the television and known that it was the end of Christmas. By the following Christmas she'd consigned him to social services and he'd taken to the streets, consumed by grief, anger and mis-ery. Then finally he'd decided to take control—to leash the demons and channel his emotions in order to succeed.

With an abrupt movement he stood back. 'I'm done.'

Seeing the snap of concern in her blue eyes, he forced his lips into a smile. Ruby's way wasn't his way, but that wasn't to say it wasn't a good way—and she was right. If her way could help even one of these teenagers then it was worth every moment.

'It looks spectacular.'

That pulled an answering smile, though her eyes still surveyed him with a question. 'It's a work of art.'

It was definitely a work of *something*—though Ethan wasn't sure what.

'Hang on,' she said. 'We need to do the star. It's the *pièce de résistance*.' She walked across the room and rummaged around in a box before twirling round. 'What do you think?'

Ethan blinked, all darkness chased away by a star that could only be described as the Star of Bling. 'Wow. That's...'

'Eye-catching?' Ruby handed it up to him. 'I think you should do the honours. Really.' Her voice softened. 'This is your scheme. I know I'm banging on about the magic of Christmas, but without you these teens wouldn't be going anywhere. So I think it's right that you should put the star on top.'

Ethan hesitated, a frisson of discomfort rippling through him at her tone. Too much admiration, too much emotion... best to get this whole interlude over with.

In an abrupt movement he placed the star on top of the tree, nestled it into the branches and jumped down off the stepladder.

'There. Done. Now, how about we get some work done?'

'Sure...'

Ethan frowned at the note of hesitation in her voice, saw her swift glance at her watch and sighed. 'Unless you have more Christmas magic to sort?'

'Not magic...just something I need to do. But I can do it later. It's not a problem.'

Curiosity warred with common sense and won. 'Okay. I'll bite. What needs to be done?'

'Now I'll sound like Pollyanna on a sugar rush. I've bought them all gifts. Out of my own money,' she added quickly.

'The money's not an issue.' Affront touched him that she'd thought it would be.

'I know that! I just wanted to make it personal. I'll sign

the tags from you as well. Though it would be better if you—' She broke off.

'If I signed them myself? I can do that.'

'Fabulous. I'll run up and get all the gifts now. Maybe we could wrap them whilst we discuss the seating plan?'

Ethan opened his mouth and then closed it again. What he'd meant was that Ruby could give him the tags to sign. No need for him to see the presents—presumably she'd bought them all chocolates or key rings. But she looked so pleased...

'Sure,' he heard his voice say.

'I'll be back in a mo...'

'Bring them to my office.' At least that way he could pretend it was work.

Ruby toted the bags out of her bedroom and paused on the landing. Time for a pep talk. It was wonderful that Ethan had bought into her ideas, but she had to grab on to the coat-tails of perspective before it disappeared over the horizon. Sure, he'd helped decorate the tree, but that was because she had given him little choice—he'd done it for those teens and so that she could resume her restaurant manager duties more quickly. Not for *her*.

It was time to get these gifts wrapped and get on with some work.

So why, when she entered his office, did she feel a small ripple of disappointment to see Ethan behind his desk, intent on his computer screen, exuding professionalism?

His glance up as she entered was perfunctory at best.

She hesitated. 'If you want to get on with some work I can wrap these later.'

'No, it's fine.' One broad hand swept the contents of the desktop to one side.

'Right. Here goes. I've got a list that details each person and their gift.'

His body stilled. 'You bought individual gifts?'

'Yes. I called the social workers, got a few numbers for foster carers and residential home workers and chatted to some people. Just to find out a bit about them all, so I could buy something personal.'

His eyes rested on her with an indecipherable expression.

'Hey... Like you would say, it's no big deal.'

'Yes, it is.'

'No—really. To be honest, it's kind of therapeutic. In a weird way I feel like I'm doing it for myself. The me of all those years ago. Because I can remember what it was like in care, being the person with the token present. That was the worst of it—having to be grateful for gifts that were impersonal. Don't get me wrong—some carers really tried. But they didn't know me well enough to know what I wanted. Others couldn't be bothered to get to know me. So I'd get orange-flavoured chocolate when I only liked milk, or a top that I loathed and that didn't fit.'

For heaven's sake!

'That all sounds petty, doesn't it? But I want these kids to get a gift they *want*—not something generic.'

'Like a key ring or a chocolate bar?' he said, and a rueful smile touched his lips.

'Is that what you thought I'd bought?'

'Yes. I guess I should have known better.' Ethan rose to his feet. 'Come on.'

'Where to?'

'Let's do this properly. We'll wrap in the bar and you can show me what you bought everyone and brief me on what you found out about them. I'll light the fire and we'll have a drink.'

'What about work?'

The rueful smile became even more rueful, mixed with charm, and Ruby concentrated on keeping her breathing steady.

'I think we have done all we can do. The seating plan looks fine, the food is sorted, the wine is sorted, the auction is sorted and the band is booked. The banqueting hall furniture arrives after the Christmas period. All in all, I think we may have run out of work.'

He was right—and she knew exactly why that smile was now packed with regret…because without work to focus on what would they do with themselves?

She looked down at the presents she carried. The answer to that problem was to wrap fast, then flee to bed. *Alone.*

CHAPTER NINE

RUBY WATCHED AS Ethan lit the fire, his movements deft, the tug of denim against the muscles of his thighs holding her gaze as he squatted by the flames.

Stop with the ogling.

She forced herself to lay out the silver paper patterned with snowflakes and the list of gifts on the table. A sip of the deep red wine Ethan had poured for them both and then she waited until he sat opposite her.

'Here,' she said, and handed over the first present. 'This one is for Max: he's one of the boys in residential care and he's really into music—specifically rap, which I have to admit I know nothing about. So I did some research, conferred with his key worker at the home, and we came up with this T-shirt. It's the right size, and it's a cool label, so…'

Ethan shook the T-shirt out and nodded approval at the slogan. Folding it up again, he kept his eyes on her. 'It must have taken a fair amount of time to research each and every one of them and then find what you wanted. You should have told me. I'd have lightened your workload.'

'No way. I was happy to do it on my own time. Plus, you've hardly been idle yourself. You've briefed the surf instructors, sourced the caterers, the billiards table, coordinated all the paperwork—and you're also running a global business.'

Ruby frowned, wondering why he never seemed to realise just how much he did.

He broke off a piece of tape with a deft snap. 'What I've

done is generic—I could have set this up for any group of teenagers in care. You've made it personal.'

'Yes, I have. But I couldn't have done that if you hadn't set it up in the first place. Plus...' She hesitated. 'What you've done is personal too. You're giving them what helped you. The opportunity to surf, to do other water sport, to expend energy and vent frustration in a positive way. So what you've done isn't generic, and I won't let you believe it is. You care about these kids.' With a sudden flash of insight she blurted, 'Did *you* grow up on an estate? Like the one some of these kids are from?' The one he'd described as 'notorious'.

For a second she thought he wouldn't answer; the only sound was the crackle of the logs. Then he dropped the wrapped T-shirt into a bag and lifted his broad shoulders in an I-suppose-there's-no-harm-in-answering shrug.

'Yes, I did. So I relate to where these kids have come from—a tough background, maybe abuse, neglect, parents on drugs and alcohol or in prison. It's easy for them to get into trouble, join a gang, because there's nothing else to do and no one to stop them. And then they do what their parents did—steal, deal...whatever it takes. All these kids are in that cycle, and I'd like to show them there are other choices. Not just by giving them Christmas, but by giving them incentive. If they can go away from here and stay clean for a few months they can come back and take other opportunities if they want to. I want to give them a chance to get off the wheel.'

'Like you did?'

'No.'

His voice was harsh now, and the dark pain that etched his features made her yearn to reach out.

'I didn't have their excuse. My dad was a lowlife—apparently he yo-yoed in and out of prison—but my mum tossed him out when I was tiny. The time he went down for armed robbery she said enough was enough. Mum didn't drink or do drugs, and any neglect was because she was out at work all day so she could put food on the table. God knows, she did her best—but it wasn't enough. I jumped onto the wheel all by myself. Like father, like son.'

The words sounded like a quote, the derision in them painful, and Ruby tried to gather her scrambled thoughts. 'I'm guessing you got into trouble—but it's like you said yourself. In an environment like a troubled estate that's understandable. The point is you got off that wheel and out of trouble. Look at you now—your mum must be proud.'

It was the wrong thing to have said; his face was padlocked and his eyes flecked with ice. Surely his mother hadn't been the one to make the father-son comparison?

Disbelief morphed into anger as she saw his expression. 'You are *not* a lowlife.'

'That's a matter of opinion.' His eyes were dark now, his voice vibrating with mockery, though she wasn't sure if he was mocking her, himself or the world.

'I don't care. Opinion doesn't make you into your father. It doesn't work like that. I know that because *I* am not my parents. Not either of them. And I never will be.'

Her fingers clenched around the edges of the table as she faced him.

'My parents were addicts. Booze, heroin—whatever they could get their hands on, whenever they could get their hands on it. At whatever cost. Food and paying bills and shoes were all irrelevant.'

She gestured down to the reams of Christmas wrapping paper.

'For them the festive period was an excuse to justify extra excess—which led to extra verbal violence or extra apathy. Turkey, decorations and presents didn't feature.'

For a moment she was back there—in the past. Feeling the tingle of childish anticipation that scratched her eyelids as she lay on the verge of sleep. The twist of hope that Santa was real…that she'd open her eyes and see four stuffed stockings for her siblings and herself. More importantly her parents, groomed and sober, would watch them opening them with love. Then reality would touch her with the cold fingers of dawn. The smell of stale cigarettes and worse would invade her nostrils and she'd know it would be another Christmas of playing avoid-the-abuse and hide-from-notice, ensuring her siblings stayed out of the line of fire.

The memory gave steel to her voice. 'I am not like them. I won't ever let addiction become more important than my children. *Ever.*'

His hands clenched on his thighs and his whole body vibrated with tension. His foot jumped on the wooden floor. As if he wanted to somehow change her past for her.

'Ruby. I am so sorry. I don't know what to say—except that it sucks that you had to go through that.'

She gave an impatient shake of her head. 'It did suck, but that's not the point. The point is *I* am not my parents and *you* are not your father.' His jaw was set and she could almost see her statement slide off him unheeded. 'I mean, do you even know where he is now?'

'No. My guess would be in a prison cell.'

'Well, you aren't. You are here, trying to make a difference and do good.'

'In which case I'd better get on with it.' His tone was light, but with an edge that emphasised the end of the subject. 'But first…' and now his gaze was filled with warmth and compassion '… I can't imagine what you went through, but I am full of admiration for the wonderful woman that child has become.'

'Thank you.'

Frustration mixed with a yen to get close to him—to make him see that his achievements deserved kudos just as much as hers. Yet already she could see the shutters had been pulled down to hood his eyes as he picked up the tape again.

'We'd better get a move on,' he said. It's a big day tomorrow.'

'Wait.'

Something—she had to do *something*. Loathing touched her soul at the idea that Ethan had such a deep-rooted, downright skewed vision of himself. Without allowing herself time to think she moved round the table and took his hand, tugged at it to indicate she wanted him to stand. He rose to his feet and she kept her fingers wrapped around his, tried to ignore the frisson that vibrated through her at the feel of his skin against hers.

'Come here.'

The small frown deepened on his forehead as she led him to the ornate gold Victorian mirror—an oval of gilt curls and swirls.

'Look at yourself,' she said firmly, 'and you will see you. Ethan Caversham. You are you. You may look like your dad, but you are not like him. This I know.'

His reluctance palpable, he shrugged. But he complied, and as he glanced at his reflection she hoped against all hope that he would see what she could. It was an optimism that proved foolhardy as his jaw hardened and a haunting mockery speckled his blue-grey eyes.

She stepped forward and turned so that she faced him, stood on tiptoe and cupped his jaw in her palms. The six o'clock shadow was rough against her skin as she angled his face and met his gaze.

'You are a good man,' she whispered, and reached up to kiss him.

Heaven knew she'd had every intention of pressing her lips to his cheek, but instinct overcame common sense and the burning of need to imprint her sincerity onto his consciousness prevailed. Her lips brushed his and she gave a small sigh as desire shimmered and sizzled, and then his broad hands spanned her waist and pulled her against him.

For a second she thought he'd kiss her properly, deepen the connection that fizzed, but as if he'd suddenly caught sight of his reflection he gently moved her away and stepped backwards instead. He lifted a hand and ran a finger against her cheek in a gesture so gentle she felt tears threaten.

'Thank you, Ruby. I appreciate the endorsement.'

A smile redolent with strain touched his lips and then he turned and headed back to the table, sat down and picked up the scissors.

This was a *good* thing, right? Of course it was. Kissing Ethan was a bad, bad idea—that was an already established fact. So she needed to crush the absurd sense of disappointment and follow suit.

Two days later Ethan watched the busload of teenagers depart round the curve of the driveway. A sideways glance showed Ruby still waving, a smile on her face, though he knew she must be exhausted.

'Come on,' he said. 'I'll make you a cheese toastie and a cup of tea.'

'We've just had lunch.'

'No. You just made everybody else lunch. You didn't actually eat. No protests.'

'Okay. I am hungry. Thank you.'

Twenty minutes later he made his way to the lounge, to find her curled up on an overstuffed armchair, dark head bent over her phone as she texted.

'Hey…' she said, looking up as he deposited the tray on a small table next to her. 'I'm texting Tara. To tell her I meant it when I said I'd keep in touch.'

Her expression was serious, her brow creased, as she picked up the sandwich.

He eased onto the sofa opposite and stretched his legs out. 'You bonded with her, didn't you?'

'Hard *not* to bond with someone who scares the bejesus out of you!'

Ethan shook his head; he could still feel the cold glug of panic that had hit his gut two days earlier.

Everything had been going so well. Nearly all the kids had wanted to have a go at the bake off, and had gathered in the kitchen with no more than some minor banter. Ruby had set up each person with a station with all the ingredients set out. There were recipes and she was at the front to demonstrate the technique. There had been a few flour-bomb incidents but after a couple of interventions by the social worker they settled down and soon everyone had been absorbed in the tasks at hand. The scent of cinnamon and ginger pervaded the kitchen and Ethan had relaxed enough to start a conversation about the following day's surf trip.

It had all happened so fast.

A dark-haired boy had been in discussion with his neighbour a blonde petite teenager. Ethan clocked the violent shake of her head and just as his antennae alerted him that there was trouble, the youth stepped too close. Uttered a profanity so crude Ruby's head whipped round from where she'd been helping someone else. As Ethan headed over, the girl whipped out a flick knife.

Ethan's lips straightened to grim as he strode forward but before he could get there Ruby had put herself directly in the girl's path and Ethan's gut froze. The girl looked feral, her pupils wide and he could only hope that she wasn't doped up on anything.

The knife glinted in her hand. Behind Ruby, the dark-haired boy had tensed and Ethan knew any second now the situation would blow. No way would that boy be able to keep face if he backed down to a girl—the only reason he hadn't launched yet was the fact that Ruby was in the middle.

She held her hand out to the girl. 'Tara, give me the knife. No one is going to hurt you. Not now and not later. Not Max, not anyone.' Ruby's voice betrayed not a flicker of fear. She swept a glance at Ethan and gave a small shake of head and he slowed his stride. Ruby clearly didn't want him to spook the girl. Instead Ethan ducked round so that he could manoeuvre Max out of the equation, saw the boy open his mouth and moved straight in.

'Quiet.' Max took one look and kept his mouth shut.

'Come on, Tara,' Ruby said. 'It's OK. Look round. You're safe. Look at me. You have my word. Now give me the knife and it will all be fine.'

Tara had shaken her head. 'It'll never be fine,' she stated with a flat despair that chilled Ethan's blood. Then the knife fell to the floor, the clatter as it hit the tiles released some of the tension in the room. Ruby put her foot over the weapon, then stooped to pick it up.

'You want to keep going?' she asked Tara. 'It's OK. No repercussions.' She turned to Max and there was something in her stance that meant business. 'No repercussions,' she repeated.

Next to him Ethan saw the social worker open his mouth as if to intervene and he stepped into action. 'I second that. No repercussions from anyone. This is not what this all about. You guys want to make a difference to your lives. It starts here. And this incident ends here.'

'Now back to baking,' Ruby said.

Looking back now, it occurred to Ethan how seamlessly he and Ruby had acted together, so attuned to the nuances of the scene, the risks, the threat, the best way to defuse the tension.

Ruby picked up her mug and cradled it. 'You know what she told me?'

Ethan shook his head. His chest panged at the pain sketched on Ruby's features.

'She told me she wished there *had* been repercussions. That if she'd ended up inside it would have been better for her than her life now.'

Ruby's voice was sad and heavy with knowledge.

'I don't blame her for having that knife. Her home life makes mine look like a picnic in the park. Her dad is a violent loser and she is so damaged no carer can cope. That's why she's in a residential home. That's why she reacted to Max like that—he was in her space and she panicked. Oddly enough after the incident Max tried to befriend her.' She glanced at him. 'Your doing?'

'I did talk to him.' He had tried to tell him there were other ways—told him that there were consequences to actions.

'That's fab, Ethan. Maybe they can help each other. I hope they'll all come back in September. Once they let their guard down they were all so full of potential—I mean, did you see them after surfing? They had a blast.'

So had he. All the teenagers had been stoked to be in the water and he'd watched them—some of them carbon copies of himself and Rafael. Tough...so tough...and always out to prove it. Because if they didn't there was the fear of being taken down. All swagger, all bravado—but up against the waves, up against the spray and the sea salt, they had met an element stronger than themselves that they could challenge with impunity. And they'd loved it. Enough, he hoped, to incentivise them to keep out of trouble until September.

A soft sigh escaped her lips. 'I wish...I wish I could help. Take them all in and house the lot of them.' She placed her empty plate down with a *thunk*. 'Maybe one day I will. No—not maybe. Definitely.'

'How are you going to do that?'

Her chin tilted. 'I'm going to adopt,' she said. 'That's my single parenthood plan.'

Maybe it shouldn't surprise him—after all, Ruby had been in care and he understood why she would want to help children like the child she had been. Hey, *he* wanted to do that. But adoption by herself...

Her eyes narrowed. 'You don't think it's a good plan?'

'I didn't say that.'

'Then what? You think I can't hack it?'

'I didn't say that either.'

'Then say something. What do you think?'

'I think it's a very, very big thing to take on.' He raised a hand. 'I'm not saying you couldn't do it. I think you would be a fantastic person for any kid to have in their lives.' And he meant that—he'd seen the way she'd interacted with all the kids, seen her capacity for care and love. 'But taking on older children... It's a huge commitment—especially on your own.'

'I know that.'

There was no uncertainty in her voice and he couldn't help but wonder at the depth of her need to do this even as he admired her confidence in herself. The idea of any-body—let alone a child...let alone a child who had already been through the system—being dependent on him for their well-being made his veins freeze over. To those kids Ruby would be their salvation, and he knew that saving wasn't part of his make-up.

But concern still niggled. 'You said you'd decided on single parenthood because you can't pick good father ma-terial. Don't you think you should rethink that strategy?'

'What do you mean?'

'I mean why not open yourself up to the idea of a rela-

tionship? Find a man who will support you emotionally
and be a great father to your family. You're too young to
give up on having love and a family.'

'You have,' she pointed out.

'That's because I don't want love *or* a family. You can't
give up on something you've never wanted in the first
place. You do want love—you'd never have been sucked
in by Hugh or those other two losers otherwise.'

'See?' Tucking her legs beneath her, she jabbed her
finger at him. 'That's exactly it. Three out of three losers.
That's a one hundred per cent miss rate. I can't risk what
is most important to me—having a family—by taking a
side quest for love. Plus, if I pick wrong it could have a
terrible effect on any children. I need to stay focused on
my ultimate goal. I thought you of all people would get
that. You want Caversham world domination and I want
children. I won't be sidelined by anything else.'

Well, what could he say to that?

'I can see the "but" written all over your face, Ethan. I
know it will be tough but it will be incredibly worthwhile.'
The finality in her tone suggested that any argument would
be futile. 'Like these past two days have been.'

'Two days is one thing. A lifetime is another.'

He pressed his lips together. Ruby was right—she had
her goal and he had his, and hers was none of his business.
What did he know? It was not as if he thought love was a
good idea, so why push Ruby towards it? He didn't want
the bright light of hope to be extinguished from those eyes
by some idiot. But that wasn't his problem or his decision
to make—it was Ruby's. So...

'You're right I think the past two days were a success—
and a lot of that is thanks to you. The tree, the gifts,
the food...and the karaoke carols were superb. You did
a great job.'

Relief touched her face at the change of subject and he wondered if she regretted telling him of her plans.

'So did you. Thanks muchly. And thanks for letting me be part of it.' A glance at her watch and she straightened up in the chair. 'Right. I'll start the clear-up procedure and then I'll be on my way. Leave you to your Christmas plans.'

Her voice was a smidge too breezy, and her eyes flicked away from his as she rose to her feet.

'Don't worry about clearing up,' he said as he stood, his eyes fixed on her expression. 'You've already spent so much time and effort on this—I want you to start your break as soon as possible.'

Deliberately casual, he stepped towards her.

'Where did you say you were going, again?'

'Um…' For a heartbeat she twisted her finger into a stray curl, then met his gaze with cool aplomb. 'I didn't.' As she moved towards the door she gave him a small smile. 'Any more than you shared *your* plans.'

Her pace increased to escape speed and instantly he moved to bar her path.

'That's easily remedied. My plan is to stay here.'

Surprise skittered across her face. 'Alone?'

'Yup. My original plan was to host the teens over Christmas—when that changed I didn't bother making different plans for Christmas Day. It's just another day, after all. But I know you don't agree with that. So what are your plans, Ruby?'

Her eyes narrowed slightly as she realised she'd walked straight into that. 'I… Look, why does it matter to you?'

'Because you have worked so hard, and made such a difference to those teenagers—I don't want to think that doing that has ruined your plans.'

'Oh. It hasn't. Truly.' A gust escaped her lips as he raised his eyebrows. 'You aren't going to let up, are you? Look, I haven't got any specific plans. I never did.'

A slight look of surprise tilted her features.

'It's odd, actually. My original plan was to shut myself away with some weepie movies and a vat of ice cream. But now I don't want to do that. In fact if I wanted to I could go out and paint the town red. Since your press release lots of people who had dropped me like the proverbial hot root vegetable are now keen to be my friend again. Or I could probably even rustle up an invite from a real friend. But I don't really want to do any of that either. So I think I'll just head home and use the time to relax. Read a book. Watch some sappy Christmas movies.'

Ever so slowly she started to edge around him for the door.

'Not so fast.' The idea flashed into his mind like a lightning bolt, zigzagged around and sparked a mad impulse. 'I have a better idea.'

'What?'

'Let's go away for Christmas.'

'Who? You and me?' Incredulity widened her eyes— clearly the idea was risible.

'Yup. We've worked incredibly hard and we deserve a break. You said you wanted snow—how about the Alps?'

The realisation that he was making this up as he went along triggered a ring tone of alarm.

'Are you serious?'

For a second excitement lit her blue eyes and Ethan ignored the warning blare of instinct—the reminder that mad impulses never ended well.

'Of course I'm serious. Why wouldn't I be?'

'Because... Well... We can't just up and leave.'

'Last time I looked I was the boss and I say we can.'

The idea gave him a sudden surge of exhilaration— the kind he usually felt on a surfboard. It morphed into a mad desire to take her hands and twirl her round the room.

Which was every kind of nutty—from peanuts to Brazil. *Rein it in, Ethan.* What exactly was he suggesting, here?

Welcome rationalisation kicked in. 'I'd like to check out the Alps anyway—as a possible Caversham location.'

'But you haven't even opened the castle yet.'

Ethan shrugged. 'Gotta keep on moving, Ruby. I told you I want to make it big, and momentum is key.'

Plus, it made sense—it would make this a business trip and not a mad impulse at all. With any luck he'd get there, feel the buzz of a new venture—and the odd, unwanted emotions that Ruby stirred within him would dissipate. Come to that, once the ball was over—which was a few scant days away—he wouldn't need to spend as much time here. He'd see Ruby less, and his life would regain its status quo.

'So what do you think? Shall we go and get a feel for the place?'

Ruby wasn't sure she *could* think. Or at least think straight. His idea had conjured up cosy warm scenes. Snow, mountain peaks, magical Christmas card scenery... Ethan and Ruby walking hand in hand...

As if.

Ruby hauled in a breath and instructed her brain to think, to oust the temptation that had slunk to the table— a late and uninvited guest at negotiations. Ethan had probably never held hands with anyone in his life, and the very fact that the picture had formed in her mind meant she needed to be on her guard.

In fact... 'It's a crazy idea.'

'Why? We both deserve a break. I have a good gut feeling about the Alps as a Caversham location, you've done a lot of research into the Caversham ethos, and I'd value a second opinion from you.'

It all sounded so reasonable. His words slipped into her consciousness like honey. From a professional viewpoint her boss had asked her to go on a business trip. It was a no-brainer.

Plus, if she said no would he take someone else? A sudden vision of gorgeous blondes and curvy brunettes paraded in her brain and her nails scored into her palm in instinctive recoil.

'I think it sounds fabulous. Let's do it.'

Temptation gave a smug smile of victory and panic assailed her nerves. Because all of a sudden thrills of anticipation shot through her veins. *Chill, Ruby.* Who wouldn't look forward to Christmas in the Alps? Obviously those little pulse-buzzes had zilch to do with the prospect of one-on-one time with Ethan. Because that would be personal. To say nothing of certifiably stupid.

Ethan nodded, his expression inscrutable. 'Okay. I'll check flights and we'll take the first available one.'

'Fantastic.'

Though it occurred to Ruby that this whole idea could be better filed under 'Terminally Stupid'.

CHAPTER TEN

RUBY GLANCED ACROSS at Ethan and tried to stop her tummy from a launch into cartwheels. Tried to tell herself that her stomach's antics were a Braxton-Hicks-type reaction to non-existent air turbulence. Why on earth had she consented to this? Why in this universe had *he* suggested it?

Because it was work. That was why. Ethan wanted to scout out the French Alps and had decided that this was an ideal time. Plus he was a generous man, and this was his way of showing appreciation for all her hard work.

Work, Ruby. That was what this was and she had best remember that. After all it was Christmas Day, and apart from a perfunctory 'Merry Christmas' Ethan hadn't so much as referred to the fact.

Though she could hardly blame him. Organising their departure had been his priority, and she could only admire the efficiency that had achieved a super-early trip to her London apartment to pick up her passport, followed by a trip to the airport that had given her sufficient time to pick up the extra cold-weather clothes she needed as well as time for a spirited argument over who would pay for said clothing.

Now here they were, on board a flight to Geneva, where they would pick up a car. So who could blame Ethan for not making a hue and cry about it being Christmas—he was taking her to a magical Christmas place after all.

On a business trip.

What else did she want it to be?

Yet as she studied the strength of his profile, the potent

force of his jaw, an obscure yearning banded her chest—as if she were a girl with her nose pressed against the glass pane of a sweet shop. Gazing, *coveting*, but unable to touch.

As if he sensed her gaze he turned to look at her and the breath hitched in her throat. The man was so gorgeous— but it was more than that. The way he had been with those teenagers had filled her with admiration. He'd shown them respect and invited respect in return—the fact that he'd cared about them had shone through, and it had triggered this ridiculous gooeyness inside her.

Enough. Say something. Before you embarrass yourself.

To her relief panic mobilised her vocal cords and she burst into speech. 'I was wondering—where are we staying?'

'The travel agent managed to find us a chalet; there weren't many options but she assured me that it would be perfect. And I've organised an itinerary.'

For a second his voice sounded almost gruff…even vulnerable…and she thought there was a hint of colour on the strong angles of his face.

'What sort of an itinerary?'

'The kind that will give us an idea of what other resorts offer.' Now his tone had segued to brusque—she was an idiot. What had she thought? That he'd picked things out for her?

'Great.'

The chalet was presumably part of a resort—which would be good. There would be hustle and bustle and other people, and they would be kept so busy with work that the two days would pass by in a flash.

'Sure is.' Ethan nodded a touch too enthusiastically. 'I've got the address, so once we land we'll pick up the hire car, put the location into the satnav and be on our way.'

This had to be a joke right? Ethan stared through the windscreen of the four-by-four that had negotiated the curving mountain roads and treacherous hairpin bends to bring them to the chalet that the satnav had announced was their destination. He'd swear the robotic voice had a gloat to it.

He was going to track down that travel agent and have serious words. She had described the chalet as 'just the place' and left Ethan with the impression that it was part of a busy resort, awash with people and activities. Though maybe he'd been so distracted by Ruby, so caught up in the mad impulse of the moment, that he'd heard what he'd wanted to hear.

Because it turned out that the chalet was a higgledy-piggledy structure nestled in the fold of a valley and it looked like it had come straight out of a fairy tale. Set in a circular grove of snow-heaped birches, the property was made completely of wood. It practically *glowed*. Quaint wooden shutters boxed in the windows and there wasn't another person in sight.

It looked as if it had descended from the clouds especially for Christmas. It was a surprise that it wasn't wrapped up in festive paper with a bow on top.

Ethan resisted the urge to thunk his forehead on the chunky steering wheel. Instead he glanced across at Ruby, who had fallen asleep on the motorway and slept like the proverbial infant for the entire drive. Perhaps if he started the car he could drive them to the nearest hotel and blag them two rooms. Or he could phone the travel agent and…

Too late.

Next to him Ruby stretched sleepily and opened her eyes; her sleep-creased face looked adorably kissable.

'Can't believe I fell asleep.' Her blue eyes widened as she took in the scene. 'Oh, my goodness me! We get to stay here?'

'Looks like it.'

'It's as if we've been beamed into a fairy tale. Or a Christmas card.'

Or a nightmare.

'It's magical. I reckon it may even be made of ginger-bread.'

'Which wouldn't exactly be very useful, would it?'

Chill, Ethan. Snapping wouldn't change the setting.

'Plus, I don't much want to be trapped in a cage by a wicked witch and fattened up. In fact maybe we should go and find somewhere else to stay.'

Her gurgle of laughter indicated that she'd missed the fact he'd meant it as a genuine suggestion. 'I didn't have you down as a fairy tale expert.'

'I'm not.'

For a second he remembered Tanya reading to him, his laughter at the funny voices she'd used for the different characters.

'You should go on stage,' he'd told her, and she'd shaken her head.

'I'd be too shy, Thanny,' she'd said in her soft voice. 'But I love reading to you.'

He pushed the memory away and glared at the chalet. 'I'm serious. Wouldn't you rather stay somewhere busier? Less isolated? Less over-the-top?'

'I…' She gave her head a small shake. 'Sorry, Ethan, I must still be half asleep. It just looks perfect for Christmas, but I guess it's not a good idea to stay somewhere so…' She trailed off.

So romantic, so small, so intimate.

Conversely the words challenged him—was he really saying that he was incapable of being in a romantic fairy tale chalet with Ruby? Talk about an overreaction. In truth the cutesy atmosphere should serve as a reminder that romance was anathema to him. Plus he could see from her expression that she had fallen for the place.

After the amount of work she'd put in these past weeks she deserved the chance to stay where she wanted to. With all she had been through in life she deserved a Christmas with some magic in it just as much as those teenagers had. Ethan might not believe in the magic of Christmas but Ruby Hampton did, and he would be a real-life Grinch if he denied her this.

'Why don't we go in and have a look round? Then decide what to do. The agent said the key would be outside, under a pot.'

Minutes later they crossed the threshold and irritation touched his brow as he realised he was holding his breath. What did he expect? A wolf dressed up as a grandma to jump out at them?

Instead he saw an open-plan area that brought the words *cosy*, *intimate* and *snug* to mind. Timber walls were decked with bright, vivid textiles and prints, there was a purple two-seater sofa, a fireplace piled with freshly chopped logs, a circular rustic pine table. Bright light flooded through the floor-to-ceiling window that looked out onto the crisp snow-covered garden. One corner of the room showcased an abundant Christmas tree decorated with beautifully crafted wooden decorations interspersed with red baubles.

'This is…dreamy…' Ruby said as she headed over to the table. 'Hey! Look! It's a hamper. Christmas coffee… Gingerbread… Nougat… Champagne…' Picking up a card, she twirled to face him. 'The larder and fridge are stocked with supplies as well.'

Okay, Ruby loved it, and for one disorientating second the look of wonder on her face made Ethan want to give her whatever she wanted.

A sudden sense that he was losing control sent an unfamiliar swirl of panic through his gut, caused him to strive for practicality. One swift glance took in the kitchen area, tiled and warm with pine and pottery, and another door through which he glimpsed a washing machine and a shower room. Which left…

'Oh!' Ruby gasped. 'Look! The ladder must lead up to the next storey. It's like a scene from *Heidi*.'

If there was a hayloft up there he would definitely sue the travel agent.

Ruby headed towards the ladder and started to climb, her long dark ponytail swinging a jaunty rhythm, her pert denim-clad bottom snagging his gaze.

Jeez. Get a grip, Ethan. They were in enough trouble.

Ruby stepped forward from the ladder-top and gazed around the cosy confines of the bedroom. The view from the window pulled her across the floor. Mountains sculpted the horizon, almost impossible in their precipitous snow-crested magnificence. A miracle of nature, of strata and formations that had resulted in a strength and enormity that dazzled— added to the swirl of emotions that pulsed through her. It was as if the chalet had indeed exerted some kind of Christmas spell over her.

Made her forget that this was a business trip, that any glimmer of attraction between them was impossible. Instead all that mattered to her was the fact that this place reeked of romance, oozed intimacy from every wooden beam and panel.

So much so that she couldn't think straight: images waltzed and corkscrewed through her mind. Cast her as the princess and Ethan as the knight in spotless armour. Setting the scene as the place where they would...

Her gaze plunged to the snug double bed, with its patterned quilt and simple wooden headboard. More vivid pictures tangled in her imagination: herself snuggled up to Ethan, falling asleep in dappled moonlight, warm and safe from the bitter cold outside, seduced into wakefulness by the trail of his fingers on her skin...

'On my way up.'

The sound of Ethan's voice was like an ice bucket of

reality. What was the matter with her? Panic knotted her tummy as she leapt across the room to an interconnecting door and wrenched it open.

She swung round as Ethan mounted the ladder, willed her heart-rate to slow down, ordered her brain to leave the mushy fantasy world it had stupidly decided to inhabit. She should never have fallen asleep in the car. Falling asleep on a motorway and waking up in fairyland had obviously decimated her brain cells.

'The bedrooms...' she said.

Talk about a statement of the obvious.

He crossed the mezzanine floor and poked his head into the second room, so close that she had to close her eyes to combat the urge to touch him, to inhale his clean sandalwood scent. Whatever influence this place exerted had to be shaken off.

Holding her tummy in, she sidled past him towards the ladder-top.

'It's tiny,' Ethan said. 'It's for children. It's only got a minuscule bunk bed in it. That decides it. We can't stay here.'

A glitter of relief flecked his eyes and she clocked the almost imperceptible sag of those broad shoulders.

Ruby knew it was wrong, but the knowledge that Ethan Caversham was worried about staying here with her triggered a feminine satisfaction.

The fact that she had managed to breach the professional wall he'd built up since that near-kiss prompted her to step forward.

'I wouldn't mind sleeping in there. There's no way you could manoeuvre your way into the room, let alone the bed. But I'll be fine. I'm flexible.'

Unable to help herself, she gave a little shimmy to demonstrate the point and his jaw clenched again. *Whoa.* Probably best not to bite off more than she could nibble. But this chalet called to something deep inside her. It was a magical place, made for dreams, and even though she knew dreams were a fallacy surely there could be no harm in two days of magic? It was Christmas, for crying out loud.

'I think we should stay here. I mean, it's quirky—it's different. Maybe you could build a resort with places like this. Plus, it's a good place to work. No distractions.'

Bwa-ha-ha-ha! went her hormones as they rolled on the floor with mirth. As a small voice shrieked in the dark recesses of her brain, pointed out that all those diversions she'd dissed would have equalled an effective chaperon service.

'I'd like to stay here, but if you think it's too difficult…'

Too late it occurred to her that Ethan had never been able to resist a challenge. His eyebrows rose and suddenly the room seemed even smaller.

'So you want to stay here?'

'Yup.'

Determination solidified inside her—her ill-advised hormones would *not* govern her actions. This place was magical, and magical was what she wanted. Not just for herself, but for Ethan as well. Surely even his cynicism, his determination to treat Christmas as just another day, wouldn't be proof against this chalet?

He gave so much—wanted to make a difference in the lives of Max and Tara and others teens like them. Maybe it was time someone tried to make a difference for Ethan. That darkness she'd sensed inside him a decade ago—the darkness that still remained despite the aura of success— she wanted to change that, to lighten him up with some magic. How could that be wrong?

That small, insistent voice at the back of her mind clamoured to be heard—warned her that he hadn't wanted her help ten years before and he didn't want it now. It was advice she knew she should heed—she didn't know how to change people…never had, never would. So she should back off. Instead she met his gaze.

'Yes,' she repeated. 'I do want to stay here.'

Two days. It couldn't harm.

His broad shoulders lifted. 'Then so be it.'

The enormity of her own stupidity nearly overcame her. 'Fabulous,' she squeaked. 'So let's go and sample some of that Christmas coffee and gingerbread.'

And get out of the bedroom.

Repeating the mantra 'We are professional' under her breath, Ruby busied herself in the small kitchen area. Focused on the beautifully crafted pottery and the blue and white ceramic tiles as she made coffee. Inhaled its nutty roasted aroma and hoped it would defuse her disastrous awareness of Ethan.

Tray loaded, she headed to the lounge area. Flames crackled in the hearth and the sweet spicy scent of the logs infused the air.

Pouring out the coffee, handing out the gingerbread and lowering herself warily onto the sofa to avoid any form of thigh-to-thigh contact consumed all of five minutes.

The search for conversation turned out to be problematic. Ridiculous. Over the past days she and Ethan had spent hours in comfortable silence. Unfortunately right now comfort had legged it over the horizon into the alpine peaks.

Next to her Ethan shifted; she sipped her coffee as the silence stretched on.

This was madness—what had she been thinking? The ideal solution would have been to have let Ethan move them out of here. *Here* was the sort of place where couples came on honeymoon, cuddled in front of the flickering logs and cooed sweet nothings. Or the sort of place for a family holiday—a place where kids could build snowmen in the garden and sleep in that storybook bunk bed.

This must be anathema to Ethan, and yet he'd agreed to remain here. So the least she could do was come up with some conversation. A sideways glance noted that he looked brooding, one hand drumming on his knee almost as if he were waiting for something. Conversation, presumably.

'So, if you go ahead here would you set up your own ski school, complete with equipment hire and guides? Or use an existing school and arrange for some sort of commission?'

'They are both options I'll consider. It depends.'

That seemed to cover that. She reached out for another piece of the spicy gingerbread—oh, so aware of the jiggling of Ethan's leg, the tap-tap of his foot on the wooden floor. Silence reigned until Ethan put his coffee cup down with a clunk just as a jingling noise came from outside.

Turning, he cleared his throat. 'Right on time,' he declared, with a glance at his watch.

'What is?'

'Look out of the window.' Rising, he gave a sudden smile, an odd mix of relief and trepidation in the tipping of his lips.

Despite the temptation to absorb the impact of that smile, she unsnagged her gaze from his mouth, rose to her feet and headed for the expanse of glass.

The breath cascaded from her lungs—outside on the snow-laden road was a horse-drawn carriage. Not any old carriage, either—this one was in the style of a sleigh, complete with large red and black wheels and a fur-hooded roof. The sturdy brown horse was adorned with a festive bridle, resplendent with images of Father Christmas, and a blanket in deep red and green. The driver was bundled in coats and a high fur hat and lifted a hand in greeting.

'It's amazing…' Ruby breathed as she turned to Ethan.

'I thought you might like it,' he said, almost abruptly.

'I don't just like it. I love it! Thank you.'

For a second that seemed infinite he met her gaze and something flickered in his eyes—only to be doused as he scrubbed a hand over his jaw.

'I thought it would have mass appeal if I were to offer high-end romantic Christmas breaks in the Alps.'

Wow—he couldn't have made it clearer that this wasn't personal. Hurt flashed across her ribcage…until she registered the slight croakiness to his tone, as if he were forcing the words out. She didn't believe him. Ethan had done this for *her*—had chosen this particular activity with her in mind—she knew it.

For heaven's sake.

She had to get a grip. Of course she didn't know it—it was another case of believing what she wanted to believe. Just as she'd believed her parents would change—had taken any stray kind word and built it up into a pointless dream. Just as she'd trusted that Gary and Steve and Hugh would change for her. Each and every time she had been blind and foolish.

Not any more.

'Let's get our coats.'

Curse words streamed through Ethan's brain—talk about acting like a class-A schmuck. What was he trying to prove? So what if he had chosen the itinerary with Ruby in mind? The whole point had been to give her a magical Christmas. To palliate the hurt of her Christmases Past—to do for her what she had done for Tara and Max and all those teenagers. There was nothing wrong with that—and yet panic continued to churn in his gut.

Deal with it, Ethan.

Sure, the last time Christmas had been magical for him had been when Tanya was alive. That magic hadn't stopped his sister from leaving this life scant months later. But that had zip to do with Ruby, and he wouldn't let his own past ruin this day for her.

'Wait!'

Ruby swivelled round on one booted foot, her poise

back in place, her initial happiness and subsequent hurt both erased.

'Yes?'

'I apologise. I'm not good at this whole Christmas scenario, but I don't want this to be awkward. I want you to enjoy the ride and the itinerary and...'

And he wanted to kiss her so badly his lips tingled and his hands ached with the need to reach out for her. Somehow a kiss would show her what he meant when words seemed to have deserted his tongue...

Somehow he needed to get with it and recall Ethan Caversham, man-in-control, to the building.

'So how about we get this carriage on the road?'

Her gorgeous lips turned up in a smile so sweet that he knew she had intuitively understood what he meant even if he didn't.

'It's a plan. But first maybe this is the right time for me to give you your Christmas gifts.'

Surprise slammed into him. 'You bought me gifts?'

'No need to sound so shocked. Yes, I did. Hang on.' Anticipation etched her features as she walked over to her case. 'This one I bought ages ago. I was going to leave it at the castle for you to find. And this one was an impulse buy at the airport.'

'Thank you.'

In truth he had no idea what to say—he couldn't remember the last time he had been on the receiving end of a personal gift. His lips twisted in a rueful smile—in a sense he was still on a par with Max and Tara, *et al*.

Slipping a hand into his pocket, he retrieved his present for Ruby and sudden trepidation shot through his nerves. 'Here's yours. Ladies first.'

'Oh... You didn't have to. I know you don't really believe in Christmas.'

Ethan shrugged. 'I...I thought that...seeing how much

effort you put into the teens' gifts...the least I could do was—' He broke off. He was doing it again. 'I wanted to.'

He had wanted Ruby to have a present that someone had thought about. Okay. Make that agonised over. How long had he spent in that stupid jewellery shop? Irritation caused his fingers to drum on his thigh as he felt his heart thud faster—he wanted her to like it way too much.

A yearning to see her eyes light up banded his chest as she carefully unwrapped the green embossed paper, held the dark blue jewellery box and then snapped it open and gasped, her lips forming a perfect O of wonder.

The pendant glittered, diamonds on white gold, shaped into an exquisite simple star. When he'd seen it an image of Ruby as she'd handed him the star to adorn the Christmas tree had popped into his mind.

'Ethan. I...I...can't accept this. It's not right. It's...'

'It's yours.'

Though by 'not right' maybe she meant she didn't like it...

An image of his mother that terrible first Christmas after Tanya's death flashed across his mind. Her wooden expression as she opened his gifts. The sear of knowledge that he'd got it wrong. That without Tanya he meant nothing to her, couldn't get it right. All those hours spent agonising for naught.

Maybe he should have learnt—stuck to something generic for Ruby. Better yet, he should have given her a Christmas bonus—a cheque, a banker's draft. Going personal had been a mistake. Ethan Caversham didn't do personal.

'You can exchange it if need be.'

'Exchange it?' she echoed. 'Why would I do that? It's beautiful. I meant it's too much.'

'It's a gift, Ruby.' It occurred to him that she was no more used to gifts than he was. 'I want you to have it.'

'Then thank you.'

As she took it from the box he thought for an instant that she would ask his help to put it on. Relief warred with disappointment when she lifted it herself—the thought of his fingers brushing the sensitive skin of her neck had strummed a jolt of pure desire through him.

'Now open yours.'

An absurd sense of excitement threaded his gut as he unwrapped the first gift, the bright paper covered in images of Father Christmas bringing a smile to his lips. It was a smile that grew as warmth touched his chest.

In his hands was a painting of Caversham Castle. The artist had captured the sheer brooding history of the craggy mound of medieval stone, imposing and grand, made to defend and dominate the landscape.

'It's perfect. Thank you.'

'Open the next one.' A small frown creased her forehead. 'Like I said, this was an impulse buy and if you don't like it I won't be offended…'

As he pulled the jumper out of its silver wrapping paper a chuckle fell from his lips. 'A Christmas jumper.' A cable knit in dark blue, it was patterned with reindeer. 'It's inspired—and what better time to wear it?'

'You mean it?'

Surprise and a smile illuminated her face, and for one heartbeat full of exhilaration he nearly succumbed to the temptation to sweep her into his arms and kiss her.

No! There was personal and there was *personal*.

Instead he tugged the jumper over his head 'Of course. Now, let's go!'

A few minutes later and they were all layered up. Once outside, Ethan sucked in the cold air; welcomed the hit to his lungs and brain. Perhaps the cold would freeze some sense into him.

CHAPTER ELEVEN

RUBY STOLE A sideways glance at Ethan and tried to confine the tornado of her thoughts. *Yeah, right.* Containment continued to elude her, effectively held at bay by the sheer nearness of Ethan as they settled under the heap of blankets on the carriage seat. Ruby clenched her jaw—she would not even contemplate the word snuggle.

Somehow she had to keep perspective, had to chillax and not read more into Ethan's actions than there was. After all, she had earned a diploma in that. Yes, he had bought her a beautiful Christmas gift—instinctively her hand rose to touch the diamond pendant—but that was because Ethan was a good man who tried to give people second chances.

No doubt he had simply wanted to do for her what he had wanted to do for all those troubled teenagers. In fact he had practically said so…so there was no point to this continued analysis.

Time instead to concentrate on the beauty of her surroundings, which was enough to catch the breath in her throat. The ground was covered in snow, as if someone had taken the time to weave a thick white duvet to cover the landscape and then sprinkled the bare branches of the trees with a dazzling glitter. It was beautiful—glorious—magical. The silence was broken only by the chime of the horse's bells, the huff of his breath and the crunch of his hooves in the snow.

'This is beyond incredible,' she murmured with a sideways glance.

Ethan's expression was unreadable, but the vibe she

got from him was edgy—as if he too battled complicated thoughts.

Her words caused him to blink and give a small shake of his head. 'I'm glad you're enjoying it,' he said. 'Not too cold?'

'Nope. The last time I saw snow was in London, and it had turned to slush before I could truly appreciate its beauty. This is spectacular.'

Now a genuine smile touched his lips as his gaze rested on her expression. 'I hope you'll like the next item on our agenda.'

'Which is…?'

'Sledging.'

'For real?'

Excitement fizzed inside her and collided with a pang of emotion as a memory jolted her brain. Years and years ago she'd taken her siblings out into the snow. She'd carried Edie, who hadn't been able to walk yet, Philippa had toddled beside her and Tom, aged just four, had raced ahead with a joyous whoop. They hadn't gone far, just to a local park to watch the children sledge.

How she had yearned to have a go. But there had been no sledge, and she hadn't wanted to draw attention to themselves. But it had still been a good day—they had made a snowman, thrown some snowballs, before Ruby had realised that there were some adults clearly wondering why they were unaccompanied and she'd quickly herded her siblings together and left.

'Is that okay?' A small frown touched Ethan's face as he studied her expression and she did her best to erase the hint of wistfulness, the shadow of memory from her face.

'It's better than okay. I've never sledged before and I would absolutely love to.'

Ruby let the memory go with the silent hope that her siblings had had plenty of opportunity to sledge with their new family. Allowed the fizz of excitement to take ascendancy.

Minutes later the carriage drew to a halt and Ethan helped her alight. 'Here we are. It's a resort, but we have passes.'

They lingered for a moment to thank the driver and pat the horse, and then she turned and once again the scenery caused the breath to whoosh from her lungs. Snow glistened in the distant trees of the forest and crunched underfoot, thick and soft all at the same time—the way she had imagined stepping on clouds would be as a child.

They entered the resort and headed to the sledge hire desk.

The woman behind the counter smiled. 'Would you like a paret, a disc or a toboggan?'

Ruby stared at the options. 'I'll go for a toboggan.' On the basis that it looked the safest. The paret looked to be a mixture of a tricycle without wheels and a stool, and the disc looked as if it might well career round and round out of control. As that was her current mental state, there was no point adding a physical element.

The woman smiled. 'I promise they are all safe, *mademoiselle*. They are designed to be safe for children as well as adults.'

'I'll try the paret,' Ethan said.

Ruby narrowed her eyes. 'Show-off.'

That garnered a smile. 'Think of it as research. It's occurred to me that I could offer moonlit paret sledging as a part of a holiday package.'

They exited the building and she inhaled the tang of snow and pine, absorbed the bustle of people and the sound of laughter. Took courage from the happy vibe.

Until they reached the top of the slope.

'Um…' Ruby peered over the edge.

Suddenly the snow was reminiscent of clouds only in

the way that if you tried to walk on a cloud you would plummet downwards. The ground was a turreted mass of white, under which surely there would lurk hidden dangers.

'You worried?'

Daft. She was being daft. This was an official slope, suitable for tiny kids. All she needed to do was look around again and observe them.

Her heart gave a sudden thump. Just a few feet away a mother with a baby in a sling helped two children get onto a sledge. A dark-haired boy and a younger little girl with blonde curls. The world seemed to fall into slow motion and for an absurd second she nearly ran towards them— until common sense drummed its beat.

That wasn't Tom and Philippa. Tom would be twenty now, and Philippa nineteen. Even if they were here she wouldn't recognise them. They were adults.

For a second, loss shredded her insides.

'Ruby?' Ethan's rich voice held a question and a heap of concern.

For a mad minute she wanted to tell him the truth, in the hope that he could soothe the pain.

With muscle-aching effort she pulled herself together. Confiding in Ethan would only add to the intimacy she was trying to fight. In any case Ethan didn't welcome emotional intensity; he hadn't ten years before and he wouldn't now.

'I'm fine. Just chicken, I guess. Why don't you show me how it's done?'

'No. You look like you've seen a ghost. We're going to the café.'

'I…'

'No arguments. First rule of snow sport. You don't do it unless you're focused.'

Maybe he was right. Either way he wasn't taking no for an answer and willy-nilly Ruby followed him towards the café.

* * *

Ethan held the café door open. The smell of coffee jumbled up with the aromas of vanilla and almond and Christmas spices. Carols filled the air with a choral hum—a festive backdrop to the chatter of families and the clink-clank of cutlery. Usually the scents would have triggered a smile, but Ruby seemed enmeshed in thought.

Even an almond croissant and hot chocolate didn't bring more than a perfunctory smile to her face.

'You want to talk about it?' Even as he spoke the words he knew it was a foolhardy query. The invitation to confide, to *share*, was not one he would ever make as a rule. Panic threatened—an echo of a decade ago. He was letting her get too close. But how could he help it? When she looked to be in such pain, with her usual vividness drained? He wanted to help, to make it better for her.

If he had any sense he would never have let things get to this point—maybe he should have let history repeat itself and cut and run.

Chill, Ethan.

Time to remember that he was ten years older now, ten years wiser, and this time he would be able to control the situation. There could be no danger in an offer of support and it would be an impossibility to withhold that support.

'If you want to talk I'm here.'

Her eyes met his with a hint of surprise, palpable hesitation, and a small determined shake of her head. 'It's Christmas. You've gone to all this trouble. I'm sorry to be a Debbie Downer.'

'You aren't. I promise. Ruby, we both know that Christmas can be an emotive time for people with difficult pasts. Talk to me. I know your childhood Christmases were grim. Maybe I can dilute some of your tainted memories.'

One more heartbeat of a pause and then she exhaled. Picked up the steaming mug of hot chocolate and cradled it, her eyes wide. 'I guess for a moment out there the past arrived from nowhere and knocked me for a half-dozen. Those children on the sledge next to us… For an instant they reminded me of my younger brother and sisters.'

The words registered in his brain—generated a host of questions. If Ruby had siblings where were they now? Why did the memory of them haunt her?

Her gloved hand pushed a tendril of hair from her face and she sighed. The noise escaped into the chatter-tinged air with the sound of age-old sorrow and weariness.

'Tom, Edie and Philippa,' she continued. 'I told you my parents were addicts. One of the ways they funded their addictions was via benefits. The more children they had, the more money they got. I was the oldest, then Tom, Philippa and Edie. I was six when Tom was born, and I can still remember the awe I felt when I first saw him— such a tiny scrap of humanity. I felt welded to him. Same with the girls. All I wanted was for us to stay together as a family, and I vowed I would do whatever it took. Mum and Dad told me that it was up to me—that they couldn't do it so I had to be strong. I had to be responsible. I had to lie to social workers and school teachers. Had to make sure everyone believed we were a happy family.'

Ethan's chest constricted at the sight of her face, whiter than the snow that glittered and glinted outside. He could picture a much younger Ruby, her expression oh, so serious, tucking an unruly curl of dark hair behind her ear as she concentrated on changing a nappy or manoeuvred a heavy pan of water onto the hob.

'That must have been tough,' he said softly.

'It was and it wasn't. I loved them all so much, you see—and I told myself that Mum and Dad loved us really. But the cold hard truth is that they used us. More fool me for ever thinking otherwise. Even after it all went wrong,

when I screwed it up, for ages I still kidded myself that
they loved me.'

'What happened?'

'I couldn't hold up the façade and it crumbled down. We
were whisked away into care. They couldn't find a carer
to take all four of us so we were split up. We went from
being a family unit to having visits in a social worker's
office once a week if we were lucky.'

'That must have been beyond terrible.'

'It was.'

Her words were flat and in that moment he knew that
it had been unfathomably horrific.

'I fought for us to be placed together, or at least near
each other. But nothing I said made any difference. The social workers said that we were better off like that than with
our parents. But it didn't seem that way to me. Sometimes
I even pictured my parents missing us so much that they
would turn over a new leaf and we'd all go back to them.'

She laughed—the noise devoid of mirth.

'I take it that didn't happen?'

'Nope. They turned up to see me once—stoned and
drunk—hurled abuse at me and the social worker ended
the meeting. I've never seen them again. No idea if they
are alive or dead.'

He placed his hand over hers, wished he could find
words to convey his feelings.

'Time went—and one day a social worker came and
told me she had good news. An adoptive family had been
found, but they would only take three children—Tom, Edie
and Philippa. I was too old and too difficult. I'd been acting out, and they figured it would be bad for the others if
I was placed with them.'

She paused, her blue eyes wide and unfocused, as if she
had teleported through time to relive the moment.

'The social worker explained that if they waited, kept

trying to find someone to take all of us, it might end up that none of us got adopted—or that Tom, Edie and Philippa would end up separated. She promised me there would still be contact. I'd still see them. But it didn't go down like that. Tom Edie and Philippa moved in with their new family and I was told there would be no contact whilst they settled in. I fought it—I went on and on to the carers, to the social workers. They told me I had to wait. That I was being selfish. Then one day I decided to take matters in my own hands. I bunked off and went to their school. I was so desperate to see if they were okay. That's all I'd ever done, you see.'

Her hands gripped the mug of hot chocolate so hard he leant over and prised her fingers free, retained her hand in his grasp. He could envisage her so clearly; frantic and determined, fuelled by a love that gave her the strength to do anything for the sake of her siblings.

'It was the end of school—I saw them run out to a woman who I knew must be their new mum. She looked so pretty, and like she adored them, and they looked so happy. It just needed Mary Poppins to make it complete. Not me.'

'Oh, jeez, Ruby…'

What could he say? What could he do to fix this? To mend the void that echoed from her voice? Helplessness gnawed at his insides and he did the only thing he could. Moved his chair round the table in the hope that his body, his presence, would offer some comfort.

'After I saw that I knew what I needed to do. I told the social worker that I didn't want to see my siblings for a while. That I understood it was better for them to integrate into their new family. Eventually, with a social worker's approval, I wrote them a letter to tell them I loved them but a clean break was better for all of us. I knew it was right—my presence in their lives would only make everyone feel bad. Their new family would feel bad for not being able to take me, and Tom and Edie and Philippa's loyalty would be divided. That wouldn't have been good for them. So I decided there and then that I would try and be happy for them.'

Her slim shoulders lifted.

'And I *am* happy for them. But occasionally I still miss them so much it hurts.'

A solitary tear seeped from her eye and he reached out and caught it on his thumb. The moisture glistened on the pad of his glove and he pulled her into his arms.

'It's okay, Ruby. Cry it out.'

Her body tensed and he rubbed her back in a gentle circular motion. Felt her relax as she snuggled into his chest and wept. From somewhere he found soothing words as he rested his cheek on the silkiness of her hair. He realised he couldn't remember a time when he had done this. Offered comfort. Oh he'd tried with his mother, after Tanya, but she'd pushed him away, her whole body stiff with grief. Her eyes had told him what she had later confirmed in words—the wish that it had been him who had died rather than his sister.

He pushed the thoughts away—right now it was all about Ruby. His past couldn't be changed or fixed—his mother had no wish to mend fences in any way. Tracey Caversham wouldn't even take his money, let alone any affection. But he was grateful that Ruby seemed to derive some comfort from his actions.

After a while she placed her palms on his chest and gently pushed herself upright. 'Phew,' she said as she looked up at him, tear-swept eyes glistening. 'I'm sorry. What you said was so beautiful, and suddenly I could see them so vividly. Memories deluged me and turned me into a watering pot.'

'There's no need to apologise. At all. I'm glad you told me. Tell me more about them. About Tom, Edie and Philippa.'

So she did, and as she spoke he could visualise the energetic, dark-haired Tom, with his cheeky grin, see the chatterbox Philippa with her blonde ringlets and quiet, straight-haired Edie who sucked her thumb.

When she'd stopped speaking Ruby squeezed his hands. 'Thank you. Mostly I try to leave the past in the past. But sharing the good memories has made the bad memories easier to bear. I feel lighter. Thank you, Ethan—and I mean that. If you ever want to talk I'm here for you.'

Her words triggered a strange reaction—for a second he allowed himself to ponder that scenario. Tried to picture the concept of sharing. Sharing with Ruby the way his mother's face had always twisted at the sight of him, the continued rain of comments as to how he reminded her of his dad. How Tanya had shielded him with her love, but how that shield had been tragically removed by her suicide. His terrible grief and its aftermath. How spectacularly he had let his mother down and the devastating consequences.

Discomfort rippled in his gut, along with a healthy dose of denial, and he felt his lips curl with distaste. *Not happening*. If there was one thing his past had taught him it was the need to control emotion—all the release of it could achieve was pain. If he had only retained control after Tanya's death then he wouldn't have walked the road that had led to his mother handing him over to social services. To confide in Ruby would open up an emotional vortex and that was not going to happen.

So… 'I'll bear it in mind,' he said as he pushed her plate towards her. 'So what now?'

Ruby picked up the almond croissant. 'I'd like to eat this, and then—if it's okay with you—I'd still like to sledge.'

'Then that's the plan.'

It truly felt as if a bulk had been hefted from her very soul. The sadness was still there, but more manageable. As they exited the café the snow seemed even brighter, and now the sight of children filled her with a sense of hope and determination. Because one day she would adopt, and she vowed that she would take her children sledging.

A sideways glance at Ethan filled her with relief—his blue-grey eyes rested on her with warmth, but not a hint of pity, and she honoured him for that. For his innate re-alisation that pity would be anathema to her.

There was a bond between them now—she could see it shimmer in the air between them. They had both pulled themselves from the gutter and survived events that had had the potential to destroy. That was worthy of admi-ration—not pity. But she knew she felt more than admi-ration, and she needed to be careful. Because right now that gooey warmth had multiplied, and instead of being mortified at having wept all over him she felt energised… awash with dangerous feelings of intimacy. An intimacy he would abhor.

Sure, he had just proved himself capable of emotional understanding, but his withdrawal at the thought of shar-ing his own past had been crystal-clear.

She had to rein it in. Her goals and Ethan's goals were as far apart as it was possible to be. Ethan wanted to sit in his un-rocked boat on his own—he wanted a life alone—and she wanted as many children as she could manage. So her best hope was that she and Ethan could become friends.

Yet right now she wanted more…couldn't help herself. The tug of attraction, the tug of emotion, the tug towards him in general asserted a magnetism she somehow had to control. Because there couldn't be anything else, and she couldn't let herself fall headlong for yet another unsuitable man. Another man who would not or could not change his lifestyle for her.

Instead it would be better to focus on what she could share with Ethan—like this wonderful Christmas Day he had given her. Maybe she needed to focus on a headlong ride on a sledge… A peek down the slope and she felt a surge of anticipation.

'Take it away, maestro,' she said.

His smile was the genuine article—it lit his grey-blue eyes and her tummy clenched in response.

'As you wish,' he said, and he turned, dropped down onto the disc sledge and launched himself down the slope. Tore down the slope, swerved and manoeuvred, flew over the snow.

Once at the bottom he looked up and gave her the thumbs-up sign before beginning his ascent. She watched him climb back up, legs strong and body lithe. What was it about him that made him stand out? Maybe his aura— one that meant she would be able to spot him anywhere in the world.

'There—see. Easy.'

Ruby looked down at the toboggan doubtfully. 'I'm still not convinced I won't fall off.'

'It's all about balance.'

'Very Zen…'

His chuckle caught on the crisp breeze, and unlocked something inside her. The sight of his smile and the tang of snow made her breath catch, made her heart hop, skip and jump. and she felt her lips tilt into a grin.

'Zen or not, you are going down that slope, Ruby. We'll go together. This is one childish dream that you *will* fulfil. Come on. Sit. I'll fit in behind you.'

Huh?

She squatted, placed the plastic toboggan on the snow and wriggled on, intensely aware of him as he lowered himself behind her. This was daft—they were both in Eskimo-level layers of clothing on a populated slope— not sunbathing on an isolated beach in bikini and trunks.

Ethan placed one arm round her waist and she swallowed her small gasp. His touch defied physics, felt electric through all the layers.

'So all you have to do to steer is use this stick on the side, or your hands or feet.'

Was it her imagination or was his voice deeper than normal—the sort of deep that made her think of dark chocolate with a hint of ginger and spicy mulled wine? Panic mixed with a tummy-tingle of need.

Do something, Ruby.

'Let's go!'

They took off, skimmed over the snow. Exhilaration heated her veins as she let go, with no time to think or analyse or worry. She existed in the second, fuelled by adrenalin and sheer excitement as the world flew by until they reached the base and glided to a stop.

Pure elation frothed inside her as she shifted to look up at Ethan. 'That was incredible. Like an out-of-body experience.'

Ruby stared at him. He looked…utterly gorgeous. And in this mood of sheer instinct she knew with a blind, horrible clarity that she wanted him to kiss her. That the tingles that coursed through her body were no longer due to her sledging experience. This attraction existed. No—it did more than that. Right now it burned…just like his gaze that was focused on her parted lips.

His pupils darkened; desire flared.

'Ethan…?'

The question whispered across the snow-tinged air. Her heart pounded in her ribcage as her lips parted and she twisted round, propelled by an instinct older than time, her body no longer at home to the voice of reason.

CHAPTER TWELVE

ETHAN COULDN'T TEAR his gaze from her—she was so incredibly beautiful. Her cheeks flushed from the cold, her entire face animated by desire. And, heaven help him, he couldn't help himself—couldn't stop himself.

Leaning forward, he covered her lush lips with his own as precipitous need overcame all capacity for thought. It felt so right. He could taste Ruby—the tang of almond with a hint of chocolate. Her lips, cold at first, heated up and she gave a small mewl. The sound triggered a further yearning for more and he pushed his fingers under the hood of her parka, tangled his fingers in the silk of her hair. Her lips parted and her tongue touched his in a tentative flick. And he was lost in a desire to block out the world and kiss her until…

Until what?

The knowledge that the universe could not be ignored was one he carried with him every second of the day; there were always consequences. Problem was at this instant he couldn't care less—which was dangerous beyond belief. He mustn't let her close. For both their sakes. Ruby wanted a family and she deserved to have that—she might believe now that she wanted single parenthood, but he hoped that one day she would find love with a man who could give her everything she deserved. Ethan was not that man—and he would not mess with her head.

With a supreme effort of will he pulled back and for a long second they gazed at each other, puffs of breath mingling in the cold.

'I…' Her voice trailed off as she lifted her fingers to her lips again. As if they stung in sheer frustration.

Well he could empathise with that. All of him was tingling with spikes of unfulfilled need.

'I…um…what now?'

'I don't know.'

What could he say? There was no point trying to dismiss what had happened. That kiss had been off the Richter scale and it had changed everything. Which was a problem.

'But I apologise.' From somewhere he pulled a smile—this Christmas Day would *not* be ruined by his stupidity. 'We need to forget that happened. And whilst we try to do that let's keep sledging.'

Truth be told, he couldn't think what else to do. The alternative was to hotfoot it back to the chalet and haul her into the bedroom.

A silence, and then she essayed a small, determined nod. 'Okay,' she agreed. 'This is such an amazing place to be, and I am having a wonderful Christmas Day, so don't apologise. We can chalk it up to an inevitable moment of foolishness.'

To his surprise there was no awkwardness in the next few hours—Ruby took to the snow like the proverbial duck to water, and swerved and dipped and dived over the slopes. They raced each other and laughed over the results, argued with mock ferocity over a handicap system, and sledged until dusk hit.

'Time for the next stop,' Ethan said. 'Gaston should be back with the carriage and then it's time for Christmas drinks and dinner in town.'

The knowledge was a relief, because despite all his efforts the air still hummed with the undercurrent of attraction and they needed time before they returned to the problematic fairy tale chalet, with its solitude and adjoining bedrooms.

'Great.' Ruby clapped her hands together to get rid of the last vestige of snow and leant with natural grace to pick up her toboggan.

The carriage journey into town was silent—but not a silence of an awkward or grim calibre. Ethan would have classed it as one infused with an undercurrent he wasn't sure he grasped. Every so often Ruby would glance at him with a sideways sweep, her eyes wide in thought as one finger curled a tendril of dark hair that escaped from her red bobble hat.

And then the horse came to a halt and they disembarked into the Christmas card scene of the Alpen town. The atmosphere was lively, and the artful array of high-end shops was combined with an olde-worlde charm.

'It's gorgeous…' Ruby breathed.

As was she.

They walked down the snow-dusted street, illuminated by the glow of lights from the multitude of bars and restaurants and the twinkle of lights that decked the air. Next to him Ruby had subsided back into silence. She broke it with a quick look up at him.

'Where are we having dinner?'

'A Michelin-starred restaurant owned by the resort. We're a bit early, but we can have a drink before.'

'How about in here?' she suggested, stopping outside a bar that resembled an old coaching inn.

'Sure.'

They stepped over the threshold into the warmth of the bar. Chatter in a variety of languages mingled with universal laughter and the chink and rattle of glasses and cutlery. The aroma of fondue and beer was mixed with the tang of snow.

'What would you like?'

'A small glass of white wine, please.' Ruby eyed him with something very near speculation as she tugged her bobble hat off.

'Coming right up.' He shrugged out of his jacket and dropped it on the back of a chair whilst she seated herself at the round wooden table. As he headed through the throng to the bar he was aware of her eyes as they followed his progress.

Minutes later he returned and placed her wine and his tankard of beer on the table. He sat down and surveyed her thoughtful expression. Something had shifted and he wasn't sure what it was. The idea that they were on the brink of new territory sent a conflict of anticipation and panic to his synapses.

Ruby lifted her glass. 'To us. And how far we've come.'

Her words seemed imbued with meaning. The crowd and the hum of conversation seemed to fade, to leave only Ruby and himself. Perhaps he should make a stalwart attempt to pull the conversation round to work, but the idea refused to be translated into words.

The moment they had avoided so dextrously refused to be ignored any longer. That kiss—the mammoth in the room—was sitting right next to them, drink in hand. All he could think about was how her lips had felt, the wonder and the beauty and the sheer pleasure of that kiss. A kiss he'd waited a decade for...the desire he'd run from all those years ago. And now...

Ruby leant forward, her sapphire eyes sparkling as she tucked a stray tendril of hair behind her ear. 'I've been thinking, and I want...' Her cheeks flushed with a tinge of pink. 'I want...I want—' She broke off. 'Maybe it's better to start with what I don't want. I don't want a relationship with you. I don't want to climb into your boat or to rock it in any way whatsoever. My goal is adoption, and I will not let anything stand in my way.'

A pause whilst she sipped her drink.

'But I would like to explore this further. You and me. Just whilst we're here. Like a bubble of time between our pasts and our futures. I'd like to enjoy the now. With you. A two-night holiday fling. That's what you normally do, isn't it?'

No! It was an enormous effort to haul the syllable back. But instinct revolted, because Ethan knew that whatever happened between him and Ruby it didn't class with his usual liaisons.

'No.' The word was gentle. 'No, Ruby. You are different. If we do this I need you to know that.'

If they did this.

Ethan tried to think—when all he wanted to do was punch the air in triumph, sling Ruby over his shoulder caveman-style and get back to the chalet pronto. But he couldn't do that. Ruby had thought this through and he needed to do that as well.

Hours before he had ended their kiss because he had believed it was a bad idea—succumbing to emotion and impulse would land him in trouble. Worse, it could land *Ruby* in trouble, and he wouldn't let that happen. She'd been messed around enough by the men in her life—he wouldn't add to that.

'Ethan, I won't get hurt.'

Great. Clearly she could read him like a picture book.

'This is *my* idea. As soon as we get on the plane back home we revert to normal. Boss and employee. And we throw ourselves into making the ball a success. This will work.'

Her words held conviction and sense. Ruby did not want a relationship with him—she wanted a fling. There would be no further expectation, so he would not be messing with her head. Ruby wanted a family—he didn't. There could be no future. Her words.

For a scant second a warning bell clanged at the back of his brain—he didn't want to let Ruby close, remember? But Ethan wasn't in danger—how could he be? This was a fling—purely physical, no emotions on the table.

'Let's do it,' he said.

Ruby held her breath, giddy with sheer disbelief—had she really propositioned Ethan Caversham? *Yup*—she believed she had. For a scant second she wondered if she'd lost her mind. Yet if her sanity had gone walkabout she was in no hurry to get it back. Not when Ethan's eyes raked over her, glinting with a promise of fulfilment that sent shivers dancing up her spine.

'Let's go,' she said. 'Would you mind skipping dinner? I don't think I could eat a thing. But if you're hungry…'

Be quiet, Ruby. Before he changes his mind.

'I don't want dinner.'

His voice sent the tingle into acrobatic overdrive and sheer anticipation wobbled her legs as she slipped off the bar stool. As he encased her hand in his she knew her smile rivalled that of a plethora of Cheshire cats. This was all about the moment, and this moment felt fabulous, unrestricted by the past or the future.

Even the wait at the taxi stand, the journey back, felt alight with possibility—and then the magical glow of the chalet welcomed them.

Without releasing her hand Ethan manoeuvred the door open and tugged her straight across the lounge area.

Ruby disengaged her grasp to scramble up the ladder and into the bedroom. Now the reassurance of his touch had gone a sudden shyness threatened, caused her to circumnavigate the bed and approach the window.

The hairs on the back of her neck stood to attention as she sensed his presence behind her, and then his warmth enveloped her. His hands rested on her shoulders and began to knead gently. Tension ebbed away as she gazed out at the garden, where moonbeams danced on the birches and skittered in gleams on the duvet of snow.

Ethan swept her hair from her nape and she gasped as his lips grazed the sensitive flesh. An urge to see him overcame her, and as if he instinctively knew he stepped back and gently turned her to face him.

'So beautiful...' he murmured, one thick finger stroking her cheek.

His grey-blue eyes shone in the moon's illumination, the light played on the planes of his face and emphasised their strength. Her heart melted and ached and she reached up for him, greedy for the devastation of his kiss.

It was a kiss that seemed to take up from where they'd left off—only this time with the knowledge that there was more to come. There was no need to think or analyse or worry, and that added a sharp edge to a desire that dizzied her. Propelled by instinct, she gripped his shoulders and Ethan lifted her effortlessly, so her legs wrapped his waist and his hands cupped her bottom.

He carried her to the bed, their lips still locked, and Ruby moaned as he slid her down the hard length of his body before tumbling her onto the mattress.

Hours later Ruby opened her eyes, aware of an immense contentment that swathed her limbs in languorous satisfaction. For a long moment she lay and gazed up at the ceiling, cocooned under the weight of Ethan's arm, his dark brown head next to hers. A gentle shift and she could study his face, bathed in the streaks of dawn that slid through the slats of the shutters. Softer in sleep, yet still his features held a tautness—as if even in slumber he were loath to relinquish complete control.

A qualm tugged at her heart as it hopped, skipped and jumped. But there was nothing to worry about—she had decided that she wanted to grasp this opportunity, to live in the moment and just be herself. Because with Ethan that was who she could be—she'd shared her past and she'd shared her future. Now she wanted this time with him to explore their attraction.

Though somehow the theory no longer seemed so simple. Certain flaws had popped into her mind. These past hours had shown her an attraction that flamed with a heat she hadn't envisaged. But the fire would burn itself out. Though when fires burnt themselves out didn't they often leave a whole lot of collateral damage…?

His eyes opened and instantly focused—barely a fraction of a second between oblivion and awareness.

And she doused every qualm as his smile warmed her. She was being daft. They only had a day and a night left. Then it would be over. So what was the point of worry? It was not as if she had any intention of calling a halt to proceedings. Of not experiencing the wonder of the previous hours again…not falling asleep in the safe cocoon of his arms—the idea was unthinkable.

'Ruby? You okay?'

'Of course I am.'

Of course she was. *Jeez.* She really needed to work on her live-in-the-moment technique. The whole point was to enjoy each and every moment of the next twenty-four hours.

Twenty-four hours. Tick-tock went a metaphorical clock.

Concern lit his eyes and she summoned a smile. 'Just hungry. Guess it's time to eat. Not that I have a single regret for missing that Michelin-starred Christmas dinner.'

'Me neither. Our evening was spent in far more enjoyable ways. But now you mention it I am pretty hungry. I think we need to build up our strength,' he added with a wiggle of his eyebrows that made a giggle bubble up to the surface.

'And why would that be, Mr Caversham?'

Leaning over, he nuzzled her ear. 'In fact, perhaps I could muster up my last reserves of energy right now...'

'Hmm...' Desire sizzled through her with intoxicating speed—perhaps enjoying each and every moment would be a cinch after all.

An hour later he grinned lazily at her. 'Now would be a good time for breakfast.'

'How about I whip us up a brunch fondue?'

'Sounds perfect. I'll check our Boxing Day itinerary.'

'Okay. And thank you for a magical Christmas Day—the planned bits and the...the...' Her cheeks heated up.

'Impromptu night-time activities?' he supplied, with a wicked smile that curled her toes.

The morning hours swept by and she could almost see the magical motes of happiness fleck the air. Magic infused them both—brought laughter and warmth, enabled Ethan to dance round the kitchen disco-style whilst she sang along into a wooden spoon in lieu of a microphone.

Even the fondue worked—the mixture of Emmental, Gruyère and Comté provided a tang that burst onto their tastebuds, and the consistency of the bubbling cheese and wine was neither too thick nor too thin. Perfect for dunking cubes of baguette.

'Ruby, that was awesome. I am truly replete. Why don't you relax by the fire and I'll wash up?'

'You wash. I'll dry. You did help cook.'

'That's a generous interpretation of grating cheese.'

'You did an excellent job of stirring as well.'

Ruby looked over her shoulder as she carried their plates towards the kitchen area and glanced at the clock. A sudden sense of panic touched her. *Tick-tock.*

Stop it, Ruby.

This was an interlude—it couldn't go on for ever and

she wouldn't want it to. Work was way too important, along with her goals and her future life. A future in which Ethan would only feature in a professional sense.

'Anyway, we'd best get this cleared up quick—the carriage will be back to take us into town for the Boxing Day market, followed by a mountain ascent.'

'Sounds brilliant.'

Maybe Ethan was right—the key was to keep moving, garner the maximum number of precious memories from this time capsule.

The hustle and bustle of the town square soothed her. It was littered with stalls, and the air was alight with chatter, wafting with a cluster of glorious scents. As she stood and inhaled the tang of gingerbread, the scent of the pine so evocative of the Christmas Day just gone, her qualms faded away along with the concern they had created.

This was all about a magical interlude and for once she was in control. There was no question of delusions or false dreams or hopes. This fling had been her idea, entered into with the knowledge that Ethan wouldn't change, and she was good with that.

She opened her eyes to find Ethan's grey-blue eyes fixed on her and she smiled at him, drank in the craggy features, the breadth of his shoulders, his aura of strength. Desire lodged deep in the hollow of her tummy—this freaking gorgeous man was hers. For now... And that was enough. For now she would live in the moment.

'This is such a wonderful place,' she said. 'I'd come on holiday for the market alone.'

The fresh produce was enough to make her tastebuds explode in anticipation. Cheeses abounded, bowls heaped with olives glistened, dried meats and *saucissons* hung in tempting displays.

'Shall I buy ingredients for dinner tonight?' she asked, the words so deliciously intimate. The idea of the evening ahead enticed her: cosy in the chalet, preparing dinner, a glass of wine, music in the background, smooth conversation, the exchange of a kiss here and there…

Purchases made, she espied the Christmas stalls, still piled high with festive adornments. Wooden gifts, bright wrapping paper, carved toys and gaudy sweets. Simple carved Christmas decorations, each one chunky and unique. One of the reindeer looked back at her, its antlers glistening in the afternoon sun.

Surprise laced her as Ethan picked it up and studied it. Then he nodded at the stallholder. 'I'll take one of each.'

'What are you doing? We did Christmas already. Anyway, I thought you weren't into decorations.'

'They're for you. To keep for your perfect Christmas. I know it'll happen for you.'

Tears prickled the back of her eyes. 'Thank you.'

A vision strobed in her mind. But it was wrong… Because there was Ethan, standing by a Christmas tree as he helped a small brown-haired boy hang the decorations. Around the other side of a tree a slightly older dark-haired girl was being helped by a teenager to thread a garland of tinsel.

Squeezing her nails into the palms of her hands, she erased the imaginary scene and shoved it firmly into her brain's 'Deleted' file. Time to concentrate on the moment, on the here and now. On the imposing grandeur of Mont Blanc as it towered over the town…on the fact that she was about to ascend a high mountain peak with this gorgeous man.

The stallholder handed her the bag and she smiled. 'They are perfect. Now, we had better get going—before we miss the ascent.'

CHAPTER THIRTEEN

ETHAN STRODE DOWN the street, an unfamiliar warmth heating his chest. It was as if this bubble of time theory had freed him to...to what? To *feel*? A soupçon of worry trickled through the fuzzy feel-good haze. Feelings netted nothing but pain and loss.

Chill.

Once they got on that plane in less than twenty-four hours everything would snap back to normal. Work would become paramount and all these strange feelings would dissipate.

'You okay?' she asked.

'I'm good.'

Without thought he took her hand in his and they made their way towards the ticket office. Picked up their tickets and joined the press of people in the gondola. When was the last time he had held someone's hand? Not since childhood, when he'd teetered along holding Tanya's hand.

The concept was strange, and for a moment he stared down at their clasped hands before releasing Ruby's hand under the pretence of losing his balance. The motion was abrupt, and it left him with a strange sense of bereavement as he fixed his eyes on the view as they ascended the steep elevation.

Ruby too was silent, until they disembarked at very top, when she halted, her lips parted in a gasp that denoted sheer wonder. Ethan stared too. The incredible vista was one that emptied the lungs and constricted the throat. Panoramic didn't cover it.

They walked slowly across the terrace and Ruby hesitated as she approached the rail.

'You okay?' he asked. 'The altitude could be making you dizzy.'

'I do feel a little light-headed, but I think that's because I am awestruck.'

'Ditto.'

The snow-covered expanse stretched and stretched; the sky surrounded them in a cerulean blue cloak.

Ruby gestured towards the now far-distant town that looked as if it might be made from building bricks. 'Wow! Being up here, encompassed by Nature's might—it puts things into perspective. We are here for such a minuscule slice of time compared to this universality. It makes me feel insignificant.'

'You could never be insignificant.'

Not this woman, with her determination, courage and her capacity to give.

She tugged her hat further down her head and he stepped closer to her to share his body warmth; the icy temperature permeated their thick padded layers.

'That's kind, Ethan, but it's not true. One day I hope I *will* be significant—help turn someone's life around. But until then...'

'No.' The idea that she believed herself insignificant did not sit well with him. 'You have already touched so many people's lives. Look at what you did for your brother and sisters.'

She shook her head. 'I did my best, but you know the saying—the road to hell is paved with good intentions. If I'd been stronger I wouldn't have shielded my parents for so long. I believed what they said—believed they would turn their lives around for us. So I lied, I pretended, but I was a fool. There were times when there wasn't enough food, when we slept in squalor—parties when things could have gone so horribly wrong. If I'd spoken up Tom, Edie and Philippa would have had a better start in life. I let them down.'

'No!' The syllable was torn from him. 'You didn't let anyone down. You gave Tom and Edie and Philippa the right start in life, you kept them safe and you gave them love. I promise you, hand on heart, that you gave each one of them something incredibly precious. Something every baby and every child deserves. Your parents let you all down. The system let you down. *You* didn't let anyone down. This I know.'

'Thank you.' The words were polite, but she turned away as she spoke them to survey the vast expanse and he knew she had dismissed his words as so much bunkum.

'Why don't you ask them?'

That caught her attention and she twisted to face him, her breath white in the crisp cold air.

'I'm sure you would be able to trace them.'

'I won't do that.' Her chin tilted in a stubborn determination that spoke of a decision made.

'Why not? I understand the decision you made back then. But now... Now surely it would be good for you all to reconnect?'

She shook her head. 'I don't want to rock *their* boat. You should understand that. They are young adults now, and they have their own lives to lead. The last thing I want to do is complicate those lives. That's partly why I changed my name years ago—a clean break, a fresh start.'

'It sounds like there was a deep bond between you. I think they would want to hear from you.'

A sigh puffed from her lips and stricken eyes met his. 'They have each other and their adoptive parents. They don't need me.'

Ethan frowned, hearing the stubborn lilt to her voice.

'It's not about need, Ruby. Maybe they'd like to hear from you. Maybe they want to know what happened to you.'

He knew that if he could turn back time and somehow spend even five more minutes with Tanya he would move heaven and earth to do so.

His body tensed as Ruby turned again, rested her arms on the railing and stared out into the cold vastness of unforgiving beauty.

'It's a bit more complicated than that.'

'How?'

'What if I try and contact them and they say thanks, but no thanks? I've already lost them once and…' She gestured over the terrace rail. 'It was like plummeting into that chasm. I'm out of the pit now and I've got my life together. I can't face the prospect of falling back in.'

Her voice was small and lost and compassion touched him. 'It's okay to be scared. But that doesn't mean you shouldn't take the risk.'

'That's easy for you to say. You're never scared, and risk is your middle name. Given half a chance you'd leap off here and ski down the mountain.'

'That's different. That's about physical fear—it helps create a buzz; it's a good feeling. The fear of contact with your brother and sisters not working out is an emotional one, and it takes far more courage to overcome that then it does to climb a mountain.'

'But you don't have any emotional fears either.'

That was because he didn't let himself feel any emotion that he couldn't control. 'This isn't about me. This is about you. And I believe you should do this. Otherwise you're letting your fear conquer something that could make an enormous difference to your life and theirs.'

Her eyes shot anger at him—a dark blue laser. 'It's not your decision to make. All due respect, Ethan, but you don't know how this feels.'

'No, I don't. But…'

His turn now to look away, to absorb the vast chill of white that would remain there long after he and Ruby had returned to normality.

'But what?'

The exasperation had left her tone and she shifted closer to him, placed a hand on his forearm. Her touch brought a soothing heat and somehow gave him the incentive to step into the chasm. To help Ruby make the decision he felt to be right.

'But I do know what it feels like to lose a sibling. I had a sister.' His voice cracked—the word was rusty with disuse. 'An older sister. Tanya. She died, and I would do pretty much anything to have the chance to see her again. So I am telling you, Ruby. Contact them. You have the chance of a future that has them in it. Take that chance.'

Her body stilled next to him and then she let out an exhalation of shock as her grip tightened on his arm. 'I am so sorry. I don't know what to say or do, but I am so very sorry.'

She closed the gap between them completely, so that her body pressed against his, and he took comfort from her closeness. For a long moment they stared out at the view, and then he heard her intake of breath.

'Do you want to talk about it?' she asked.

Did he? Disbelief rippled in his gut at the fact he was even considering the hitherto impossible. But he was. Because he knew that once they left the Alps there would be no more of this. It was too emotional; too many layers were being unravelled and he couldn't risk his emotions escalating out of control.

But here and now the temptation to share his memories of Tanya nigh overwhelmed him, and images of his beautiful gentle sister streamed in his mind. He realised that he wanted Ruby to 'know' Tanya—to 'see' the sister he missed so much. Ruby had told him that talking about Tom, Edie and Philippa had reminded her of the good memories. Maybe Tanya deserved that—to be remembered.

His voice caught as he nodded his head. 'I think I do. But not here. Let's go back to the chalet.'

As they entered the chalet Ruby fought down the urge to throw herself onto his chest, wrap her arms around him and just hold him. Though…why not? For the next few hours at least she could be herself, could show feelings and emotions, and right now the desire to offer comfort overrode all else. But she knew that this was unmapped territory for both of them.

He shrugged his jacket off and hung it on a peg, watched her almost warily as she approached. Standing on tiptoe, she kissed his cheek, inhaled his woodsy scent, felt the solid bulk of his body against hers. She stepped back and took his hands in hers. The smile he gave was a little twisted, but his grasp tightened around hers as she tugged him towards the sofa.

'I'll light the fire,' he said.

Sensing that it would be easier for him to talk whilst in action, she nodded. 'That would be great. You want coffee?'

'No, thanks.'

He busied herself with the fire, loaded the logs, and Ruby curled up on the purple cushions, her whole being attuned to him.

'Tanya was three years older than me. Mum was always out—she worked so many jobs to make ends meet—and that made Tanya and I extra close. Tanya was…'

His deep tone faltered and he paused, scraped a match against the side of the box and lit the wood. Sat back on his haunches and gazed at the flicker of red and orange.

'She was so very gentle, so kind.' Wonder touched his voice. 'It was as if she was something rare and beautiful and fragile on that estate. She had chestnut hair, long and thick, and brown eyes, and the warmest smile in the world—the kind that made you feel like you could do anything.'

The fire whoomphed and caught, illuminated the planes of his features, touched with sadness now. Ruby slipped off the sofa, and as if aware of her movements he shifted, so that they both ended up on the floor with the sofa at their backs. Without speaking she placed a hand on his thigh, tucked her body next to his.

'She wanted to make something of her life. Her dream was to write, to travel, to see the wonders of the world. Mum encouraged her, and Tanya flourished—she loved books, absorbed information like a sponge. She'd tell me about all the countries out there and we'd hatch dreams of travel.'

'She sounds wonderful—and it sounds like you loved each other very much.'

No wonder Ethan had rejected love—he'd had the most important person in his world snatched by death. Yet the darkness of his expression told her that it was even worse than that.

'We did. It was Tanya who kept me on the straight and narrow for a long time. But as I got older it became harder for her.'

'What about your mum?'

'Mum was… Mum and I… It was difficult. I am the spitting image of my father. She hadn't actually wanted a second child with him and she never really engaged with me.'

Ruby felt her nails score her palm—it sounded as though Ethan felt he'd deserved the indifference she read from his words. 'That wasn't your fault.'

A shrug greeted this and she held her peace.

'No, but my behaviour was my own choice. The estate was my reality and I began to believe that Tanya's aspirations could never happen. I started to bunk off school, began to go off the rails. But Tanya held me in check; I would have done anything for her. If she'd let me.'

Foreboding touched Ruby, drizzled her skin with dread. 'What happened?'

'She was bullied. I didn't know—she didn't tell me, and we were at different schools by then. Tanya was doing A levels, and that meant a bunch of kids had it in for her. It started out as small-time stuff, teasing with a nasty edge, and then it became sabotage of homework, and then it became worse and worse. They stalked her, threatened her with rape, and eventually she couldn't take it any more. She killed herself.'

The words buzzed in the air like dark, malignant insects, and for a moment Ruby couldn't take in the enormity of his words. Once they hit her she raised her hand to her mouth to stifle the cry of protest. 'Ethan...' The anguish on his face was enough to make her weep.

'I found her. She'd overdosed—she'd found a stash of Mum's sleeping pills and swallowed the lot.' His voice jerked the words out, raspy and abuzz with a raw, jagged pain. 'At first I thought she was asleep, and then...'

Ruby swallowed the lump of horror that clogged her throat, pressed her lips together to stop herself from crying out. The image was so clear in her brain—she could only imagine how etched it was on his. A younger Ethan— lanky, tall, unsuspecting—calling his sister, entering the room... And then the awful paralysed second when he would have realised the grim truth and his life had changed for ever.

'Ethan...' Her voice was a whisper as compassion

robbed her breath. 'I am so very sorry. I cannot imagine what you and your mother went through.'

The words were inadequate against such calamity, and she could only hope that the tragedy had brought mother and son closer.

'Mum was devastated. It was a dark time.'

For a long moment he stared into the flames and then he shifted slightly. Scored his palm down his face as if in an attempt to erase the memories.

'Do you think we could change topic? I'm kind of talked out.'

'Of course we can.'

Ruby tried to pull her thoughts together, her heart aching for what he had been through. For what he had told her and for the troubled relationship that he had with his mother. But now she wanted to lighten the mood, hoping that their conversation had been cathartic.

'How about a picnic and some board games?'

Surprise touched his face, and then his lips tipped into a small smile. 'That sounds perfect.' As she rose he followed suit and placed a hand on his arm. 'Thanks for listening.'

He cupped her jaw in his palms and dropped the lightest and sweetest of kisses on her lips. And her heart ached all the more.

As dawn slipped through the shutter's slats Ethan slipped quietly from the bed, pulled on his jeans and gazed down at Ruby, her cheek pillowed on her hand, her dark hair in sheer contrast to the white of the pillowcase and the cream of her skin. Her beauty touched him on a strata that he didn't want to identify and, turning away, he reached down for his shirt, thrust his arms into the sleeves and headed for the ladder.

Panic strummed inside him, made him edgy. Somehow Ruby had got right under his skin, and the idea caused angst to tighten his gut as he prowled the lounge and kitchen.

Memories of the past evening itched and prickled— they'd drunk cocoa in front of the lambent flames of the fire, talked of anything and nothing, laughed and philosophised. Then they'd gone to bed and… And there weren't words, truth be told, and he wasn't sure he even wanted to find any.

The panic grew—as if his actions had opened the floodgates. Letting her in had been a mistake, and nothing good could come of it. He wasn't capable of closeness.

'Ethan?'

He swivelled round, saw her at the top of the ladder. How long had she been there, watching him pace?

With an effort he forced his lips up into a relaxed smile. 'Morning!' he said, and his heart thumped against his ribcage as he took in her tousled hair, the penguin pyjamas.

Silence stretched into a net of awkwardness as she climbed down the ladder, paused at the bottom to survey him. Impulse urged him to walk over and carry her right back upstairs, and he slammed his hands into his jeans pockets and rocked back on his heels. No more impulses—because his emotions were already ricocheting off the Richter scale.

'Coffee?' he offered.

'Yes, please.'

Trying to keep his body rhythm natural, he headed to the kitchen. The endeavour was a fail and he passed her, breath held, unsure what to do, ultra-careful not to touch her. Yesterday he'd have teased her mercilessly about the penguins, dropped a kiss on her lips, taken her hand… Now he sidled past.

Ruby stood stock-still, one finger tugging a strand of hair. 'I'll…I'll go change,' she said, the words stilted, and relief rippled with regret touched his chest.

Because he knew she'd gone upstairs to armour herself in clothes. For this bubble of time she had been herself—no façade needed. Same for him. But now... Now it was time to go back to normal. Because being himself was too raw, too hard, too emotional. And emotion was not the way he wanted to go—he wanted the status quo of his un-rocked boat.

So he filled the kettle and assembled the ingredients for breakfast. The bread they had bought yesterday, the succulent strawberry jam, the pastries Ruby loved so much.

The sound of her shoes tapping on the wooden floor forced him to look up.

'Looks great,' she said, the words too bright, underscored with brittleness.

Her glorious hair was tamed into a sleek ponytail, not even a tendril loose. The knowledge sucker-punched him—never again would he run his fingers through those smooth silky curls, never again would he touch her soft skin, hear the small responsive gasp she made...

Enough.

A sudden urge to sweep the breakfast off the table, to get rid of the false image of intimacy, nearly overwhelmed him. The intimacy was over, and the sooner they exited this cloying atmosphere the better.

Too many emotions brewed inside him now, but at all costs he had to remember this was not Ruby's fault. If he had miscalculated it would not rebound on her. Instead he would haul back on all this feeling and return to professional normality. Though right now, in the line of her direct gaze, work seemed almost surreal. Which was nuts. Work was his life.

Jeez, Ethan.

Now he'd gone all drama king. Maybe he'd actually shed some brain cells these past days. In which case it was time to use the ones he had left. Fast.

No point in rueing the fact that he'd agreed to this fling in the first place. His eyes had been open to the fact that it would be different from his usual liaisons—he simply hadn't realised how that difference would play out. But there was no time for regrets. None at all. Regret was an indulgence—the important thing now was momentum.

With determination he lifted a croissant, went through the motions of spreading butter and jam. Then he glanced at his watch. 'We'll need to hit the road soon. I thought we could do a drive-round and get a visual of any areas or properties suitable for Caversham. I'll do a computer trawl whilst you pack up. Then maybe you can take over whilst I pack.'

'No problem.'

The cool near formality of her tone smote him even as he forced himself to pick up his coffee cup.

A gulp of coffee and she pushed her plate away. 'I'm on it.'

CHAPTER FOURTEEN

RUBY LOOKED AROUND the banqueting hall of Caversham Castle and tried to summon more than a token sense of pride and achievement. It looked fabulous, and she knew the sight would usually have prompted a victory dance or three around the room.

Actually it looked better than fabulous—she had worked flat-out the past two days, and all the work she had put in prior to Christmas had paid off. Medieval-style trestle tables fashioned from oak were arranged round the restaurant floor. The ceiling boasted an intricate mural depicting knights, princesses and acts of valour. The whole room seeped history, with maps of Cornwall through the ages and Cornish scenes from centuries ago adorning the walls.

Soon enough the room would be filled with the bustle of one hundred celebrity guests, the sound of troubadours and the scent of a genuine historic feast and Ruby knew the evening would be a success.

If only she cared.

She resisted the urge to put her head in her hands—of course she cared. This would be a career-tilting event—it would show the world that Ruby Hampton was the business. The restaurant at Caversham Castle would be launched in style, and she had little doubt that by the time they opened for normal custom in two weeks they would be booked up months in advance. Which was even better, because then she would be rushed off her feet.

Which would hopefully be the catalyst for the cessation of the stupid, mad feelings that swamped her every time she saw Ethan. The strange ache in her tummy when she wasn't with him…the stranger ache in her heart when she was. It would almost be preferable to discover that it was an ulcer rather than what she suspected—she missed him. Missed the Ethan she had glimpsed for forty-eight precious hours.

Unfortunately that Ethan had vanished—had donned the cloak of professionalism and left the building. How did he do that? Maybe the same way she did. After all, hadn't she been the epitome of a perfect restaurant manager? Could there be a possibility that he was hurting as she was?

But even if he was…what difference did it make? There could be no future. Her plan was to adopt and Ethan didn't want a family. Ethan didn't want *anything*.

In two days the ball would be over—it would be a new year and a new start. Ethan would waltz off to his usual business concerns and she would be able to get her head back together.

The back of her neck prickled and her whole body went to code red—a sure indicator that Ethan was in the vicinity.

'It's looking good,' he said. 'I need the final auction list, please. Rafael's on his way and he wants to look at it en route.'

'Sure. It's good of him to be auctioneer.'

'Yes.'

The terse edge of near indifference that veiled his tone made her foot itch with the urge to kick him even as she matched it. 'I'll email him the list straight away.'

'Ruby?'

The sound of Cora Brookes's even, well-modulated voice had her swivelling on her heel in relief. Cora, the new hotel administrator, had arrived two days before, and already Ruby was impressed by her smooth competence— though Cora had equally smoothly avoided all attempts at anything other than professional conversation.

'I thought you should see this.'

'What's up? Don't tell me the caterers have cancelled? Rafael Martinez has pulled out?'

For a second a faint look Ruby couldn't interpret crossed Cora's face. Then the redhead shook her head. 'Nothing like that. Why would he? It's great publicity for him... Plus it's not often a playboy like him gets to feature in a celebrity magazine in a charitable light.' She shook her head. 'Anyway, here you are.'

Ruby accepted the netbook and looked down at a celebrity magazine's website.

Breaking News!
Hugh Farlane engaged.
'This time it's the real thing,' Hollywood star proclaims.

What?

Disbelief churned in her tummy. She'd barely given Hugh a thought in the past days. Apart from feeling a vague relief that he had obviously decided to stop offering her up as sacrificial goods to the press.

Mere weeks after his break-up with Ruby Hampton, now working within the Caversham Holiday Adventures empire, Hugh has announced his engagement to his long-term PA, Portia Brockman.

Portia? Beautiful, devoted to Hugh's interests, she'd worked for him for years—the woman had to know him better than anyone else, so why on earth would she marry him? Surely it was another stunt. Or... She looked down at the image of Portia, who was gazing up adoringly at Hugh. Maybe a better question would be did Portia *know* it was a stunt?

Next query—what was Ruby going to do about it?

Which led on to another question: if she thrust a spoke in Hugh's wheel what would he do? A flicker of fear ignited at the memory of his expression, taut with threat, as he'd ensured her silence.

It was a flicker she knew she had no choice but to ignore.

With a start she realised Ethan had removed the tablet from her grasp and was reading the article. A formidable frown slashed his brow as he handed it back to Cora.

'I'll have to go and sort this out,' Ruby said briskly. 'I'll get a train up to London—I should be back late this evening. Cora, thanks for bringing this to my attention. Can I leave a few things for you to do while I'm gone?'

'Of course.'

'Great. I'll catch you before I leave.'

Ruby nodded and turned, headed for the door.

'Hold on.' Ethan's stepped into her path, his tone peremptory.

'Yes?' Slamming to a halt, she tried to sound cool, as if her proximity to his chest, delectably covered in a white T-shirt, wasn't playing havoc with her respiratory system. Who wore T-shirts at the end of December, anyway?

'I'll come with you.'

'That is not necessary.'

Cora glanced from one to the other. 'Let me know what you need, Ruby. I'll be in my office or you can call me.'

Once the redhead had glided away, with admirable discretion, and the door had clicked shut, Ruby glared at Ethan.

'*So* not necessary,' she amended.

'I disagree—I told you I stand by my employees.'

All of a sudden a wave of pure white-hot anger flooded her—as if every molecule of built-up frustration from the past four days had all exploded into rage simultaneously.

'So you're going to hop on your charger and come and protect me because I am your *employee*?'

'What is wrong with that?'

'Everything. Everything is wrong with that.' Had he forgotten Christmas? Had some sort of brain transplant? 'Forget it. You have made it perfectly clear that you want our relationship to be professional.'

'We agreed that once we got back here we would revert to being professional.'

There was no arguing with that—if he took it a step further he might even point out that it had been *her* fool idea in the first place.

'You're right. So since my business with Hugh is *personal* I will deal with it myself.'

There was no indication that he'd even heard her. 'I don't want you to face him alone.'

'Why not? I'm sure I'll have to face plenty on my own when I adopt. There will be social workers and carers and teachers and who knows what else? Will you be there when it gets tough then?'

'That is hardly a valid argument.'

'It is extremely valid from my side.'

The air was tinged with exasperation as he folded his arms. 'That scenario is set in the future. This situation with Hugh is now. He's threatened you in the past, the man is a liar and a bully, and I don't see the problem with you accepting some support.'

Oh, crap!

As she stared at him, absorbed the frown that slashed his brow and the determined set of his mouth, drank in his sheer strength, the icy cold fingers of realisation dawned. Seeped into her soul. She knew exactly why this was a problem—she *wanted* Ethan to come with her. But she wanted his presence because he cared about her as person, not as an employee.

Panic squeezed her chest. She'd fallen for Ethan Caversham. Again. Or maybe she'd never got over him. This stubborn, generous, flawed man had called to something deep within her and her heart had responded without her permission.

She wanted him in her present *and* in her future.

Shock doused her veins, made her skin clammy. How had this happened? Ethan would never want a family. Would never change from being the workaholic, driven man he was. So why was her heart—the self-same heart that wasn't supposed to be involved—aching with a deep, bitter sting?

His frown deepened as he studied her expression and she desperately tried to think—tried to work out what to do with this awful, awesome knowledge.

Nothing. That was what she should do.

Ethan had made it more than clear that he had negative desire for a relationship, let alone a family. It wasn't his fault she'd been stupid enough to fall for him. If she told him how she felt he would recoil, and she wasn't sure she could bear that. Let alone the fact that it would make any work relationship impossible.

Maybe that would be impossible anyway. Maybe her best course of action would be to leave. Otherwise she would have to spend her life erecting a façade of lies, playing a part, watching him from afar, living in hope that one day he'd return her love. The idea made her tummy churn in revolt. It would be a replay of her childhood.

'Ruby?' There was concern in his voice now, as well as an assessing look in his blue-grey eyes that indicated the whirring of his formidable brain.

With an effort she recalled their conversation. 'Ethan, I need to do this by myself. Plus, tomorrow night is too important to blow—too important for kids like Tara and Max. You need to be here to supervise any last-minute glitches.'

He shook his head. 'Cora can cover that. So can Rafael.'

Somehow she had to dissuade him—all she wanted to do now was run. Achieve some space. Get her head together. Enough that she could hold the façade together for a while longer until she could find him a replacement restaurant manager.

'No. Cora and Rafael are great, but you need to be here. This is your show.' For a heartbeat she felt the sudden scratch of tears—this would be one of the last times they were together, and emotion bubbled inside her. 'You're doing such good here.'

Instinct carried her forward, so close to him that she could smell the oh-so-familiar, oh-so-dizzying woodsy scent of him. One hand reached out and lay on his forearm as she gazed up at him, allowed herself one last touch.

'Don't.' His voice low and guttural.

'Don't what? Tell the truth?'

He shook his head, stepped back so that her hand dropped to her side. 'Don't look at me like that. Don't make me a hero. Because I'm not.'

'I didn't say you were a hero. But you are a good man, and you do so much good. Why won't you acknowledge that and accept something good in your life.'

What was she doing? The sane course of action would be to get out of there at speed, but some small unfurling of hope kept her feet adhered to the floor.

'Whatever you did in the past can't change that.'

'You don't know about my past, Ruby.'

'Then tell me.'

For a long moment he looked deep into her eyes, and for a second she feared that he could read her thoughts, her emotions, could see the love that she was so desperately trying to veil.

His gaze didn't falter, though the clench of his jaw and the taut stance of his body betrayed his tension.

'I told you that even before Tanya died I was beginning to go off the rails—I'd bunk off school every so often… I'd taken up smoking, graffitied the odd wall. But after she died I was so angry; I wanted vengeance on those bullies who'd made her last months on this earth a torment. But what could I do? I couldn't take them all on myself—they were a group, part of one of the most intimidating gangs on the estate. Mum was falling apart, and I was full of frustration and rage.'

Her lungs constricted as she imagined how the teenaged Ethan must have felt. So helpless, so alone. With a mother prostrate with grief and the sister he'd looked up to driven to take her own life.

'So it all went downhill. School became ancient history. I took up petty crime—shoplifting. I got into fights. I did dope…I drank. I swaggered around the estate like an idiot. I became everything Tanya would have abhorred.'

'Tanya would have understood. You were a child full of anger, pain and grief. Didn't your mum do anything?'

'She was too immersed in grief to notice.'

There was no rancour to be heard, but it seemed to Ruby that everything he had done must have been in an effort to make his mum notice—step in, *do* something. She couldn't bear the fact that he'd judged himself so harshly—that he couldn't see the plethora of mitigation around his actions.

'God knows what might have happened, but finally I got caught stealing from one of the high-street clothes stores. I went nuts—went up against the security officer. I lost it completely and they called in the cops. I was arrested, taken down to the police station, and they contacted my mother.'

'What happened?'

'As far as she was concerned it proved I'd morphed into my father. Reinforced her fear that history would repeat.'

'But…but she must have seen that this was different?'

His silence was ample testament to the fact that she hadn't, and the dark shadow in his eyes was further proof that neither had he. Foreboding rippled through her. 'What did she do?'

'Packed my stuff and handed me over to social services.'

Words failed her as anger and compassion intertwined—no wonder Ethan had judged himself as guilty when his own mother had disowned him.

'Hey. Don't look like that. For Mum the loss of Tanya was more than a tragedy—it was innately wrong. It should have been me.'

'Did she say that?'

'Yes.'

The syllable was spoken as if it was to be expected and Ruby's heart tore.

'I get that. She had a point.'

'No, she did not!' The words were a shout, but she couldn't help it.

'I let her down, Ruby. It is as simple as that. No one made me act that way.'

'You were her *son*, Ethan—her child. You were acting out of your own grief and anger.'

Ruby clenched her fists. Why was he being so obdurate? But, of course, she knew the answer. Hope. Why had she persisted in believing in her own parents, long after they had proved they would never change? Same answer. Hope.

'Have you seen your mum since?'

'No. She is still on the estate, and every year I send her a cheque and a letter. Every year she doesn't bank the cheque and she doesn't answer the letter.'

The unfairness, the tragedy of it, banded her chest. 'I understand that your mother had her own issues, but they were *her* issues. Would you ever do to a child what she did to you?'

Something flashed across his eyes and then he rubbed

his hand down his face, made a derisive sound in his throat. 'Jeez. Let's end this conversation. Okay? I've come to terms with it all and it's no—'

'If you say it's no big deal I'll scream. It's a *huge* deal. You told me to fight for justice, that right and wrong matter. This matters, and this is injustice. Ethan, you told me you thought I would be a good parent.'

'You will be.'

'Well, a social worker told me once that damaged children like me repeat their parents' mistakes. I don't believe that has to be true and neither do you. That's why you want to help kids like Max and Tara—because you believe they deserve a chance. So do you.' Ruby hauled in breath. 'You have judged yourself and you've judged wrong. Whether your mum can see it or not, you're a good man, Ethan Caversham.'

For a second she thought she'd made some sort of impact, but then his broad shoulders lifted.

'Sure, Ruby. Whatever you want. I'm a good man.'

The self-mockery evident.

'You are. And you deserve love. Real, *proper* love.'

It all seemed so clear to her now—exactly why Ethan had his heart under such a guard, his emotions in lockdown. The only person who had loved him was the sister he felt he had let down—a sister he had lost so tragically. The mother who should have loved him had condemned him from birth.

'You do not have to be alone in that boat, Ethan. All family relationships do not have to end in tragedy. Love doesn't always have to go wrong.'

Discomfort etched his face, was clear in his stance as he rocked back on his heels, hands in his pockets. 'Leave it, Ruby.'

'I can't. You deserve love.' How could she make him see that? 'For what it's worth, I love you.'

His face was leached of colour; blue-grey eyes burned with a light she couldn't interpret. Eventually he stepped back.

'It's not love. It's what you felt for Hugh, for Steve, for Gary. You said it yourself—you're not a good judge of character.'

'Ouch. That is below the belt.'

'No, it isn't. You don't love me—you want to heal me because you see me as broken. And I don't need to be healed. As for deserving love—that is irrelevant. I don't want love; I don't need love. I have come to terms with my past and I am moving forward. I'm not going to change. Any more than Gary, Steve or Hugh. So please don't waste your time thinking you love me. Find someone who will be good for you and to you. Someone who will father your children, whichever way you choose to have them. That man isn't me.'

The words were so final, so heavy, that she could feel her heart crack.

'Then I'd best get to London.'

What else was there to say?

CHAPTER FIFTEEN

THE CLICK OF the door unglued Ethan's feet from the floor, sent him striding forward, her name on his lips. Only to stop. What was he doing? He'd rejected her love so why was he following her? To do what?

His gut churned. He didn't want to hurt Ruby—hadn't wanted to a decade ago and didn't want to now. Somehow he had to make her see that he was right—she did not love him, whatever she believed. All he needed to do was convince her of that.

Maybe she'd work it out herself. See that every word he'd said was the truth. The past was over and he had come to terms with it. Had worked out that the best way forward was to move on, to channel his anger into becoming a success and using that success to help others. That worked for him—he didn't need love or a family. Didn't want love.

So why did he sound as if he was trying to convince himself?

The door swung open and Ethan swivelled round, his heart hammering in irrational hope that she had come back. Instead he saw Rafael Martinez, his expression creased in a small puzzled frown. 'A red-haired woman brought me here. Who is she?'

Pull it together, Ethan.

'Cora Brookes. My new hotel administrator.'

'I see.' Rafael frowned and rubbed his jaw. 'I had the distinct impression that Cora Brookes doesn't like me. She walked me here at the rate of knots and avoided all eye contact. Yet she looks familiar. Anyway it doesn't matter.

I'm here, and ready to auction like a pro tomorrow. I also have a business proposition I want to discuss with you. But you look as though business is the last thing on your mind.'

He needed to get it together. This was Rafael Martinez and this was business.

'I'm fine. Happy to talk business. Why don't we go to my office?'

Get away from this banqueting hall with all its memories of Ruby.

Rafael's dark eyes surveyed him with what looked like amusement. 'And how is the lovely Ruby Hampton?'

'Fine.' If Rafael was about to show even the most tepid interest in Ruby, Ethan had every intention of ramming his teeth down his throat. Business or no business. 'Why do you ask?'

'Whoa!' Rafael lifted his hands in the air. 'I was just curious. I get that she is off-limits.'

'Yes, she is.'

Rafael's eyebrows rose. 'Well, if you have an interest there you should know she has left the castle at speed—with a suitcase.'

Ethan paused as his brain attempted to compute the situation. Why would Ruby have taken a suitcase when she planned to return the same day? Unless she'd figured the journey there and back was too far? Needed some space? That must be it. Yet panic whispered in his gut.

There was a knock at the door and Cora entered, glanced at Rafael and then away again. 'Ethan. I'm not sure if I should mention this or not, but Ruby seemed upset and I'm not sure she's coming back.'

'What do you mean? It's the ball tomorrow.'

'I know.' Cora hesitated. 'It's just… She gave me the whole breakdown of the event in intricate detail—as if it was possible that she wouldn't be here. I mean…to be honest I can cover the admin side, because you and Ruby have planned it all down to the last detail. But I can't meet and greet or mingle with the guests. We agreed that.'

Her even voice held the hint of a quaver as her turquoise eyes met his and Ethan nodded. She was right. They had.

As if aware of Rafael's gaze as he studied her expression, Cora shifted so her back was to him. 'And, more importantly, as Ruby put all the work in I think she should be here to see the success I am sure it will be. I thought you should know.'

Ethan hauled in breath, tried to think.

Of course Ruby wouldn't leave.

You sure, Ethan?

The truth was the ball could go ahead without her and she knew it. It could be she was running—exactly as he had a decade ago. The irony was more than apparent.

Images of Ruby filtered through his brain. Her elfin features illuminated by enthusiasm, haunted by sadness, etched with compassion, lit up by desire. The gurgle of her laugh, the beauty of her smile… The idea of losing her, the idea that she might not return, sent a searing pain to his very soul.

Alongside that was fear…the terror of what it would feel like to let go, to allow his emotions full rein. Fear that he would somehow let Ruby down. If he allowed love to take hold he would screw it up, not be the man she deserved. That added up to a whole lot of scared.

The question now was what was he going to do about it?

Ruby approached the swish London hotel—the very same one where she had discovered Hugh's infidelity and perfidy in a double whammy. For a scant second she wondered why the idea of facing Hugh now didn't have the power to intimidate her. Possibly because she felt numb—had felt a cold, clammy sense of 'ugh' since she'd filled her suitcase and fled Caversham Castle.

Right now all she wanted was to get this over with, because she didn't want Portia to go through the same pain and disillusionment. In addition, it was about time she stood up to Hugh Farlane.

As she entered the imposing lobby—all fancy uniformed staff, marble and fluted pillars—one of Hugh's assistants rushed over to her.

'Come with me,' he said, his eyes roving the area. 'We don't want any bad publicity.'

'Hi, Greg. Good to see you again. Thanks for arranging this.'

The young man flushed. 'Sorry. It's good to see you too. But Hugh is very emphatic that I get you up there fast.'

'So he hasn't decided how to spin it yet?'

Greg declined to answer, shifting from foot to foot in an agony of discomfort, and then hustled her to the lift.

Once inside the sleek metal box, she felt a sliver of worry permeate the anaesthetic of hurt. Hugh Farlane had the power to crush her like an insignificant bug, and she didn't have Ethan's protection to fall back on now. In her own mind at least she was no longer a Caversham employee.

The irony was that she'd come full circle.

No! Not true. Weeks before she hadn't had the courage to stand up to Hugh. Now she did. In the past weeks she'd learned so much—on a professional *and* a personal level.

Before, the thought of any contact with her siblings had been an impossibility—now the idea seemed feasible. Because Ethan had shown her a new perspective. Somehow he had shown her her own inner strength. Which was a further irony. Because now she would have need of that strength to get over Ethan.

Not now. Put the pain aside and channel that inner power.

Her vertebrae clicked as she straightened up. The lift

doors swooshed open and she stepped forward and followed Greg along the plushly carpeted floor to the ornate door of the penthouse suite.

'Good luck,' Greg murmured as he knocked and then faded discreetly away.

The click as the door swung open set her heart pounding but she managed a smile.

'Ruby…' Hugh stepped forward, the familiar smile full of charm on his lips. 'Great to see you. Come right on in.'

Could the man have had some sort of amnesia attack?

'Drop the charm, Hugh,' she said. 'I've come here to give you fair warning.'

'Of what?'

'If this is another scam I won't stand by and let it happen. I will not let you do it to Portia.'

A roll of his deep brown eyes. 'And what exactly do you think you can do to stop me? Wait.' He raised his hand. 'I can answer that for you. There is nothing you can do. Portia believes in me, and as far as she is concerned you are a gold-digging vixen. And that's the way it's going to stay. In fact…' A casual shrug accompanied his words. 'It may get a bit heated for you in the press again. We'll be giving interviews, and Portia does feel very strongly about you.'

'That's a joke, right?' Her imagination went into boggled mode. 'You want me to take the flak *again*?'

'Yes.' Hugh smiled—a smile that would reduce half the population to its knees but left her utterly unmoved. 'That's not a problem, is it?'

'What if I say it is?'

Goodbye to the smile and any pretence of charm. 'Then you'll leave me no choice. I'll take you for everything you have. You'll lose your job like a shot. You may think Ethan Caversham will protect you, but how long do you think he will do that if I really go to war? Threaten to get one of my friends to sue him?'

'Sue him for what?' Disbelief and a smidge of fear touched her.

'For improper safety procedures—I could rig an accident, no sweat.' Tipping his hands in the air, he switched the smile back on. 'I don't *want* to do it, Rube. I don't… But I need this marriage to happen. Those Forsythe sisters have got a bit suspicious…my agent is on my back again. Yada-yada.'

'In other words you've reverted to type,' Ruby interjected.

'Whatever. Point is, Portia is my salvation.'

Ruby stared at him, and suddenly so much seemed clear to her. 'Ethan will never cower before your so-called might. And neither will I. Not any more. So I suggest you tell Portia the truth. Because if you don't, I will. And if you lie about me one more time in the papers then I will call you on it. I will give an interview of my own and then if you want to retaliate you go for it. Bring it on.'

A burst of adrenalin shot through her system. Ethan was right—the only way to deal with a bully was to stand up to him.

Hugh's eyes narrowed. 'I could drag you through the mud.'

'Go right ahead. But I will not let you do this to Portia. Or to me. I want you to tell her the truth and I want you to issue a statement saying that we have sorted our differences and you were mistaken about my gold-digging tendencies.'

He deflated before her eyes, sank onto a chair. 'You don't understand. I'm scared I'll lose my career…'

'Then fight for it. Clean up your act. Change. But do it for real and fight clean.'

Even as she spoke the words it occurred to her that she had hardly put her own money where her lips were. With Ethan she'd accepted rejection as if it were only to be expected. She hadn't put up so much as a vestige of fight—had let him write off her love as false.

Was that the person she'd become? Sure, years ago she'd lost the fight to keep her family together, but that did not mean she had to lose every fight. The truth was, it was easier, less painful, to expect and accept defeat. After all, the harder you fought the more you risked losing.

A hard rock of determination formed inside her. 'Your choice, Hugh. I've got to go.'

'Okay. I'll do it.'

Ruby nodded, already en route to the door. Her thoughts swirled as she figured out how long it would take her to get back to Cornwall. Should she call first? Text? Email?

The elevator felt claustrophobic, stupidly slow, and she jogged from foot to foot as impatience seized her.

Finally the doors opened and she stepped outside—and there was Ethan.

Thank goodness. Ethan's heart thumped against his ribcage as Ruby erupted from the elevator—he'd already paced a layer off the marble floor of the lobby.

Ruby skidded to a stop and stared at him as if he could be some sort of hologram. 'Ethan?'

'In the flesh.'

'But…what are you doing here?'

'We need to talk. How did it go with Hugh?'

'Good. All sorted. He'll tell Portia the truth and issue an apology to me.'

'That's fabulous, Ruby.'

'Is that why you came here? To check I could cope with Hugh?' Wariness tinged her expression now as she tugged at an errant strand of hair.

'Nope. Were you planning on coming back to Caversham Castle?'

'No. But…'

Ethan held a hand up, not sure he could bear to hear any more. Fear strummed him. She had believed the sheer baloney he had spouted earlier. Somehow he had to convince her to give him another chance.

'Not here. We need to talk properly.'

She nodded. 'There are loads of cafés round here. Or…'

'It's okay. I have it covered. Come on.'

Within seconds of leaving the lobby Rafael's loaned car glided to a halt in front of them. The chauffeur climbed out and opened the car door for Ruby, who slid inside with a puzzled look.

'Why didn't you drive your own car?' she asked.

'Actually, Rafael lent me his helicopter, as well as Robert and this car, to meet me on arrival.'

'You *flew* here from Cornwall?' Her eyes widened and a half-laugh dropped from her lips. 'Why?'

Ethan shrugged. 'Impulse. I needed to see you. To apologise and…'

Her eyes narrowed. 'Apologise for what?'

Here goes.

Time to put himself on the line. Along with some emotional honesty. 'For my reactions. I panicked. Just like I did ten years ago. I've been alone a long time; the only person who has ever got close has been you. Ten years ago I ran. I told myself I did it for you, because I could see that you had developed a misguided crush on me, but in reality I panicked.'

'And this time?' The question was soft, almost tentative.

Clenching his hands round his knees, he hauled in breath. 'This time I don't want to run, and I don't want you to run. For ten years I have avoided emotion, locked it down because I associated emotion with bad choices, rejection and tragedy. I decided to channel my anger and use it to create momentum—to build Caversham into something bigger and bigger, to allow me to do good via charitable efforts.'

'And you succeeded—you turned your life around.'

A twist of her body and she faced him now, her face illuminated in the dusky light of the limo's interior, her cinnamon scent whirling in his head.

'You should be proud of that.'

'I am. But the whole time I have been scared of emotion, scared of rocking the boat, because I thought my whole new life would tumble down. These past few weeks you have shown me that doesn't have to happen. With you I have run the gamut of emotions—each day I have felt more and more. Caring, desire, happiness, sympathy, a need to give and take comfort. You've unlocked something inside me. You've helped me remember Tanya as she deserves to be remembered—not just with bitterness and guilt, but with the memory of all the good she did in my life. You've let me look down the dark tunnels of the past and realise that along with the darkness there was also light. And there's something else you did too...'

'What?'

Her voice caught and fear and anticipation rollicked through him.

'You taught me how to love. I love you, Ruby.'

For a heartbeat her expression registered no more than shock, and the fear escalated. What if she had changed her mind—realised that loving him was foolhardy? Then he would change her mind if it took him his whole life to do it. Then her expression morphed into a smile that touched and warmed him as she launched herself across the limo seat and into his arms.

'I love you too. So very, *very* much. And I swear to you it is nothing to do with a need to heal you. Because I don't need to do that—I love you exactly as you are. You're kind and generous and caring and stubborn and demanding and deep and complicated, and I love you for all those traits. You don't need to change for me.'

She nestled onto his lap, her hands cupping his jaw, and he felt a thrill of happiness. This woman loved him, and he knew he was the luckiest man in the universe.

'That realisation has been an epiphany for me. You see, all my life I have associated love with need. I wanted to be needed. My parents didn't love me enough to change their lifestyles for me, so I equated someone loving me with them being willing to change for me. Because that would give me self-worth. You've taught me how to have self-worth all by myself. You've shown me how to be brave, to stand up for what is right, and you've taught me to risk again—to risk rejection, to risk pain, because sometimes that is the right thing to do. So you don't have to change to prove your love or mine. I love *you*.'

'And I love you.'

He could quite cheerfully have continued in this conversational vein all day. His heart gave a happy jump and his whole body fizzed with a joy he could barely believe.

The limo glided to a stop and he dropped a kiss on her lips. 'Now that is sorted you need to come with me.'

'Where to?'

'Wait and see.'

The door opened and Ruby scrambled off Ethan's lap, sneaking a quick glance at the impassive face of the chauffeur and figuring he'd probably seen worse as Rafael Martinez's driver.

She looked around in an attempt to work out where they were. Not that it mattered—all that mattered was Ethan's proximity and the sheer sense of wonder that doused her. Ethan *loved* her. The urge to cartwheel, to grab passersby and tell them of her sheer happy feelings nigh overwhelmed her.

Instead she looked round and took in a tree-lined canal, with moored narrowboats of all colours bobbing up and down on the water. Cream Georgian architecture abounded, and the whole area felt like a quirky peaceful oasis in the midst of London's sprawl.

A quick tour of her mental knowledge told her they were in Little Venice.

'Come on,' Ethan said.

His grin was so boyish, so relaxed, that her heart threatened to burst.

'Close your eyes.'

Ruby scrunched her eyes shut and wrapped her fingers round Ethan's capable hand, anticipation unfurling as he guided her along the pathway.

'Okay. You can look.'

A small gasp escaped her lips as she surveyed the boat—gaudy, cheerful, bright red. It looked as though it had a personality all its own.

'Ta-dah!' Ethan beamed at her. 'Welcome to the *Oasis*. Fifty-eight feet long, six foot ten inches wide, she'll be able to take us all over England's canals.'

The grin dropped from his face, to be replaced by a serious expression, his blue-grey eyes full of passion and determination. 'It's symbolic. I want you on board my boat, Ruby, and I don't care how much it rocks or rolls or even if it capsizes, as long as we are on it together.'

The words caused a prickle of tears and he looked at her, consternation written all over his face.

'Hey, don't cry!'

'I can't help it. That is so beautiful and...' She gulped. 'I can't believe you bought a boat!'

'Come and see.'

Ruby followed him inside and felt an instant sense of home. The interior had a clean, homey, compact feel, with the space used to incredible effect. The kitchen area gleamed with pine, and as she explored she gave a small gurgle of delight at the dexterity of the storage space. Already she could picture rustling up meals as they chugged along England's canalways.

Walking further in, she saw the tiny but functional bathroom and shower room. 'There's even a dining area!'

'Well, meals are an important consideration. And look—when we don't need the table it can be folded away and we convert it into a lounge. Plus there are two cabins—a double room and a twin. Tight fit, but…'

Ruby stilled. 'Why the twin bedroom?' she asked.

'Because one day I hope that we will have children. Adopted or birth or a mixture of both.'

His words caused her to freeze, unsure whether to believe him or not, and needing him to understand that she truly loved him for himself. Only him. That he was way more than enough.

'You don't have to say that. I meant what I said. You are who I want. I want my future to be with you—to wake up every day wrapped in your arms.'

'I get that, Ruby, but you have changed me. You've opened my heart. And I have enough love in there for you and for children. Of course I'm scared—scared I'll mess it up, terrified I'll let them down—but I also know I will strive every day to be the best parent I can. Because you were right earlier. I don't blame my mum for what she did, but I could never do that to my child. I would never give up and I would never stop loving them. I'll be there for them, Ruby. I swear I will.'

'There is no doubt in my mind, or in my heart.'

Of course he was scared—after his childhood how could he not be? But she knew that Ethan would be a wonderful dad, and she wanted to whoop with joy that he too wanted a family.

'I know you will be a wonderful dad, and I so want us

to be a family. I've decided to try to trace Tom, Edie and Philippa as well. Make some new memories.'

The idea still scary, but with Ethan by her side, there to catch her if she fell, as she would be there for him, it seemed less daunting.

'I'll support you one hundred per cent. In this and everything, Ruby. Now and for ever.'

His smile was so full of love her breath hitched in her throat.

He gestured towards a corner of the lounge area. 'And right now why don't you have a look in your stocking?'

'Huh?' Following the trail of his hand, her eyes alighted on a small Christmas tree, still in its pot, decorated with silver strands of tinsel and red, purple and gold decorations. Pinned next to it was a bulging striped stocking, with a candy cane poking out of the top.

'I know it's not Christmas anymore. But I figured there was still some Christmas magic left in the air,' he said.

There were those tears of joy. *Again.* 'How on earth did you manage to do all this?'

A grin and the wicked wiggle of his eyebrows banished her tears in favour of a chuckle.

'Consider me all-powerful. Actually, it wasn't too hard. The helicopter only took an hour or so… Rafael's driver picked me up at Battersea… A few stops on the way and then straight here to Little Venice, where the ex-owner of *Oasis* waited. I cleaned the place, set up the tree, and then I went back to the hotel to wait for you.' Eagerness lit his expression as he shifted from foot to foot. 'Come on—open it.'

Unhooking the stocking, Ruby sank onto the cushioned sofa and dived her hand inside. Pulled out a heart-shaped box of chocolates, a gorgeous bath bomb that exuded lavender and chamomile, a pair of fluffy woolly socks… And then, nestled in the toe, her questing fingers found a box.

Heart pounding, mouth parched, she tugged it out and opened it. Inside was a ring—a glorious cluster of sapphires and diamonds.

'Sapphires to match the sparkle of your eyes,' Ethan said. 'Diamonds because diamonds are for ever. Will you marry me, Ruby?'

'Yes.' The assent dropped from her lips and happiness blanketed her as he slid the ring onto her finger. 'It's *so* beautiful.'

'Not as beautiful as you. Now, look up.'

There above them was a sprig of mistletoe, and as Ethan's lips covered hers she knew that her happiness was complete. They would sail their boat together over the horizon, into a life that would hold ups and downs, rain and sunshine. But she knew with all her heart that their love would ride every swell, weather every storm and bask in each ray of happiness.

EPILOGUE

The Caversham Castle Ball

RUBY FELT AS if she were walking, floating, *dancing* on
air as she greeted each and every guest at the ball. Time
seemed spun with the shining threads of pure happiness
as she rested her gaze on Ethan, listened to his speech—
his words powerful, emotive and drenched with compassionate belief in his cause.

'He's a good man.'

Ruby turned to see Cora Brookes by her side.

'He is.'

Instinctively she looked down at her left hand, even
though she and Ethan had decided to keep their engagement under wraps until the end of the ball. Ruby had insisted that the ball was about fundraising—she didn't want
to dilute the impact in any way.

They watched as Ethan introduced Rafael and the tall,
dark-haired man took the podium; his aristocratic lips
upturned in a captivating smile—within minutes he had
them riveted by his words as the bids climbed to outra-
geous heights.

Cora gazed at him. 'He has the charm of the devil,' she
murmured under her breath.

'He's putting it to a good cause.'

'Men like Rafael Martinez only have one cause—their
own.' A strand of bitterness tinged Cora's tone. 'I'm surprised he and Ethan are so close.'

Ruby frowned. 'Ethan sees the good in everyone, and he

is a great believer in second chances. Plus, you shouldn't believe everything you read in the papers. Trust me on that. Unless, of course, you know Rafael?'

Cora hesitated. 'No,' she said finally. 'I don't.' A perfunctory smile and then she gestured towards the door. 'I'll go and check the champagne is ready for midnight.'

Ruby turned as Ethan headed towards her.

'All okay, sweetheart?' he asked. 'Why the frown?'

'I was just wondering why Cora doesn't like Rafael…'

'Lots of people don't like Rafael. But he has his good points. Or at least I hope he does. He and I have decided to invest in a business venture together. Spanish vineyard holidays.'

'Maybe we could honeymoon in Spain?'

Ethan shook his head, his expression serious. 'We are *not* going on a working honeymoon, my love. I have way better plans than that, I promise you.'

'I can hardly wait.'

He grinned down at her—a smile that lit his face— and his blue-grey eyes were flecked with a love that stole her breath.

'I think Rafael has everyone's attention,' he murmured. 'So let me snag us a glass of champagne…I want to toast our future under the stars.'

And as he twined his strong hand in hers Ruby basked in the healing lessons learnt from the past, the wondrous glow of joy of the present, and the glorious promise of the future.

* * * * *

CHRISTMAS WITH HER MILLIONAIRE BOSS

BARBARA WALLACE

For Peter and Andrew,
who put up with a stressed-out writer
trying to juggle too many balls at one time.
You two are awesome, and I couldn't ask
for a better husband and son.

CHAPTER ONE

OH, WHAT FRESH hell was this?

A pair of ten-foot nutcrackers smiled down at him with giant white grins that looked capable of snapping an entire chestnut tree in half—let alone a single nut. Welcome to Fryberg's Trains and Toys read the red-and-gold banner clutched in their wooden hands. Where It's Christmas All Year Round.

James Hammond shuddered at the thought.

He was the only one though, as scores of children dragged their parents by the hand past the nutcracker guards and toward the Bavarian castle ahead, their shouts of delight echoing in the crisp Michigan air. One little girl, winter coat flapping in the wind, narrowly missed running into him, so distracted was she by the sight ahead of her.

"I see Santa's Castle," he heard her squeal.

Only if Santa lived in northern Germany and liked bratwurst. The towering stucco building, with its holly-draped ramparts and snow-covered turrets looked like something out of a Grimm's fairy tale. No one would ever accuse Ned Fryberg of pedaling a false reality, that's for sure. It was obvious that his fantasy was completely unattainable in real life. Unlike the nostalgic, homespun malarkey Hammond's Toys sold to the public.

The popularity of both went to show that people loved

their Christmas fantasies, and they were willing to shovel boatloads of money in order to keep them alive.

James didn't understand it, but he was more than glad to help them part with their cash. He was good at it too. Some men gardened and grew vegetables. James grew his family's net worth. And Fryberg's Toys, and its awful Christmas village—a town so named for the Fryberg family—was going to help him grow it even larger.

"Excuse me, sir, but the line for Santa's trolley starts back there." A man wearing a red toy soldier's jacket and black busby pointed behind James's shoulder. In an attempt to control traffic flow, the store provided transportation around the grounds via a garishly colored "toy" train. "Trains leave every five minutes. You won't have too long a wait.

"Or y-you could w-w-walk," he added.

People always tended to stammer whenever James looked them in the eye. Didn't matter if he was trying to be intimidating or not. They simply did. Maybe because, as his mother once told him, he had the same cold, dead eyes as his father. He'd spent much of his youth vainly trying to erase the similarity. Now that he was an adult, he'd grown not to accept his intimidating glower, but embrace it. Same way he embraced all his other unapproachable qualities.

"That depends," he replied. "Which mode is more efficient?"

"Th-that would depend upon on how fast a walker you are. The car makes a couple of stops beforehand, so someone with…with long legs…" The soldier, or whatever he was supposed to be, let the sentence trail off.

"Then walking it is. Thank you."

Adjusting his charcoal-gray scarf tighter around his neck, James turned and continued on his way, along the path to Fryberg's Christmas Castle. The faster he got to his meeting with Belinda Fryberg, the sooner he could lock in his sale and fly back to Boston. At least there, he only had to deal with Christmas one day of the year.

"What did you say?"

"I said, your Christmas Castle has a few years of viability in it, at best."

Noelle hated the new boss.

She'd decided he rubbed her the wrong way when he glided into Belinda's office like a cashmere-wearing shark. She disliked him when he started picking apart their operations. And she loathed him now that he'd insulted the Christmas Castle.

"We all know the future of retail is online," he continued. He uncrossed his long legs and shifted his weight. Uncharitable a thought as it might be, Noelle was glad he'd been forced to squeeze his long, lanky frame into Belinda's office furniture. "The only reason your brick-and-mortar store has survived is because it's basically a tourist attraction."

"What's wrong with being a tourist attraction?" she asked. Fryberg's had done very well thanks to that tourist attraction. Over the years, what had been a small hobby shop had become a cottage industry unto itself with the entire town embracing the Bavarian atmosphere. "You saw our balance sheet. Those tourists are contributing a very healthy portion of our revenue."

"I also saw that the biggest growth came from your online store. In fact, while it's true retail sales have remained constant, your electronic sales have risen over fifteen percent annually."

And were poised to take another leap this year. Noelle had heard the projections. E-retail was the wave of the future. Brick-and-mortar stores like Fryberg's would soon be obsolete.

"Don't get me wrong. I think your late husband did a fantastic job of capitalizing on people's nostalgia," he said to Belinda.

Noelle's mother-in-law smiled. She always smiled when speaking about her late husband. "Ned used to say that Christmas was a universal experience."

"Hammond's has certainly done well by it."

Well? Hammond's had their entire business on the holiday, as had Fryberg's. *Nothing Says Christmas Like Hammond's Toys.* The company motto, repeated at the end of every ad, sung in Noelle's head.

"That's because everyone loves Christmas," she replied.

"Hmm." From the lack of enthusiasm in his response, she might as well have been talking about weather patterns. Then again, his emotional range didn't seem to go beyond brusque and chilly, so maybe that was enthusiastic for him.

"I don't care if they love the holiday or not. It's their shopping patterns I'm interested in, and from the data I've been seeing, more and more people are doing part, if not most of their shopping over the internet. The retailers who survive will be the ones who shift their business models accordingly. I intend to make sure Hammond's is one of those businesses."

"Hammond's," Noelle couldn't help noting. "Not Fryberg's."

"I'm hoping that by the end of the day, the two stores will be on the way to becoming one and the same," he said.

"Wiping out sixty-five years of tradition just like that, are you?"

"Like I said, to survive, sometimes you have to embrace change."

Except they weren't embracing anything. Fryberg's was

being swallowed up and dismantled so that Hammond's could change.

"I think what my daughter-in-law is trying to say is that the Fryberg name carries a great deal of value round these parts," said Belinda. "People are very loyal to my late husband and what he worked to create here."

"Loyalty's a rare commodity these days. Especially in the business world."

"It certainly is. Ned, my husband, had a way of inspiring it."

"Impressive," Hammond replied.

"It's because the Frybergs—Ned and Belinda—have always believed in treating their employees like family," Noelle told him. "And they were always on-site, visible to everyone." Although things had changed over the last few years as Belinda had been spending more and more time in Palm Beach. "I'm not sure working for a faceless CEO in Boston will engender the same feelings."

"What do you expect me to do? Move my office here?"

He looked at her. His gaze, sharp and direct, didn't so much look through a person as cut into them. The flecks of brown in his irises darkened, transforming what had been soft hazel. Self-consciousness curled through Noelle's midsection. She folded her arms tighter to keep the reaction from spreading.

"No. Just keep Fryberg's as a separate entity," she replied.

His brows lifted. "Really? You want me to keep one store separate when all the other properties under our umbrella carry the name Hammond?"

"Why not?" Noelle's palms started to sweat. She was definitely overstepping her authority right now. Belinda had already accepted Hammond's offer. Today's meeting was a friendly dialogue between an outgoing owner and the new CEO, to ensure a successful transition. She couldn't help it. With Belinda stepping down, someone had to protect what Ned had created. James Hammond certainly wasn't. To hear him, Fryberg's Christmas Castle was one step ahead of landlines in terms of obsolescence. She gave him two years tops before he decided "Hammond's" Christmas Castle didn't fit the corporate brand and started downsizing in the name of change. Bet he wouldn't blink an eye doing it either.

Oh, but she really, really, *really* disliked him. Thank goodness the corporate headquarters were in Boston. With luck, he'd go home after this visit and she'd never have to deal with him again.

"Our name recognition and reputation are important elements to our success," she continued. "All those people who line up to see Hammond's displays every Christmas? Would they still remember to make the pilgrimage if Hammond's suddenly became Jones's Toys?"

He chuckled. "Hammond's is hardly the same as Jones."

"Around here it might as well be."

"She makes an interesting point," Belinda said. Noelle felt her mother-in-law's sideways gaze. When it came to giving a pointed look, Belinda Fryberg held her own. In fact, she could probably do it better than most since she always tossed in a dose of maternal reproach. "While you may think our physical store has a limited future, there's no need to hasten its demise prematurely. Maybe it would make more sense for Fryberg's to continue operating under its own name, at least for now."

Leaning back in his chair, Hammond steepled his fingertips together and tapped them against his lips. "I'm not averse to discussing the idea," he said finally.

I'm not averse… How big of him. Noelle bit her tongue. Her mother-in-law, meanwhile, folded her hands and smiled. "Then why don't we do just that over lunch? I made reservations at the Nutcracker Inn downtown."

"I don't usually have lunch…"

No surprise there. Noelle had read once that sharks only ate every few days.

"Perhaps you don't," Belinda replied, "but for a woman my age, skipping meals isn't the best idea. Besides, I find business always goes smoother when accompanied by a bowl of gingerbread soup. You haven't lived until you've tried it."

Either Hammond's cheek muscles twitched at the word *gingerbread* or else they weren't used to smiling. "Very well," he said. "I have some calls to make first though. Why don't I meet you at the elevator in, say, fifteen minutes?"

"I'll see you there."

Returning Belinda's nod, he unfolded his lanky self from the chair and strode from the room. If only he'd keep walking, Noelle thought as she watched his back slip through the door. Keep walking all the way back to Boston.

"Well, that was a surprise." Belinda spoke the second the door shut behind him. "I hadn't realized you'd joined the mergers and acquisitions team."

"I'm sorry," Noelle replied. "But the way he was talking…it sounded like he planned to wipe Fryberg's off the map."

"You know I would never allow that."

She hung her head. "I know, and I'm sorry. On the plus side, he did say he would consider keeping the Fryberg's name."

"Even so, you can't keep getting angry every time he says something that rubs you the wrong way. This is Hammond's company now. You're going to have to learn to bite your tongue."

She'd better hope Noelle's tongue was thick enough to survive the visit then, because there was going to be a lot of biting.

"I just…" Starting now. Gritting her teeth, she turned and looked out the window. Below her, a school tour was lining up in front of the reindeer petting zoo, the same as they did every year, the Wednesday before Thanksgiving. Later on, they would make wish lists for their parents and trek over to the Candy Cane Forest to meet Santa Claus.

Her attention zeroed in on a little girl wearing a grimy pink snow jacket, the dirt visible from yards away, and she smiled nostalgically at the girl's obvious excitement. That excitement was what people like James Hammond didn't understand. Fryberg's was so much more than a toy store or tourist attraction. When you passed through that nutcracker-flanked gate, you entered a different world. A place where, for a few hours, little girls in charity bin hand-me-downs could trade their loneliness and stark reality for a little Christmas magic.

A warm hand settled on her shoulder. "I wish things could stay the same too," Belinda said, "but time marches on no matter how hard we try to stop it. Ned's gone, Kevin's gone, and I just don't have the energy to run this place by myself anymore.

"Besides, a chain like Hammond's can invest capital in this place that I don't have."

Capital, sure, but what about heart? Compassion was part of the Fryberg DNA. Noelle still remembered that day in sixth grade when Kevin invited her to his house and she felt the family's infectious warmth for the very first time.

"I don't fault you for wanting to retire," she said, leaning ever so slightly into the older woman's touch. "I just wish you hadn't sold to such a Grinch."

"He is serious, isn't he?" Belinda chuckled. "Must be all that dour Yankee heritage."

"Dour? Try frozen. The guy has about as much Christmas spirit as a block of ice."

Her mother-in-law squeezed her shoulder. "Fortunately for us, you have enough Christmas spirit for a dozen people. You'll keep the spirit alive. Unless you decide to move on, that is."

Noelle tried for tongue biting again and failed. They'd had this conversation before. It was another one of the reasons Belinda sold the business instead of simply retiring. She insisted Noelle not be tied down by the family business. A reason Noelle found utterly silly.

"You know I have zero intention of ever leaving Fryberg," she said.

"Oh, I know you think that now. But you're young. You're smart. There's an entire world out there beyond Fryberg's Toys."

Noelle shook her head. Not for her there wasn't. The store was too big a part of her.

It was all of her, really.

Her mother-in-law squeezed her shoulder again. "Kevin and Ned wouldn't want you to shortchange your future any more than I do."

At the mention of her late husband's wishes, Noelle bit back a familiar swell of guilt.

"Besides," Belinda continued, heading toward her desk. "Who knows? Maybe you'll impress Mr. Hammond so much, he'll promote you up the corporate ladder."

"Him firing me is more likely," Noelle replied. She recalled how sharp Hammond's gaze had become when she dared to challenge him. Oh, yeah, she could picture him promoting her, all right.

"You never know" was all Belinda said. "I better go get

ready for lunch. Don't want to keep our Mr. Hammond waiting. Are you joining us?"

And continue bonding with Mr. Hammond over a bowl of gingerbread soup? Thanks, but no thanks. "I think Mr. Hammond and I have had enough contact for the day. Better I save my tongue and let you and Todd fill me in on the visit later."

"That reminds me. On your way out, can you stop by Todd's office and let his secretary know that if he calls in after the funeral, I'd like to talk with him?"

"Sure thing."

Her answer was buried by the sound of the phone ringing.

"Oh, dear," Belinda said upon answering. "This is Dick Greenwood. I'd better take it. Hopefully, he won't chat my ear off. Will you do me another favor and give Mr. Hammond a tour of the floor while I'm tied up?"

So much for being done with the man. "Of course." She'd donate a kidney if Belinda asked.

"And be nice."

"Yes, ma'am."

The kidney would have been easier.

"You're not going to have an insubordination problem, are you?"

On the other end of the line, Jackson Hammond's voice sounded far away. James might have blamed the overseas connection except he knew better. Jackson Hammond always sounded distant.

Struggling to keep the phone tucked under his ear, he reached for the paper towels. "Problem?" he repeated. "Hardly."

With her short black hair and red sweater dress, Noelle

Fryberg was more of an attack elf. Too small and precious to do any real damage.

"Only reason she was in the meeting was because the new general manager had to attend a funeral, and she's the assistant GM." And because she was family. Apparently, the concept mattered to some people.

He shrugged and tossed his wadded towel into the basket. "Her objections were more entertaining than anything."

He'd already come to the same conclusion regarding the Fryberg name, but it was fun seeing her try to stare him into capitulation. She had very large, very soulful eyes. Her glaring at him was like being glared at by a kitten. He had to admire the effort though. It was more than a lot of—hell, most—people.

"All in all, the transition is going smooth as silk. I'm going to tour the warehouse this afternoon." And then hightail it back to the airstrip as soon as possible. With any luck, he'd be in Boston by eight that evening. Noelle Fryberg's verve might be entertaining, but not so much that he wanted to stick around Christmas Land a moment longer than necessary.

"Christmas is only four weeks away. You're going to need that distribution center linked into ours as soon as possible."

"It'll get done," James replied. The reassurance was automatic. James learned a long time ago that his father preferred his world run as smoothly as possible. Complications and problems were things you dealt with on your own.

"If you need anything from my end, talk with Carli. I've asked her to be my point person while I'm in Vienna."

"Thank you." But James wouldn't need anything from his father's end. He'd been running the corporation for several years now while his father concentrated on over-seas and other pet projects—like his new protégé, Carli, for example.

Then again, he hadn't needed his father since his parents' divorce. About the time his father made it clear he didn't want James underfoot. Not wanting their eldest son around was the one thing Jackson Hammond and his ex-wife had in common.

"How is the trip going?" James asked, turning to other, less bitter topics.

"Well enough. I'm meeting with Herr Burns in the morning…" There was a muffled sound in the background. "Someone's knocking at the door. I have to go. We'll talk tomorrow, when you're back in the office."

The line disconnected before James had a chance to re-mind him tomorrow was Thanksgiving. Not that it mat-tered. He'd still be in the office.

He was always in the office. Wasn't like he had a family.

Belinda was nowhere in sight when James stepped into the hallway. Instead, he found the daughter-in-law waiting by the elevator, arms again hugging her chest. "Belinda had to take a call with Dick Greenwood," she told him.

"I'm sorry" was his automatic reply. Greenwood was a great vendor, but he was notorious for his chattiness. James made a point of avoiding direct conversations if he could.

Apparently, the daughter-in-law knew what he meant, because the corners of her mouth twitched. About as close to a smile as he'd seen out of her. "She said she'll join you as soon as she can. In the meantime, she thought you'd like a tour of the retail store."

"She did, did she?" More likely, she thought it would distract him while she was stuck on the phone.

Noelle shrugged. "She thought it would give you an idea of the foot traffic we handle on a day-to-day basis."

He'd seen the sales reports; he knew what kind of traffic they handled. Still, it couldn't hurt to check out the store. Hammond's was always on the lookout for new ways to engage their customers. "Are you going to be my guide?" he asked, reaching across to hit the elevator button.

"Yes, I am." If she thought he missed the soft sigh she let out before speaking, she was mistaken.

All the more reason to take the tour.

The doors opened, and James motioned for her to step in first. Partly to be a gentleman, but mostly because holding back gave him an opportunity to steal a surreptitious look at her figure. The woman might be tiny, but she was perfectly proportioned. Make that normally proportioned, he amended. Too many of the women he met had try-hard figures. Worked out and enhanced to artificial perfection. Noelle looked fit, but she still carried a little more below than she did on top, which he appreciated.

"We bill ourselves as the country's largest toy store," Noelle said once the elevator doors shut. "The claim is based on square footage. We are the largest retail space in the continental US. This weekend alone we'll attract thousands of customers."

"Black Friday weekend. The retailers' best friend," he replied. Then, because he couldn't resist poking the bee's nest a little, he added, "That is, until Cyber Monday came along. These days we move almost as much inventory online. Pretty soon people won't come out for Black Friday at all. They'll do their shopping Thanksgiving afternoon while watching TV."

"Hammond's customers might, but you can't visit a Christmas wonderland via a computer."

That again. He turned to look at her. "Do you really

think kids five or six years from now are going to care about visiting Santa Claus?"

"Of course they are. It's Santa."

"I hate to break it to you, but kids are a little more realistic these days. They grow fast. Our greeting card fantasy holiday is going to get harder and harder to sell."

"Especially if you insist on calling it a fantasy."

What should he call it? Fact? "Belinda wasn't kidding when she said you were loyal, was she?"

"The Frybergs are family. Of course I would be loyal."

Not necessarily, but James didn't feel like arguing the point.

"Even if I weren't—related that is—I'd respect what Ned and Belinda created." She crossed her arms. Again. "They understood that retail is about more than moving inventory."

Her implication was clear: she considered him a corporate autocrat who was concerned solely with the bottom line. While she might be correct, he didn't intend to let her get away with the comment unchallenged.

Mirroring her posture, he tilted his head and looked straight at her. "Is that so? What exactly is it about then?"

"People, of course."

"Of course." She was not only loyal, but naive. Retail was *all* about moving product. All the fancy window dressing she specialized in was to convince people to buy the latest and greatest, and then to buy the next latest and greatest the following year. And so on and so forth.

At that moment, the elevator opened and before them lay Fryberg's Toys in all its glory. Aisle upon aisle of toys, spread out like a multicolored promised land. There were giant stuffed animals arranged by environment, lions and tigers in the jungle, cows and horses by the farm. Construction toys were spread around a jobsite, around which cars zipped on a multilevel racetrack. There was even a wall of televisions blasting the latest video games. A special display for every interest, each one overflowing with products for sale.

"Oh, yeah," he murmured, "it's totally about the people."

A remote-control drone zipped past their heads as they walked toward the center aisle. A giant teddy bear made of plastic building bricks marked the entrance like the Colossus of Rhodes.

"It's like Christmas morning on steroids," he remarked as they passed under the bear's legs.

"This is the Christmas Castle, after all. Everything should look larger-than-life and magical. To stir the imagination."

Not to mention the desire for plastic bricks and stuffed animals, thought James.

"Santa's workshop and the Candy Cane Forest are located at the rear of the building," she said pointing to an archway bedecked with painted holly and poinsettia. "That's also where Ned's model train layout is located. It used to be a much larger section, but now it's limited to one room-size museum."

Yet something else lost to the march of time, James refrained from saying. The atmosphere was chilly enough. Looking around he noticed their aisle led straight toward the archway, and that the only way to avoid Santa was to go to the end, turn and head back up a different aisle.

He nodded at the arch. "What's on the other side?" he asked.

"Other side of what?"

"Santa's woods or whatever it is."

"Santa's workshop and Candy Cane Forest," she corrected. "There's a door that leads back into the store, or they can continue on to see the reindeer."

"Meaning they go home to purchase their child's wish item online from who-knows-what site."

"Or come back another day. Most people don't do their Christmas shopping with the kids in tow."

"How about in April, when they aren't Christmas shopping? They walk outside to see the reindeer and poof! There goes your potential sale."

That wouldn't do at all. "After the kids visit Santa, the traffic should be rerouted back into the store so the parents can buy whatever it is Little Susie or Johnny wished for."

"You want to close off access to the reindeer?"

She needn't look so horrified. It wasn't as though he'd suggested euthanizing the creatures. "I want customers to buy toys. And they aren't going to if they are busy looking at reindeer. What's that?"

He pointed to a giant Moose-like creature wearing a Santa's hat and wreath standing to the right of the archway. It took up most of the wall space, forcing the crowd to congregate toward the middle. As a result, customers looking to walk past the archway to another aisle had to battle a throng of children.

"Oh, that's Fryer Elk, the store mascot," Noelle replied. "Ned created him when he opened the store. Back in the day, he appeared in the ads. They retired him in the eighties and he's been here ever since."

"He's blocking the flow of traffic. He should be somewhere else."

For a third time, James got the folded arm treatment. "He's an institution," she replied, as if that was reason enough for his existence.

He could be Ned Fryberg standing there stuffed himself, and he would still be hindering traffic. Letting out a long breath, James reached into his breast pocket for his notebook. Once the sale was finalized, he would send his operations manager out here to evaluate the layout.

"You really don't have any respect for tradition, do you?" Noelle asked.

He peered over his pen at her. Just figuring this out, was she? That's what happened when you spent a fortune crafting a corporate image. People started believing the image was real.

"No," he replied. "I don't. In fact…" He put his notebook away. "We might as well get something straight right now. As far as I'm concerned, the only thing that matters is making sure Hammond's stays profitable for the next fifty years. Everything else can go to blazes."

"Everything," she repeated. Her eyes narrowed.

"Everything, and that includes elks, tradition and especially Chris—"

He never got a chance to finish.

CHAPTER TWO

FOUR STITCHES AND a concussion. That's what the emergency room doctor told Noelle. "He's fortunate. Those props can do far worse," she added. "Your associates really shouldn't be flying remote-control drones inside."

"So they've been told," Noelle replied. In no uncertain terms by James Hammond once he could speak.

The drone had slammed into the back of his head, knocking him face-first into a pile of model racecar kits. The sight of the man sprawled on the floor might have been funny if not for the blood running down the back of his skull. Until that minute, she'd been annoyed as hell at the man for his obvious lack of respect toward Fryberg tradition. Seeing the blood darkening his hair quickly checked her annoyance. As blood was wont to do.

That was until she turned him over and he started snarling about careless associates and customer safety. Then she went back to being annoyed. Only this time, it was because the man had a point. What if the drone had struck a customer—a child? Things could have been even worse. As it was, half of Miss Speroni's first grade class was probably going to have nightmares from witnessing the accident.

Then there was the damage to James Hammond himself. Much as she disliked the man, stitches and a concussion were nothing to sneeze at.

"How long before he's ready for discharge?" she asked.

"My nurse is bandaging the stitches right now," the doctor replied. "Soon as I get his paperwork written up, he'll be all yours."

Oh, goodie. Noelle didn't realize she'd gotten custody. She went back to the waiting room where Belinda was finishing up a phone call.

"Bob is working on a statement for the press," her mother-in-law told her. "And we're pulling the product off the shelves per advice from the lawyers. Thankfully, the incident didn't get caught on camera so we won't have to deal with that. I doubt Mr. Hammond would like being a social media sensation."

"I'm not sure Mr. Hammond likes much of anything," Noelle replied. She was thinking of the remark he made right before the drone struck him. "Did you know, he actually said he doesn't like Christmas? How can the man think that and run a store like Hammond's?" Or Fryberg's.

"Obviously, his disdain hasn't stopped him from doubling Hammond's profits over the past two years," Belinda replied. "What matters isn't that he like Christmas, but that he keeps the people in Fryberg employed, which he will."

"Hope they like working for Mr. Frosty. Did you know he wants to get rid of Fryer?"

"Well, some change is bound to happen," Belinda said.

"I know," Noelle grumbled. She bowed her head. She really did. Same way she understood that the retail industry was changing. She also knew she was acting irrational and childish about the entire situation. Ever since Belinda announced the sale, however, she'd been unable to catch her breath. It felt like there were fingers clawing inside her looking for purchase. A continual churning sensation. Like she was about to lose her grip.

James Hammond's arrival only made the feeling worse.

"Doesn't mean I have to like it though," she said referring to the prospect of change.

Belinda nudged her shoulder. "Sweetheart, you wouldn't be you if you did. Cheer up. Mr. Hammond will be out of your hair soon."

"Not soon enough," she replied.

"What wouldn't be soon enough?" Hammond's voice caused her to start in her chair. Turning, she saw a nurse pushing him toward her. He was slouched down in a wheelchair, a hand propping his head. Noelle caught a glimpse of a white bandage on the back of his scalp.

"The bandage can come off tomorrow," the nurse told them.

"How are you feeling, Mr. Hammond?" Belinda asked.

"Like someone split my head open. Who knew such a little device could pack such a wallop?"

"Lots of things pack a wallop when they're going thirty miles an hour. We pulled the toy from the shelves. Though I doubt it would have been popular anyway, once parents heard what happened."

"Don't blame them. Thing could slice an ear off." Groaning, he leaned forward and buried his face in both hands as though one was suddenly not enough to hold it up. "I'm going to have Hammond's pull them too as soon as I get back to Boston," he spoke through his fingers.

"That won't be anytime soon, I'm afraid. You heard what Dr. Nelson said," the nurse warned.

"What did she say?" Noelle asked. She didn't like the sound of the nurse's comment.

Hammond waved a hand before cradling his head again. "Nothing."

"Mr. Hammond has a slight concussion. He's been advised to rest for the next couple of days. That includes no air travel."

"You mean you're staying here?" No, no, no. Noelle's stomach started to twist. He was supposed to go away, not stick around for the weekend.

"The doctor merely recommended I rest," James replied. "No one said it was mandatory."

"Perhaps not, but it's generally a good idea to take doctors' advice," Belinda said.

"We're talking about a handful of stitches. Nothing I haven't had before. I'll be fine. Why don't we go have our lunch as planned and finish our conversation? I could use some food in my stomach. What kind of soup did you say they made?"

"Gingerbread," Noelle replied.

"The only place you should be going is to bed," the nurse said.

Much as Noelle hated to admit it, the nurse was right. He was looking paler by the minute. She remembered how unsteady he'd been right after the accident; he could barely sit up.

Funny, but he still looked formidable despite the pallor. A virile invalid. Noelle didn't think it possible. Must be the combination of square jaw and broad shoulders, she decided. And the dark suit. Black made everyone look intimidating.

Again, he waved off the nurse's advice. "Nonsense. I rested while waiting for the doctor. Why don't we go have our lunch as planned and finish our conversation? I could use some food in my stomach. What kind of soup did you say they made?"

"I just told you."

A crease deepened between his eyes. "You did?"

"Uh-huh. Two seconds ago."

"That only proves I'm hungry. I'm having trouble listening." He pushed himself to a standing position, squaring his shoulders proudly when he reached his feet. His upper body swayed back and forth unsteadily. "See?" he said. "Fine. Let's go."

Noelle looked over her shoulder at Belinda who shook her head in return. "I'm not going to negotiate anything while you're unsteady on your feet," her mother-in-law said. "I won't be accused of taking advantage when you're not thinking straight."

James laughed. "You're a smart businesswoman, Belinda, but I can assure you, no one ever takes advantage of me."

"That I can believe," Noelle murmured.

He looked at her and smiled. "I'll take that as a compliment, Mrs. Fryberg. Now how about we go get that lunch we missed…"

It took two steps for him to lose his balance. His eyes started to roll back in his head, and his knees started to buckle.

Noelle reached him first. "Okay, that's enough," she said, reaching around his waist. Thanks to the size difference, it took a minute to maneuver him, but eventually she managed to lower him into the wheelchair. Unfortunately, the downward momentum pulled her along as well. She landed with one hand pressed against his torso and knee wedged between his thighs. Man, but he was solid. A tall, lean block of granite.

She looked up to find herself nose to nose with him. Up close, his eyes were far more dappled than she realized, the green more of an accent color than true eye shade.

He had freckles too. A smattering across the bridge of his nose.

Cold-blooded businessmen weren't supposed to have freckles.

"Think you might listen to the nurse now?" she asked.

"I was lightheaded for a moment, that's all."

"Lightheaded, huh?" She pushed herself to her feet. To her embarrassment, the move required splaying her hand wider, so that the palm of her hand pressed over his heart. Fortunately, he was too dizzy or distracted to comment.

"Any more lightheaded and you would have hit the floor," she told him. "Are you trying to get more stitches?"

"I'm not…"

"Face it, Mr. Hammond, you're in no condition to do anything but rest," Belinda said. "We'll talk when you're feeling better. Monday."

"Monday?" He'd started to rest his head in his hands again, but when Belinda spoke, he jerked his head upward. The pain crossing his face made Noelle wince. "Why wait until then? I won't need that many days to recover."

"Maybe not, but that is the next time I'll be able to see you. Tomorrow is Thanksgiving. The only business I'll be discussing is whether the stuffing is too dry."

"What about Friday?"

Noelle answered for her. "Black Friday, remember? Around these parts, it's the kickoff for the annual Christmas festival, the biggest weekend of our year."

"I'll be much too busy to give you the proper time," Belinda added.

Noelle watched the muscle twitching in Hammond's jaw. Clearly, he preferred being the one who dictated the schedule, and not the other way around.

"Let me get this straight." Whether his voice was low by design or discomfort, Noelle couldn't guess. His tension came though nevertheless. "I'm not allowed to fly home for the next twenty-four hours…"

"At least," the nurse said.

The muscle twitched again. "*At least* twenty-four hours,"

he corrected. "Nor will you meet with me for the next five days?"

"That's correct," Belinda replied. "We can meet first thing Monday morning, and conclude our preliminary negotiations."

"I see." He nodded. Slowly. Anyone with two eyes could tell he didn't appreciate this change in plans at all. Noelle would be lying if she didn't say it gave her a tiny trill of satisfaction. Payback for his wanting to toss Fryer.

"Fine," he said, leaning back in his chair. "We'll talk Monday. Only because my head hurts too much to argue." Noelle had a feeling he wasn't kidding. "What was the name of that hotel?"

"The Nutcracker Inn," she replied.

"Right, that one. I'm going to need a room, and something to eat. What did you say that soup was?"

"Gingerbread." It was the third time he'd asked. She looked at the nurse who nodded.

"Temporary short-term memory loss can happen with concussions. It should recede soon enough. However, I think you might have a more pressing problem."

"I do?"

"He does?"

The two of them spoke at the same time. "I'm not sure the Nutcracker has any rooms," the nurse replied. "You know how booked it gets during the holidays."

"Wait a second." James tried to look up at the nurse, only to wince and close his eyes. "Please don't tell me there's no room at the inn."

"Wouldn't be the first time," the nurse replied. "Did you know that once we even had a baby born—"

"I doubt Mr. Hammond will have to do anything quite as dramatic," Noelle interjected. No need for the conversation to head down that particular road.

The nurse offered a tight-lipped smile. Apparently, she didn't appreciate being cut off. "Either way, you're going to need someone to look in on you. Doctor's orders."

"The concierge will love that request," Hammond muttered.

"We could arrange for a private duty nurse."

"Good grief," Belinda said. "That doesn't sound pleasant at all."

"Pleasant isn't exactly on the table right now." Hammond's eyes had grown heavy lidded and his words were slurred. It was obvious the entire conversation was exhausting him, and Noelle couldn't help but feel bad.

Although she doubted he'd appreciate the compassion. A man like Hammond, with his disregard for sentiment and tradition, would despise showing any hint of vulnerability.

"Of course pleasant is on the table," Belinda said. "This is Fryberg." The meaning behind her emphasis was obvious.

Hammond let out a low groan. Still feeling compassionate, Noelle decided the noise was coincidental.

Her mother-in-law continued as if the noise never happened. "We're not going to let you spend your weekend in some hotel room, eating room service and being attended to by a stranger. You'll spend the weekend with me. That way you can recuperate, and enjoy a proper Thanksgiving as well."

The strangest look crossed Hammond's face. Part surprise, part darkness as though her mother-in-law's suggestion unnerved him. Noelle didn't picture him as a man who got unnerved. Ever.

"I don't want to put you out," he said.

"You won't. I have plenty of room. I'll even make you

some…oh, shoot." A look crossed her features, not nearly as dark as Hammond's, but definitely distressed.

"What is it?" Noelle asked.

"The Orion House Dinner is this evening. I completely forgot."

In all the craziness, so had Noelle. Fryberg's was being honored for its fund-raising efforts on behalf of homeless veterans. "Would you mind?" her mother-in-law asked. "I don't want Orion House to think I don't appreciate the honor. The project meant so much to Ned."

"I know," replied Noelle. After Kevin's death, her father-in-law had channeled his grief into helping as many veteran programs as possible. Orion House had topped the list. "He was very passionate about wanting to help."

"That he was," Belinda said, getting the faraway look she always got when they discussed Ned. The family had been through a lot these past years, and yet they continued to channel their energy into the community. Their dedication in the face of grief made her proud to bear the Fryberg name.

"Would you mind stepping in instead?"

"Not at all," she told her. "I'd love to." It'd be an honor to accept an award for them.

"Thank goodness." The older woman let out a long sigh. "I was afraid that because of our words earlier… Never mind." Whatever her mother-in-law had been about to say she waved away. "Let me pull my car around. I'll help you get Mr. Hammond settled, and then go home to change."

Help her…? Wait… What exactly had she agreed to do?

Noelle opened her mouth, closed it, then opened it again. Nothing came out though. That's because she knew what she'd agreed to. As surely as the sickening feeling growing in her stomach.

Somehow, James Hammond had become *her* responsibility. She looked over to her mother-in-law, but Belinda was busy fishing through her purse. And here she thought she would be free of the man. Talk about your sick karmic jokes. If only she'd been the one hit in the head.

"Do you need an extra copy of the discharge instructions?" the nurse asked her.

"No," Noelle replied with a sigh. "I know what to expect."

There was only one consolation, if you could call it that. Hammond looked about as thrilled over this change of events as she was.

Goodie. They could be miserable together.

A few minutes later, James found himself being wheeled outside behind a tiny bundle of annoyance, who marched toward the waiting sedan with her arms yet again wrapped tightly across her chest. A voice behind his headache wondered if they were permanently attached to her body that way.

"Why don't you take the front seat?" Belinda opened the passenger door. "I've pulled it all the way back so you'll have plenty of leg room."

Front seat, back seat. Didn't make much difference. Neither were the cockpit of his private plane. His head felt split in two, the world was tipping on its axis and he wanted nothing more than to be in his bed back in Boston. Damn drone.

He pushed himself to his feet only to have the world rock back and forth like a seesaw. A second later, an arm wrapped around his biceps, steadying him, and he smelled the sweet scent of orange blossoms. The elf. He recognized the perfume from the confines of the elevator. Funny, but he expected her to smell Christmassy, not like Florida sunshine. Maybe they were out of sugar cookie perfume this week.

"Something wrong?"

Turning his head—barely—he saw her frowning at him and realized he'd snorted out loud at his joke. "Do you really need to ask?"

He was being an ass, he knew that, but with stitches in his scalp, surely he was entitled to a little churlishness?

The frown deepened. "Watch your head," she replied.

James did as he was told, and as his reward, the orange blossoms—as well as her grip—disappeared. In their absence, his headache intensified. He found himself slumped against a leather armrest with his fingers pressed against his temple to hold his head up.

"Fortunately, we don't have to drive too far," he heard Belinda say. "Noelle only lives a short distance from town."

"Great." What he really wanted to say was that two feet was too far what with the lights outside dipping and rocking as they passed by. Thankfully the sun had set. If those were buildings bobbing, he'd be lurching the contents of his stomach all over his Bostonians. He closed his eyes, and did his best to imagine orange blossoms.

"The nurse seemed to think the worst of the dizziness would pass by tomorrow," Noelle said from behind him.

"Thank God," he whispered. If true, then maybe he could snag a ride to the airport and fly home, doctor's orders be damned. He bet the elf would drive him. After all, she didn't want him at her house any more than he wanted to be there. He'd caught the look on the woman's face when Belinda foisted him on her.

Foisted. What a perfect word for the situation. Stuck

where he didn't want to be, dependent on people who didn't want him around.

Story of his life.

Great. He'd moved from churlish to pity party. Why not round out the trifecta and start whining too?

How he hated this. Hated having no choice. Hated being weak and needy. He hadn't needed anyone since he was twelve years old. Needing and foisting were incompatible concepts.

"It's too bad you can't look out the window," Belinda said. "The town looks beautiful all lit up."

James pried open one eye to see building after building decorated with Christmas lights. *Ugh*. One in particular had a giant evergreen dripping with red and green.

"That's the Nutcracker Inn. The Bavarian market is next door. It'll be packed on Friday for the festival."

"I doubt Mr. Hammond is very interested in a tour, Belinda."

"I'm merely pointing out a few of the landmarks since he's going to be here all weekend."

Not if he could help it, thought James.

"The man can't remember what kind of soup they serve—I doubt he'll remember what the place looks like."

"There's no need to be harsh, Noelle Fryberg."

"Yes, ma'am."

Actually, James rather liked the harshness. Beat being treated like a patient. "Pumpkin," he replied.

"Excuse me?" Belinda asked.

"The soup. It's pumpkin."

"You mean gingerbread," Noelle replied.

"Oh. Right." He knew it was some kind of seasonal flavor. His cheeks grew warm.

Belinda patted him on the knee. "Don't worry about

it, Mr. Hammond. I'm sure you'll be back to normal by tomorrow."

"Let's hope so," he heard the elf mutter.

James couldn't have agreed with her more.

CHAPTER THREE

THE NEXT MORNING James woke to what had to be the best-smelling candle in the universe—sweet with traces of allspice and cinnamon—which was odd since he didn't normally buy candles. Maybe the smell had something to do with the stinging sensation on the back of his head and the vague memories of dark hair and kitten eyes dancing on the edge of his brain.

And orange blossoms. For some reason, the first thought in his mind was that as delicious as the candle smelled, it wasn't orange blossoms.

Slowly, he pried open an eye. What the…?

This wasn't his Back Bay condo. He sprang up, only to have a sharp pain push him back down on the bed.

Sofa, he amended. He was lying facedown on a leather sofa, his cheek swallowed by a large memory foam pillow. Gingerly, he felt the back of his skull, his fingers meeting a patch of gauze and tape.

The drone. This must be Noelle Fryberg's living room. Last thing he remembered was leaning into her warm body as she led him through the front door. Explained why he had orange blossoms on the brain. The memory of the smell eased the tension between his shoulder blades.

Once the vertigo abated, he surveyed his surroundings. Given her slavish devotion to Fryberg's vision, he pictured his hostess living in a mirror image of the Christmas Castle, with baskets of sugarplums and boughs of holly. He'd been close. The house definitely had the same stucco and wood architecture as the rest of the town, although she'd thankfully forgone any year-round Christmas motif. Instead, the inside was pleasantly furnished with simple, sturdy furniture like the large pine cabinet lining the wall across the way. Brightly colored plates hung on the wall behind it. Homey. Rustic. With not a chandelier or trace of Italian marble to be found.

"You're awake."

A pair of shapely legs suddenly appeared in his line of vision, followed seconds later by a pair of big cornflower-colored eyes as the elf squatted down by his head. "I was coming in to check on you. I'm supposed to make sure you don't fall into a coma while sleeping," she said.

"I haven't."

"Obviously."

As obvious as her joy over having to play nursemaid.

She looked less elfish than yesterday. More girl next door. The red dress had been shucked in favor of a white-and-red University of Wisconsin sweatshirt and jeans, and her short hair was pulled away from her face with a bright red headband. James didn't think it was possible to pull back short hair, but she had. It made her eyes look like one of those paintings from the seventies. The ones where everyone had giant sad eyes. Only in this case, they weren't sad; they were antipathetic.

He tried sitting up again. Slowly this time, making sure to keep his head and neck as still as possible. He felt like an awkward idiot. How was it that people in movies bounced back from head wounds in minutes? Here he was sliding his legs to the floor like he was stepping onto ice.

"How did I end up here?" he asked.

Her mouth turned downward. "Do you mean the house or the sofa?"

"The sofa."

"Good. For a minute I was afraid you didn't remember anything." She stood up, taking her blue eyes from his vision unless he looked up, which didn't feel like the best idea. "You collapsed on it soon as we got through the door last night," she told him. "I tried to convince you to go upstairs to the bedroom, but you refused to budge."

That sounded vaguely familiar. "Stairs were too much work."

"That's what you said last night. Anyway, since you refused to move from the sofa, I gave you a pillow, threw an afghan over you and called it a night."

Out of the corner of his eye, James saw a flash of bright blue yarn piled on the floor near his feet. Tightness gripped his chest at the notion of someone tucking a blanket around his legs while he slept. Cradling his head while they placed a pillow underneath.

"Wait a second," he said as a realization struck him. "You checked on me every few hours?"

"I had to. Doctor's orders."

"What about sleep? Did you…"

"Don't worry—I didn't put myself out any more than necessary."

But more than she preferred. He was but an unwanted responsibility after all. The tightness eased, and the familiar numbness returned. "I'm glad. I'd hate to think you had to sacrifice too much."

"Bare minimum, I assure you. Belinda would have my head if you died on my watch. In case you hadn't guessed, she takes her responsibility to others very seriously. Especially those injured in her store."

His store now. James let the slip pass uncommented.

"Good policy. I'm sure your lawyers appreciate the extra effort."

"It's not policy," she quickly shot back. Her eyes simmered with contention. "It's compassion. The Frybergs have always believed in taking care of others. Belinda especially. I'll have you know that I've seen her literally give a stranger the coat off her back."

"I apologize," James replied. "I didn't mean to insinuate…"

She held up her hand. "Whatever. Just know that lawsuits are the last thing on Belinda's mind.

"You have no idea how special the Fryberg family is," she continued. Driving home the point. "Ned and Belinda were…are…the best people you'll ever meet. The whole town loves them."

"Duly noted," James replied. Must be nice, having a family member care so much they sprang to your defense at the slightest ill word. "I'll watch my language from now on."

"Thank you."

"You're welcome."

They both fell silent. James sat back on the sofa and rubbed his neck, an uncomfortable itch having suddenly danced across his collar. Normally silence didn't bother him; he didn't know why this lapse in conversation felt so awkward.

Probably because the entire situation was awkward. If they were in Boston, he would be the host. He would be offering to whip up a cappuccino and his signature scrambled eggs, the way he did for all his overnight guests. Instead, he was sitting on her sofa, feeling very much like the obligation that he was.

And here he'd thought he was done feeling that way ever again.

Noelle broke the silence first. Tugging on her sweatshirt

the way an officer might tug on his jacket, she cleared her throat. "I'm heading back into the kitchen. You might as well go back to sleep. It's still early. Not even seven-thirty."

"You're awake."

"I have cooking to do. You're supposed to rest."

"I'm rested out." Headache or not, his body was still on East Coast time, and according to it, he'd already slept several hours past his usual wake time. "I don't think I could sleep more if I wanted to."

"Suit yourself," she said with a shrug. "TV remote's on the end table if you want it. I'll be in the kitchen." The unspoken *Stay out of my way* came loud and clear.

She turned and padded out the door. Although James had never been one to ogle women, he found himself watching her jean-clad rear end. Some women were born to wear jeans, and the elf was one of them. With every step, her hips swayed from side to side like a well-toned bell. It was too bad the woman disliked his presence; her attractiveness was one of the few positive things about this debacle of a trip.

He needed to go back to Boston. It was where he belonged. Where he was…well, if not wanted, at least comfortable.

Slowly, he pushed himself to his feet. The room spun a little, but not nearly as badly as it had yesterday, or even fifteen minutes earlier, for that matter. If he managed to walk to the kitchen without problem, he was leaving. Grant him and Noelle a reprieve.

Plans settled, he made his way to the kitchen. Happily, the room only spun a little. He found his hostess in the center of the room pulling a bright yellow apron over her head. The delicious aroma from before hung heavy in the air. It wasn't a candle at all, but some kind of pie. Pumpkin, he realized, taking a deep breath.

His stomach rumbled. "I don't suppose I could get a cup of coffee," he said when she turned around.

She pointed to the rear cupboard where a full pot sat on the coffee maker burner. "Cups are in the cupboard above. There's cereal and toast if you want any breakfast. Do you need me to pour?" she added belatedly.

"No, thank you. I can manage." He made his way over to the cupboard. Like everything else in the house, the mugs were simple, yet sturdy. He was beginning to think she was the only delicate-looking thing in the house. "You have a nice place," he remarked as he poured.

"You sound surprised."

"Do I?" he replied. "I don't mean to."

"In that case, thank you. Kevin and his father came up with the design."

That explained the resemblance to the Christmas Castle.

"I'm curious," he said, leaning against the counter. She had bent over to look in the oven, giving him another look at her bottom. "Is there some kind of rule that the houses all have to look…"

"Look like what?" she asked, standing up.

"Alike." Like they'd all been plucked off a picture post-card.

"Well the idea *is* to resemble a European village. That's part of what makes us such a popular tourist attraction."

She was tossing around his words from yesterday. He'd insulted her again.

Which he knew before asking the question. Hell, it was why he'd asked it. Their exchange earlier reminded him how much he'd enjoyed her backbone yesterday. Next to her cute figure, pushing her buttons was the only other thing that made this trip enjoyable. "I'm sure it does," he replied.

"What is that supposed to mean?"

James shrugged. "Nothing. I was simply noting the town had a distinctive theme is all, and wondered if it was by design. Now I know."

"I'm sure you already knew from your research," she said, folding her arms. She had the closed-off pose down to a science. "You just felt like mocking the town."

"Actually…" What could he say? He doubted she'd enjoy knowing her anger entertained him. "Maybe I did."

She opened her mouth, and he waited for her to toss an insult in his direction. Instead she closed her lips again and spun around. Immediately, James regretted pushing too far. What did he expect? Surely, he knew she wouldn't find him as entertaining as he found her. Quite the opposite. She disliked him the same as everyone else. Pushing her buttons guaranteed the status quo.

There was one thing he could say that she might like.

"Your pie smells delicious, by the way. I'm sorry I won't get to taste it."

That got her attention. She turned back around. "Why not?"

Leaning against the counter, he took a long sip of his coffee. Damn, but she made a hearty cup. "Because as soon as I have my coffee and grab a shower, you're driving me to the airstrip so I can fly back to Boston."

Noelle almost dropped the pie she was taking out of the oven. Had she heard right? Not that she wouldn't be glad to see the back of him, but… "I thought the doctor said no flying."

"Doctors say a lot of things."

"Yeah, but in this case…" She flashed back to his falling into her at the hospital. "You could barely stand without getting dizzy."

"That was yesterday. Clearly, that's not the case today."

No, it wasn't. He appeared to be standing quite nicely against her counter, all wrinkled and fresh with sleep as he was.

The guy might be annoying, but he wore bedhead well.

Still, she couldn't believe he was serious about flying an airplane less than twenty-four hours after getting whacked in the head. What if he got dizzy again and crashed the plane? "It doesn't sound like the wisest of plans," she said.

From over his coffee mug, he looked at her with an arched brow. "You'd rather I stick around here with you all weekend?"

"No, but..."

"Then why do you care whether I fly home or not?"

Good question. Why did she care? She looked down at the golden-brown pie still in her hands. Setting it on the cooling rack, she took off her oven mitts, then nudged the oven door shut with her hip.

"I don't care," she said, turning back around. "I'm surprised is all. In my experience, doctors don't advise against things without reason.

"Why are you so eager to leave Fryberg anyway?" she asked. She could already guess the answer. It'd been clear from his arrival he didn't think much of their town.

Unless, that is, he had a different reason for returning to Boston. Something more personal. "If you have Thanksgiving plans with someone, wouldn't they prefer you play it safe?"

His coffee cup muffled the words, but she could swear he said "Hardly." It wasn't a word she'd expected him to use. *Hardly* was the same as saying *unlikely*, which couldn't be the case. A man as handsome as Hammond would have dozens of women interested in him. Just because he rubbed her the wrong way...

She must have misheard.

Still, it wasn't someone special calling him home. And she doubted it was because of Black Friday either. He could get sales reports via his phone; there was no need to physically be in Boston.

That left her original reason. "I'm sorry if our little town isn't comfortable enough for you to stick around."

"Did I say it wasn't comfortable?"

"You didn't have to," Noelle replied. "Your disdain has been obvious."

"As has yours," he shot back.

"I—"

"Let's face it, Mrs. Fryberg. You haven't exactly rolled out the welcome mat. Not that I mind," he said, taking a drink, "but let's not pretend the antipathy has been one-sided."

Maybe it wasn't, but he'd fired the first shot.

Noelle's coffee cup sat on the edge of the butcher-block island where she'd set it down earlier. Seeing the last quarter cup was ice-cold, she made her way to the coffee maker to top off the cup.

"What did you expect," she said, reaching past him, "coming in here and announcing you were phasing out the Christmas Castle?"

"No, I said the castle was near the end of its lifespan. You're the one who got all overprotective and jumped to conclusions."

"Because you called it a fading tourist attraction."

"I said no such thing."

"Okay, maybe not out loud, but you were definitely thinking it."

"Was I, now?" he replied with a snort. "I didn't realize you were a mind reader."

"Oh, please, I could hear it in your voice. I don't have

to be psychic to know you dislike the whole concept, even before you started making efficiency suggestions."

She set the pot back on the burner, so she could look him square in the eye. The two of them were wedged in the small spot, their shoulders abutting. "Or are you going to tell me that's not true?"

"No," he replied, in an even voice, "it's true. You shouldn't take it personally."

"Are you serious? Of course I'm going to take it personally. It's Fryberg's." The store represented everything good that had ever happened in her life since she was seven years old. "You didn't even want to keep the name!"

"I already conceded on that point, remember?"

"I remember." And considering how quickly he conceded, he'd probably already decided he didn't care. "That doesn't mitigate the other changes you want to make." The reindeer. Fryer. Those suggestions were the tip of the iceberg. Before anyone knew, her version of Fryberg's would be gone forever.

"Forgive me for wanting to improve the store's bottom line."

"Our bottom line is perfectly fine." As she glared into her coffee cup, she heard Hammond chuckle.

"So what you're saying is that you all would have been better off if I'd stayed in Boston."

"Exactly," she gritted.

"And you wonder why I don't want to stay in Fryberg."

Noelle's jaw muscles went slack. She looked back up in time to see Hammond tipping back the last of his drink. "I don't make a habit of staying where I'm not wanted," he said, setting the cup on the counter. "I'm certainly not about to start now. Would you mind if I grabbed that shower now? Then you can drop me off at the airstrip, and we'll both be free from an uncomfortable situation."

While he walked out of the kitchen, Noelle went back to contemplating the contents of her cup. She was waiting for a sense of relief to wash over her. After all, he was right; his leaving did free them both from an uncomfortable situation.

Why then wasn't she relieved?

Maybe because your behavior helped drive the man out of town? her conscience replied as she rubbed away a sudden chill from her right arm.

Perhaps she had been...prickly. Something about the man got under her skin. Everything he said felt like a direct assault on her life. Between the company being sold and Belinda moving to Florida, she felt cast adrift. Like a part of her had been cut away. The only things she had left were the castle, the town and its traditions. Without them, she'd go back to being...

Nothing. No, she'd be worse than nothing. She'd be the nameless little girl whose mother left her in the stable. She'd rather be nothing.

Still, regardless of how angry Hammond made her, she still had a responsibility as a host. Belinda would have never been as argumentative and...well, as bratty...as she'd been.

She found Hammond in the living room folding last night's cover. As he bowed his head to match one corner to another, he wobbled slightly, clearly off-balance. A stab of guilt passed through her. No way was he better.

"You're going to have to keep your head dry," she said, taking one end of the afghan for him. After making sure the folds were straight enough, she walked her end toward him. "That glue the doctor used to cover your stitches needs to stay dry until tomorrow. I could draw you a bath though." They met in the center, their fingers tangling slightly as he passed her his end.

"Anything that gets me clean works fine. Thank you."

Hammond's index finger ran along the inside of hers as he spoke. Coincidence, but Noelle got a tingle anyway. It had been a long time since a man's fingers touched her even accidentally. "It's the least I can do," she replied.

Tucking the afghan under her arm, she headed upstairs. The claw foot tub was going to be a tight fit for his long legs, she realized. Kevin had never been one for baths, and she'd never had any trouble, but Hammond was going to have to sit with his knees bent. Folded like a card table, as Belinda might say.

She felt another stab of guilt. Her mother-in-law would be mortified by Noelle's behavior this morning. In Belinda's world, everyone was welcome, no matter who they were. Hadn't she embraced Noelle that first afternoon? The Frybergs didn't pick fights like bratty children.

Or encourage men with concussions to fly home.

If he crashes, it's on your conscience.

He wasn't going to crash. He wouldn't take the risk if he didn't feel secure in his abilities. Right?

I don't make a habit of staying where I'm not wanted.

"That looks deep enough." Hammond's voice from behind her made her start. Looking at the water, Noelle saw the tub was three-quarters filled. Hammond's blurry reflection shimmered beside hers in the water. Tall and icy blue next to small bright red.

"The water?" he repeated.

Stupid her. "Spaced out for a moment, there," she said, reaching for the faucet handle. "I'll let some of the water out."

"No need. I think I can handle it. I didn't hit my head that hard."

"Right. Let me grab you a towel then and I…"

She sucked in her breath. Hammond had unbuttoned his shirt, revealing a white T-shirt beneath. Tucked tight in his waistband, the thin cotton emphasized the muscles in a way the dress shirt couldn't possibly. You could see the outline of his ribs. The bottom of the cage cut away to a narrow, trim waist. Above the ribs, a cluster of dark curls playing peekaboo at the V. It was to that spot that Noelle's gaze immediately zoned. Drawn by the contrast, of course, not by any memory of her hand splayed against the firmness.

Cheeks warming, she quickly yanked her gaze upward.

"There's blood on your collar," she said. It was the first thing that sprang to mind, and she needed something to explain her sudden loss of words. "Your shirt is ruined."

"Looks like the drone claims another victim." Hammond fingered the stiff corner. The red-brown stain covered most of the right side. "I'll toss it out when I get home. Who knew something so small could cause so much damage?"

"Consider yourself lucky it wasn't something bigger," Noelle replied. Her senses regained, she continued toward the linen closet. "Could have been a remote-control C-130."

"Or a crystal tumbler."

"What?"

"They can cause a lot of damage, is all."

"If you say so."

Was this knowledge from personal experience? Considering she'd thought about tossing a thing or two in his direction, she wouldn't be surprised. Taking a pair of towels from the cabinet, she piled them on a stool next to the tub along with a spare toothbrush.

"If you don't need anything else," she said, looking in his direction. Hammond had shed his dress shirt completely, and stood in his T-shirt studying the bloodied collar. Noelle struggled not to notice the way his biceps stretched his sleeves.

This sudden bout of awareness disturbed her. She'd never been one to check out other men. Of course, the fact that this was the first time a man had stood in her bathroom since Kevin probably heightened her sense of awareness. And while she didn't like Hammond, he was handsome. She had been struck by how much so when she'd checked on him during the night. He had been blessed with the most beautiful mouth she'd ever seen. Perfect Cupid's bow, full lower lip.

"What time do you have to be at Belinda's?"

His question jerked her back to the present. Dear God but she was having focus issues all of a sudden. "Not for a couple hours," she replied.

"Good. You'll have time to drive me to the airstrip."

Her stomach twisted a little. "So you're still planning to fly home today, then."

"What's the matter? Worried I changed my mind between the kitchen and here?" He grinned. Something else she'd noticed this morning. His mouth was capable of an annoyingly attractive smile.

Noelle scoffed. "Hardly. I doubt you ever change your mind."

"Only if I'm well and truly persuaded."

The intimate atmosphere made the comment sound dirtier than it was. Noelle fought to keep a flush from blossoming on her skin.

"That's what I thought," she said. He'd stick to his decision, even if the idea was a bad one. Nothing she could say would change his mind.

Oh, well. He was a grown man. If he wanted to risk his safety, it was his concern. She started to leave. "Do you need anything else?"

"No. I won't be long." From the corner of her eye, she saw him start to shake his head, then close his eyes.

He probably doesn't think I can see him.

Once again, Noelle's conscience twisted her stomach.

"You know…" she started. "Belinda isn't going to be happy with you. She was expecting you for Thanksgiving dinner."

"I'm sure she'll survive." There was an odd note to his words. Disbelief or doubt?

I don't make a habit of staying where I'm not wanted. His comment seemed intent on repeating itself in her brain.

"Survive? Sure," she replied. "That doesn't mean she won't be disappointed. Thanksgiving is a big deal to her. God knows she cooks enough for the entire state—and we're talking about a woman who gave up cooking when Ned made his first million. She'll hunt you down if you aren't around to try her sweet potato casserole."

"There's an image," he said with a soft laugh.

"But not far off. I'm willing to bet she was up early making something special for you."

"Something special?"

"That's the way the Frybergs do things. Seems to me the least you can do is stick around long enough to try whatever it is."

Noelle watched as his eyelashes swept downward and he glanced at the tile floor. He had pretty eyelashes too. When he raised his gaze, his eyes had an odd glint to them. The light looked right through her, and her argument.

"Is this your way of asking me not to fly?"

"I'm not asking you anything," she immediately replied. "I'm thinking of Belinda's feelings."

What was supposed to be nonchalance came out sounding way too affected, and they both knew it. Truth was, she didn't want to deal with a guilty conscience should something happen. "Belinda likes you."

The corners of Hammond's mouth twitched like they

wanted to smile. "Nice to know one member of the Fryberg family likes me."

"Don't get too flattered—Belinda likes everyone." Apparently, her conscience wasn't bothering her too much to stop being bratty.

To her surprise, he laughed. Not a chuckle, like previously, but a bark of a laugh that seemed to burst out of him unexpectedly. "Well played, Mrs. Fryberg. Tell me, are you always so upfront with your opinions?"

Honestly? Quite the opposite. She much preferred adaptation and assimilation to challenge. Hammond brought out an edge she hadn't known she had. "Not always," she replied.

"I'll take that as a compliment then." He crossed his arms, causing the T-shirt to stretch tighter. "There aren't a lot of people in this world who would say boo to me, let alone challenge me as much as you have these past twenty-four hours. It's been very entertaining."

Noelle wasn't sure if she should be flattered or feel condescended to. "I wasn't trying to entertain you," she said.

"I know, which makes me appreciate it even more. You've got backbone."

So, flattered it was. "You're complimenting me for being rude to you."

"Not rude. Honest. I like knowing where I stand with people. You may not like me, but at least you don't pretend, which is more than I can say for a lot of people."

He may have meant to be complimentary, but his words struck her uncomfortably. They pressed on her shoulders along with his comment from earlier. If he was trying to prick her conscience this morning, it worked. She took a long look at him. Tall, handsome, arrogant, and yet... Maybe it was the concussion misleading her, or maybe the injury shifted a mask, but she was seeing something in his expression she hadn't noticed before. It almost looked like...

Vulnerability.

The chip slipped a little off her shoulder. "I don't dislike you," she said, toeing the tile. "Not entirely. Like, I'd feel bad if you crashed your plane and died or something."

"Your kindness overwhelms."

"What can I say? I'm a giver." They smiled at one another, the air between them thawing a little more. The guy wasn't so bad when he wasn't talking about gutting tradition.

"Seriously," she said, "I wouldn't want to see anyone— you—do anything foolish."

"So now you're calling me foolish, are you?"

"I—"

"Relax, I'm joking. I know what you were trying to say. And I thank you."

"For what?" She hadn't done anything special.

His expression softened like she had, however, and she saw the man she'd watched sleep. "Caring about my safety," he replied. "Not many peop— That is, I appreciate it."

A tickle danced across the back of her neck at the gentleness in his voice. If he kept it up, they'd be friends before the bath water grew cold. "Does that mean you'll consider staying for dinner? I wasn't kidding about Belinda being disappointed."

"Well..." He ran his fingers across his mouth and along the back of his neck. "I'd hate to disappoint the woman who sold me her company. I suppose sticking around a few more hours wouldn't hurt."

"Good. Belinda will be glad."

"No one else?"

The cheeky question demanded a shrug in reply. "I

might be a little bit relieved. Lack of blood on my hands and all. Enjoy your bath, Mr. Hammond."

She closed the door before he could see in her eyes that she was way more than a little relieved.

Or that she was starting to like him.

CHAPTER FOUR

JAMES ADDED A LOG to the fireplace. The wood smoked and sputtered for a moment, before being hidden by the flames rising from the logs beneath. Warmth wrapped around his legs. Legs that were now clad in khakis, thanks to Noelle. She'd cajoled the Nutcracker's concierge into opening the hotel boutique so he could buy a fresh change of clothing. The casual pants and plaid sports shirt were more stylish than he'd expected, a fact Noelle took great pleasure in mocking once he'd completed his purchase. His rescue elf had a terrifically sharp sense of humor.

Then again, so did he. Tossing retorts back and forth in the car had him feeling as much like his old self as the bath and clean clothes.

Behind him, cheers erupted in the downstairs family room. Someone must have made a good play. A politer man would head down and join the other guests, lest he be labeled unsociable. Since James had stopped caring what people thought of him when he hit puberty, he stayed upstairs. He was content sitting in one of a pair of wingback chairs, studying the fire.

"People were wondering where you were." Noelle's heels click-clacked on the hard wooden floor until she drew up beside him. "Don't tell me you're not a football fan. Isn't that against the law in New England?"

"Only a misdemeanor," he replied. "I'll be down shortly. I was enjoying the fire. It's soothing."

"Hmm. Soothing, huh?" Perching on the arm of a wing-back chair, she looked up with a tilted glance. Before leaving the house, she'd swapped her sweatshirt for an angora sweater. The neon blue reflected in her eyes, giving them a gemlike glow. "Let me guess," she said, "you're not a fan of crowds either. Can't say I'm surprised."

"I don't dislike them," he replied. "But you're right, I prefer being by myself." It was easier that way. Less picking up on the negative vibes.

He shifted in his seat. The small space between the chairs caused their knees to knock. Laughing, they both pushed the seats back. "Let me guess," he said, "you love crowds."

"I don't love them, but they don't bother me either. I spent most of my childhood having to share my space, so I'm used to it."

An interesting choice of words. "You came from a big family then?"

"Not really."

Then with whom was she sharing space?

"Did you get enough to eat? There's more cornbread casserole if you'd like some."

"Dear God no," he replied. "Four servings is enough, thank you." Why such an abrupt change of subject? He was under the impression she was all about family. "I can't believe I ate as much as I did."

"That's what you get for sitting next to Belinda and her ever-moving serving spoon."

"Plus almost two days without eating." He literally had been the starving man at the buffet. The perfect match for Belinda's serving spoon.

Noelle wasn't joking when she said her mother-in-law cooked up a storm for the holiday. The woman must have served three times as much as the guests could eat. Granted, the turkey and side dishes were nothing like the five-star fare the family chef set out—on those rare occasions he and Jackson celebrated together—but James had enjoyed eating them ten times more. The food today came with wine and laughter and conversation. Real conversation. The kind where people debated, then joked the tension away. No stilted dialogues or pretend interest in each other's lives.

And not a single tumbler hurled across the room.

Funny how that memory had reappeared today, after twenty years of staying buried. Especially since it happened on Christmas Eve. Thanksgiving had been a Tiffany candlestick. Or had that been the dinner plate? The flying objects blended together after a while.

"You're frowning," Noelle said. "Is your head okay?"

"My head's fine." A faint headache at the base of his neck was all. The bulk of his dizziness had ebbed as well. Unless he whipped his head around quickly or hung upside down, he wouldn't have a problem.

"Guess that means you'll be able to fly home without a problem."

"Don't see why not," he replied. His original reason still stood. So long as he could control when and where he stayed, he would. "No sense overstaying my welcome, right?"

"Definitely not," Noelle replied. "Is it a long flight?"

"A few hours. One of the benefits of being the pilot, you save all that time waiting at the airport."

"No security pat down either. Is that why you fly? So you can avoid lines at the airport?" While she was talking, she slid backward off her perch and into the chair. The move left her sitting sideways with her calves balanced on the arm. "Wow, you really do hate people, don't you?"

Her smirk told him she was teasing. "Very funny," James replied. "I fly because it's more efficient. I don't like wasting time."

"Really? Who would have guessed?"

This time he smirked. Her sitting in such a cozy, casual position had made his muscles relax as well. He was at ease, he realized. An unusual experience outside the cockpit. The sky was the one place he felt truly at home. He would never tell that to anyone though. At thirty-nine-thousand feet, the sound of the engine roaring in your ears drowned out your thoughts. There was nothing to prove, nothing to forget.

"I was studying Belinda's mantel." He nodded toward the fireplace, and the collection of photographs and knick-knacks that lined the thick pine. Diverting the attention away from himself once more. "Couldn't help noticing you and she have a lot of the same pictures."

"No big surprise, considering I married into her family."

Family was definitely the theme. The largest photograph was a portrait of a man in a military uniform smiling from the passenger seat of a truck. Pushing himself to his feet, James walked over to take a closer look. A copy of the photo was on Noelle's mantel as well. "Kevin?" he asked. He already knew the answer. Who else could it be?

"He emailed the photo from Afghanistan a few months before the accident."

His jeep flipped over. James remembered from researching the sale. He'd been surprised to hear the Fryberg's heir had been in the military.

"He looks like he enjoyed being in the army."

"Guard," she corrected. "Signed up our senior year of high school." James heard a soft rustling noise, which he realized was Noelle shifting in her chair. A moment later, her heels tapped on the wood floor again. "He was so excited when his unit finally deployed. All he ever talked about was getting overseas. Ned and Belinda were crushed when they learned he'd been killed."

Was it his imagination or did all her answers go back to Ned and Belinda? "Must have been hard on you too."

"I was his wife. That goes without saying."

He supposed it did. It was odd is all, that she focused on her in-laws' grief instead of her own.

Then again, maybe it wasn't. Maybe that was how real families behaved.

The picture on the left of Kevin was from their wedding. The Fryberg quartet formally posed under a floral arbor. It too had a duplicate at Noelle's house. "How old were you when you got married anyway?" She looked about ten, the voluminous skirt of her wedding dress ready to swallow her.

"Twenty-one. Right after graduation. We were already living together, and since we knew Kevin was scheduled to leave after the first of the year…" She left the sentence hanging with a shrug.

No need to say more. "You didn't have a lot of time together."

"Actually, we had almost twelve years. We were middle school sweethearts," she added, in case that wasn't obvious. She smiled at the photograph. "I did a lot of growing up in this house."

"There you two are! Detroit's almost done letting everyone down." Belinda came strolling through the living room along with Todd Moreland, Fryberg's general manager. "I promised Todd here some pie for the road." When she saw he and Noelle were looking at her son's photo, she smiled. "I always liked how happy he looked in that photo."

"He was a real special kid," Todd added. "The whole company liked him. We always figured we'd be working for him one day. No offense, Mr. Hammond."

"None taken," James replied stiffly. "Everyone has their preferences." And it usually wasn't him.

"Noelle was filling me in on some of the family history," he said, turning to Belinda.

"You picked the right person for the job. She remembers more about the family history than I do at this point. In fact, she can tell you who those people in the portrait are. I forgot a long time ago."

"Ned's great-grandparents from Bamberg."

"See what I mean?" The older woman tugged at her companion's arm. "Come on, Todd. I'll get you that pie."

"So, keeper of the family history, huh?"

"Someone has to. Family's important."

"That, Mrs. Fryberg," he said, shuffling back to the chairs, "depends upon the family."

He shouldn't have said the words out loud; they invited a conversation he didn't want to have. Taking a seat, he steered the conversation back to her. "What about your family? Do you maintain your own history as diligently as your in-laws'?"

A shadow crossed her face. "Like you said," she replied. "Depends upon the family."

It appeared they had both dropped curious comments. In her case, she'd dropped two. Was it possible they had more in common than he'd thought?

Catching her gaze from across the space, he held it in his. Trying to tell her he understood. "What's that old saying about families? You can't live with them...you can't take them out and bury them in the woods."

"I don't think those are the words."

Her expression clouded again as she added, "Besides,

you can't bury something you don't have." The words came out low and hesitant. Her gaze broke from his and returned to the photographs on the mantel as though she was speaking more to them than James.

Normally when a woman made coy remarks, he ignored them, seeing how coy was nothing more than an attempt at attention. Something about Noelle's remark, however, cut through him. There was weight to her words that spoke to a piece inside him.

Maybe that's why he decided to ask. "You don't have a family?"

Her sigh rattled signs in Chicago. "What the hell. Not like it's a secret.

"I was raised by the state," she said. "My mother left me in the town crèche on Christmas Eve and disappeared never to be heard of again."

That wasn't necessarily a bad thing, he thought. Better that she disappear altogether than sell you a fantasy and then unceremoniously pop the bubble.

He stared at the crease in his new pants. No wonder her comment affected him the way it had.

The two of them had more in common than she realized.

"Anyway, I grew up in the foster system. The Frybergs were the first real family I ever had. If it weren't for them, people would still be calling me the Manger Baby."

"The what? Never mind." He figured it out as soon as he asked. She said she'd been left in the crèche.

Something else dawned on him as well. "Is that how you got your name? Because you were found at Christmas?"

Her cheeks turned crimson as she nodded. "Nothing like advertising your past, huh? I shudder to think what they'd have called me if I were a boy."

"Trust me, I can imagine."

They both chuckled. When they were finished, he sat

back in his chair and took a fresh look at the woman he'd spent the last twenty-four hours with. "It suits you," he said. "The name."

He wasn't surprised when she rolled her eyes. "So I've been told by half the town."

"Half the town would be right." There was a brightness about her that reminded him of a Christmas ornament. He could only imagine what she'd looked like as a kid. All eyes and luminosity.

No wonder Kevin Fryberg fell for her.

Knowing her story, a lot of things made sense now. Her loyalty. Her attachment to every tradition Ned Fryberg ever started.

He sat back in his chair. "You know, hearing all this, I've got to say I'm surprised Belinda sold to me when she had you around to take her place."

The muscle on her jaw twitched. He'd clipped a nerve. "I said the same thing. I suggested she retire, and let Todd run the place while he groomed me to be his replacement, but she said this was the best move for the store. Hammond's would give us the capital we needed to stay modern. Plus, she thought selling would give me more freedom to do other things. She didn't want me to feel trapped in Fryberg because I was tied to the business."

Interesting. Made sense. While Noelle professed loyalty now, she was also young, with a host of options in front of her. Better to sell the business while Belinda could control the deal. That's what he would do. His father as well. Hell, if James weren't so good at making money, Jackson probably would have sold the store years ago—and not because he wanted his son to have freedom.

Still, he could hear the disappointment in Noelle's answer. A part of her felt rejected. Cast aside. He knew that sting. It made him want to pull her into his arms for a hug, which was unsettling, since he didn't do comfort. And even if he did, she would deny the feelings.

Meaning they shared another trait in common as well: neither liked to show weakness.

"Look on the bright side," he said instead. "She could have fired you."

"You don't fire family."

"Speak for yourself, sweetheart. Not everyone is as family oriented as you are. There are as many people on the other side of the line who value profits over DNA."

She tilted her head. "I'm curious? Which side do you fall on?"

James didn't even have to pause and think. His answer was that reflexive. "The side that doesn't believe in family period."

Noelle stared at him. Unbelievable. No sooner did she catch a spark of warmth, then his inner Grinch came along to snuff out the flame.

"You do know how ironic that statement sounds, coming from the heir of Hammond's, right?"

Ask anyone in the industry and they'd tell you, Hammond's Toy Stores was the epitome of old-fashioned family values. Their history put Fryberg's hundred-year-old tradition to shame.

James's lashes cast shadows on his cheeks as he studied the palm of his hand. "Things aren't always what they seem," he said.

"They aren't? 'Cause I've studied Hammond's." And the last time she checked, Hammond's sure looked like a fifteen-decades-old success story. The Boston store dwelled in the same building where Benjamin Hammond originally opened it. Over the decades, the store had become a touchstone for people looking to recapture childhood innocence. Their window displays and decor was like walking into a magical piece of frozen history. And at Christmas time…

Noelle had seen the photos. It was the Christmas Castle, Santa's workshop and Rockefeller Center all rolled into one. "There's too much heart in your branding for it to have been pulled from a hat."

His reply was somewhere between a cough and a snort. "I'll let the marketing department know you appreciate their efforts. They put a great deal of effort into creating that 'heart.'"

She could feel the air quotations. There were exclamation points on the sarcasm.

"I hate to break it to you," he said, "but my family has made a small fortune selling a fantasy."

"For one hundred and fifty years? I don't think any company can fake their corporate culture for that long."

"Maybe once, a long time ago, someone believed in it," he said in a softer voice. "My grandfather or someone like that."

His fingers traced the plaid pattern on the chair arm. "Who knows? Maybe back then, life was different. But holidays are all manufactured now. There's no such thing as a 'family Christmas' except on TV. Divorce, dysfunction… most of the world's just trying to get through the day without killing each other."

Noelle didn't know what to say. She couldn't call him on his sarcasm, because he wasn't being sarcastic. He delivered his words in a flat, distant voice tinged with hopelessness. It took squeezing her fists by her sides to keep from hugging him. What was it he had said about glass tumblers?

"I'm sorry," she murmured.

"For what?"

Good question. She wasn't sure herself. "That you don't like Christmas."

Hammond shrugged before returning to his pattern tracing. "Don't have to like it to make money off it," he said.

"No," she said, "I don't suppose you do." And Hammond did make money. Lots of money. So, he was right. Who cared if he liked Christmas or not?

Except that the notion left her incredibly sad. Noelle didn't know if it was the cynicism of his words or something else, but this entire conversation left a pang in her stomach. She couldn't look at Hammond without wanting to perch on his chair and press him close.

To chase away his sadness. Talk about silly. Twenty-four hours ago she disliked the man and now here she was thinking about hugging him? As though a hug from her would solve the problem anyway. She didn't even know if he was sad, for crying out loud. Imagine what he would think if he suddenly nestled up against that hard torso.

That she was crazy, no doubt.

Still, possible personal demons aside, she wondered how long it would take before Hammond's cynicism bit him in the behind? She didn't care how good a marketing team he had, a store that didn't believe in its own brand couldn't last. Sooner or later the phoniness, as he put it, would seep through.

You can only bury the truth of your feelings for so long before the truth wins out.

The corner of her gaze caught the photo on the edge of the mantel. Noelle turned her head.

And thought of Fryberg's. Without sincerity at the helm, the castle would truly become a cheesy tourist destination. Wouldn't take long after that for Hammond to close the store down, in favor of his giant shipping warehouse.

The store was on borrowed time as it was. His cynicism shortened the timetable.

"Bet if you spent time here, you wouldn't be so negative."

"Excuse me?"

Oh, jeez. She'd spoken out loud, hadn't she? The point had merit though. "The magic of the place has a way of growing on you," she said.

"Is that so?"

Interesting that he hadn't said *no.* "Yeah, it's so. Do you think this cottage industry of a town sprang up because people wanted to live in Bavaria again?"

Her question made Hammond chuckle. "The thought crossed my mind."

It crossed a lot of people's. "The people here love the holidays. You want to see the Christmas spirit you need to see tomorrow's Christmas season kickoff. It'll convert the most frozen of hearts into holiday fans."

A light flickered in his eyes, along with an emotion Noelle couldn't quite recognize, but made her pulse quicken nonetheless. "Are you asking me to stick around, Mrs. Fryberg?"

"No. I mean, yes. Sort of." Articulating herself would be easier if he weren't chuckling. "So you could see how we do Christmas, is all."

"I've seen how you do Christmas. Part of the celebration struck me in the head yesterday, remember?"

"I meant how the town did Christmas. I thought, if you spent time with people who enjoy celebrating Christmas, it might make you less cynical."

"I see. Worried my cynicism will kill the Christmas Castle sooner rather than later?"

In a word? "Yes," she replied. Wasn't he already turning things upside down in the name of efficiency?

Damn if he didn't chuckle again. A throaty rumble that slid under a person's skin and brushed across her nerve endings. The sound left goose bumps on Noelle's skin. "No offense to your Christmas magic," he said, "but I highly doubt a few gingerbread cookies and a tree lighting will make me less cynical."

He had a point. She probably was giving the magic too much credit. "Once a Grinch, always a Grinch. Is that what you're saying?"

"Precisely. I always thought he was misunderstood."

"As misunderstood as a man with a tiny heart could be," Noelle replied.

This time, instead of chuckling, Hammond let out a full-on laugh. "I wasn't trying to be funny," she said when he finished.

"I know. I was laughing at how easily you're abrupt with me. It's so damn refreshing."

So he'd said this morning. "I'm not trying to be," she told him. "The words keep popping out before I have a chance to mentally edit."

"Making it all the more refreshing, knowing it's organic." He settled back in his chair and assessed her with, based on the tingling running up her arm, what had to be the longest look in the world.

"You know, I have half a mind to bring you along when I fly out of here so you could follow me around and make snarky comments."

"Excu—"

"Don't worry, I'm kidding." He wiped the words away with a wave of his hand. "I have no desire to move you from Fryberg. *Yet.*"

Noelle let out her breath.

"What's this about flying to Boston?" Todd asked. He and Belinda came around the corner from the kitchen. The general manager had on his coat and carried a plastic bag filled with Tupperware.

"You're not planning to fly back tonight are you, Jim? They showed Foxborough on TV and the rain looks miserable there."

Partially hidden behind the chair wings, Hammond winced at the nickname, leaving Noelle to fight back a smirk. If there was anyone who looked more unlike a Jim…

"I've flown in rain before," he said. "I doubt it'll be a problem."

"If you say so. All I can say is better you than me. That wind was blowing so strong the rain was sideways. Won't be much of a passing game, that's for sure."

"How strong is this wind?" Hammond asked, swiveling around to face the man. Noelle noticed he already had his phone in his hand. Checking the forecast, probably.

"No clue. They didn't say."

"Maybe you should stay like you planned," Belinda replied. "I would hate for you to be bounced around during a storm and hit your head again."

"I'm sure I'll be fine. We fly above the weather."

"What about you?" he asked Noelle, once the others had departed. "You want to ask me to stay again too?"

The sparkle in his eye caused a rash of awareness to break out along her skin. "I didn't ask you to stay. I *suggested* staying for tomorrow's Christmas Kickoff might change your mind about the holiday. There's a difference." One of semantics maybe, but she clung to the argument anyway. "Besides, you made it quite clear this morning that you make your own decisions. If you want to risk flying in the wind, that's your business."

She fought back a frown. That last sentence sounded a

little passive-aggressive. It was his business and she didn't care—not that much anyway.

"You're right. It is my business," he replied.

Noelle watched as he tapped the keys on his phone and pulled up the Boston weather. An odd feeling had gripped her stomach. A cross between nervousness and disappointment. Something about Hammond had her emotions skittering all over the place. One minute she detested him, the next she felt a kinship. The man had turned her into a collection of extremes. It wasn't like her, being this mass of shifting energy.

Rather than continue staring, she turned to the pictures on the mantel. Kevin smiled at her from the Humvee and her insides settled a little. Good old Kevin who she'd loved for nearly fifteen years.

Loved like a brother.

No sooner did the thought rise than she stuffed it back down. How she felt about Kevin was her secret and hers alone. No one need ever know the truth.

Besides, she *had* loved him. He was her best friend. Her shoulder. Her rock. He'd given her so much. A home. A family. When she became his girl, her world went from being cold to one full of love and meaning. Kevin turned her into someone special. Wasn't his fault she couldn't feel the passion toward him that he deserved.

"Looks like you got your wish." Hammond's voice sounded above her ear. Startled, Noelle stepped back only to have her shoulders bump against his muscled chest, causing her to start again.

"What wish?" she managed to say as she turned around.

"Todd was right. There's a high-wind warning up and down the New England coast. Logan's backed up until the nor'easter moves on."

"What does that mean?" she asked. Focused on putting distance between their bodies, the significance of his words failed to register.

"It means…" He reached out and cupped a hand on the curve of her neck. His thumb brushed the underside of her jaw, forcing her to look him in the eye. The sparkle she saw in his left her with goose bumps.

"It means," he repeated, "that you're stuck with me another day."

It was the perfect time for a sarcastic remark. Unfortunately, Noelle was too distracted by the fluttering in her stomach to think of one. The idea of his continuing to stay around didn't upset her nearly as much as it had yesterday.

In fact, heaven help her, it didn't upset her at all.

James was disappointed when the barbed comment he'd been expecting didn't come. Instead, he found himself standing by the fire while Noelle went to tell Belinda he'd changed his plans. Again. Oh, well, what good was flying your own plane if you couldn't control your flight schedule, right?

He twirled his smartphone between his fingers. Christmas Kickoff, he thought with a snort. He'd go, but there was no way he'd change his thoughts on the holiday. The Hammond dysfunction was far too ingrained.

Turning his attention from the now empty doorway and back to his phone, James tried to settle the disquiet that was suddenly rolling in his stomach. He wished he could blame the sensation on being stuck in Christmas Land, but his phone screen told the truth. The conditions weren't that bad in Boston; he'd flown in worse dozens of times.

He'd used the wind as an excuse. To hang around.

He didn't rearrange his schedule on a whim for anyone, let alone a woman, and yet here he was making up reasons to spend additional time with Noelle Fryberg, a woman he was sure wasn't one hundred percent happy about the decision. He was breaking his own number one rule and staying where he might not be wanted. All because she made him feel energized and connected in a way no one ever had.

No wonder his stomach felt like it was on a bungee.

CHAPTER FIVE

Someone had shot off a Christmas bomb. How else could he explain it? Overnight, fall had disappeared and been replaced by poinsettias and tiny white lights. There were wreaths and red bows on doorways and evergreen garlands draped the fascia of every downtown building. It was even snowing, for crying out loud! Big, fluffy flakes straight out of central casting. An inch of the white stuff already coated the ground.

"What the heck?" he said as he looked out the passenger window of Noelle's SUV. "Did you drag a snow machine over from one of the ski resorts?"

"Nope. A happy coincidence is all," Noelle replied. "Makes a nice touch for the start of the Christmas season, doesn't it? Snow always puts people in the Christmas spirit."

"Keeps people off the roads too. People hate driving in snowstorms."

"Maybe back in Boston, but in this town, we deal perfectly fine with snowstorms."

"Residents maybe, but what about all those out-of-town shoppers?"

"Oh, I wouldn't worry about them," she replied.

They turned onto the main drag, where the bulk of the

shops and restaurants were located. First thing James noticed was the steady flow of people looking into windows.

"See? The town will do very well economically over the next few weeks, weather or no weather."

"Yeah, but will they drive from downtown to the toy store?" That was the real issue. No one minded walking a few blocks; it was risking the roads that made people balk. Today, Black Friday, was the day retailers counted on to jumpstart their yearly profits. A healthy turnout was vital. "Conditions like this are one of the reasons why I want to push the online business," he said. "Bad weather encourages people to stay inside and shop online." Where there was a lot more competition for their attention.

Not surprisingly, she ignored his comment. "I wouldn't worry too much. We've got things under control."

She pointed ahead to where a bus stop had been decorated with a big gold sign that read Trolley to Christmas Castle Every Fifteen Minutes. "Like I said, we're used to snow. There's already a line too. Everyone loves to visit Santa's workshop."

The smugness in her voice begged to be challenged. "Crowds don't necessarily equal sales. Half the people coming to see the foolish window displays at the Boston store never buy a thing. Not a very good return considering how much we spend on them every year."

She gave him a long look. "If that's how you feel, then why continue having them? Why not scale back?"

"Because…"

James frowned. Why did he continue doing the windows on such a grand scale? Not even his own father wanted to continue the tradition. Yet, every year, he saw the numbers, and then turned around and approved something equally lavish for the following December. It was the one budget item where he deviated from his own rules of business and he didn't have a decent explanation.

"People have come to expect them," he replied. That was the reason. He was preserving Hammonds' reputation with the public. "Those window displays are part of the Hammond brand."

"I'm surprised you haven't figured out a way to support the brand in a less expensive way. Building brand new, custom animatronic exhibits every year is expensive."

Tell me about it, he thought. "Cutting back would send a negative message to the public. They might equate it with financial difficulties that don't exist." James could imagine how the business press might speculate.

"In other words, it's not always a good idea to mess with tradition."

"Unfortunately, no."

"You mean like Fryer and the Santa's reindeer corral at the castle."

Damn. She'd boxed him in. Quite neatly too.

Shifting in his chair, he tipped an imaginary hat. "Well played, Mrs. Fryberg. I see your point."

"I thought you might, Mr. Hammond," she said, nodding her head in return.

Neatly playing him, however, did not mean she was getting all her own way. "You still can't have people leaving Santa's workshop, and not reentering the store. The idea is to keep them around the toys as long and as much as possible."

He waited for a response, half expecting another argument. Instead, she daintily flicked the turn signal handle with her fingers. "Fair enough. What about Fryer?"

"Fryer?" Parts of the other day were still a bit fuzzy. James had to think a moment about whom she was talking about. Finally, he remembered. "You're talking about the giant stuffed moose eating up space at the rear of the store."

"Elk," she corrected.

"What?"

"Fryer. He's an elk, and people love taking selfies with him. In fact, customers have been known to bring friends specifically to see him. Much like your window displays."

So it was the moo—elk she wanted to save. Strange item to draw a line over. Then again, she did mention something about Ned Fryberg using the creature in his early ads and as he'd learned yesterday, his hostess had a very strong attachment to Fryberg history.

"Fine," he said. "The elk can stay. But only until I get a good look at the profit per square foot. If we need to redesign the floor plan, I make no promises."

"But he stays for now?"

"Yes," James replied, his sigh sounding more exasperated than he truly felt. "He can stay."

She turned and smiled. "Thank you."

That made twice in three days that she'd managed to convince him to bend on a decision. Granted, neither were major sticking points. Still, she had a better record than most of the experienced negotiators he'd faced.

Beginner's luck, he told himself. It definitely didn't have anything to do with how her eyes got bluer when she smiled.

He continued studying her after she'd turned her eyes back to the road. Today she was dressed for the holidays in a red sweater and a brightly colored scarf. Candy cane stripes, naturally. A matching knit cap sat on her head. The outfit made her look like a tiny character from *Where's Waldo*, only she'd stand out in any crowd, regardless of her size.

A blush worked its way into her cheeks as she sensed

him studying her. "How's your head this morning?" she asked. "You never said."

"Better," he replied. Better than better actually. The spot around his stitches was still tender, but the dull ache had disappeared and he could bend and turn his head without the room spinning. "Being able to shower this morning helped." Nothing like being able to stick your head under a stream of water to erase the cobwebs. "Having a bed helped too. No offense to your sofa."

"I'm glad you were awake enough to climb the stairs this time," she replied. "I was thinking that considering how tired you were last night, it was a good thing you couldn't fly home after all."

"Yeah, a good thing." James forced his expression to stay blank. When they'd returned from Belinda's, he'd gone straight to the bedroom, telling Noelle he was too tired for conversation. In reality, he wanted the solitude so he could process his decision to stay. He wanted to say it boiled down to attraction. Noelle wasn't stereotypically beautiful—more cute really—but the more he studied her eyes, the more he found her gaze hypnotically compelling. If that was even a thing. And her curves…he did love those curves, no doubt about it.

Problem was, attraction didn't seem like a complete enough answer. It wasn't the challenge either, even though she clearly challenged him. He was drawn to her in a way that went beyond attraction. What that meant, he didn't have a clue, other than knowing he liked her in a way that was different from other women he'd known. Whatever the reason, he didn't like feeling this way. He didn't want someone getting under his skin. Didn't want the awkwardness when things inevitably blew up.

Why break his cardinal rule then by sticking around

last night? To spend time with a widow devoted to her late husband and his family, no less?

Hell. Maybe he did want the awkwardness. Maybe he had some subconscious desire to punish himself.

Certainly would explain a lot of things.

A flash of color caught his eye. They were passing an open-air market of some kind, the perimeter of which was marked off by a banner of rainbow-colored flags.

"That's the *Christkindlmarkt*," Noelle said. "It's German for Christmas market."

"Yes, I know. I've seen them in Europe."

"Really? Only other one I've seen is in Chicago. Ned and Belinda told me about the one they visited in Berlin. Sounded wonderful."

James watched as they passed a woman moving her collection of knit scarves out of the snow. "If you like flea markets," he said.

"It's a lot more than a flea market," Noelle replied. Even with his head turned to the window, he could feel her giving him the side-eye. It made his stitches tingle. "We hold the market every year. There are crafts, baked goods. Did you even spend time at the market in Europe? Or were you too busy studying the traffic patterns?"

"Contrary to what you might think, I don't analyze every retail establishment I visit. And no, I didn't have time to visit the market in Germany. My car drove past on the way to a meeting."

"No wonder you are being so derisive!" she said. "We'll visit this one on our way back from the store. Besides the castle, it's the linchpin of our Christmas Kickoff festival. One of the vendors, Heineman's Chocolatiers, has the most amazing hot chocolate you've ever tasted. Kevin and I made a point of visiting his stall first thing every festival. Mr. Heineman would never forgive me if I skipped it."

"God forbid you break tradition," James replied. The strangest flash of emotion passed through him when she mentioned Kevin. Not jealousy—he hadn't known Noelle long enough to feel possessive—but the sensation had the same sharp kind of pang. Like a tear in the center of his chest.

He'd been feeling a lot of odd things these past two days. Maybe that drone had jarred something loose when it struck him.

All he knew was the idea of Noelle and her beloved late husband strolling through the Christmas fair made his sternum ache.

"I owe you an apology. That was the most organized chaos I've ever seen."

Noelle's chest puffed with pride. Store management had spent years perfecting their Black Friday routine, so she knew James would be impressed. What she hadn't counted on was how his positive reaction would make her feel. She took his compliments as a personal victory. Unable to contain her smirk, she let the smile spread as she looked to the passenger seat. "I take it you no longer think of the castle as a fading tourist attraction then."

"I still think our retailing future lies online," he replied, "but I'll concede that you all know what you're doing here. Those handheld wish list scanners are genius."

"Thank you. Ned installed them shortly before he passed away."

Borrowed from the supermarket industry, the scanners let kids record items they fell in love with. The lists were downloaded to share with Santa as well as their parents. Moms and dads could purchase the items then and there and have them stored for pickup at a later date.

"We've boosted our Black Friday numbers by thirty

percent since installing them," she told him. "Of course, our numbers drop a little at the back end, but we prefer to start the season high rather then sweat it out at the end of the quarter."

"Don't blame you there." He smiled again, and this time Noelle got a little flutter in her stomach.

Her assessment of his smile hadn't changed in the last twenty-four hours; if anything, she was finding it more magnetic. Especially when he let the sparkle reach his eyes. That didn't always happen. Noelle found those smiles— the ones with shadows—intriguing too.

Despite the voice warning her the shadowy smiles were the more dangerous of the two.

"When I was a kid, the store made paper lists. Kids wrote down ten items and put the letter in a mailbox for Santa. Parents could come by and pick up their child's list at the front desk."

James had taken out his phone and was typing a note. "This is much more efficient," he said. "I'm sending a message to our logistics department about the scanners right now."

"I had a feeling the system would appeal to you. Although, I've got to admit…" She paused to back out of her parking space. "There was something special about folding up the letter and dropping it into that big red-and-white mailbox." Christmas always brought out the nostalgic in her. "Scanning bar codes doesn't feel the same."

"Even Santa's got to keep up with technology," James replied.

"Yes, he does. By the way, did you see how popular Fryer was with the crowd? I had a half dozen people ask me if we were bringing back our stuffed animal version."

"So you told me in the store. Twice," he replied, as he

tucked the phone back into his coat. "I take it this is your way of saying 'I told you so.'"

"You've got to admit. I did tell you." A chuckle bubbled out of her, cutting off the last word. Didn't matter. He got the point.

In the grand scheme of things, Fryer's continued existence was a small victory, but one that made her happy. She'd saved part of Fryberg's, which was like saving part of her family.

"Don't hurt yourself gloating," James said.

His comment only made her chuckle a second time. Heaven help her, but she was starting to enjoy their verbal jousts. "I'm trying, but it's hard when I was so right. People really love that elk. We should have taken your picture."

"Why? For you to hang in your office?"

"Uh-huh. With a piece of paper underneath that reads The Time I Told James Hammond So." She waved her hand over the wheel as though painting the words in the air.

"Oh, well. Guess my memory will have to do."

From the corners of her eyes, she saw him shifting his position until he faced her. "Anyone ever tell you that you're cute when you're being smug?"

"No," Noelle replied.

The feel of his eyes on her turned her skin warm. It had been a long time since a man had studied her, let alone one with eyes as intense as his. She'd be lying if she didn't admit she found his scrutiny flattering. All morning long, she'd sensed him stealing glances here and there, checking her out as she reached for an item from a shelf or adjusted her rearview mirror. The sensation left goose bumps on her skin, not to mention a warm awareness deep inside her.

It felt good, being noticed by a man. That was, a man like him. Someone smart and savvy. Who took charge of a space simply by entering it. His scrutiny left her feeling decidedly female.

Plus, it kept her from feeling guilty about her own stolen glances. She'd been looking his way since their conversation in front of the fire.

She was stealing a look now.

"Getting ready to gloat more?" James's eyes had slid in her direction, catching her. Try as she might to stop them, her cheeks started to burn.

"No," she said. "I'm done gloating."

"Glad to hear it. Why the look then? You looked like you were about to say something."

Had she? "I was looking at your shirt," she replied. "You…" Her cheeks burned hotter. "You wear plaid well."

"Thank you." The compliment clearly took him by surprise, which was okay, because she was surprised she'd said it out loud. "I'm glad you like it since it's going to be a wardrobe staple while I'm here."

Interestingly, he didn't say anything about leaving. But then, the snow probably made flying impossible.

More interesting was how relieved she felt about his staying.

Again.

And heaven help her, it wasn't only the banter she was enjoying. She was enjoying James's company. A lot. "We can stop at the boutique and grab you a new shirt if you'd like."

"Are you saying you don't like this shirt?" he asked.

"Not at all. I mean, I like the shirt," she corrected when his brows lifted. "I told you, you look good in plaid."

"Thank you. You look good in…red-and-white stripes."

Sensing that another blush was working its way to the surface, she quickly turned her face to scan the left lane. "Color of the day," she murmured.

"Shouldn't it be black? Being Black Friday and all."

"Technically, maybe, but red is far more festive." They were stuck behind a returning trolley. Flicking her turn signal, she eased into the left lane to pass. A little boy with his face pressed to the window saw the car and waved. "I'm not sure a bunch of people running around in black would inspire Christmas spirit," she continued.

"Good point. All that really matters is that the red color stays on the people and not on my balance sheet."

"Said every retailer everywhere today."

"No one said we weren't predictable," he observed with a laugh.

"You can say that again," Noelle replied. Bad Black Friday jokes were as much a tradition as Santa in her office. Hardly surprising that a man raised in the retail industry knew his share of them. "Although not every retailer was born into a retail dynasty."

On his side of the car, James made what sounded like a snort. "Lucky me," he replied.

"I'm sure some people would think so. Ned used to tell me about the early days, when his parents weren't sure the store would survive. He considered it a point of pride that Kevin would inherit a thriving business. I know we're not talking the same thing as a multimillion-dollar national chain…"

"Yeah," James said, reaching back to rub his neck, "if there's one thing my father knows how to do, it's make money."

"As do you. According to Belinda anyway. It's one of the reasons she chose to sell to Hammond's in the first place. Because she liked the idea that you would be stepping into your father's shoes. As she put it, the apple didn't fall far from the tree."

"That isn't necessarily a compliment," James replied.

No, thought Noelle. She supposed it wasn't. Especially if his father was like the man who'd arrived at their store two days ago. She thought him brusque and unsentimental. Absolutely hated the way he'd been focused solely on product and profit.

Oddly enough, James's comments today didn't upset her. Oh, sure, he was just as focused on profit and efficiency, but rather than annoy her, James's suggestions this time around had sounded incredibly astute. Probably because this time around, she liked him better.

Which might also explain why she detected a bitter edge to James's voice when she compared him to his father. "Don't you and your father get along?" she asked.

"Let's say my father does his thing, and I do mine," he said when she cast him a look. "It's a system that's worked quite well for us for a number of years."

Work or not, it sounded lacking. "I can't help but wonder," she said, "if some of these cynicisms of yours are exaggerated."

"I beg your pardon?"

"Well, you can't hate your family too much if you work for the family business."

He stiffened. "I work for the family business because I'm good at it. Like you said, the apple doesn't fall far from the tree. Not to mention that if I didn't, Hammond's wouldn't be a family business anymore," he added in a softer voice.

"There aren't any other family members?"

"None that are around," he said in a chilly voice. Clearly, it was a touchy subject.

Figuring it best to move on, Noelle focused on the rhythm of her windshield wipers going back and forth in the snow. Too bad the wipers couldn't swipe away the awkwardness that had overtaken the car.

As they got closer to downtown Fryberg, the road narrowed to one lane. Thanks to the snow, the already slower than normal traffic was reduced to a crawl. Only the castle trolley, which traveled in the bus lane, made any progress. Looking to the passenger seat, James was attempting to lean against the headrest without pressing on his stitches and not having much luck. His brow was furrowed and his mouth drawn into a tense line. Was he agitated because he was uncomfortable or from her uncomfortable question? Either way, it made Noelle anxious to see.

The sign for Bloomberg's Pharmacy caught her eye, giving her an idea. "Think your head can handle the snow?" she asked.

"It won't melt, if that's what you're asking," he replied.

"Good." With a flick of her directional handle, she eased the car to the right.

"From here until the central parking lot, traffic's going to be slower than molasses. I'll park at the drug store and we can walk."

James's frown deepened. "Walk where."

"To the Christmas market, remember?"

"Hot chocolate and gingerbread cookies. How could I forget?"

"You left out Christmas spirit," she said. "I thought maybe we could find you some. That way you don't have to rely on your marketing department to give your business heart."

"I told you yesterday, it's going to take a lot more than some midwestern Christmas craft fair."

Maybe, but a day at the market might make him smile. And for some reason, that was suddenly important to her.

Noelle swore the Christmas Kickoff got larger every year. At least the crowds did. Seemed to her that in middle school, she and Kevin darted from booth to booth without having to fight the flow of traffic.

James cut through the crowd like it was human butter. Hands in his coat pockets, he walked past the various stalls and vendors with such authority, the people naturally parted upon his approach. Noelle walked beside him and marveled.

Part of the deference had to be caused by his looks. He was, by far, the most handsome man there. The wind had burned his cheekbones pink while his hair and coat were dappled with snowy droplets. Dark and bright at the same time.

He looked over at her with eyes that refracted the light. "Where is this chocolate maker of yours?" he asked.

"I'm not quite sure." Rising on tiptoes, she tried to scan the aisle, but there were too many people taller than her. "In the past, Mr. Heineman liked to take a stall toward the rear."

"Then to the rear we go," he replied. "Like salmon heading upstream. This cocoa better be everything you claim it to be."

"Better. I promise, you'll be addicted." Mr. Heineman had a secret recipe that made the cocoa smooth and spicy at the same time.

"Addicted, huh? You're setting a pretty high bar, Mrs. Fryberg."

"It's not high if it's true," she told him with a grin.

And there it was. The start of a smile. Like a lot of his smiles, it didn't reach his eyes, but they had all afternoon. After the way he'd closed off in the car, she was determined to pull a bona fide grin out of him before they were finished.

She'd contemplate why the mission mattered so much later.

"Coming through!" Four teenage boys wearing match-ing school jackets were pushing their way through the crowd with the obnoxious aggression of teenage boys. The tallest of the four crashed his shoulder into Noelle. As she pitched sideways, an arm grabbed her waist. Instead of tak-ing a face full of snow, she found herself pressed against cashmere-covered warmth.

"Looks like it's your turn to get knocked over," James said, his chest vibrating against her cheek as he spoke. "You all right?"

"Right as rain." His coat smelled faintly of expensive aftershave while his shirt smelled of her orange body wash. A subtle combination that tempted a woman to rest her head. Okay, tempted *her*. Instead, she pressed a palm to his shoulder to steady herself. "We do have a habit of fall-ing around each other," she said. "Thank you for catching me. In this crowd, I might have gotten trampled."

"That would definitely kill your Christmas spirit." Among other things. "Maybe you should hold on in case you get jostled again."

Noelle stared at the arm he was holding out for a mo-ment, then wrapped a hand around his biceps. The curve of his muscles was evident even through the coat, remind-ing her that his vulnerability over the past few days was an exception. All of a sudden she felt decidedly dainty and very female. Her insides quivered. To steady herself, she gripped his arm tighter.

"Hey? Everything all right?"

He was looking down at her with concern, his eyes again bending the light like a pair of brown-and-green prisms.

"F-f-fine," she replied, blinking the vision away.

"You sure? You seemed a little unsteady for a moment."

"Must be your imagination. I'm steady as can be," she told him. Or would be, so long as she didn't meet his gaze.

She met his gaze.

"Are you sure? Because we could…"

It had to be a trick of the light because his pupils looked very large all of a sudden.

"Could what?" she managed to ask.

"Go…" His gaze dropped to her lips.

Noelle's mouth ran dry.

CHAPTER SIX

"Go," JAMES REPEATED. "I mean… Back to the sidewalk. Where it's not as crowded." He shook the cotton from his brain. Was that what he meant? He'd lost his train of thought when she looked up at him, distracted by the sheen left by the snow on her dampened skin. Satiny smooth, it put tempting ideas in his head.

Like kissing her.

"Don't be silly," she replied. For a second, James thought she'd read his mind and meant the kiss, especially after she pulled her arm free from his. "It's a few inches of snow, not the frozen tundra. I think I can handle walking, crowd or no crowd. Now, I don't know about you, but I want my hot cocoa."

She marched toward the end of the aisle, the pom-pom on her hat bobbing in time with her steps. James stood and watched until the crowd threatened to swallow her up before following.

What the hell was wrong with him? Since when did he think about kissing the people he did business with? Worse, Noelle was an employee. Granted, a very attractive, enticing one, but there were a lot of beautiful women working in the Boston office and never once had he contemplated pulling one of them against him and kissing her senseless.

Then again, none of them ever challenged him either. Nor did they walk like the majorette in a fairy band.

It had to be the drone. He'd read that concussions could cause personality changes. Lord knows, he'd been acting out of character for days now, starting with agreeing to stay for Thanksgiving.

It certainly explained why he was standing in the middle of this oversize flea market when he could—should—be working. Honestly, did the people in this town ever do anything at a normal scale? Everywhere he looked, someone was pushing Christmas. Holiday sweaters. Gingerbread cookies. One vendor was literally making hand-blown Christmas ornaments on the spot. Further proof he wasn't himself, James almost paused because there was one particularly incandescent blue ornament that was a similar shade to Noelle's eyes.

The lady herself had stopped at a booth selling scented lotions and soaps wrapped in green-and-gold cellophane. "Smell this," she said, when he caught up with her. She held an open bottle of skin cream under his nose, and he caught the sweet smell of vanilla.

"It's supposed to smell like a Christmas cookie," she said. "What do you think?"

"I like the way your skin smells better." He spoke automatically. It wasn't until her eyes looked down and away that he realized how his answer sounded.

"I'm not a huge fan of vanilla," he quickly amended. "I prefer citrus smells."

"We have a holly berry scent which is fruity," the vendor said, reaching for a different sample. "Maybe you'll like this one better."

"I don't think…" Before Noelle could finish, the saleswoman grabbed her hand and squirted a circle of pale pink cream on her exposed wrist. "Scents smell different on than they do in the bottle," she said as she massaged the lotion into Noelle's skin. "That's why it's always best to try the sample out before you buy. What do you think? Fruity, eh?"

She started to lift Noelle's wrist, but James intercepted. Keeping his eyes on hers, he raised her wrist to his nose and inhaled. Traces of berry mingled with the orange blossom. "Better," he said.

Noelle was staring at him, her lower lip caught between her teeth, and he instantly thought about nibbling her lip himself. "But you don't need it," he finished. The scent and/or the nibbling.

He, on the other hand, was definitely going to see a neurologist when he got back to Boston.

For the second time, she slipped free of his touch. "I—I'll have to think about it," she told the saleswoman.

"Don't think too long," the woman replied. "I sell out every year."

"We'll keep that in mind," James replied. Noelle had already moved along.

"Sorry about that," he said when he caught up. He noticed she'd stuffed both her hands deep into her coat pockets. "I didn't realize she was going to make me smell your skin."

"The lady was definitely working for the sale."

"Vendors at these things always are."

They were conveniently ignoring that James was not a man who people made do anything, as well as the fact he could have sampled the scent without brushing the tip of his nose across her skin. "I hope my comment didn't stop you buying something."

"Of course not. I know what I like and don't like."

"I'm sure you do," he replied. In this case, as she'd twice

demonstrated, she didn't like sharing any more personal space with him than necessary.

Message received. Copying her, he stuffed his hands in his pockets.

"Heineman's Chocolatiers is straight ahead," she said, nodding toward the red-and-white-striped stall fifty yards away. "Doesn't look like there's too much of a line either."

Considering the crowds, that didn't bode too well for the chocolate. One would think the greatest cocoa in the world would have lines a mile long.

A burly man with gray bushy hair peeping out from beneath a Santa hat waved to them as they approached. "There's my Noelle! I wondered when I would see you!" Leaning over the table, he wrapped Noelle in a hug. His arms were so massive she nearly disappeared from view. "It's good to see you, child. Merry Christmas!"

Noelle replied something that sounded like "Murry Chrfmaf!" before breaking free. "It's good to see you too. I've been dreaming about your hot chocolate since last December."

"You say that every year."

"I mean it every year. You know it's not Christmas until I have my Heineman's Hot Chocolate fix."

James got a twinge in his stomach. Noelle wore a smile brighter than anything he'd seen on her face. Brighter than anyone had ever smiled around him actually.

"This is James Hammond," she said. "His company purchased the store."

"I read in the paper that Belinda had retired and sold the business. I'm surprised she lasted as long as she did after Ned's death. The store was always more his, and with Kevin gone…"

The man paused to wipe at a spot of dried chocolate with his hand. An impromptu moment of silence.

"I'm surprised she didn't have you take over," he said once the moment ended.

"I'm afraid I haven't worked long enough to have the experience," Noelle said. "I also didn't have the kind of money Mr. Hammond put up."

"I read that in the paper too. Nice to meet you, Mr. Hammond."

"Same here," James replied. "Noelle has been raving about your hot chocolate all day. She swears it has magical properties."

"I didn't say that," Noelle shot back. "I said it tasted magical."

"Auch! You and that man of yours were always saying that. Ever since you were in junior high."

"Did she tell you about her man?" he asked James.

"Some," he replied.

The old man nodded. "Kevin Fryberg. Belinda's son. Fine young man. A true hero."

"So I've been told."

"Left a hole in the town when he died," Mr. Heineman continued. "A huge hole. Can't imagine how Belinda coped. Or this one."

Noelle was looking down and fingering a tiny tear in the plastic tablecloth. Her cheeks had turned a darker shade of pink. "Mr. Heineman…"

But the vendor didn't get her hint. "Did she tell you how he died?" James shook his head, eager to learn details his research couldn't. "Truck rolled over and blew up while he was trying to pull one of his men free."

A true hero, like the man said. Bet he was a great guy through and through. The kind of guy who was easy to fall for. "Pretty amazing," James replied.

"The whole town loved him," Mr. Heineman repeated. "Isn't that so?"

Noelle, who still hadn't said anything beyond his name, nodded. "Everyone," she repeated softly.

"And this one… Joined at the hip, the two of them. Kevin Fryberg and the little Manger Baby. They made the perfect couple."

"Mr. Heineman…" This time, the words came out a little stronger, whether because of unwanted memories or the Manger Baby comment, James wasn't sure. Probably unwanted memories, considering how she started twitching the moment Kevin's name came up.

Personally, James wanted to hate the man—Kevin—but he couldn't. It was impossible to hate a saint. Instead he jammed his hands down deeper into his pockets.

"I don't mean to be rude, but I promised Mr. Hammond hot chocolate, not a trip down memory lane." Noelle did her best to smile brightly as she cut the older man off. "I need to prove to him that the drink's worth bragging about."

"Of course it's worth bragging about. Two cups of Heineman's Hot Chocolate coming right up."

"Prepare to be blown away," she said to James with an enthusiasm she no longer felt.

"My taste buds can hardly wait."

"Go ahead and joke. I will be vindicated."

Naturally, his responding smile didn't reach his eyes.

Dragging James to the market had been a bad idea. If she hadn't let his eyes get to her in the first place, they wouldn't have had to stand here listening to Mr. Heineman go on and on about Kevin. Normally, the man's effusiveness didn't bother her; people always talked about Kevin. Their marriage. His heroism. Being Kevin Fryberg's widow was part of who she was. This afternoon though, Mr. Heineman's reminiscing was too much like a spotlight. It left her feeling guilty and exposed.

Oh, who was she kidding? She was feeling guilty and exposed before they ever reached Mr. Heineman's booth.

It was all James's fault. Him and his stupid, sad, kaleidoscope eyes. Twice now, he'd looked at her in that intense way of his, and twice she'd had to move away before her knees buckled. Twice, she'd held her breath thinking he might kiss her. Which was stupid, because if a man like James wanted to kiss a woman, he would simply go ahead and kiss her.

And, since he hadn't kissed her, he obviously didn't want to. A point she should feel relieved over, but she didn't. She felt foolish. Mr. Heineman waxing on about her great love affair only made her feel worse.

James's voice pulled her from her thoughts. "Seems you and your late husband made quite an impression," he said.

"After a dozen years of buying hot chocolate, I should hope so." Her attempt at lightness failed, so she tried again. "That's the kind of person Kevin was. Everyone loved him. He didn't even have to try."

"Some people are naturally lovable," he replied.

"Only some?" Something about his comment struck her as odd. Looking over at him, she waited for his answer only to get a shrug.

"Not everyone is on that side of the bell curve," he said.

"Bell curve? What the heck's that supposed to mean?"

Mr. Heineman's arrival prevented him from answering. "Here you go. Two cups of Fryberg's finest hot chocolate. On the house," he added, when James reached for his wallet. "To celebrate you buying Belinda's company."

"That's very kind of you."

The old man waved off the compliment. "My pleasure. Besides, it's the least I can do for my longest and most vocal customer. You come back later in the season, okay?" he said to Noelle.

"Don't I always, Mr. Heineman?" There were customers waiting behind them. Leaning over the counter, she gave the chocolatier another hug and left him to his business.

"Moment of truth," she said to James. "What do you think?"

He took a long sip.

"Well…?" She was waiting to drink herself until she heard his verdict.

James smiled. "This is good. Like truly good."

"Told you." Her thrill at seeing his pleasure was ridiculously out of proportion. "And here you thought I was exaggerating."

"Yes, I did," he replied, taking another, longer sip, "and I take every thought back. This chocolate definitely qualifies as amazing. What's in it?"

"Beats me. Mr. Heineman won't share the recipe with anyone. Claims he'll take the secret to his grave." She took a sip and let the familiar delicious thrill wash over her. "That'll be a dark day for sure."

James was studying the contents. "I can't believe no one's suggested he bottle and sell it. A drink this good, sold in stores, would make him a fortune."

"He's been approached. So far as I know he's turned all the offers down. I think he feels it would lose what makes it special if you could have the drink all the time."

"Sort of like a store celebrating Christmas every day?" James replied.

"That's differ— Jerk."

He chuckled, forcing her to nudge him with her shoulder. It was like poking a boulder, and had as much effect, which made him chuckle again. Noelle hated to admit it, but the sound slid down her spine with a thrill similar to the cocoa. It was certainly as smooth and rich.

Quickly she raised her cup to her lips, before her reaction could show on her face. "You know exactly what I mean," she said.

"Yes," he replied, "I do. He's also a rare bird. Most people would willingly sell out for the sake of a fortune."

"Would you?" she asked.

His face had *Are you joking?* written all over it. "Weren't you listening yesterday? Hammond's already has."

Right. Their family fortune made by selling a fantasy.

Cocoa mission accomplished, the two of them began walking toward the market entrance. As their arms swung past one another, Noelle's muscles again tensed with a desire to make contact. She thought back to the lotion display and the way James's nose brushed her skin. Barely a wisp of contact, it nonetheless managed to send tingles up her arm. Now here she was having the same reaction from the memory.

Didn't it figure? All day, she'd been pulling away from his touch only to wish for it now, when the moments had passed.

But what if she touched him?

She snuck a glance through her lashes. Walking in the snow had left James's hair damp and shiny. At the back of his head, where the doctor had woven the stitches, there was a tuft sticking out at an odd angle. What would he do if she reached over and smoothed the unruliness with her fingers? Would his pupils darken the way they had before?

Would his eyes fall to her mouth?

She took a long swallow of cocoa. Thoughts like those were only asking for problems. Better to purge them from her brain.

"Before Mr. Heineman brought us our cocoa, you were talking about bell curves," she said. "You never explained what you meant."

He shrugged. "Ever take statistics?"

"In high school."

"Then you remember how results look when plotted for a spectrum, with the bulk of responses falling in the middle."

"The bell." Memories of mountain-shaped graphs popped into her head. "With the outliers on either end. I remember."

"Same thing works with personality traits, intelligence, etc. Most people are average and therefore fall in the middle. Every now and then, however, you meet someone who skews way over to one side. Like your late husband. He was clearly an outlier when it came to being well liked."

Noelle thought of how Kevin could charge a room with his presence. "He had a lot of personality. Like a big, enthusiastic teddy bear. It was easy to get caught up in his energy." So much so, a person could misread her own emotions. "All the Frybergs are like that."

"Having met Belinda, I know what you mean."

"I wonder where I would have fallen on the bell curve if I hadn't been with Kevin," she mused. "Probably in the middle." The poor little orphan girl dropped in the manger.

"Are you kidding?" They were passing a trash can, so he took their empty cups and tossed them away. "You are definitely an outlier."

"Don't be so sure. I'm talking about me without the Fryberg influence."

"So am I," he replied. "From where I'm standing, you'd be impressive, Frybergs or not."

Noelle was surprised the snow didn't melt from the blush spreading across her body. He'd looked her square in the eye as he spoke, with a seriousness to his gaze that matched his voice. The combination made her insides flutter. "Really? I mean, th-thank you." She cringed at the eagerness in her voice. Sounded like she was leaping at the approval.

Still, she'd been entwined with the Frybergs for so long. It was the first time anyone had ever suggested she was unique on her own. Well, Belinda had, but that was more maternal affection.

"You're welcome," he replied. "And..." He reached over and smoothed her scarf. Right before pulling away, his gloved fingers caught her chin. "Really."

Her insides fluttered again. Double the speed this time. "Wait a second."

They'd resumed their walk when the rest of his comment came back to her. "Didn't you say you were on the other side of the bell curve? That doesn't make sense."

"Why not?" Again, he shrugged. "We can't all be warm, huggable teddy bears. The world needs cool and efficient as well."

"True," Noelle replied. Why did his indifference sound forced, though? He was leaving something out of his comparison. Whatever that something was, its unspoken presence made her want to tell him he was wrong.

She settled for saying nothing. For his part, James seemed happy to see the subject dropped. "Traffic's eased up," he noted.

He was right. With the snow done and the bulk of the day over, there were fewer cars on the road. Most of the tourists were either on their way home or warming up before the evening festivities. "They'll start blocking streets for the Santa Light Parade soon." A few hardy souls were already setting up lawn chairs. "Santa will drive his sleigh down Main Street to light the town tree, and then Christmas season will be officially here."

"And you all do this every year?"

"Like clockwork," she told him. "I'm not the only one

who takes traditions seriously. You've got to admit it definitely kicks up the Christmas spirit."

"I'll admit the town has a certain marketable charm to it, but I still prefer Boston and its other three hundred and sixty-four days."

"Marketable charm? You spend a day surrounded by Christmas and that's the best you can come up with?" Worse, he still had those far away shadows in his eyes. "You really don't like Christmas, do you? I know…" She held up a hand. "We covered this last night."

They were coming up on the Nutcracker Inn. The hotel had been decorated to look like a real gingerbread house. "So much for my theory that Fryberg's enthusiasm could inspire anyone."

"Sorry." To her surprise, his apology sounded truly sincere. "You shouldn't take it personally. When it comes to Christmas…"

He paused to run a hand over his face. "Let's say my history with the holiday is complicated, and leave it at that."

In other words, sad. After all, people didn't hate the holidays because of happy memories.

"And here I thought I was the one with the juicy Christmas story," she said. "In fact, we're passing my birthplace now."

She pointed to the old nativity scene which had been relocated to the Nutcracker's front lawn. "Back when I was born, Mary and Joseph hung out in the park next to the Christmas tree. The Nutcracker took them in a few years ago."

"I'll refrain from pointing out the irony," James said.

"Thank you." Pointing to the baby in the center, she said, "That's where they found me. Bundled up next to the baby Jesus. I guess my mother thought he'd keep me warm."

They stopped in front of the display. "Anyway, a group of people walking by noticed there were two babies, alerted the authorities and a Fryberg legend was born."

"Manger Baby," James said.

"Exactly. And you say your Christmas history is complicated."

Noelle could make light of it now, but when she was a kid? Forget it. Being the odd man out, even at home. The foster families were decent enough and all, but she was never truly a part of them. Just the kid the state paid them to take care of. Whose mother abandoned her in a plaster nativity display.

Thing was, she could justify her mother giving her up, but why couldn't she have picked a fire station or somebody's doorstep? Why did she have to go with the cliché of all clichés on Christmas Eve, thus saddling her child with a nickname that wouldn't die?

"I hated that nickname," she said. "Every Christmas, without fail, someone would dredge up that story, and that's all I'd hear on the playground."

"I'm sorry."

"Don't be." Reaching across the gap separating them, she touched his arm. "I've gotten over it. People don't call me the name anymore, haven't since I was in high school." Or maybe they did, and she didn't notice because she'd had the Frybergs.

James looked down at her hand on his arm. Feeling her fingers begin to tingle with nerves, Noelle moved to break away only for him to cover her hand with his. "It's a wonder you don't hate Christmas as much as I do," he said. "Considering."

"Never even crossed my mind." She stared at the manger. "Christmas was never a bad holiday. I mean, yeah I got stuck with that nickname, but there was also all of this too."

With her free hand, she gestured at the decorations around them. "How can you dislike a holiday that makes an entire town decorated for your birthday?

"Besides," she added. "There was always Santa Claus. Every year, the school would take a field trip to Fryberg's and we'd tell him what we wanted. And every year, those very toys would show up under the tree.

"I found out when I was in high school that Ned Fryberg made a point of granting the low-income kids' wishes," she said. "But when I was six or seven, it felt like magic."

"At six or seven, everything seems like magic," James replied. Noelle could feel his thumb rubbing across the back of her hand. Unconsciously, probably, but the caress still comforted. "But then you grow up and stop believing."

"In Santa Claus maybe. Doesn't mean you have to stop believing in holiday magic. I believe that special things can happen at Christmas time. Like Ned making sure kids got their gifts. People come together during the holidays."

She waited for James to chuckle, and give her one of his cynical retorts. When none came, she looked up and saw him staring at the manger with sad, faraway eyes. "They also rip apart," he said in a low voice.

CHAPTER SEVEN

JAMES'S WORDS—or rather the way he said them—caught her in the midsection. Taking her free hand, she placed it on top of his, so that he was caught in her grasp. "Ripped apart how?" she asked.

"My parents broke up on Christmas," he replied. "Christmas Eve actually. I woke up on Christmas morning and my mother and my little brother were gone. Moved out."

"Just like that? Without a word?"

"Not to me."

Wow. Noelle couldn't imagine. At least she'd been a newborn when her mother dropped her off. Unable to notice the loss. "How old were you?"

"Twelve. Justin, my brother, was ten."

Definitely old enough to understand. She tried to picture James coming downstairs that Christmas morning and discovering his world had changed. "I'm sorry," she said, squeezing his hand. The words were inadequate, but she couldn't think of anything else.

"It wasn't a complete surprise. Whenever my parents got together it was a drunken screamfest. Mom liked her whiskey. Especially during the holidays," he said with a half smile. "And Justin had always been her favorite, so..." He shrugged. Noelle was beginning to realize it was his way of shaking it off whenever the moment got heavy. Or in this case, touched too close to a nerve.

"I'm sure she would have…" She stopped, realizing how foolish what she was going to say sounded. Mothers didn't always want their children; she of all people should know that. "Her loss," she said instead.

The right side of James's mouth curved upward. "From the woman who's only known me for seventy-two hours. And disliked me for at least twenty-four of them," he added, his smile stretching to both sides.

"Meaning I've warmed up to you for forty-eight. Besides," she added, giving a shrug of her own, "I don't have to know you for a long time to realize your mother missed out on knowing you. Same as my mother. Far as I'm concerned, they both didn't recognize what they had."

He squeezed her hand. Even trapped between her hands, his grip was sure and firm. Noelle felt it all the way up her arm and down to her toes. "Are you always this positive?" he asked.

"Me? Positive?" She laughed. "Only by necessity."

She let her gaze travel to the nativity set again. "For a long time, I dreamed about my mom coming back. She didn't have to take me away with her…"

"Just tell you why she left you behind."

Noelle nodded. He understood. "But she didn't. So, what else can I do but focus on being happy without her? Best revenge and all that, right?"

"You're right," James said. A chill struck her as he pulled his hand free from hers. Before the shiver could take true hold, however, gloved fingers were gripping her chin, and gently lifting her face skyward. James's eyes had a sheen to them as he smiled down at her. "Your mom lost out. Big time."

It might have been the nicest thing a man—anyone

really—had ever said to her. While the Frybergs—and Kevin, of course—complimented her, they always made a point of avoiding any mention of her mother. For as long as she'd known them, her past had been the great elephant in the room. Known but not spoken aloud.

She'd had no idea how good having her past acknowledged could feel. "Yours did too," she said, meaning it. "Your brother might be a modern-day saint for all I know, but your mom still missed out. On the plus side, though, at least your father didn't."

He dropped his hand away. "That, I'm afraid is debatable."

While he sounded self-deprecating, she'd clearly said the wrong thing. There was a cloud over his features that hadn't been there before. It made Noelle's stomach hurt. "I'm…"

"It's all right," James said, holding up a hand. "My father isn't the most lovable man himself.

"It's all right," he repeated. Noelle waited for the inevitable shrug to punctuate the sentence; she wasn't disappointed.

James was wrong though. It wasn't all right. The implication that he wasn't lovable wasn't right. Granted, she'd only known him a few days, but the man she was standing with right now seemed very lovable indeed.

She couldn't help herself. Rising on tiptoes, she wrapped her arms around his neck and pulled him into a hug. He stiffened, but only for a moment before sliding his arms around her waist.

"I think they're both idiots," Noelle whispered in his ear before laying her head on his shoulder. One of James's hands slid up her back to tangle in her hair.

They fit together well, thought Noelle.

Scarily so.

* * *

"What was I supposed to do? I mean, the guy's mother left him behind. On Christmas Eve, no less. I had to offer some kind of solace, didn't I?"

The photograph on the nightstand smiled knowingly. Kevin always did know when she was overjustifying. He would listen patiently, and when she finished talking, cock his head and say, "Who you trying to convince, Noelle? Me or you?"

"Me," she told the memory and flung herself face-first across the bed. Why else would she be in her bedroom talking to a picture?

Letting out a long breath, she splayed her fingers across her plaid duvet. The fresh air and snow had taken their toll. Fatigue spread through her body, causing her to sink deeper into the down filling. If she lay here long enough, she'd fall asleep.

James wouldn't care. He was locked in his own room, having retreated there as soon as they returned home. His head was bothering him, he claimed.

Could be true. Embarrassed was more like it though. Who wouldn't be when one of their new employees suddenly starts clinging to them in the middle of Main Street?

He'd hugged her back though. With warm, strong arms that made her feel safe all over. "Like the ones you used to give," she told Kevin.

Except for the way she'd flooded with awareness.

There had been a moment, when James slid his arm around her shoulder, that she swore the awareness was mutual. Apparently not. If James had wanted her, she thought, tracing the threading on her comforter, he would have kissed her. He wouldn't have retreated to his bedroom alone.

"Sorry," she said to Kevin. "S'not like I'm looking to

move on or anything. It's just I haven't been kissed in a long time—by a man, your mom doesn't count—and the idea is kind of nice."

Especially if the kiss came from a man with a mouth as beautiful as James's.

"You had a pretty mouth too, Kev," she said. Everyone in town used to say his smile was brighter than a Christmas tree. Once, when they were in high school, he'd taken her skiing, and face-planted in the snow getting off the ski lift. His laughter could be heard all over the mountain. God, but she missed that laugh.

She missed him. The private jokes. The Friday Old-Time Movie Nights.

"None of this would be a problem if you were here." She certainly wouldn't be drawn to her boss-slash-houseguest.

But, as her eyelids started to close, it was damp cashmere teasing her cheek, not brushed flannel, and the memory of warm arms cradling her close. Kevin's voice sounded in her ear. *Who you trying to convince, Noelle? Me or you?*

By all rights, James should have gone straight to bed, risen early and called a taxi to take him to the airport before Noelle was up for breakfast. Steps one and two went according to plan. Step three, on the other hand, had run into some difficulty. Instead of doing his preflight check, he was sitting on Noelle's leather sofa downing coffee number two and staring at her mantel.

She'd hugged him.

Flirting, kissing, sexual aggression, those he could handle. If Noelle had thrown herself at him, he would have gladly reciprocated, and the two of them would be waking up in tangled sheets.

But a hug? Hugs were tender. Caring. They reached into

vulnerable parts of you and offered compassion. How was he supposed to respond?

He'd hugged her back, that's how. Hugged her and took the comfort she was offering.

And when she put her head on his shoulder, it was like all the air had suddenly rushed to his throat. He'd nearly choked on the fullness. The last time anyone had bothered to comfort him was…

He couldn't remember. Certainly long before his mother left. God knows, she'd checked out on him long before that. His father even earlier. Was it any wonder he couldn't take the moment further?

Or were you afraid she'd say no?

The thought made his shoulders stiffen. Rejection had never been an issue before. Then again, a woman had never hugged him before either, or left him feeling so… so exposed. That made him want her even more, and he didn't mean sexually. He wanted to make her smile. Her eyes light up like a Christmas tree. To give her a dose of that magic she believed in so strongly.

Dear God. His mouth froze against his mug. He sounded like a sappy teenager. Could it be he was falling for Noelle?

"It can't be," he said.

"Can't be what?"

Noelle stood on the stairway in her Wisconsin sweatshirt and a pair of flannel sleep pants. Baggy plaid pants that obliterated her curves. He hated them.

"James? Everything okay?"

He blinked. "I was looking at your pajamas. They're very…" He sought for a decent adjective. "Plaid."

"Thank you," she replied, padding down the last couple steps. Barefoot, James noted. "I wasn't expecting you to be awake this early," she continued. "And you're dressed."

"You sound surprised. I didn't think you'd want me wandering around your kitchen in my briefs."

"Now that would have been a surprise. Is everything okay?"

"Huh?" James missed the question. He was too busy studying her bare feet. They were runner's feet—no painted toes for her—and to his horror he found them as attractive as the rest of her.

"I asked if you were feeling all right," she repeated.

"I'm fine. Why wouldn't I be?"

"Well, you didn't look good last night when you booked it to bed. I was worried you overdid it and made your headache return."

Dammit. Did she have to ask with concern increasing the vibrant blue of her eyes? It made his chest squeeze again, like yesterday.

"I'm fine," he said. "No headache. I got up to check the forecast."

"Oh." Was that disappointment darkening her eyes? "And what did you find out?"

"Actually…" He'd been too busy arguing with himself to look at his phone. It lay dormant on the coffee table.

"Is there coffee left?" Noelle asked.

He nodded, embarrassingly relieved that he didn't have to look quite yet. "I made a whole pot."

"Great. I'm going to grab a cup. Give me yours and I'll get you a refill." She held out her hand and waited while he finished the last swallow. "You can tell me about the weather when I get back."

Okay, the pajama bottoms weren't so bad after all, James decided as he watched her walk to the kitchen. Although, he would much prefer her bare legged.

The woman was definitely under his skin, big time.

Leaning forward, he picked up the phone and pressed

the weather app. As the radar loaded on his screen, he saw it was clear all the way to the coast. No excuse against flying home.

Fantastic, he thought, shoulders feeling heavy.

What a difference a few days made. Two days ago he couldn't wait to get out of the place. Now here he was dragging his feet.

Again.

"So, what's the verdict?" Noelle asked as she came around the corner.

Handing him one of the mugs, she took a seat in the opposite corner and waited.

"Smooth sailing," he replied. "Not a snowflake in sight. I'm back to thinking you had a hidden snow machine yesterday for ambience."

"Wouldn't surprise me if Ned considered it," she replied. "I know at one point he was looking for a way to make snow in July."

"Did he?"

"Apparently years ago he used soap flakes, but they got in the water and caused all sorts of problems. After that, Belinda put the kibosh on summer snow plans."

"Good thinking." He was beginning to think Ned Fryberg had been more than a little on the eccentric side. Envy twisted in his stomach. "Must have been fun, hanging out at their house as a kid."

"More like insane," she replied with a grin. "Ned was forever coming up with ideas. And they weren't all for the store. He went crazy at home too. You should have seen the to-do he made over Halloween. One year, he turned their living room into a haunted tableau. Kevin and his mom played haunted mannequins." James tried to picture the scene in his head. "What were you?" he asked.

"A flying monkey. Ned thought scary mannequins should be bigger than the fifth graders."

"I'm afraid he had a point there." Turning sideways, James rested his elbow on the back of the sofa, and propped his head with his hand. "I bet you made an adorable flying monkey."

"Scary! I was supposed to be scary!"

"Were you?" He waited while she sipped her coffee, noting her cheeks had grown the tiniest bit pink.

"No," she replied. Leaning in, she set the mug on the coffee table. The action brought along the orange blossom scent James had come to associate only with her. He breathed in deep through his nostrils. "I'm not surprised," he said once she'd left his senses. "I can't picture you as anything but adorable."

"Explains why we decided to decorate only outside the following year," she said, the blush James had been trying to deepen coming through. "Anyway, Ned was always coming up with something different. The neighborhood kids loved coming to the house to get candy."

"They sound like a fun family," he said. A true Rockwell painting. "My parents had the housekeeper pass out the candy." Bags of Hammond's brand goodies assembled by employees and doled out from a silver tray.

A hand suddenly covered his. Noelle's eyes were incandescent with unreadable emotion. "I'm sorry—I didn't mean to send us down that road again," she said.

"Road?"

"You know, our collective lousy childhoods."

James knew. But he wanted to hear how she framed the conversation.

"Bad enough we opened up all those wounds last night." She paused, reached for her coffee then changed her mind and pulled back. "I hope I didn't make you feel uncomfortable when I hugged you."

A loaded question. Depended upon her definition of uncomfortable.

"No," he lied. "Not at all."

"Good." He could hear her relief. "Because the moment seemed to call for one, you know? I didn't mean to overreach."

"You didn't," he told her. *You were the first person I'd ever shared my childhood with.*

Her eyes widened, and for a brief second, James wondered if he'd spoken his thoughts aloud. "So, you didn't go to bed early because you were avoiding me?"

Yes, I did. "Don't be silly. I had work to do, and I was tired."

"That's a relief. I... That is, we were..." A frown marred her features as she stared at their joined hands. "I wanted yesterday to jumpstart your Christmas spirit, not make things all awkward between us."

"They didn't make anything awkward," he told her. "As for the hug...it was nice. I liked it."

Soon as the words were out, his insides relaxed with a vengeance, as if they'd been gripped by tension for weeks, not a few days. He played with the fingers holding his. "I enjoyed spending time with you," he added.

"Me too," she said softly. "Even if we did get off on the wrong foot."

"More like wrong feet," James said, smiling. He took a good long look at her.

With one leg tucked under her body, she looked small and delicate against the dark leather. Only she wasn't delicate, was she? She was as resilient a person as he'd ever known. Strong, smart, loyal, gorgeous. A rare package.

Suddenly it struck him. Why he couldn't leave.

"What are you doing tonight?" he asked her.

As he suspected, her eyes got wide again. "Nothing. Why?"

"Because," he said, "I'd like to take you to dinner." And he knew the perfect place too.

"Dinner? You mean, like on a date?" From the look on her face, the question caught her by surprise. A good surprise, he hoped.

"Exactly like a date. Two minutes ago, we both said we enjoyed each other's company. I don't know about you…" Lifting his hand, he risked brushing the hair from her face. "But I'd like to continue enjoying it a little longer."

Wow. Noelle didn't know what to say. She'd gone to bed last night convinced she'd embarrassed both of them by hugging him, that this morning he would be flying back to Boston as soon as possible. Instead, he was asking her out. "But you're my boss," she blurted out. "Isn't that against some kind of rule?"

James chuckled. Noelle hated when he chuckled because the rumbling sound tripped through her every time. "I promise, where we're going, we won't run into a single coworker."

"Is that so?" Goodness, when did her voice grow husky? She sounded breathless.

"Absolutely. What do you say? Spend a few more hours with me? We can call it a thank-you for taking me in during my time of need."

His fingers were brushing her cheek again. Feathery light touches that made her mouth dry and turned her insides warm and liquid. Who exactly was supposed to be thanking whom in this proposal?

"All right," she said, fighting to keep from closing her

eyes and purring. His touch felt that good. "I'd love to have dinner with you."

"Fantastic. You have my word you won't regret a single second. This is going to make your Christmas Kickoff look like a roadside yard sale."

She laughed. Good to know his audacity was alive and well. "I'll have you know I happen to like yard sales."

"You'll like this better. Now…" To her dismay, he took both his touch and the hand beneath hers away. "Why don't you go get dressed while I make the arrangements? If we hurry, we'll have time to walk around before the show."

Show? There weren't any shows going on in Fryberg. The closest performances she knew of were at least a two hours' drive away.

"Are we going to Chicago?" she asked.

James was on his feet and taking her coffee cup. A man in command. "Not Chicago. I'm taking you to Radio City Music Hall."

"Radio what?" She'd heard wrong. "Isn't that in New York City?"

"Yes, it is," he replied. "Which is why you'd better hurry and get dressed."

CHAPTER EIGHT

Six hours later found Noelle sitting in the back of an airport town car on her way to Manhattan, and wondering when—or if—her head would stop spinning. New York City for dinner? That was the sort of thing they did in movies. Yet there was the Empire State Building on the skyline ahead. And the Statue of Liberty alone on her island.

James's hand brushed her knee. "You haven't said much since we left the airfield. Everything okay?"

"I can't believe I'm actually in New York City for dinner" was all she could manage to say. "It's…"

"Amazing?"

"Yes. And overwhelming. When you said dinner, I never dreamed you meant—is that the Freedom Tower?" She pointed to a gigantic building with a large antenna, on top of which waved an American flag. She'd seen pictures of the structure built to replace the Twin Towers, but they were nothing compared to the real thing. "It's huge. Even from this far away."

"That was the idea," he replied before shifting a little closer. "To make a statement to the rest of the world about our resilience."

"They won't keep New York down."

"Precisely. New York Strong, as we'd say in Boston," he replied. He shifted again and unbuttoned the top of his coat. Noelle caught a glimpse of pearl gray. Before leaving Fryberg, they'd stopped at the boutique so he could purchase another set of clothes, the plaid, he'd said, having worn out its welcome. The soft color was a toned-down version of the executive she'd met three days ago. That man, she thought with a smile, would never have flown her to New York.

His hand slid along hers, breaking her train of thought. "Would you like to see it up close?" he asked.

"Careful how often you ask the question. I want to see everything up close."

Now that she'd accepted the ginormousness of where they were, excitement was quickly replacing disbelief. "I've always dreamed of going to New York ever since I was a little girl, but never got the chance."

"Never?"

"I almost went. Once. Right after Kevin and I got engaged. There was a merchandising conference I thought of attending."

"What happened?"

"The conference conflicted with an awards banquet Kevin had to attend. People expected me to be there too, so I cancelled. I could always go to Manhattan another time. Wasn't like the city was going to go anywhere."

"At least not last time I looked," James replied. "And now you're here."

"Now I'm here." She sat back against the leather seat and watched the traffic. Despite being the middle of the afternoon on a Saturday, the streets were lined bumper to bumper, with more cars than ten Fryberg Christmas Kickoffs. Everywhere she looked, buildings reached toward the sky. Big, square buildings jammed with people. She could feel the city's energy pulsing through the limousine's windows. It was fantastical.

Next to her, James was watching the window as well, his long fingers tapping on the armrest. He looked quite at home with the traffic passing by them. Same way he'd looked at home in the cockpit of his plane. Noelle had watched him the entire flight, his deftness at the controls far more interesting than the ground below. Surely he knew how gracefully he moved. If he didn't, the universe really should hold up a mirror for him to see.

"What?" He turned his face to hers. "Why are you staring at me?"

"Thank you," she replied, the words bubbling out of her. "For today."

"You haven't seen anything worth thanking me for yet."

Was he kidding? They were passing the biggest Christmas billboard she'd ever seen that very minute. "I don't have to see anything," she told him. "Being here is already amazing."

His eyes really did turn into sparkling hazel diamonds when he smiled. "You ain't seen nothing yet. You, Noelle Fryberg, are going to get the full New York Christmas experience."

"I can't wait."

It wasn't until she felt his squeeze that she realized they were still holding hands. Their fingers were entwined like puzzle pieces. Yet again they fit together with unnerving perfection.

James instructed the driver to pull over at the corner of Fifth and West Thirty-Third. Looking at the block of office buildings, Noelle frowned. "I might be a New York City virgin, but even I know this isn't Radio City Music Hall."

"There's no moss growing on you, is there?" James replied. Opening the door, he stepped outside and offered her a hand. "Since we have time before the show, I figured you'd enjoy a bird's-eye view of the city. Watch your step."

A blast of cold east coast air struck Noelle as she stepped onto the sidewalk. If not for James's warm hand holding hers, she might have shivered. His grip, however, left her impervious to the wind. "Bird's-eye view?" she said. "I don't under... *Ohhhh!*" Spying the crowd ahead, it clicked where they were. The Empire State Building.

"Precisely. Best view in the city, if you don't mind getting cold."

What a silly comment. "I'm from the Midwest, remember?" she replied. "We invented cold. Or have you already forgotten what it was like walking around yesterday?"

Despite James's warnings of cold, the outside observation deck was lined with tourists. The two of them had to wait before finding a space near the rail. When they finally made their way to a viewing spot, Noelle leaned as close to the barricade as possible. Below, the city spread for miles. She squinted past the rooftops and spotted Lady Liberty. From up there, the majestic statue looked no bigger than an action figure. "It's like standing at the top of the world," she said, only to cringe a little afterward. "Not that I'm being clichéd or anything."

"Hey, phrases become cliché for a reason." A pair of arms came around to grip the rail on either side of her, blocking the wind and securing her in a cashmere cocoon.

Noelle's fingers tightened their grip. She could feel the buttons on his coat pressing through hers, letting her know how close he was. So close that she need only relax her spine to find herself propped against his body. Did she dare? If she did, would he wrap his arms tighter? Her stomach quivered at the thought.

"I wonder if you can see the Christmas tree from the other side," she said.

"The one at Rockefeller Center? I haven't a clue."

Turned out she didn't need to slouch, because James stepped in closer. "Want to know a secret?" he whispered in her ear. His breath was extra warm against her cold skin. "I've been to Manhattan dozens of times over the years and this is my first visit to the top of the Empire State Building."

"Really?" The sheepish nod she caught over her shoulder made her smile. "You're a virgin too?"

Several heads turned in their direction, earning her a playful shoulder nudge. "Say it a little louder," James replied. "There are a couple of people below that didn't hear you."

"Okay. James Hammond is a—"

The rest of her sentence died in a giggle as he grabbed her by the waist and pulled her to him. Her head leaned back against his collarbone. "I'm glad we could experience this together," she told him.

For a second there was silence, then his voice was back at her ear. "Me too," he murmured. Noelle swore he brushed the shell of her ear with his lips.

Like a kiss.

They took their time on the deck, making sure they saw all four views. Each was spectacular in its own right, and Noelle decided that if her tour ended then and there, it would still be an unforgettable day. "You really need to stop thanking me," James said as they left the observation deck. "I'm feeling self-conscious."

"Then you shouldn't have sprung for such a marvelous day," she told him. "Isn't the whole point of a day like today to make a woman feel grateful?"

She meant it as a tease, but he took her seriously, looking down at her with eyes filled with sincerity. "Not this time," he said. "Not you."

If they weren't trapped in a line of tourists, Noelle would have kissed him then and there.

The crowd herded itself downstairs and into the gift shop. "I see they've got the traffic flow issue managed," she remarked, hoping shop talk would distract the fluttering in her stomach. It didn't help that James's hair was windblown. The bonded strands around his stitches stuck out at an angle. "Considering all their years of practice, I'd be disappointed if they didn't," he replied.

Noelle only half listened. She was too distracted by those errant strands. Her fingers itched to run through them. Because those mussed-up strands looked all wrong, she argued. If she were him, she'd want someone to adjust his appearance, right?

"Hold on a second." Grabbing his arm, she stopped him from heading toward the doorway. "Let me…" As gently as possible, she combed his hair smooth, making sure her fingers barely grazed the bump on the back of his head. "Much better."

Did she just purr? Wouldn't surprise her. Stroking his hair was nearly as soothing as being petted herself.

"You realize the wind is going to mess up my hair again the second we step outside."

"Then I'll simply have to fix it again." She smoothed a patch around his ear, which was really an excuse to continue touching him.

Her reward was a smile, and a brush of his fingers against her temple. "Well, if that isn't incentive to spend the day stepping in and out of the wind, I don't know what is. Now, what do you say? Should we continue exploring?"

Noelle shivered. Explore could mean so many things. Whatever the meaning, she had the same answer. "Absolutely," she said. "Lead the way."

* * *

They were walking out of Radio City Music Hall when James's phone buzzed. "Maybe you should answer," Noelle said. "That's what? The fourth call today?"

While she was flattered he considered her to be the higher priority, she knew from experience that not all calls could be ignored. "Generally speaking, people only bother the boss on weekends if there's an emergency."

"And what makes you so sure these calls are from the office?" he asked. "How do you know I don't have an expansive social life?"

Like a girlfriend back in Boston? The thought passed as quickly as it popped into her head. James wasn't the type to play around. He was, however, the type to work all hours. "Okay, Mr. Social Life," she challenged, "what would you be doing right now if you hadn't been stuck with me all weekend?"

"A person can be dedicated to his job and have a social life, I'll have you know. And I'm not stuck with you."

Still, her point had been made and he pulled out his phone. "I was right. Nothing that can't wait," he said. He rejected the call. Not, however, before Noelle caught the name on the call screen—Jackson Hammond—and the frown that accompanied it.

Curiosity got the best of her. "You don't want to talk to your father?"

"Not particularly," he replied. "I'm sure all he's looking for is a trip update. I can fill him in when I get home."

Ignoring the unexpected pang that accompanied the words *get home*, Noelle instead focused on the rest of his comment. "I'm sure he wants to hear how you're feeling as much as he cares about the trip."

The sideways glance he sent her said otherwise. She thought about what he said yesterday, about his father and he doing their own thing. "He does know about your accident, doesn't he?" she asked.

James shrugged. "Word's gotten to him by now, I'm sure. I left a message with his 'protégé' that I was detained by a drone attack. She makes sure he's kept abreast of things."

"So you haven't spoken to him at all since your accident?"

"No." He stepped aside to let her exit the building first. "I told you," he continued, once he joined her, "my father and I aren't close. We don't do the family thing. In fact, I think I've made it pretty clear that the Hammonds are the anti-Frybergs."

Selling the world a clichéd myth. So he'd told her. Ad nauseum. "Still, your father is trying to reach you. You don't know it's all about business."

"I know my father, Noelle. When I was a kid and broke my leg, he didn't come home for two days because he was in Los Angeles meeting with a distributor."

Poor James. "How old were you?" Not that it mattered. A child would feel second-best at any age.

"Twelve and a half."

Right after his mother left. A time when he needed to feel wanted and special. Her heart clenched on preteen James's behalf. Being abandoned by her parents sucked. Still, James had something she didn't, and she needed to point that out. "He came eventually. I know it doesn't sound like much," she said when he snorted, "but I would have killed for even that much parental attention."

"Don't take this the wrong way, but you got the better end of the deal. At least you knew where you stood from the start."

"More like where I didn't stand. My parents were out

of my life from day one. So long as your father is around, you still have hope for a relationship."

Up until then, the two of them had been strolling the sidewalk. Now James stopped to look at her and for a moment, Noelle saw the twelve-year-old boy who'd been struggling to keep his hurt at bay. "Why hope for something that won't happen?"

And yet he did hope. She saw how his eyes flashed when she'd suggested his father might be worried.

"Never say never," she replied. "You can call me naive, but there's always hope. Look at me. For years, I burnt my Christmas wish on wanting a family, and then the Frybergs came into my life and poof! My wish came true."

"What do you wish for now?"

"I—" She resumed walking. "We're talking about you, remember?"

"We're also talking about hopes and dreams. You said you used to wish for a family. Since your wish was granted, you must hope for something else. What is it?"

"Peace on earth."

"I'm serious," he said.

"So am I." Every year, she, like every Fryberg's employee, filled out her Christmas wish list, and asked for large, conceptual things like peace or good health for all. There was no need for her to hope for anything personal. After all, hadn't she'd gotten everything she wanted when she'd become Noelle Fryberg? What more could she want?

James took her hand.

"This conversation is getting way too serious," he said. "Today is supposed to be about you getting the New York Christmas Experience. What did you think of the show?"

Noelle shook off her somberness with a laugh. "I loved it." She loved how he described the day with capital letters more. "If I were six inches taller, I'd start practicing my high kicks so I could audition."

"That's something I'd pay to see—you kicking your leg past your ears. I had no idea you were that limber," he added, leaning in to her ear.

Noelle's knees nearly buckled. It wasn't fair, the way he could lower his voice to the exact timbre to zap her insides. "Who said anything about ears? Waist-high is more like it.

"S'all a moot point anyway," she added. "With my size, I'd be more likely to get cast as one of the elves."

"And a right adorable one at that."

Noelle tried to shove him with her shoulder. Unfortunately, the impact had no effect. Instead, she found herself trapped against his side when he snaked his hand around her waist. The position left her arm no choice but to respond in kind and slip her arm around his waist as well.

"I mean it," he said, adding a side hug for good measure. "First thing I thought when I saw you was that you were Belinda's attack elf. So much feistiness in such a tiny package."

"I'm not sure if I should be flattered or actually try to attack you," she replied. With her luck, she'd end up wrapped in both his arms.

"Definitely flattered," he told her. "My second thought was I didn't know elves could be so beautiful. Are your knees all right?"

They wouldn't be if he kept purring compliments in her ear. "Careful," she purred back. "Keep up the sweet talk, and I'll get a big head."

"You deserve one. I've never met a woman like you, Noelle."

"You must not get out much."

Once more, he stopped, this time to wrap a second arm around her. Noelle found herself in his embrace. Heavy-lidded heat warmed her face as his eyes travelled to her mouth. "I'm not joking," he said. "You're an original."

If this were Fryberg, his features would have been hidden by the early darkness, but being the city that never slept, she could see his dilating pupils beneath his lashes. Their blackness sucked the breath from her lungs. She parted her lips, but couldn't take more than a shallow breath. Her racing heart blocked the air from going farther.

"I want to kiss you," she heard him say. "Right here, on this sidewalk. I don't care if people stare or make rude comments. I need to kiss you. I've wanted to since I—"

"Shut up, James." She didn't need to hear any more.

Standing on tiptoes, she met him halfway.

Kissing was something James thought he had a handle on. He'd kissed dozens of women in his lifetime, so why would kissing Noelle be any different?

Only it was different. With other women, his kisses had stemmed from attraction. He'd kissed them to stoke his sexual desire—and theirs. But he'd never *needed* to kiss a woman. Never had a bone-deep ache to feel their mouths on his.

The second his lips met Noelle's, a feeling he'd never felt before ballooned in his chest. Need times ten. It was the blasted hug all over again. Talking about his father and hope, she'd ripped open a hole inside him and now he couldn't get enough, couldn't get *close* enough.

Which was why he surprised himself by breaking the kiss first. Resting his head against her forehead, he cradled her face in his hands as they came down to earth.

"Wow," Noelle whispered.

Wow indeed. *Wow* didn't come close. "I think..." He inhaled deeply, to catch his breath. "I think we should get some dinner."

Noelle looked up her lashes. Her brilliant blue eyes were blown black with desire. "Is that what you want?" she asked. "Dinner?"

No.

And yes.

Some things were meant to simmer. "We've got all night," he said, fanning her cheek with his thumbs. The way her lips parted, he almost changed his mind, but inner strength prevailed. "Dinner first," he said with a smile. "Then dessert."

She nodded. Slowly. "All right. Dinner first."

"Wow. That might be one of the first times this weekend that you haven't disagreed with one of my suggestions." Maybe miracles could happen.

"What can I say?" she replied. "I'm hungry. Although…" The smile on her face turned cheeky as she backed out of his embrace. "Since you decided to postpone dessert, I'm going to make you work for it."

Her words went straight below his belt. Snagging a finger in the gap between her coat buttons, he tugged her back into his orbit. He leaned in, feeling incredibly wolfish as he growled in her ear. "Challenge accepted."

As seemed to be the theme of the past few days, James was completely wrong about the restaurant. He made their reservation based on an internet article about New York's top holiday-themed restaurants and wrote off the writer's ebullience over the decor as a marketing spin. For once, though, spin matched reality.

"Oh. My." Noelle gave a small gasp as they stepped inside. The place was completely done in white and gold to resemble an enchanted winter forest. Birch branches trimmed with tiny white lights formed a wall around the central dining room, making it look as though the tables were set up on the forest floor. There were Christmas ornaments and stockings strung about, as well as fluffy cottony-white snow on the window edges.

"Talk about a winter wonderland," Noelle said.

Indeed. Silly as it was, he actually felt the need to hold her hand tighter, in case some woodland creature tried to whisk her away. This was what she'd call magical. "I'm glad you like it," he said.

"Like it? It's unreal." She had her phone out and was snapping away at the various objects. Suddenly, she paused. "I'm not embarrassing you, am I?"

"Not at all." She was enchanting. "Take as many photos as you want. We'll be eating in a different room."

She frowned, and James almost felt bad for disappointing her. *Almost.* "You mean we're not eating in the forest?"

"Mr. Hammond requested a table in our crystal terrace," the maître d' informed her. He gestured to the elevator on the other side of the birch barricade. "Upstairs."

"We're eating on the roof," Noelle said a few moments later. He smiled at her disbelief as she stated the obvious.

Actually a glass atrium, the famed Crystal Terrace was decorated similarly to downstairs, only instead of recessed lighting, patrons ate under the night sky.

"I figured since this was our only meal in the Big Apple you should eat it with a view of the skyline," he told her. "By the way, this time you can see the Rockefeller Christmas tree. *And* the Empire State Building."

"Amazing."

Letting go of his hand, she moved toward the window while he and the maître d' exchanged amused glances.

"I had a feeling you'd like the view," James replied. He waited until the maître d' had disappeared behind the elevator doors before joining her at the glass. Noelle stood like a child pressed to a window display with her hands clutching the brass guardrail. Her lower lip was caught between her teeth in wonder. James stood behind her and captured her between his arms, the same way he had on the observation deck. "As good as the Fryberg town tree?" he asked.

"The Empire State Building really is red and green. I've read about how they projected the colors, but I had no idea they would be so vivid. The building looks like a giant cement Christmas tree."

"I'm not quite sure that's the analogy the city was going for, but…"

"I love it. Thank you for bringing me here."

Still trapped in his arms, she whirled around to face him. Up close, her smile knocked the wind out of him. He had to swallow before he could find his voice.

"I thought we agreed this afternoon that you could stop thanking me."

"We did, but a place like this deserves a special thank-you." She slipped her arms around his neck. "Makes sense now, why you wanted to have dinner. I'd have been disappointed if I'd learned… Are we the only people here?"

He was wondering when she'd notice. "No. There's a waiter and a bartender on the other side of the room."

"I don't mean the staff. I mean dinner guests. The other tables are empty."

"Are they, now?" He pretended to look over his shoulder. The Terrace only housed seven tables; the limited seating was part of how the place got its exclusive reputation. All seven tables were unoccupied.

"Well, what do you know. So they are empty," he said before turning back to her. "Must be because I booked them."

"You what?" Noelle's expression was worth every cent he'd paid too. Her eyes widened, and her lips formed an

O. She looked so charming; he had no choice but to press a kiss to her nose.

"You know how I like efficiency," he told her. "Service is so much better when you don't have to compete with other patrons for the server's attention. Besides, I wanted to give you something special since you took me in these last few days."

"I was under the impression flying me to New York was the something special," she replied. "This is…"

Shaking her head, she slipped from his arms. "Do you do this sort of thing often? Buy out restaurants?"

James wasn't sure of the right answer. Had he gone too far? The impulse had popped into his head when he'd read the internet article. Yes, it was over the top—this whole day was over the top—but he'd wanted to make it memorable.

Face it: he'd wanted to impress her. Because he liked her. And how else was he supposed to compete with a dead war hero who gave her the family she'd always dreamed of?

"I didn't mean to make you uncomfortable," he replied. "If you want, I can tell the maître d' to open the other tables…"

"No." She shook her head again. "You went to a lot of trouble, and I'm sounding ungrateful. It's just that you didn't have to do all this. Any of this. I would have been perfectly happy having dinner with you at the Nutcracker."

"I know. I told you, I wanted to do something special. To make you feel special. Because I kind of think you're worth it. Hell, after kissing you, I know you're worth it."

He scuffed the ground with his foot. Stumbling for words wasn't like him. But once again, she had him feeling and thinking uncharacteristically.

"Thank you," Noelle replied. Unlike the other times,

she spoke in a gentle, tender voice that hung in the air. "No one has ever put so much effort into trying to impress me. Ever. You've made me feel very special. I think you're crazy. But you make me feel special."

James smiled. So what if he was crazy? The satisfaction he was feeling right now far surpassed that of any deal or successful investment. "So does this mean you'll stick around for dinner?"

"What do you think?" she replied.

Turning to the first table within reach, James pulled out a chair. "After you."

CHAPTER NINE

"HERE'S WHAT I THINK." It was an hour later, and the wine had loosened Noelle's tongue. "I think that you're not as anti-holiday as you claim."

"I'm not?"

"Nope." Giving an extra pop to the *p*, she leaned forward across the table. Shadows cast by the flame in the hurricane lamp danced on the planes of James's cheek, giving his handsome features a dark and mysterious vibe. She'd been thinking about this for a while, analyzing the clues he'd dropped. Tonight's rooftop surprise sealed her theory. "I think you're sentimental and I think you're a romantic," she told him.

He rolled his eyes. "Why? Because I bought out a restaurant? Hate to break it to you, honeybunch, but that doesn't mean I'm romantic—it means I'm rich and trying to seduce you."

And he was succeeding. Not even the wine and duck with truffles could wash the kiss they'd shared off her lips. James kissed like a man in charge. She might have met him halfway, but there was no doubt who dominated whom once the kiss began, and frankly, so caught up was she in the moment, that she didn't care. She liked being overwhelmed.

Right now, however, she didn't like him distracting her.

"Why are you so quick to paint yourself negatively?" she asked, getting back on track. "Last time I checked, a person could be rich and seductive and a sentimental romantic. This restaurant is only one example. The entire day…"

"Again rich and…"

"Trying to seduce me. I know," she replied.

James reached for the bottled water to pour himself a glass. "So far, I've got to say that your argument isn't too compelling."

"I have other examples."

"Such as?"

"You were tapping your toe during the show."

"It was a catchy tune!"

And the enthusiastic smile he wore at the end of the performance? He'd probably say he was rewarding a job well done. "What made you pick that particular show in the first place, huh? Why not that hot hip-hop musical everyone's gushing about, if you were simply out to impress me? Don't tell me you couldn't have scored tickets to that if you'd wanted them. Instead, you picked a Christmas show, and not just any show. The Christmas Spectacular. Heck, even your choice of restaurant," she said, gesturing at the winter wonderland around them, "is Christmassy."

"I didn't exactly pluck the theme out of thin air. Since I arrived in Fryberg, you've made your attachment to Christmas quite clear. For crying out loud, your in-laws celebrate Christmas year-round."

"All the more reason for a person who hates holidays to show me something different," she replied. "But you didn't. You went full-on Christmas. What's more, you enjoyed everything as much as I did. And not—" she wagged her finger "—not simply because I was having fun."

James raised his glass to his lips. "How could I not have a good time with such amazing company?"

Noelle blushed at the compliment. There was more though. She'd stolen enough looks during the day when he thought she wasn't looking. Saw the enjoyment on his face. Their adventure today had touched something inside him. The same sensitive part that was inspired to rent out the dining room.

She still couldn't believe he'd rented an entire rooftop for her. Talk about intimidating. She'd never been the focus of attention before, not by herself. Not without a Fryberg attached. The notion unsettled her.

Her thoughts were getting off track. "You're trying to distract me with compliments," she said, shaking her index finger. "No fair."

"*Au contraire.* I'm pretty sure all's fair," he replied.

"This isn't love or war."

"Yet."

He was joking. It was one date and, possibly, a few hours of intimacy. Neither of them expected anything more. Nevertheless, her stomach fluttered anyway. She reached for her wine, changed her mind, picked up her water and took a long drink to drown the sensation.

"Do you have any good memories of Christmas?" she asked, changing the subject.

He made a noise in his throat that sounded like an unformed groan. "We're back to talking about Christmas, are we?"

"We never left," she said. In spite of his efforts to dissuade her. "Surely, you must have some decent memories before your parents' marriage went sour." She was curious. There was a different James Hammond behind the cynicism, one that believed in moonlight dinners and making a woman feel like a princess, not for seduction purposes, but because he thought that's what a woman deserved. She wanted to get to know that James.

If she could coax him to talk.

He sat back and let out a long breath. "Easier asking for the Holy Grail. My parents never got along. Even before they separated, as soon as they spent extended time together, they would end up screaming and tossing dishes."

"Glass tumblers." She remembered.

"Exactly. Honestly, it's amazing they managed to have two kids." Frowning, he pushed his plate toward the center of the table. "There was this one Christmas. I was four. Maybe five. Hammond's was having some kind of event, for charity I think—I'm not sure. All I know is Santa was supposed to be there so my parents took Justin and me into Boston to see him. We had these matching wool coats and hats with flaps on them."

"Stylish," she said.

"Best-dressed kindergartener in the city."

His frown eased into a nostalgic-looking smile. "It was the first time I'd ever seen the Hammond's window displays. First time I remember seeing them anyway. We stood outside and watched them for hours. Although now that I say it out loud, it was probably more like ten minutes."

"Time has a way of slowing down when you're a kid."

"That it does," he said. "I read somewhere the passage of time changes based on how much of your lifetime you've lived. The author was very scientific. All I know is, on that afternoon, I could have watched those window displays forever."

He chuckled. "In one of the windows, a bunch of animals had broken into Santa's workshop. There was this squirrel inside a pot on one of the shelves that kept popping up. Every time he did, Justin would squeal and start laughing. Every time," he repeated. "Like it was the first time." And he rolled his eyes the way Noelle imagined his four-year-old self had. The image made her heart turn over.

"But you knew better," she teased.

"Totally. Who cared about some stupid squirrel when there was a polar bear looking in the window? At least the squirrel was inside the workshop. The bear was obviously in the store. What if he ate Santa Claus?"

"Obviously."

"Hey, don't laugh. Polar bears can be ruthless creatures."

"I'm not laughing." Not much anyway. His exaggerated earnestness made staying completely serious impossible. She could picture the moment in her head. Little James, his eyes wide and serious, worried about Santa's safety. "What did you do?"

"I thought we should call the police so they could tranquilize him, but my father assured me that all the polar bears at the North Pole were Santa's friends, and if there was one in the store, he was probably Santa's pet. Like a puppy."

"And that worked?"

His gaze dropped to the table. "Yeah, it did. If my father said the polar bear was a pet, then I believed him. Funny how at that age, you believe everything your parents tell you."

"The voice of definitive authority," Noelle said.

"I guess," he replied. "Anyway, we saw Santa, he told me the bear was taking a nap when I asked, and that Christmas I found a stuffed polar bear in my stocking. Damn thing sat on my bureau until junior high school."

When his world fell apart.

Afraid he'd come to the same conclusion, she reached

across the table and took his hand. He responded with a smile and a fan of his thumb across her skin.

"I bet you were an adorable little boy. Protecting Santa Claus from danger."

"More like worried I wouldn't get presents. I'd have gladly sacrificed Justin if it meant finding a race car set under the tree."

"Did you?"

"You know, I don't remember."

But he remembered the window displays, and the polar bear toy, and his childhood wonder.

"You know," she said, "they say Christmas brings out the child in people. That's why adults go so gung ho for the holiday."

"Oh, really?" He entwined their fingers. "In your case, I'd say that's definitely true."

"It is for you as well. Seriously," she said when he rolled his eyes. "You can talk about hating Christmas all you like, but today's little adventure proves that little boy who watched the window displays is in there, way down deep."

"That little boy also pulled off Santa's beard."

He was so determined to pretend he didn't have a soft side. "Fine, be that way," she told him. "I know better. Thou protest too much."

"I beg your pardon?"

"You heard me," she said, reaching for her glass. "You may act all cynical and talk about greeting card fantasies, but you don't one hundred percent believe it. If you did, you'd convince your father to redo the Boston store, tourist attraction or no. We both know you could do so successfully." Instead, he doubled down on the Christmas fantasy every year. The reason hadn't hit her until tonight, as she looked around the winter wonderland he'd rented.

He may never have had a greeting card family Christmas, but he wanted one. Over the years, whenever she'd looked at photos of the Boston store, she had sensed a secondary emotion hovering behind the nostalgia and charm, but she could never give the feeling a name. Until tonight. Like a completed jigsaw, now that the pieces had fallen in place, she could recognize the emotion clear as day. It was longing.

Hope.

That was why James authorized the window displays every year, and why he kept the Boston store unchanged despite his insistence they focus on the future. The Boston store wasn't selling a greeting card fantasy to tourists. It represented *his* Christmas fantasy.

How on earth had she missed it? If anyone knew what it was like to hope on Christmas... She'd bet he didn't even realize what he was doing.

"You're staring," James said.

"Am I?" Lost in thought, she hadn't realized. "I didn't mean to stare. I was thinking how stubborn you are."

"Me, stubborn? Says the woman who refused to move a moose?"

"Elk, and that's different. Fryer is part of our great tradition. And at least I fought to protect something the town has had for years. You're going out of your way to avoid looking sensitive."

As expected, he rolled his eyes again. At least, there was a blush accompanying it this time. She was making progress. "You know," she said, sitting back in her chair. "There's nothing wrong in admitting a vulnerable side. Some people might even be impressed."

He laughed. "Some people being you."

"Maybe." She shrugged. Truthfully, she was already impressed. Probably too impressed, if she stopped to think about it.

She waited while he studied their hands, a smile playing on his lips. "I never should have told you I enjoy it when you challenge me," he said.

"Yeah, well, hindsight is always twenty-twenty," she teased before sobering. "What I'm trying to say—very badly, apparently—is that it's okay for you to let your guard down around me. That is, you don't have to feel awkward about showing…"

Thinking of all the ways he'd already opened up, she realized how foolish she sounded. Psychoanalyzing and advising him on his feelings. "Never mind. You don't need my encouragement."

Slipping her hand from his, she pushed her chair away from the table and started folding her napkin. "I wonder what time it is? We probably won't get back to Fryberg until after midnight."

"Once," James said.

"Once what?" She set her napkin on the table and waited. James hadn't moved. His eyes remained on the spot where their hands had been.

"You wanted to know how often I bought out restaurants to impress women. The answer is once." He lifted his eyes. "Tonight."

Holy cow.

His answer rolling around her brain, Noelle stood up and walked to the window where, a few blocks away, the lights of Rockefeller Center created a glowing white canyon amid the buildings. "I was pretty sure you were joking about the whole rich-and-trying-to-seduce-you thing, but at the same time, I thought for sure you'd done stuff like this before."

She heard his chair scraping against the wood floor. A moment later, her back warmed with his presence. "Stuff?"

"You know… Sweeping a girl off her feet. Making her feel like Cinderella at the ball."

"Nope," he replied, mimicking the way she'd said the word earlier. "Only you."

She pressed a hand to her stomach to keep the quivers from spreading. "What makes me so special? If you don't mind my asking."

Silence greeted her question. The warmth disappeared from behind her, and then James was by her side, leaning against the chair rail. "I've been trying to answer that same question for two days," he said, "and damned if I know. All I know is you've had me acting out of character since Thanksgiving.

"Damn disconcerting too," he added under his breath.

"Most men would have answered a little more romantically," she said.

"I thought you knew by now that I'm not most men. Besides, you wanted me to drop my guard and be honest."

"Yes, I did," she replied, and James did not disappoint. What she hadn't expected was how enticing his honesty would be. Romantic words could be laughed off or discounted, but truth? Truth went right to your heart. Noelle liked that he didn't know why. Liked that his behavior frustrated him. That made her feel more special than any word ever could.

Suddenly, James wasn't close enough.

She moved left until they stood face-to-face, hip to hip. "I can't explain why you get to me either."

There was heat in his eyes as he wrapped her in his arms. "Then we'll just have to be confused together."

CHAPTER TEN

"I KNOW WHAT'S topping my Christmas list this year."

Beneath Noelle's cheek, James's chest rumbled with his husky voice. She tucked herself tighter against his ribcage and let her fingertips ghost across his bare chest. "What's that?" she asked.

"A couple hundred more nights like this."

Sounded perfect. "You think Santa can fit them all in his sleigh?"

"He'll have to make them fit, because I won't settle for anything less. Wouldn't want to have to give him a bad online review. You know how he is about naughty and nice and all that."

"Sounds like someone gets silly when they're tired," she said, before planting a kiss on his skin. She liked silly. It was a side of him, she imagined, very few people got to see.

James rolled over and surrounded her in his embrace. They lay together like opposing spoons, with her head on his shoulder. "I'm not that tired," he said.

A yawn belied his words.

"All right, maybe a little. That was…"

"Amazing?" The word washed warm over her, causing her already boneless body to melt a little more.

"Mmm."

Noelle hadn't known. Sex with Kevin had been fine—she hadn't known anything else—but this... Her skin still hummed from being stroked. It was as if in touching her, James marked her inside and out, each caress and kiss seared into her skin like a brand.

The sensations went beyond physical though. She felt she'd woken from a long, unproductive sleep. When James sent her over the edge, he sent her to a place beyond her body. A place so high and bright, she swore she saw white. She'd wanted to float there forever.

And very nearly did.

James's fingers were tracing patterns along her arm. In her mind, she imagined them painting lines along her skin. To match the other marks he'd made.

"How about we fly to Boston in the morning, and lock ourselves in my apartment?" he suggested. "We can stay in bed until next year."

"We'd have to move though." Physical separation didn't seem possible at the moment. "Wouldn't it be easier to stay right here?"

"Nuh-uh. Boston's better." Sleep was turning his voice into a slur.

"Better than New York?"

"Better than anywhere. You'll see."

"I wouldn't say anywhere," she replied. "Fryberg's pretty special too, you know."

A soft snore stopped her from saying anything more.

So much for pillow talk. Shifting onto her elbow, Noelle used her new position to steal an uninterrupted look at the man beside her. Like she had on his first night in Fryberg, she marveled at James's beauty. The way all his features worked together to create the perfect face. Not perfect as in perfection, but perfect as in captivating. His cheekbones. His lashes. His parted lips. Leave it to him to make snoring seem attractive.

Awake, he looked older. There was a weight of the world behind his hazel eyes. When he slept, that weight faded, and hints of the boy he must have been leaked through. She would have liked to have known James as a boy. She would have told him he wasn't alone. She would have made him feel like he belonged, same way the Frybergs did her.

The Frybergs.

Her heart started to race. What had she done? She'd slept with another man. No, not slept with, *connected* with. What happened between her and James went beyond sex. Her entire love life with Kevin paled in comparison.

She felt awful just thinking the words. But they were the truth. She didn't feel guilty for sleeping with James; if anything, she felt guilty for enjoying the experience. She wanted to curl up in his arms and when James woke up, make love with him again. For crying out loud, she couldn't even use the word *sex*, because it was too inadequate a word.

"Damn you," she whispered. Why couldn't he remain the annoyingly dislikable boss she'd met on Wednesday morning? Why'd he have to get all romantic and vulnerable? Someone she could fall for?

If she hadn't fallen for him already.

She sat up, causing James's arm to slip away. He grumbled softly before rearranging himself, his head coming to rest on her hip while his arm wrapped around her thigh.

Reflexively, her fingers started combing his hair. The bump under his stitches was beginning to recede, she noticed. That was a good sign. She combed around the unruly patch where the hair and stitches met and tried to ignore the way her heart was expanding.

She *was* falling for him. Hard. And he was falling for

her—there was no way that tonight had been one-sided. No, they might be at the very beginning, but the emotions in this bed had the potential to become something very real and special. It was the last thing she'd expected, but there it was.

The air in the room was suddenly getting close. Her lungs wouldn't fill. She tried breathing in as hard as she could, but it was as if the air wouldn't flow past her lips.

Fresh air. That's what she needed. To clear her head so she could think.

Slipping out from beneath the covers, she padded toward the window only to find it couldn't open. Apparently New Yorkers didn't believe in throwing up the sash like they did in Fryberg. Very well, she'd risk a walk. A couple of moments of fumbling in the dark later, she was dressed and slipping out the door.

The brightness caught her off guard. She was used to seeing stars after midnight, not soft drink billboards and scrolling news feeds. After the soft lighting of their hotel room, the contrast hurt her eyes. Noelle leaned against the icy marble, and inhaled. The air was cold and sour smelling. A mixture of body odor and exhaust. A few blocks away, a trio of young women giggled their way toward her. They looked cold with their short jackets and exposed legs. Just looking at them made Noelle stuff her hands deeper into her pockets. If she were smart, she'd turn around and head back inside.

Back to James. No sooner did she think his name than her heart started racing again.

She was scared. She didn't want to be falling in love.

Was that what was happening? James certainly was someone she *could* love. Being with him these past two days, she'd felt like a different person. Not Kevin Fryberg's widow or the infamous Manger Baby, but like *herself*. For the first time that she could remember, she hadn't felt grateful for the attention. Maybe it was because they shared similar pasts, but when she was with James, she felt worthy. As though she was the gift.

She should be thrilled by the feeling. Why then was she standing panicked and shivering on a New York sidewalk?

"Like I would even be interested in the loser... Not that desperate... She's such a skank!" The female trio was crossing the street, talking simultaneously. They had their arms linked. Holding each other up, no doubt, since they swayed back and forth as they walked. A blonde on the far end looked to be swaying more than the others, and as they got closer, Noelle realized it was because she was bouncing to a song she was singing. Her movement caused the middle one to pitch forward and stumble.

"What are you looking at?" she slurred as they stumbled past.

Noelle blinked. "Nothing," she replied, but the trio had already passed on, the blonde turning the air blue as she heaved a string of crude obscenities in her direction. Half the words, Noelle had never heard a person actually say out loud. Feeling like she'd been punched, she tried to flatten herself farther against the building.

Something fuzzy brushed her ankle.

Oh, God, a rat! Noelle shrieked and jumped forward. City rats were rabid, weren't they? She whipped her head back and forth to see which direction the horrid creature went.

Except it wasn't a rat at all. It was a hand. A rattily gloved hand that had slipped free of a dark lump. In her distraction, she hadn't noticed the body rolled up tight against the building. The person moaned and rolled over to reveal a weathered dirty face partially covered by a winter hat. White eyes stared out at her in the darkness as he moaned again. Despite the late hour, there was enough light to see his lips moving. He was trying to tell her something.

Swallowing in nerves, she moved closer and crouched down so she could hear. As she did, she realized he was the source of the sour smell from earlier. Body odor and alcohol swamped her nostrils.

"Do you need something?" she asked, opening her pocketbook. She only had a few dollars on her, but if it would help…

The vulgar name he called her brought her up short.

Her head snapped back. "Wh-What?"

"You ain't takin' my vent. Get your own fraking spot. I ain't sharin' my heat with nobody."

The rant pushed her backward. Stumbling, she sat down hard. Tears sprang to her eyes from the impact, but she ignored them as she pushed herself to her feet. The homeless man was waving her off now as well, his voice growing loud and angry.

"I'm—I'm…sorry. I'm leaving right now." Dropping a handful of bills by his hand—which he snatched while continuing to swear at her—she scurried backward, afraid to turn around until she'd put a safe distance between them. She traveled no more than a yard or two when her foot slipped off the curb. A horn blared. A taxicab had stopped in the intersection.

"Hey, lady. Watch where you're going!"

Nodding, she hurried across the street, and didn't stop until she reached a sign indicating an all-night coffee shop. There was a waitress behind the counter playing with her phone. She looked up when Noelle entered, and pointed to an empty stool.

"Counter service only," she said, before going back to her phone.

Noelle took a seat between two bulky customers, both of whom glared at her desire for space. "Sorry," she heard herself murmur again.

"Coffee?" the waitress asked.

Not really, but Noelle was too shy to ask for anything else. "Yes, please," she replied.

The waitress slapped down a mug and a bowl of plastic creamers. Noelle shivered and wrapped her hands around the cup. Everything was so cold all of a sudden. Cold and angry. This was nothing like the New York James had shown her. But then, he'd gone out of his way to show her only the magical parts. What she was seeing now was the other New York, the part that dwelt beneath the twinkling lights and Christmas trees.

The realistic part, James would say. She'd been trying to keep this part of the world at bay since foster care.

What if falling in love with James was like that?

Sure, everything seemed wonderful now, but what if being with him was like New York and what looked beautiful at the beginning turned out to be filled with garish lights and cold, burnt coffee? It had happened before with Kevin. Hadn't she convinced herself he was the love of her life? What if she woke up one morning and discovered she'd made another mistake? Where would she be then? *Who* would she be then? She wouldn't be a Fryberg, not after betraying Kevin's memory, and they were the only family she'd ever had.

She'd be alone again. Back to the days when she was an outsider at the dinner table. Present but not truly belonging.

Manger Baby.

Suddenly, she felt very small and alone. Add in a few

schoolyard taunts and she'd be ten years old again. Lost and longing for a family to call her own.

"You want anything else?" a voice asked.

Noelle looked up to find the waitress looking in her direction. *Yeah*, she thought, *I could use a hug.* "No thanks. I'm good."

If she were home, Belinda would hug her. Like her son, she hugged fiercely. When a Fryberg encircled you in their arms, nothing in the world could harm you.

You come visit us anytime you want, Noelle. Any friend of Kevin's is a friend of ours.

Tears sprang to her eyes as Noelle remembered that wonderful first afternoon at Kevin's house. Had Mr. Lowestein known what he was giving her when he assigned Kevin as her lab partner? One step over the threshold and she had the family she'd always wanted.

And now, Kevin and Ned were dead. Belinda was moving. The store had changed hands. Everything she cared about and deemed important was slipping out of her fingers. If she lost Belinda's love along with everything else...

She couldn't lose it. She couldn't go back to being alone. She needed...

Needed...

"I need to go home."

Her announcement fell on deaf ears, but it didn't matter. Noelle knew what she had to do. With any luck, James would understand.

Slapping a five-dollar bill on the counter, she headed outside.

James woke up to the sound of his cell phone buzzing. At first he tried ignoring the noise by putting the pillow over his head, but no sooner did the call stop, than the phone started buzzing again.

"Whoever it is, they're fired," he groaned. Leaning over the side of the bed, he groped along the floor until he found his jacket and dug the phone from the breast pocket. The name on the call screen made his shoulders stiffen.

"It's the crack of dawn," he said. "Is something wrong?"

"It's early afternoon here," his father replied. "You're usually up this hour."

"I slept in." Sort of. Raising himself on his elbows, he looked to the other side of the bed, only to frown at the empty sheets. Noelle must have slipped into the bathroom. "Is everything all right?" he asked. "You don't usually call on Sunday mornings."

"Shouldn't I be asking you that question?" Jackson said in return. "Carli said there was an…" He cleared his throat. "An issue at the Fryberg store the other day."

How like Jackson to call his being struck in the head an "issue." "I had a minor accident is all," he said.

"So everything is all right there?"

"Everything is fine." He told his father he had the Fryberg deal under control. A bump on the head wouldn't change anything.

Jackson cleared his throat again. "I'm glad to hear it. Carli didn't have too many details so I wanted to make certain myself. When I had trouble connecting with you, I thought perhaps there had been a problem."

"No," James said. "No problems. I've just been very busy here, and with the time change and all…"

"Right. Right. I'm glad…things…are going smoothly." There was a pause on the other end of the line, like his father was reading something. Multitasking and distraction were par for the course with Jackson. "When do you think you'll be back in Boston?"

"I'm not sure." The irony of his answer made him smile.

Three days ago, he'd been champing at the bit to leave. "There are some…developments I want to look into."

"Developments?"

"Nothing problematic, I assure you."

On the contrary. If last night was any indication, he was on the cusp of something very significant. Noelle made him feel… He couldn't think of how to articulate his feelings. Special? Important? Neither word fit. How did he describe his heart suddenly feeling a hundred times larger?

"You'll keep me advised though, won't you? I want to know if there are any complications," his father said. "Doesn't matter if they are big or small. I'd prefer you not go silent again."

"Of course. I didn't mean to give you cause for concern."

"James, I'm always…" There was another pause. A longer one this time.

James couldn't help the way his breath caught. If he didn't know better, he'd say his father had been worried. "You're what?" he asked.

"I've decided to stop in Copenhagen before I head home."

"Oh." That wasn't what he was going to say. He looked down at the wrinkles on the sheets beneath him. Like tiny white rivers leading to Noelle's side.

Maybe it isn't all about business, she'd said. *You still have hope.*

What the hell. It was worth a try. "Hey, Dad?" The word felt odd on his tongue from lack of use. "Do you remember going into Boston to see the window displays?"

"I'm afraid you're going to have to be more specific. I examine the window displays every year."

"This was with me and Justin and…and Mom. Back when we were…" A family. "We went to see Santa Claus."

"I remember your mother hated those trips. She only went because Justin insisted. Why?"

So much for his wonderful family memory. "I was thinking about repeating one of the designs next year. Vintage is very trendy right now."

"But will it be in fashion next year, that's the question," his father replied. "Trends fall out of favor quickly these days."

As did memories. "It was just a thought."

"Well, you know my position on those displays. They outlived their expenditure long ago. I'll be back by the middle of the week. Why don't we connect then? Over dinner, perhaps."

"Okay," James said. With any luck he would have to cancel to take a certain sexy little elf sightseeing in Boston. "Have a safe trip."

"You too, James."

He let the phone drop to the floor. Stupid, his feeling kicked in the gut over one comment. Wasn't like his father was revealing some kind of family secret. At least Noelle wanted him. The way he felt with her trumped anything—everything—else. Simply thinking her name chased his dark thoughts away.

Damn, but he was falling hard for her.

He stretched his arm to pull her close, only to remember when he struck bare sheets that she was still in the bathroom. "You can come out of hiding! I'm off the phone," he called with a smile. It was sweet that she wanted to give him privacy.

When she didn't respond, he flipped over on his back. "Noelle? Babe? You okay?"

The bathroom door was wide open.

What the hell? Jumping from the bed, he rushed across the room and slapped on the bathroom light. The room was empty. He knew it would be empty. He'd just hoped...

That was the problem with hope. It always ended with a sucker punch.

Noelle was gone. While he'd been dreaming of waking up beside her, she'd gotten dressed and left.

Maybe she went to get coffee, a small, desperate voice in his head said. He angrily shoved the idea away before it could take hold. He didn't want to entertain possibilities, didn't want *hope*. His fingers squeezed the towel rod, his body trembling with the desire to rip it from the wall. He could still see the way she looked at him in the restaurant. Like she cared.

Dammit. He smashed a fist on the marble vanity, roaring through gritted teeth at the pain. Dammit, dammit, dammit! Why couldn't she have stayed a mildly attractive employee? No, she had to crawl under his skin and make him start to believe the damn greeting card was possible? He thought yesterday had been as mind-blowing for her as it had for him. He thought they were starting something here. He thought...

He thought she cared.

Joke was on him, wasn't it? Like he could compete with her dead war hero of a husband. For crying out loud, his own parents didn't want him; what made him think Noelle would?

If only she hadn't been so damn special.

Forget it. Taking a deep breath, James pushed the rage down as deep as possible. He tucked it away along with the crazy dream he'd had of sharing the holidays with Noelle.

Turned out, he'd been right all along. Things like family and holiday cheer, hope, love—they were pipe dreams.

Marketing concepts designed to manipulate emotions and sell products. They didn't really exist. At least not for him. Lesson learned.

CHAPTER ELEVEN

IF NOELLE HEARD the guy on the sound system sing about Santa coming to town one more time, she was going to scream. The song, part of a continual loop in the store, had been playing for the past three days. Usually, she embraced Christmas carols, but she hadn't slept well since returning from New York, and the lack of sleep had left her with a throbbing knot at the back of her head. Like she'd been smacked in the head by a drone.

If only she could be so lucky. A smack to the head and temporary amnesia sounded pretty good about now. Anything would, if it meant whipping out Saturday's memories. She had her own continual loop of sounds and images tormenting her. Every night when she tried to sleep, they repeated in her head. James smiling. James propped on his elbows above her. James raining kisses on her skin. Over and over, the memories repeated until she ended up clutching a pillow to her aching insides while she waited for the clock to signal morning.

Not that daytime was all that much better. If she drove past the Christmas market, she thought of James. If she visited Santa's workshop, she thought of James. If she walked past her living room sofa…

For goodness' sake, they'd known each other four days!

Their relationship didn't warrant this kind of obsession. Yet, here she was obsessing.

Her guilty conscience didn't help. She should have gone back to the hotel and explained in person, but she'd been so freaked out by what she was feeling that she was halfway home before she'd thought things through. By then, embarrassment had kicked in, and the best she could do was a text reading *I'm sorry*. As far as regrets went, it was the stupidest, most immature thing she'd ever done.

Her gaze drifted to her telephone. It wasn't too late. She could still call and explain. What would she say? *Sorry I ran out on you, but I liked you so much I freaked?* While true, she doubted it would make a difference. When push came to shove, it was still only one night—one fantastical, mind-blowing, life-altering night—but one night all the same. And there was still the chance she'd read the situation wrong. After all, she was assuming he felt the same way. For all she knew, the way she felt after they'd made love was commonplace for James and his talk of showing her Boston was nothing more than pillow-talk promises. It had only been a few days, but he might have already moved on, and calling would simply make her look foolish.

A knock sounded on her door. Looking up, she saw Todd standing in the doorway. His arms were folded, and he wore a frown. "You okay?" he asked.

"Fine," she replied, pretending to shuffle some papers. "What can I do for you?"

"I was wondering if you've read the email from the Boston office yet."

Boston office meaning James. Her stomach did a little bounce. "No. What did it say?"

"Hammond sent a list of recommendations for how we can streamline operations and improve traffic flow in the store. Looks like he took a lot of mental notes during his tour last week. Pretty impressive for a guy with stitches in his head."

"Streamlining is his thing," she replied. Along with renting out restaurants and nipping at shoulders, she thought, fighting a blush.

Either she succeeded or Todd was too polite to say anything. "Some of his changes we won't be able to implement until after the holidays, but a few we can put in place now. Why don't you read the list and then you and I can talk?"

"Sure thing." Reaching for her mouse, she clicked on the email icon and brought up her inbox on the screen. "Has Belinda seen the list? What did she say?"

"Nothing. She officially stepped away from operations on Monday afternoon, remember?"

"Sorry. I forgot." This time, Noelle did blush.

"Totally understand," Todd replied. "It's going to take some getting used to, not thinking of her as being in charge."

Or being around, thought Noelle. The first thing her mother-in-law mentioned after Noelle's return on Sunday was that she planned to leave for Florida right after Christmas and not return until mid-April. So in the end, Noelle didn't have James or her family.

Todd cleared his throat. "You sure you're okay? You seem a little spacey."

"Sorry," she apologized again. "I was scanning the memo."

He nodded, even though the expression on his face said he didn't believe her for a second. "Soon as you've gone through it, come find me. I'm looking forward to hearing your thoughts. Especially about point number five."

Point number five, huh? She clicked open the email. Turned out, it wasn't from James after all, but rather a Carli Tynan. The suggestions were all James, however. She recognized the first two as ones he'd made during the tour. Quickly she scanned down to point five.

Remove the Elk statue from the rear of the store. In addition to taking up a large amount of space, the crowd that gathers around it impacts other shoppers' ability to maneuver in the aisles. Recommend statue be placed either outside on the grounds or in storage.

That rat! He'd promised Fryer would stay.

This was clearly revenge for her walking out. Completely unacceptable. It was one thing for him to be angry with her, but he had no business taking his anger out on a poor innocent elk. Fryer hadn't done a thing except uphold tradition.

Retrieving the Boston number from the bottom of the email, she picked up her phone and dialed.

"I want to talk to James Hammond," she snapped when the receptionist answered. There'd be plenty of time to regret her rudeness later. "Tell him Noelle Fryberg is on the phone, and that it's important."

Apparently, there was a part of her that didn't expect him to answer, because she nearly dropped the phone when James's voice drawled in her ear. "I'm in the middle of a meeting."

Nevertheless, he took her call. She might have taken that as a hopeful sign, if not for his chillingly businesslike voice.

She got straight to the point. "Fryer," she said.

"Carli sent out the memo."

"She sent it out, all right. What are you doing removing Fryer? We agreed he was a popular attraction, and deserved to stay."

"I changed my mind," James replied. "I had some time to think on my flight alone back to Boston and decided it wasn't a good idea. There's enough chaos in that store without teenagers blocking the aisles and taking selfies."

"On Friday you called that chaos organized."

"My perspective changed."

Noelle didn't think she'd ever heard his voice so emotionless, not even on his first day in Fryberg. He sounded like the warmth had been sucked out of him and it was her fault.

She grew sick to her stomach. "I'm sorry about the other night."

"I know. I received your text."

She winced. "I know I shouldn't have run out the way I did."

"Forget it, Noelle. I already have."

"You—you have?" Of course he had. Hadn't he said at the restaurant that he was a rich man trying to seduce her? She was the one who'd gone and attached deeper meaning to his behavior. Maybe all the importance had been in her head. "But Fryer..."

"Business, Noelle. The store is a Hammond's property now. It seemed silly to wax nostalgic about the previous ownership." She could hear him shifting in his chair and pictured him sitting straight and stiff behind his desk. "Besides, I'm taking the chain in a different direction after the first of the year. Your elk clashes with the new brand."

"But we agreed," Noelle said. The protest came out a whine. Worst of all, it wasn't Fryer she cared about. It was the chill in his voice. So cold and detached. She wanted the voice that scorched her skin.

"Disappointment's part of life."

Ouch. Then again, what did she expect his attitude would be? Relief? He was angry, and Noelle deserved every ounce of wrath thrown her way.

"James—" *I'm sorry.*

Too late. He'd hung up.

Noelle let the receiver slip from her fingers. What had she done? Handled the whole situation like a child, that's what. One-night stand or not, James deserved a proper goodbye.

Everything was messed up.

"Argh!" Squeezing her eyes shut, she ground the heels of her palms into her lids. "What a freaking idiot."

"Little harsh, don't you think?" she heard Belinda ask. "I'm sure whoever you're talking about isn't that stupid."

The blurry image of her mother-in-law carrying a newspaper walked into the office. She was dressed in her off-duty clothes—jeans and a soft hand-knit sweater—and looked so much like the day they first met, that Noelle immediately jumped up and ran into her arms. Immediately, Belinda's arms went around her in a bear grip more comforting than she deserved. Noelle's shoulders started to shake.

"Whoa, what's this all about?" Belinda asked. "Are you crying?"

"I c-can't help it." Noelle gulped between sobs. The safer she felt, the more she cried.

"Come now, I'm sure it's not that bad."

Did she want to bet? Sniffing back her tears, Noelle let herself catch her breath before speaking. "Fryer's gone," she said, sniffing again. "The Boston office wants him put in storage." And it was all her fault because she'd been a childish coward.

"Don't tell me all these tears are because of a battered old elk," Belinda said.

She stepped back and looked Noelle in the eye. "I know you're fond of tradition, sweetheart, but he's only an old statue. I tried to convince Ned to get rid of him for years. Thing takes up way too much space on the floor."

Great. In addition to dashing out on James, she'd been protecting a tradition no one else wanted.

How fitting.

"Then I guess you've finally gotten your wish." Backing out of her mother-in-law's embrace, Noelle turned back to her desk. "If I'd known you didn't care, I wouldn't have put up a fight."

"Don't be silly," Belinda said. "Of course you would have. You'll fight for every tradition. It's who you are. But something tells me all these tears aren't for our soon-to-be-departed mascot. Something's been bothering you all week."

"That obvious, is it?"

"Thirty seconds ago you were sobbing on my sweater. A billboard would be less obvious. What's wrong?"

Where to start? "It's complicated."

"Is it my retiring? I know my leaving for Florida is happening quickly."

"The business is only part of the problem," Noelle replied.

"I see." She wore Kevin's same skeptical expression as she folded her arms. "What's the other part?"

Shame burned in Noelle's stomach. Thinking her mistakes were bad enough, but speaking them aloud?

"I messed up," she said. "I did something really, really stupid."

"Oh, sweetheart." The older woman stepped up and rested a hand on Noelle's shoulder. "I'm sure you're exaggerating. Todd would have told me if it was super serious."

"Todd doesn't know, and worse, it's too late to fix things."

"You don't know that, sweetheart. Nothing is so horrible it can't be repaired."

"Not this time," Noelle replied, turning around. Taking a deep breath, she relayed what had happened in New York.

"Well," Belinda said when she finished, "that explains why James mysteriously cancelled our Monday meeting *and* why you were acting so strangely when you came by the house on Sunday afternoon. Why on earth would you run off and leave him like that?"

"Because I freaked out." She rubbed her forehead, the pain from the back of her head having decided to relocate there. "The way he made me feel. The emotions. They were too overwhelming. I've never felt like that before."

"Not even with Kevin?"

Noelle froze. Here she thought she couldn't mess up any further. "Kevin was… That is, I loved Kevin…"

"It's all right," Belinda said. "I know what you meant."

"Y-you do?"

"You and Kevin were practically babies when you started dating. Only natural the grown-up you would feel things a little differently.

"Maybe…" Her mother-in-law's smile was indulgent as she cupped Noelle's cheek. "Maybe even a little stronger."

How did she earn such a wonderful person in her life?

"You have to know, I loved Kevin," Noelle replied. "I wanted to spend the rest of my life with him." Who knows how things would have worked out between them if he'd returned? They'd already had a strong foundation. Passion might have blossomed eventually as well.

"No matter what, he'll always own a big piece of my heart."

Belinda smiled down at her. "I know, sweetheart. Now, the question is—does James Hammond own any of that heart? Are you in love with him?"

Was she? Noelle shook her head. "We've only known each other four days." Far too soon to fall head over heels.

"But…" She thought about how her heart felt fuller when he walked into a room.

"But you could see yourself falling in love with him someday," Belinda finished for her.

"Yes." Very much so, Noelle thought as she looked to the ground. She had the sinking feeling she was halfway in love now. Not that it mattered given her foolish behavior. "I'm sorry."

"Don't be ridiculous," Belinda replied. She forced Noelle to look up. "You never have to apologize for falling in love with someone else."

"But Kevin…"

"Kevin would want you to move on. So would Ned and I. You're much too young to spend your life alone."

Right, because Belinda was leaving. The reminder she would soon be alone in Fryberg only made the hollow feeling in Noelle's chest grow larger. "What if I'm wrong?" she asked. "What if James isn't as awesome as I think?"

"Then you try again," Belinda told her. "Relationships don't come with guarantees. Some work. Some don't."

"Yeah, but if I choose him, and we don't make it, then I'll be alone again." Her eyes had lost the battle and teared up again. One dripped down her cheek onto Belinda's fingers. "You're the only family I've ever had. I don't know what I'd do without you."

"My goodness, is that what you're scared of? Losing your family?"

She didn't see how she could move on and keep them. "I'm only family because I married Kevin. If I move on, I won't belong anymore."

"What are you talking about? Of course you'll belong. Don't you realize that with Kevin gone, I need you more than ever?"

Before she could say another word, Noelle found herself

back in Belinda's embrace. Her mother-in-law squeezed her tight. "You, Noelle Fryberg, have always been more than Kevin's wife," she said. "I love you like a daughter, and that's never going to change, whether you fall in love with James Hammond or a hundred different men. Family is forever, and you…"

She kissed Noelle's forehead. "You are my family. Got that?"

Noelle tried to keep her jaw from trembling as she nodded. What a fool she was. So busy being grateful for Belinda and Ned's affections, she couldn't see that when it came to Belinda, family wasn't an either-or proposition. Her heart was large enough to accommodate everyone. Take Thanksgiving and the mishmash of characters who joined every year. Todd, Jake from the mail room, Nadifa from sales. None of them blood related and yet all of them embraced like they were.

When she thought about it, Belinda had pulled Noelle into that welcoming web the day Kevin brought her home. She didn't inherit a family *because* she dated Kevin; dating Kevin was an added bonus. Chances are she would have been enfolded into the Thanksgiving Day group regardless. After all, the only qualification was being alone at the holidays.

"Your family was—is—the greatest gift I could ever ask for," she told Belinda. "Being a Fryberg was a dream come true. It was all I ever wanted."

By now Belinda's eyes were shining too. "Oh, sweetheart, you're my dream come true too. Don't get me wrong, I loved Kevin, but I always wanted a daughter to keep the family traditions alive."

Offering a smile, the older woman bent down and kissed Noelle on the forehead. "I never imagined I'd end up with a daughter who's more Fryberg than anyone with actual Fryberg blood."

They both laughed. "Does that mean I can still have Grandma Fryberg's recipe book?" Noelle asked, wiping her eyes.

"Absolutely. I'll even laminate the pages so you can pass the book along to your daughter.

"And you will have a daughter. Or daughter-in-law," Belinda added. Her smile faded and once again, her expression grew serious. "There's a whole world out there beyond this store and our family name. I fully expect you to build a happy life beyond Fryberg's. You deserve one."

"But I wouldn't have a life without Fryberg's," Noelle replied. Breaking out of her mother-in-law's grasp, she reached for the box of tissues on her desk. Her eyes and nose were runny with tears. "I can't imagine anything else."

"Really? Then why are you crying over James Hammond?"

All right, maybe Noelle could imagine a little more. The other night, in James's arms, she'd imagined all types of future. "Doesn't matter whether I'm crying over him or not," she said, blowing her nose. "He and I are finished."

"Are you certain?"

"Man said so himself."

Forget it, Noelle. I already have.

She blew her nose. "You should have heard his voice, Belinda." Remembering sent a chill down her spine. "I called him to discuss his email, and I might as well have been talking to a stranger."

A feeling of hopelessness washed over her. "I thought… That is, the whole reason I freaked out was because I thought we had some kind of special connection. Now I wonder if maybe I wasn't simply confusing good sex with affection and blew the weekend out of proportion."

Thankfully, Belinda chose to let the good sex comment slide. Hearing her thoughts out loud, however, made Noelle even more certain she was right, and had let the romanticism of Saturday night get the best of her. "Other than being angry with the way I took off, I wonder if James has even given me a second thought."

"I'm sure he has. He didn't strike me as someone who took…those kinds of encounters…lightly."

"Me either," Noelle replied. "He certainly sounded businesslike enough today though. Talking about the company's new direction and all."

"New direction?"

"Uh-huh. Based on the points in his email, I'd say he's back to focusing on streamlining and internet sales." She could see it now. Today Fryer. Tomorrow the Christmas Castle.

"Hmm."

Noelle frowned. "What?"

"I'm not sure," Belinda replied. "Did you see today's business headlines?"

"No."

"I think you should. There's something very interesting in it." Her mother-in-law retrieved the newspaper she'd dropped on the desk during their talk. It was folded in thirds, to highlight the headline on the weekly marketing column. Noelle's heart sank as she read.

Hammond's to discontinue iconic window displays.

The article below quoted James as saying he wanted to take the chain in a "new direction" and build a store for the next generation.

"'It's time Hammond's let go of the past,'" she read. "'We can't bring the past back, no matter how badly we may want to.'" It was a harsh-sounding quote, one she imagined marketing hadn't wanted to use.

"When I read the article this morning, something didn't hit me as right. Still doesn't, although I can't put my finger on what."

Noelle stared at the headline.

All week she'd been downplaying Saturday night to ease the giant ache in her chest, but her efforts hadn't worked. There were too many reminders in the Christmas music and lights. She wanted the holiday to go away so she could breathe again. She who held Christmas in her heart fifty-two weeks a year.

But ending the window displays? They represented the one decent family memory he had. It was why he kept them going year after year, regardless of the cost. Because there was a part of him, the ghost of that little boy, that wanted to believe family meant something. That he meant something to his family. Before his mother's midnight departure convinced him otherwise.

No. Noelle's heart seized. Dropping the newspaper, she stumbled toward a chair. The room had become a tunnel, a narrow dark tube with black all around.

"Are you all right?" she heard Belinda ask from far away. "Is something wrong? What is it?"

No. Yes. Everything. The answers flew through her head as her realization became clear.

She'd disappeared in the middle of the night without a word just like his mother. He'd spent the day revealing himself, at her urging, and she'd let her cowardice trample that vulnerability. In doing so, she solidified all of James's fears.

That was why he was closing the window displays. Not because he wanted to take the chain in a new direction—though he would and do so brilliantly—but because that little boy no longer believed in his own memory. James had retreated, quit, waved the white flag in defeat.

He had given up hope, and it was her fault.

It wasn't right. Someone needed to tell him he had too much sweetness and light inside him to hide behind profits and modern retail. Someone had to show him he was special.

Lovable.

Not someone. Her. Noelle needed to fix the horrible wrong she had done to him. And not by text or by phone either. In person.

"I need to go to Boston," she told Belinda. "As soon as possible."

She may have thrown away her chance to be with him, but Noelle would be damned if she cost him Christmas.

"Why are you still wearing your coat?" Jackson asked, as he slipped into his seat. As usual, he was dressed impeccably in a suit from his London tailor.

"I'm cold," James replied. "This table picks up a draft from the front door."

He and his father were meeting for a business lunch in the bistro across from Hammond's. Outside, Copley Square bustled with Christmas shoppers, many of who stopped to watch the Hammond's displays. In fact, there was a crowd of preschoolers clumped in front of them that very moment, watching the elves make mischief in Santa's kitchen. Why they were standing out in such blasted cold was beyond him. A shiver passed through him, and he looked away.

"If you're uncomfortable, we can move," Jackson said.

"That won't be necessary. I'll warm up soon enough." He hoped. He'd been chilled to the bone for days. At home, he'd cranked both his gas fireplace and the thermostat, and slept with an extra comforter. It was going to be a long winter, at this rate.

Maybe if he found someone to warm him up? He dismissed the idea as quickly as it appeared. Female company didn't appeal to him right now.

Meanwhile, for some reason, his father refused to let the subject drop. After the waiter took their orders, he laid his napkin on his lap and leaned forward. "Are you sure it's temperature-related and not something to do with the 'issue' you had in Fryberg?"

"I'm sure." Other than a minor case of temporary insanity, his "issue" had been side-effect-free. "A cup of hot coffee and I'll be fine."

Jackson stared at him for a beat or two. "If you say so," he said finally, before reaching for his water glass. "I saw the article in the *Business Journal* today about the window displays. I have to say I didn't think you would ever agree to eliminate them."

"What can I say? Even I couldn't ignore the numbers."

"I'm glad you finally came around. Although it would have been nice if you'd alerted me to your decision. I realize you handle these kinds of day-to-day operations, but…"

"You were in Copenhagen," James interrupted. "And I wanted to make the announcement early enough to take advantage of the entire Christmas season. I didn't mean to blindside you."

"*Surprise* is a better word."

James returned his father's flat smile and sipped his coffee. "Marketing tells me we're getting quite a bit of local press attention from the announcement. This could turn into a public relations bonus for us."

"That reminds me," Jackson said, "you need to talk to whoever wrote the press release. They should have drafted a less caustic quote."

James had written the quote himself. Molly, their communications assistant, had clearly wanted something else, but she hadn't argued.

Noelle would have. He suppressed a shiver. "Actually, I thought the quote went straight to the point."

"'We can't bring the past back, no matter how badly we may want to'?" Jackson quoted. "I would have preferred something a little less cynical."

"Why? It's true, isn't it?"

"Yes, but we're not in the business of selling truth, James—we sell toys."

"Don't worry. I've no intention of letting sales slide." Amazing how unaffected he was about the whole thing. Not too long ago, he would have argued the window displays brought in customers. But when he'd visited the store on Sunday afternoon and saw this year's intricate displays, he'd suddenly thought *Why bother?* All that money spent and what did it matter?

"The rest of the chain does quite well without window displays," James said, reaching for his coffee again. "Boston will too. A month from now, people won't remember what the display looked like."

"I could have told you that," Jackson replied.

The waiter arrived with their food. While he waited for the man to serve his soup, James let his eyes travel back to the crowd across the street. The preschoolers had been joined by several mothers with strollers. For a moment, he thought he saw a red-and-white knit hat mixed in the crowd and his pulse stuttered. His eyes were playing tricks on him. He hadn't thought about Noelle since he left New York—prolonged thought anyway—and he wasn't about to start.

Although yesterday's phone call nearly killed him. When the receptionist said her name, a tearing sensation had gripped his chest. The first intense feeling he'd had in days, it nearly knocked him to his knees. Then there was the way she'd lowered her voice to apologize. It took all his reserves, but thankfully he kept himself from breaking and asking why she left. No need to hear her excuse. He already knew.

The sound of his father clearing his throat drew back his attention.

"Are you certain you feel all right?" Jackson asked. "Perhaps you should see a specialist."

"I'm *fine*," he insisted.

"You say you're all right, but you're clearly not acting like yourself. You're difficult to reach. You're making sudden changes in company policy."

James let out a long sigh. "So this is about my not discussing the announcement with you beforehand." He knew this sudden interest in his health had to mean something.

"This has nothing to do with the announcement," Jackson said, killing that theory immediately. "I'm simply concerned about you."

"Why? You've never been before." The words came flying out before James realized what he was saying. They landed between them, causing his father to sit back, his features frozen in shock.

"You don't think I care?" Jackson said. He actually sounded stung.

What did he do now?

Aww, heck. Might as well put this bit of the past to rest too. "I'm not making an accusation," James said, holding up a hand. "I understand that you were stuck with me when Mom left and that put you in an awkward position."

His father stared at him. A long look similar to the ones he'd given James as a teenager. And like then, James had to fight the urge to tug at his collar.

Finally, Jackson put down his fork. "Are you suggesting that I was unhappy when your mother left you behind?"

Wasn't he? "I remember the look on your face when I came downstairs that morning and you definitely weren't expecting to see me. If anything," he added, looking down at his chowder, "you looked disappointed."

"That's because I was," Jackson replied. "For you." He let out a sigh. "Your mother was a very unpredictable woman. Doing one thing one day, and something else the next. She insisted that I encouraged your analytical side to spite her, and that I didn't understand what it took to raise a child. I had no idea she'd left you behind until you came downstairs that morning.

"She was right," he said, smoothing a wrinkle from the tablecloth. "I was completely unprepared."

Silence filled the table while his father paused to sip his water and James struggled for what to say next. It was true; his mother had been high-strung. Hence the flying crystal. He remembered preferring the quiet of his father's study to being around her whirling dervish personality.

"I'm not..." Jackson took another drink. "I'm not a naturally affectionate person. Your mother complained all the time that I was too detached. Too stiff. It's how I am. Looking back, I can see how an impressionable teenager might misconstrue my behavior.

"I can assure you, though," he added, "that at no time did I ever consider myself 'stuck' with you."

Slowly stirring his soup, James digested his father's confession. So he had been wanted after all. As far as family reconciliations went, the moment wouldn't win any prizes, but he got a tightness in his chest nonetheless. "Thank you," he said. "I appreciate you telling me."

For the first time in James's life, Jackson Hammond looked bashful. "You're welcome. Son."

By unspoken agreement, they spent the rest of the luncheon discussing business, a far more comfortable subject. When they were finished, Jackson suggested they meet for lunch again the next week. "Or you could come by for dinner," he offered.

"Sure," James replied. If his father could try, then so could he. "Dinner would be great."

Jackson responded with the most awkward shoulder pat in history. Still it was a start.

Not that he would ever say so, but his father had terrible timing. Short as it was, their heart-to-heart killed the numbness he'd so carefully cultivated when Noelle left. Granted, he'd been cold, but with one or two exceptions, he'd been able to function without thinking about what a fool he'd been.

But then, Jackson decided to pat his shoulder, and the first thought that popped into his head was *Noelle was right*. Suddenly, the entire weekend was replaying in his head.

Telling his father he had an errand, James hung back on the sidewalk as Jackson entered the building. He needed to clear his head of the frustration his father's apology had unleashed. It felt like a giant fist shoving upward in his chest. If he didn't push it back down, he was liable to scream out loud.

Why was he letting one tiny woman get to him so badly?

Dammit! He'd had one-night stands before. Some of them even told him to go to hell after they discovered they were nothing more than one-night stands. None of those experiences had ever turned into an existential crisis. His weekend with Noelle shouldn't have either, late-night escape or otherwise. Yet here he was, making long overdue peace with his father and wishing it was Noelle reaching out to him instead.

He never should have let her past his defenses. From the start, he knew nothing *real* could happen between them. Relationships didn't happen on his end of the bell curve. But then she'd hugged him, shifting around his insides and allowing things like hope and longing to rise to the surface. She'd made him believe their night together went deeper than sex. He hadn't just taken her in his arms; he'd shared his soul with her. Every touch, every kiss was his way of expressing the feelings she unlocked in him. Fool that he was, he'd actually started believing in Hammond's marketing pitch.

And now, thanks to his father's apology, those feelings threatened to return, this time to mock him. He didn't want to feel. He didn't want to hope anymore.

From here on in, it was about business. Profit and efficiency.

"Ooh, look, Andre! There's a monkey swinging in the lights. Do you see him?"

Lost in his thoughts, James didn't realize he'd joined the crowd in front of the window displays. Next to him, a young mother in a leather jacket stood holding a toddler. She had a second baby, bundled in pink bunting in a stroller beside her.

The woman pointed a manicured finger toward the window. "Look at him," she said. "He's trying to steal Santa's cookies."

The toddler, Andre presumably, had a frown on his pudgy puce-colored face. "Bad monkey," he said. "No cookies."

"You don't think he should take the cookies?" the mother asked, laughing as the toddler shook his head.

"Someone's taken the naughty list concept to heart," James caught himself saying.

"Let's hope he feels that way when he's ten," she replied. "You ready to see the next window, Dre?"

Watching the trio walk away, a pang struck James in the midsection as he realized Dre and his little sister wouldn't see the displays next year. Oh, well, at their age, they wouldn't even realize the loss. Most kids wouldn't. It was just James holding on to the memory.

Did his brother ever think about the window displays? Last time he saw Justin… When was the last time he'd seen him? The boat races maybe? Jackson had said something about his brother going to business school out west somewhere. James didn't even know what college his brother had attended. Or where he did his undergrad, for that matter. Like mother, like son, Justin had had little to do with them once he left. He'd apparently built quite a nice Hammond-free life and wasn't looking back.

James needed to do the same. It helped that at least Jackson had confessed he wasn't completely unwanted.

Just unwanted by his mother.

And by Noelle. Out of the corner of his eye, he saw another flash of red and white, causing the frustration to rise anew.

Four more weeks. Come January first, Christmas would be done, they would pack away the decorations, and he would be rid of any and all reminders of Fryberg. No more thoughts of blue eyes or snow-dotted lashes.

In the meantime, James had a business to run. The numbers at their Cape Cod store were especially troublesome and needed to be addressed.

Feeling his control return, he marched into the store. His renewed focus lasted until he reached the top floor.

There, he barely managed to round the corner to his office when a red-and-white cap stopped him in his tracks.

So much for blaming his imagination.

Noelle rose from her seat. "I need to talk with you," she said.

CHAPTER TWELVE

SHE LOOKED…BEAUTIFUL. The image of her lying in his arms flashed before him, and his body moved to take her in his arms. Catching himself, James clasped his hands behind his back.

"If you're here about that blasted elk there's nothing more to talk about," he said.

"I'm not here about Fryer," she said.

"Good. Then we have even less to talk about. If you'll excuse me…"

He tried to brush past her and head into his office, but she stepped in front of him. A five-foot-two roadblock. "I read about you canceling the window displays."

"And let me guess, you're worried how the new direction will affect your Christmas Castle." Why else would she fly halfway across the country instead of emailing? All roads led to Fryberg, didn't they?

"You could have saved yourself the airfare. Our plans for the castle haven't changed. Your family business will live to bring another year of Christmas cheer."

Again, he moved to his office and again, she blocked his path. "I'm not here about the castle either."

"Then why are you here?" he asked. It was taking all his effort to keep his voice crisp and businesslike. What he wanted was to growl through clenched teeth.

"Because I owe you an apology."

Seriously? James ignored how her answer made his heart give a little jump. Not again, he reminded himself. No more being fooled into believing emotions existed when they didn't.

"You wasted your airfare. I told you on the phone, the matter has already been forgotten."

This time, he managed to pass her and reach his office door.

"I know what you're doing." Noelle's voice rang through the waiting area.

Don't take the bait. Don't turn around.

"Is that so?" he replied, turning. "And what is that, exactly?"

"You're trying to kill Christmas."

Someone dropped a stapler. Out of the corner of his eye he saw his administrative assistant picking up several sheets of paper from the floor.

"You're being ridiculous." He couldn't kill Christmas if he tried. Damn holiday insisted on existing whether he wanted it to or not.

"Am I? I know what those displays meant to you. How much you loved them…"

His assistant dropped her stapler again.

He closed his eyes. "Noelle, this is neither the time nor the place for us to have this conversation."

"Fine," she replied. "When and where would you like to have it?"

"How about nowhere and never?"

"Nice try, but I flew across five states to talk to you so I can say what I have to say now or I can say it later, but I'm not leaving until I speak my piece."

He expected her to fold her arms after her speech, but instead, she looked up at him through her lashes, and added, "Please?" Her plea totally threw him a curveball. No way he could resist those cornflower eyes.

"Fine. We'll talk." Opening his office door, he motioned for her to step in first. "But take off that hat." No way was he rehashing Saturday night with her looking adorable.

Unfortunately, she looked more adorable with tousled hat hair. He went back to clasping his hands to keep from combing his fingers through it.

Nodding to one of the chairs, he walked around to the other side of his desk and sat down figuring a three-foot cherrywood barrier would keep him from doing something stupid.

"Okay, you've got the floor," he said. "What was so important that you had to fly all the way to Boston to say?"

"Aren't you going to take off your coat?"

"No. I'm cold." Although that status was rapidly changing, thanks to his heart rate. It had started racing the second he saw her. "Now what is it you wanted?"

"Why are you closing down the window displays?"

"Because they're a financial drain on the company."

"Funny how you didn't think so before," she replied coming toward the desk.

"Well, I saw them with a new perspective. I realized we were spending a lot of money trying to sell a concept that no longer resonated." Was she coming around to his side of the desk? "My decision shouldn't be a surprise," he said. "My feelings about this kind of kitschy Christmas marketing were hardly a secret."

She stopped at the desk corner. "You didn't think them so kitschy on Saturday night when you told me about the polar bear."

"That's because I was trying to charm you into bed. And it worked. At least for a little while," he added. If she was going to stand so close, he was going to wield sarcasm.

God, but he wished she'd back away. It was easier to be furious with her when he couldn't smell orange blossoms.

"It was wrong of me to run out like that," she said. "It was stupid and childish."

The earnestness in her eyes left him aching. With his hands gripping the chair arm, he pushed himself closer to the desk. "Congratulations. We agree."

He didn't have to look to know his words hit their mark. "I don't suppose you'd let me explain," she said.

"Would it make any difference?"

"Maybe. No. I don't know."

"Thank you for summarizing everything so clearly." He didn't want to hear any more. Didn't want her orange blossom scent interfering with his anger. "I think you should go," he told her.

Noelle twisted her hat in her hands. This wasn't going at all the way she'd envisioned. Seeing him again reminded her how intimidating a presence he could have when he wanted. It also reminded her how much vulnerability there was beneath the surface. Icy as he sounded, she could see the flashes of pain in his eyes. She wanted to hug him and tell him how amazingly special he was. Only he wouldn't believe her. Not until she cleared the air.

Which was why she stood her ground. She came to explain and make amends for hurting him, and she would.

"I freaked out," she told him. "Saturday was…it felt like a fairy tale with me as Cinderella. You had me feeling all these emotions and suddenly they were too much. I felt scared and guilty and so many things. I needed to get some air."

"All the way back in Michigan? What, New York air not good enough?"

She deserved that. "At first, I only meant to stand outside for a little bit, maybe get a cup of coffee. But then there was this homeless man and these women and… It doesn't matter. Bottom line is, I got scared and ran home where I knew I'd be safe."

"I would have thought you'd find me safe, considering."

"You were. You made me feel incredibly safe. That was part of what freaked me out."

"How reassuring," James replied.

Yeah, listening to what she was saying, Noelle wouldn't buy it either. "I made a mistake," she said.

"No kidding." He shoved the chair away from his desk, causing her to jump. "I told you things I've never shared with anyone," he said, as he stood up. "I opened up to you—and you were the one who pushed me."

Shame at her behavior welled up inside her. "I know," she replied.

"You made me think…" The rest of his sentence died when he ran his hand over his face. "I should have known. When I saw that mantel full of photos, I should have known I couldn't compete with Kevin."

"What?" No, he had it all wrong. "That's not true."

"Noelle, listen to yourself. Thirty seconds ago, you said you felt guilty."

"Yes, but not because of my feelings for Kevin. I felt guilty because I realized Kevin couldn't measure up to you."

Confusion marked his features. "What?"

Noelle took a deep breath. After all his openness, he deserved to know her deepest secret. "Kevin was a special person," she said. "Every girl in school wanted to date him, so I couldn't believe how lucky I was that he wanted to be with me. Being Kevin Fryberg's girl was the best thing that ever happened to me. Being part of the Frybergs was the biggest dream come true."

"So you've told me," James replied.

"But what I didn't tell you was that Kevin was…he was like the big, wonderful brother I never had."

The confusion deepened. "I don't understand."

"That's the reason I felt so guilty," Noelle said, moving to look out the window herself. "I loved Kevin. I loved our life together, especially when his parents were around. But we never had that phase where we couldn't keep our hands off each other, and I just figured that was because we'd been together for so long. It wasn't until shortly after the wedding that I realized I didn't love him the way a wife should. But by that time, we were committed."

Her fingers ran along the blinds lining the window. "And I had the family I'd always wanted. If he and I ended… So I stuck it out, figuring I'd eventually fall more in love with him. Then Kevin deployed."

And then he died, leaving her the widow of the town hero and forced to keep pretending lest she hurt her surrogate family. She turned so she could study James with her damp gaze. "I didn't know," she whispered.

"Know what?"

"What it felt like to be truly attracted to someone. To have this continual ache in the pit of your stomach because you desperately want them to touch you. Until this past weekend. You made me feel out of control and off-balance and it scared the hell out of me."

"You could have told me," he said. "I would have understood."

"How was I supposed to tell you I could see myself falling for you, when it was those feelings that terrified me?" she replied. "Don't you get it? I was afraid my feelings would blow up in my face and cost me the only family I've ever known."

She waited, watched, while her confession settled over

him. After a moment, he ran his hand over his face again and sighed. "If it frightened you, why are you telling me now?"

"Because you deserved to know," she replied. "And because I've realized that family isn't an either-or proposition. Nor is it about being related. It's about love, pure and simple. So long as you have love, you have family."

Risking his rejection, she walked toward him. When she got close enough, she took his hand. "And maybe all that greeting card stuff you despise is a myth, but Christmas can still be wonderful if you're with someone special. Please don't close off the part of you that believes that too."

But James only looked down at their hands. Noelle could take a hint. Foolish of her to think an apology would change much. At least she'd tried. "Anyway, that's what I came to tell you. That you're on the lovable side of the bell curve, and that I wish I hadn't messed up, because there's nothing I would like more than to have been your someone special this Christmas."

"Are you still scared?"

A spark lit in her heart. There was hope in his voice. He was trying to fight it, but it was there. "Terrified," she replied.

His grip tightened around her fingers. "Me too." Slowly, he lifted his gaze and she saw brightness sparkling in his eyes. "I've never had anyone think I'm special before," he told her.

"I've never been anyone's princess," she told him back.

"So maybe…"

She held her breath and waited.

"Be a shame for you not to see Boston since you flew all the way here," he said.

A hundred-pound weight lifted from her shoulders. She

felt like she had the day she met the Frybergs, times ten. "What about my flight home?"

Letting go of her hand, James wrapped an arm around her waist and leaned in until their foreheads touched. "Don't worry," he said. "I know a pilot."

EPILOGUE

Three weeks later

FOR THE LIFE of him, James was never going to get used to those nutcrackers. They were the stuff kids' nightmares were made of. Whistling to himself, he passed under them and headed for the conductor's shack.

"Good afternoon, Ed," he greeted. "How's the train business?"

The conductor blanched. "M-M-Mr. Hammond. We weren't expecting you today. I'm afraid the castle closed early."

"Are you telling me everyone has gone home?" James asked in his sternest voice. "It's only two o'clock."

"Well, it…it is Christmas Eve…"

"James Hammond, stop scaring the employees." Noelle came bouncing out of the conductor's shack wearing a Santa Claus hat and carrying a gold-and-white gift bag. Like it always did when he saw her, James's breath caught in his throat.

"Don't mind him, Ed," she said. "He's not nearly as Grinchy as he'd like people to believe." Rising on tiptoes, she flung her arms around his neck and kissed him soundly. Completely confirming her charge, James kissed her back with equal enthusiasm. Her gift bag crinkled as she wrapped her arms tighter.

"Merry Christmas," she said, smiling. "Nice sweater. You look very festive." He was wearing a red-and-white reindeer jumper purchased at the hotel on his last visit a few days before. One of the advantages of having his own plane was that it made long-distance relationships a lot easier.

"So do you," he replied. "Careful though. If Santa finds out you stole his hat, he'll put you on the naughty list."

"Then we'd better not tell him." Giving him one more kiss, she untangled herself and held out the gift bag. "This is for you. Merry Christmas Eve."

James fingered the red polka-dotted tissue paper peering out from the top of the bag. He might as well have been five again, for the thrill that passed through him.

No, he corrected, a five-year-old wouldn't get this choked up over a simple gift bag. "I thought we agreed to wait and exchange presents tomorrow night when we were alone."

Back in Boston, there was a stack of boxes with Noelle's name on them. More than necessary, probably, but he hadn't been able to help himself. Finally, he understood the joy that came from giving to the people for whom you cared.

"I know," she replied. "This is more of a pre-Christmas present."

Meaning she'd cared enough in return to shop for him. His throat constricted a little more. As far as he was concerned, he already had the best Christmas present in the world standing in front of him.

Her hand came down to rest on his forearm. Shaking off his thoughts, he focused on her shimmering blue gaze instead. "Consider it a small thank-you for asking me if

I'd help with next year's window displays," she said. "A very small thank-you. I'm poor from all my Christmas shopping."

"You didn't have to buy anything. Asking for your assistance was a no-brainer. No one is better suited to work on our chain-wide window display extravaganza than you, my little elf." It was true. Hammond's "new direction" involved rolling out Boston's iconic displays on a nationwide basis. The new displays would be more modern and inclusive to reflect the current consumer public, and focus on the message that Christmas was a time for spreading love and goodwill. James was excited for the new project, and for Noelle's involvement since she'd be making frequent trips to Boston. He didn't want to get too ahead of himself, but if things went well he hoped Noelle might someday consider spending even more time in Boston.

Seemed hope had become a habit for him these days.

"Aren't you going to open it?" Noelle asked.

"What?" The gift. He pretended to study the bag. "Considering the size, I'll go out on a limb and say you didn't buy me a drone."

Noelle stuck out her tongue. "Ha-ha-ha. You should be sending that drone a thank-you present. If you hadn't stood in the way, we might never have gotten past the dislike stage."

"True enough."

He shook the bag, only to hear the useless rustling of paper. "It's one of those stuffed Fryer collectibles, isn't it?" After he and Noelle made up, they'd compromised—sort of. Fryer was to be given one last season and then retired with an official ceremony after the first of the year.

"How about you stop guessing and open the package?" Noelle replied. "And don't forget to read the note. It's important."

James did as he was told and discovered a bag full of gingerbread cookies. Two dozen of them.

"I baked them last night," Noelle told him. "In case we get hungry on the way to Belinda's," she said. "Or on the flight tomorrow." They were spending Christmas Eve with Noelle's mother-in-law before flying to Boston for Christmas dinner.

"If you look," she said, "I gave them all little business suits."

Sure enough, she had. "So you can literally bite my head off?"

"Or lick your tummy."

"Sweetheart, you don't need a cookie to do that."

She slapped his arm, and he laughed. Like hope, laughter had also become a regular part of his life.

Funny how quickly things changed. A month ago he'd been utterly alone, and convinced he liked life that way. Now, for the first time in years, he was having a true family Christmas. He was making tentative strides with his father, and with the reappearance of his brother within the family business, it even looked like he and Justin might regain some of the bond they'd lost.

His brother had undergone his own collection of changes this past month. As a result, the two of them had discovered the Hammond family dysfunction had left a mark on both of them. Fortunately, they—and their father—were getting a second chance.

At the end of the day, though, the only person he really needed in his life was the woman in front of him. How right she'd been that day in his office when she said Christmas was wonderful when you had someone special.

And she was special. No longer were the two of them standing on the cusp of something extraordinary; they were over-their-heads deep in the middle. And with each passing day, he fell a little deeper. As soon as the timing was right, he planned to let Noelle know he'd fallen in love with her.

"The note," Noelle said prodding him.

Pretending to roll his eyes at her eagerness, he fished out the folded piece of paper. "For our first Christmas together. Made with all my love."

Damn, if he couldn't feel his heart bursting through his chest. "All your love?" he asked.

"Every ounce," she told him. "I love you, James Hammond."

Never had five words filled him with such hope and happiness. They were Christmas, Easter and every holiday in between. "I love you too," he said, pulling her close.

It was going to be a perfect Christmas.

* * * * *

MILLS & BOON

THE HEART OF ROMANCE

A ROMANCE FOR EVERY KIND OF READER

MODERN

Prepare to be swept off your feet by sophisticated, sexy and seductive heroes, in some of the world's most glamourous and romantic locations, where power and passion collide.
8 stories per month.

HISTORICAL

Escape with historical heroes from time gone by. Whether your passion is for wicked Regency Rakes, muscled Vikings or rugge Highlanders, awaken the romance of the past.
6 stories per month.

MEDICAL

Set your pulse racing with dedicated, delectable doctors in the high-pressure world of medicine, where emotions run high an passion, comfort and love are the best medicine.
6 stories per month.

True Love

Celebrate true love with tender stories of heartfelt romance, fr the rush of falling in love to the joy a new baby can bring, and focus on the emotional heart of a relationship.
8 stories per month.

Desire

Indulge in secrets and scandal, intense drama and plenty of si hot action with powerful and passionate heroes who have it all wealth, status, good looks…everything but the right woman.
6 stories per month.

HEROES

Experience all the excitement of a gripping thriller, with an in romance at its heart. Resourceful, true-to-life women and stro fearless men face danger and desire - a killer combination!
8 stories per month.

DARE

Sensual love stories featuring smart, sassy heroines you'd want best friend, and compelling intense heroes who are worthy of
4 stories per month.

To see which titles are coming soon, please visit
millsandboon.co.uk/nextmonth

JOIN US ON SOCIAL MEDIA!

Stay up to date with our latest releases, author news and gossip, special offers and discounts, and all the behind-the-scenes action from Mills & Boon...

 millsandboon

 millsandboonuk

 millsandboon

might just be true love...

MILLS & BOON
True Love
Romance from the Heart

Celebrate true love with tender stories of heartfelt romance, from the rush of falling in love to the joy a new baby can bring, and a focus on the emotional heart of a relationship.

MILLS & BOON

MODERN

Power and Passion

Prepare to be swept off your feet by sophisticated, sexy and seductive heroes, in some of the world's most glamourous and romantic locations, where power and passion collide.

Eight Modern stories published every month, find them all :

millsandboon.co.uk/Modern